KU-531-072

# THE WEDDING
# BARGAIN

BY
YVONNE LINDSAY

MILLS & BOON

All rights reserved including the right of reproduction in whole or in part in any form. This edition is published by arrangement with Harlequin Books S.A.

This is a work of fiction. Names, characters, places, locations and incidents are purely fictional and bear no relationship to any real life individuals, living or dead, or to any actual places, business establishments, locations, events or incidents. Any resemblance is entirely coincidental.

This book is sold subject to the condition that it shall not, by way of trade or otherwise, be lent, resold, hired out or otherwise circulated without the prior consent of the publisher in any form of binding or cover other than that in which it is published and without a similar condition including this condition being imposed on the subsequent purchaser.

® and ™ are trademarks owned and used by the trademark owner and/or its licensee. Trademarks marked with ® are registered with the United Kingdom Patent Office and/or the Office for Harmonisation in the Internal Market and in other countries.

Published in Great Britain 2015
by Mills & Boon, an imprint of Harlequin (UK) Limited,
Eton House, 18-24 Paradise Road, Richmond, Surrey, TW9 1SR

© 2015 Dolce Vita Trust

ISBN: 978-0-263-25254-5

51-0315

Harlequin (UK) Limited's policy is to use papers that are natural, renewable and recyclable products and made from wood grown in sustainable forests. The logging and manufacturing processes conform to the legal environmental regulations of the country of origin.

Printed and bound in Spain
by CPI, Barcelona

# "Take me away," Shanal implored.

It was the last thing Raif expected the bride to say in the middle of her wedding ceremony.

"Take me far away, right now."

"Are you sure?" he asked.

"Just, *please*, get me out of here," she begged, her bewitching pale green eyes shining with unshed tears.

It was the tears that undid him. A taxi rounded the corner. Raif secured Shanal's small hand in his and pulled the runaway bride to her feet.

"C'mon," he said, as he bolted for the sidewalk, towing Shanal along behind him.

He raised his hand to get the cabbie's attention. Eyes round as saucers and his mouth hanging open, the cabbie stopped and Raif yanked open the back door and guided Shanal inside.

Shanal sat next to him, pale but finally more composed, as they pulled away from the curb and down the street.

Raif cast one look through the back window. The crowd on the sidewalk outside the cathedral had grown.

In its midst stood the groom, his eyes fixed on the retreating cab. Even from this distance Raif felt a prickle of unease. Burton, understandably, did not look happy.

But Raif was getting exactly what he wanted.

\* \* \*

### The Wedding Bargain
is part of The Master Vintners series:
Tangled vines, tangled lives.

A typical Piscean, *USA TODAY* bestselling author **Yvonne Lindsay** has always preferred her imagination to the real world. Married to her blind date hero and with two adult children, she spends her days crafting the stories of her heart, and in her spare time she can be found with her nose in a book reliving the power of love, or knitting socks and daydreaming. Contact her via her website: www.yvonnelindsay.com.

| MORAY COUNCIL LIBRARIES & INFO.SERVICES | |
| --- | --- |
| 20 38 64 33 | |
| Askews & Holts | |
| RF | |
| | |

I don't often get the chance to tell my editor how much I appreciate her, but I want to do it here and now. E.M., you are amazing and I feel privileged to work with you. Thank you for making my work shine.

# One

"We are gathered here today…"

The priest's perfectly modulated voice filled the cathedral as sunlight filtered through the stained-glass windows, bathing the hallowed space with jeweled tones. The heady scent of the gardenias in Shanal's bridal bouquet, imported specifically at Burton's request, wafted up to fill her senses—and left her feeling slightly suffocated.

"…to join together Burton and Shanal in matrimony…"

Was this what she really wanted above all things? She looked across to her groom. Burton Rogers, so handsome, so intelligent, so successful. So rich. He was a good guy, no, a *great* guy. And she liked him, she really did.

*Like.* Such an insipid expression, really.

"…which is an honorable and solemn estate and

therefore is not to be entered into unadvisedly or lightly, but reverently and soberly."

Words she'd spoken to her best friend, Ethan Masters, only a year ago, echoed in her mind. *You have the chance to have the kind of forever love that many people can only dream of. I envy you that because that's the kind of love I want from the man I marry, if I ever marry. And you can be certain I'm not prepared to settle for less than that, ever.*

They'd been brave words, spoken before her world had begun to crumble around her. Before she'd chosen to sacrifice the chance to find true love. Before she'd latched onto the opportunity to give her parents a secure retirement after their lives had been torn apart.

Was Burton her forever love? No. Was she settling for less? Most definitely.

Everyone in the lab at the viticulture research center had said it had been a lucky day for her when she'd caught Burton's attention. They'd teased her about finding love in their clinical environment and she guessed, on the face of things, they had a point. As her boss, Burton had a reputation for expecting excellence in everything around him. Clearly, she had fallen within that category. And on the face of it, she'd agreed about how fortunate she was—faking joy amongst her colleagues when he'd proposed marriage and offered to solve her problems. She'd convinced everyone around her until she'd nearly believed herself that her engagement had made her the luckiest woman in the world.

Everyone gathered here in the cathedral believed this to be the happiest day of her life. Everyone except the one person who'd tried to talk her out of it. She flicked a glance sideways, but she couldn't spot Raif Masters, Ethan's cousin, in the crowd of two hundred guests jammed into the pews. She knew he was here, though. From the moment she'd walked down the aisle, accompanied by both her parents—her father in his wheelchair, on a rare appearance in public—she'd felt the simmering awareness that she felt only in Raif's presence.

"Into this estate these two persons present come now to be joined."

A buzzing sound began to build in Shanal's ears and her chest grew tight. A tremor in her hands made the heavy bouquet quiver—releasing another burst of cloying scent.

"If anyone here has just cause why Burton and Shanal may not be lawfully joined together, let them speak now or forever hold their peace."

Silence stretched out in the cathedral—silence filled with the ever increasing buzz in her ears and the erratic pounding of her heart.

Forever.

It was a very long time.

She thought for a brief second of her parents. Of how her father had always loved and provided for her mother. Of how her mother had always stood rock solid by her man, even now with all the uncertainty their future promised. Would Burton ever be that rock for her? Could he be? The priest's words echoed through her mind. *...just cause...not be lawfully joined together... speak now...*

"I do," Shanal said, her voice shaking, unsure.

Burton inclined his perfectly coiffed head, a puzzled twist to his lips. "Darling? That's not your line, not yet, anyway."

She dropped her bouquet, unheeding now of the scent of the flowers as they fell heavily on the carpeted altar, and worked her three-carat, princess-cut diamond engagement ring from her finger. A princess for his princess, Burton had said when he'd slid it on her hand—its fit perfect, of course.

Shanal thrust the ring toward him. "I can't do this, Burton. I'm so sorry," she choked out.

It was the first time she'd ever seen her erudite fiancé at a loss for words. With the perfect manners that were so much a part of him, he automatically accepted his ring back from her. The moment his fingers curled around the symbol of their future together, Shanal turned away from the priest in his raiment, her groom in his hand-finished tuxedo, and gathered her voluminous skirts in her hands.

"I'm sorry," she whispered in the direction of her parents, who sat in the front pew, their faces masks of shock, dismay and concern.

Then she ran.

Raif Masters had listened to the priest intoning the ceremony—a ceremony he was attending only as a favor to Ethan, who was away on his own honeymoon. Shanal Peat and Ethan had been friends for so long that it was almost as if she was part of the Masters family. It was only right that someone from the family be there for her today. He just wished it wasn't him. If Raif had had his way he'd have been anywhere but here. The idea of watching his cousin's best friend marrying Raif's nemesis was only slightly more appealing than spending the day passing a kidney stone.

He was already plotting his escape from the festivities at the earliest opportunity when he heard the objection request. He had, in fact, briefly considered standing up himself, because he did object to this wedding—on more than one level. But Shanal had made it perfectly clear a couple months ago that it wasn't his place to say anything. She hadn't wanted to hear it when he'd tried to explain to her that Burton Rogers was not the kind of man she should be tying herself to—literally or figuratively. Not for five minutes, let alone the rest of her life. But she had blinders on as far as Rogers was concerned, which, no doubt, was exactly as the other man liked it.

When Ethan had asked him to attend the wedding in his stead, Raif had objected quite emphatically, pointing out that he had no desire to see Rogers stand up to marry Shanal. In fact, he had no desire to see the other man, period. Even before the messiest parts of their history there had always been something about Burton that made Raif want to plant a fist in his arrogant face.

Ethan had brushed over his objections, reminding him that with all that was going on at The Masters, their family's resort and winery, he was the only one who could get away for the ceremony. Even so, it made Raif sick to his gut to see her willingly link herself to a man who lived by a single-minded agenda—doing whatever it took to make his life perfect, no matter who got hurt along the way. In Raif's experience, Burton was careless with others and only out for what he could get. He was the man Raif still held responsible for the death of his ex-girlfriend, Laurel Hollis, no matter what the coroner's findings had delivered.

Rogers had managed to walk away from the canyoneering accident without an ounce of blame, but while Raif hadn't been witness to it he had always believed there was more to the incident than had been disclosed. And he hadn't given up on finding out the truth one day, either. But for now, he had to sit and watch the woman he'd desired ever since he was a schoolboy with a crush that had lasted for longer than he cared to admit, marry a man he neither liked nor trusted.

Younger than her by three years, Raif had always found his relationship with Shanal awkward, right from when they'd first met fifteen years ago. Once she'd embarrassingly shattered his more intimate aspirations toward her—and in front of his entire family into the bargain—their interactions had been peppered with veiled barbs and verbal sparring when they'd crossed paths. But his attraction toward her had never dimmed, in spite of it all. And while they had never been close, he did truly care about her and wanted her to be happy.

He'd borne all that in mind when he'd gone to see her when the engagement was announced. Raif didn't believe that Burton Rogers was capable of making any woman lastingly happy, and had wanted to warn Shanal. He should have known better. Once she'd overcome her surprise at his visit, she hadn't hesitated to tell him he was wasting his time when he'd strongly urged her to reconsider her marriage to her boss. In fact she'd told him, with her usual economy with words, to butt out. And he had.

Now the entire cathedral was paralyzed in disbelief—Raif no less so than the people seated on the pew next to him.

Had his words been the catalyst that now sent her flying past him in a flurry of tulle and diamantes on her way down the aisle and out the front doors?

The stricken expression he'd spotted on her face galvanized him into action. Whatever their differences, she needed help. And since the reason she needed help was that she'd taken the advice *he* had given, he felt he owed it to her to be the one to come to her aid.

The doors of the church clanged closed in front of

him and he pulled one heavy wooden panel open and shot down the steps in hot pursuit of the vision in white that raced across the road without looking, and into the gardens beyond. That was where he found her—she'd stopped running by the time he caught up. Her breath was coming in great gasps and her usually glowing, light bronze skin now looked pale and sallow. Raif guided her to a bench and pushed her head down between her knees before she collapsed right there on the gravel path.

"Breathe," he instructed, ripping off his suit jacket and draping it over her bare, shaking shoulders, dwarfing her delicate frame. Adelaide in July was not warm, and dressed as she was in a strapless gown, she'd freeze in no time. "Slow and deep. C'mon," he said encouragingly. "You can do it."

"I…had…to get…away," she gasped.

He was shocked by how anxious she was. Shanal was always the Queen of Calm. Nothing unnerved her. Except maybe the carpet python he'd slipped in her bag when he was fifteen.

He rubbed her shoulders through the fine wool of his jacket. "Don't talk, just breathe, Shanal. It's going to be okay."

"No, no it's not."

Her words came out strangled, panicked.

"You'll work it out," he said, as reassuringly as he could under the circumstances.

Even as the words left his mouth he was reminded of the expression on Burton's face as he'd been left standing at the altar. An expression Shanal had missed seeing completely, thank God, or she might not have stopped running at all.

Raif had long known Burton was avaricious—he'd

always had to both *be* the best and *have* the best, by any means possible. But there was another edge to him, as well—and that edge had been clear on his face for a split second as he'd seen his latest intended acquisition flee from him. Raif might not have had much to do with him over the past three years, but he knew that Burton Rogers was not a man who enjoyed being thwarted.

Shanal struggled to sit upright, tugging flowers and her veil from her jet-black hair without any heed to the pins that must be raking her scalp. She tossed the destroyed blooms and filmy material to the walkway at her feet. She turned to Raif and grabbed his hands. He was shocked at how cold she felt already. As if she was chilled to her bones.

"Take me away," she implored. "Take me far away, right now."

It was the last thing he'd expected her to say.

"Are you sure?" he asked.

"Just, *please*, get me out of here," she begged, her bewitching, pale green eyes shining with unshed tears.

It was the tears that undid him. He thought about his Maserati, parked a good two blocks away. Only a handful of people had come out of the cathedral so far, but more were bound to follow soon. He and Shanal would never make it to the car before someone reached them, he thought, and once the crowd got to them, Shanal would be fielding questions left and right from a slew of concerned family members and friends wanting to know why she'd walked out on her own wedding. She didn't look as if she was up to conversation right now. As he swiftly considered their options, a taxi rounded the corner. Raif secured Shanal's small hand in his and pulled her to her feet.

"C'mon," he said, as he bolted for the sidewalk, towing Shanal along behind him.

He raised his hand to get the cabbie's attention. To his immense relief the guy pulled over, his eyes as round as saucers and his mouth hanging open as Raif yanked open the back door and guided Shanal inside. He barked his address to the startled driver as he yanked the door closed behind them.

Shanal sat next to him, pale but finally seeming more composed, as they pulled away from the curb and down the street. Raif cast one look through the back window. The crowd on the sidewalk outside the cathedral had grown. In its midst stood Burton, his eyes fixed on the retreating cab. Even from this distance Raif felt a prickle of unease. The groom, understandably, did not look happy.

Raif faced forward again. Burton's happiness had never been a priority of his, and as long as the man didn't take his anger out on Shanal in any way, Raif admitted to himself that he was delighted that his nemesis's day had been ruined.

He and Shanal had little privacy in the cab and Raif maintained his silence until, nearly forty-five minutes later, they reached his home. His phone, already on Silent for the ceremony, vibrated continuously in his trouser pocket. He knew exactly who was calling—and he had no intention of answering him.

"What are we doing here?" Shanal asked as the cab drew away, leaving them outside Raif's single-level home nestled at the edge of the family's old and well-established vineyard. "It's the first place he'll look, isn't it? He's bound to have seen us getting into the cab together."

Raif's eyebrows shot up. "I hadn't realized we were

meant to be hiding from him. You really don't want him to know where you are? You're absolutely certain you don't want to work this out with him?"

In response, Shanal shuddered. "No, I can't. I...I just can't."

Raif reached past her to unlock his front door, then gestured for her to precede him. The incongruity of the situation struck him. He'd always imagined bringing a bride back here to his home one day—just not exactly like this. But if she wanted to get away from Burton, then the least Raif could do was let her freshen up before she headed off to...wherever it was she planned on going from here.

"Can I get you something to drink?"

"Some water, please."

She followed him into the open-plan living area, her heels clicking and the multilayered skirts of her gown making a swooshing sound on the hard surface of the tiled floor. In the kitchen, he poured her a glass of mineral water from the fridge and handed it to her. She took a long drink.

"Thanks," she said, putting the glass down on the granite countertop with a click. "I needed that. Now where are you taking me? We can't stay here."

Taking her? What made her think he was taking her anywhere? She'd asked him to get her away from the wedding. He'd done that. Surely that was where his involvement began and ended. Not that he was unwilling to help her, but she'd always been so aloof toward him, had always kept him very firmly at a distance. Why would she be depending on him now? It was so unlike her.

Shanal obviously realized what he was thinking. "I'm

sorry, that was presumptuous of me. What I meant was, can you help me to get away for a bit? I'm kind of stuck."

She held her arms out from her dress in a gesture of helplessness. She was right. She was stuck, and in what she was wearing right now. She didn't even have a purse with her.

Raif studied her carefully. Her face was stretched into a tight mask of strain and her eyes had the look of a frightened animal. Even though this shouldn't be his problem right now, he racked his brains for something he could do to help her—somewhere she could go to get away from this whole mess. Ethan had chosen a fine time to marry his long-time fiancée, Isobel, and head away on a honeymoon cruise in the Caribbean, Raif thought uncharitably. A smile twisted one side of his mouth as an idea bloomed in his mind.

"How about a cruise?"

"A cruise?" Shanal looked surprise.

"Yeah. On a riverboat. I have a friend who has just re-engined and refurbished one of his fleet. He was moaning about not having time to run the motor in before it gets repositioned farther up the Murray. A nice, slow trip up the river sounds like just what you need and you'd be doing Mac a favor by getting some hours on the engine, as well."

"How soon can we leave?"

"You're serious? You want to do that?"

She nodded.

"Let me make a call."

He stepped out of the living area and into his office on the other side of the hall. He checked his phone. Yup, there were several messages, most of them from the same number—Burton Rogers. He deleted those without listening. Let the guy simmer in his own juices for a while. He frowned a little when he recognized Shanal's parents' number. He'd have to let them know she was okay, but first he needed to contact his friend.

Now, where had he put Mac's contact details... Aha! Raif spied the business card his friend had given him when they'd last caught up for a drink in Adelaide, and keyed the number into his phone. A few minutes later it was all set.

Shanal was standing at the large bifold glass doors that faced the vineyard when he came back into the room. She'd slid his jacket off her shoulders and had pulled the last of the pins from her hair, leaving it to cascade down her back like a long, wavy black river of silk. His hand itched to reach out, to touch her hair, to stroke it. Stupid, he told himself. The persistent physical attraction that had ignited back when he was a schoolboy continued to simmer beneath the surface, but he knew better than to act on it. Shanal herself had taught him that lesson. He'd gotten this far through his life without setting himself up for another smackdown like the one she'd dealt him twelve years ago, and he certainly wasn't going to set himself up for one now.

"You okay?" he asked.

She sighed, her body wilting from its strong stance. She shook her head. "No, I'm not. I don't think I'm ever going to be okay after this."

"Hey, of course you will. I've spoken to Mac and he's happy to make the boat available. With the school holidays over it's pretty quiet for him right now, so you can take all the time you need. It'll be good for you, the perfect getaway. You'll have time and space to think, and when you come back you can tackle what happens next with a fresh mind."

Her lips twisted into a semblance of a smile. "Somehow I don't think a fresh mind is going to make a big difference in resolving my problems, but thank you for all you've done. How soon can we leave?"

Raif calculated. It was just over an hour's drive to Mannum, where Mac would have the houseboat waiting.

"I'll need to get changed first. Do you want me to see if Cathleen left anything here that you can change into? We can always pick you up some more clothes on the way to the marina if you like."

His younger sister had house-sat for him when he'd gone to France on a recent fact-finding mission relating to the family vineyard operations. Not that the place needed to be minded, but while Cathleen for the most part loved living with the rest of their family at The Masters, when the opportunity to be on her own arose from time to time, she clutched at it with both hands. He could understand why she felt like that. It was, after all, why he'd chosen to build here, on the fringe of the family's oldest vineyard, as opposed to taking a suite of rooms in the family home. Sometimes a person just needed to be alone.

"Please," Shanal said, plucking at the skirts of her gown. "I really want to get out of this. It's a little attention seeking, don't you think?"

It was good to see she still had a touch of the acerbic humor he'd borne the brunt of so often in the past.

"A little," he agreed with a quirk of his lips. "Come with me and let's see what we can find."

He led her down the hall toward the guest wing of the house and to the room Cathleen had used. There, he slid open one of the wardrobe doors. For the first time ever he silently thanked his sister for her habit of leaving her things wherever she went. A clean pair of jeans and some tops were neatly folded on a shelf in the wardrobe. A lightweight jacket hung on the rail and there was even a pair of sneakers in a box on the floor.

"You two are about the same size, aren't you?" he said, gesturing to the garments in the cupboard.

"Close." Shanal nodded and reached for the jeans and one of the long-sleeved T-shirts, which she put on the bed behind them. "But even if the clothes aren't a perfect fit, given the circumstances, I'd rather wear anything else than this dress. Can you help me get out of it? The buttons are so tiny I can't do it on my own."

Raif swallowed against the dryness that suddenly hit his throat. Undress her? Hell, he'd dreamed about this moment on and off since he was fifteen years old. He slammed the door on his wayward thoughts. This was neither the time nor the place to indulge in his fantasies, he informed himself firmly. She needed a friend right now, and that was what he'd be. Nothing more. Now and always, she didn't want anything more from him—and he wasn't going to set himself up for yet another rejection from her.

Shanal turned her back to him and lifted the swathe of her hair to one side. A waft of her fragrance, an intoxicating blend of spice and flowers, enticed him. Urged him to dip his head and inhale more deeply. He fought the impulse and breathed through his mouth. She wasn't his to touch, or taste, *or anything*, he reminded himself.

She'd just run from her fiancé, and while every cell in his body was thrilled to bits about that—some cells more than others—he wasn't the kind of guy to take advantage of it. Not out of any respect for Burton, because the man deserved nothing but his contempt. But for Shanal's sake. Whatever had driven her to leave her wedding in the middle of the ceremony—and in the back of his mind he ached to know what it was that had triggered her last-minute change of heart—she was clearly shaken and upset. Unwanted attentions from a guy she'd rejected a dozen times over were the last thing she needed.

Raif took in a deep breath, then applied himself to his task. Shanal's skin was a delicate bronze above the edge of her strapless dress. A color that signaled the mixed heritage of her Indian mother and Australian dad.

"I'm surprised you didn't wear a sari," Raif commented, determined to distract her from the fact that his fingers, usually dexterous and quite capable of the job at hand, had become uncharacteristically clumsy in the face of her proximity and the way that the tiny buttons, undone one by one, revealed more of her beautiful skin.

His fingers slipped on a button, brushing against her. Her skin peppered with goose bumps and he heard her gasp.

"Sorry," he said, forcing himself to take more care.

"It's okay," she said, her voice a little husky. "And as to your question about the sari? Burton said he preferred me to dress more traditionally."

Raif frowned and was unable to keep the irritation from his voice when he spoke. "Traditionally? For whom?"

Shanal didn't answer his question. "I think I can manage the rest myself," she said, stepping just slightly out of his reach and pressing her hands against the crystal-encrusted bodice of her gown to stop it from sliding farther down. "Thank you."

"No problem. I'll be down the hall getting changed myself. Just holler if you need me."

Her pale eyes met his and he felt her trust in him as if it was a tangible thing. It was a surprisingly heady feeling. Shanal had always been so cool, so untouchable and in control. He'd never seen her this vulnerable, and the fact that she chose to put her trust in Raif when her guard was down… It meant a lot.

She gave him a small nod, then collected Cathleen's clothes off the bed and turned to the bathroom. "I won't be too long."

"Take as long as you need," he said, and left the room. *In fact, take longer*, he added silently. Because it sure as hell was going to take him a while to get his raging hormones under control.

# Two

Shanal closed the bathroom door behind her and stripped away her wedding dress. Without caring about any possible damage to the delicate and expensive fabric, she let it drop to the floor. She shuddered. Right now she felt so cold, deep down into her bones.

She quickly tugged on the jeans and sucked her tummy in a little to do up the zipper. Cathleen's curves were just a bit more subtle than her own and it showed in the cut of jeans that she favored. Too bad, Shanal thought as she slid her arms into the sleeves of the T-shirt and pulled it over her head. Beggars couldn't be choosers. That final thought held a painful irony she didn't want to think about right now. She had enough on her plate.

There was still an air of unreality about what she'd just done. In fact, she could barely believe she'd done it. Run away from everything—everyone.

Burton would be angry, she knew. Justifiably so?

Very likely. They'd had an agreement, and if she'd learned anything about Burton Rogers it was that he couldn't bear to be thwarted, not to mention being humiliated in front of a cathedral packed with his peers. She certainly wasn't in any headspace to face that right now.

It wasn't that she was worried he'd get physical with his rage—no, that would be beneath his dignity—but how did you explain to a man, especially one who on the surface was every woman's dream, that you no longer wanted to be his bride? All she knew was that she couldn't go through with it. She needed space—time to think, to form a strategy to overcome this situation she'd put herself into.

Another shudder ran through her and she felt her chest constrict anew. Her breathing became difficult again and she closed her eyes and focused on one breath in, one long breath out. When the tightness began to ease, she reached for the logical side of her brain. The one that had weighed the options of Burton's offer of marriage so carefully and had accepted it, knowing she didn't love him. The tension returned twofold. No, she couldn't even think about it. She felt so close to the breaking point. The two people who now depended upon her most, her mum and her dad, would be beside themselves with worry. For her. For themselves. Her father's medical expenses aside, in a few months they would be struggling to meet paying their utilities, let alone affording the basics like food.

Her decision to run away from Burton would affect them all.

She'd find a way around it. She had to. The alternative simply wasn't an option. And maybe it wouldn't be so bad, after all—maybe it was just her panicked mind that was making it seem worse than she thought. Right now, though, she needed distance. Distance *and* a healthy dose of perspective. Raif had offered her both unquestioningly.

But what was his angle? Was he doing this because he wanted to help her—or just because he wanted to hurt Burton? He'd come to see her at her parents' home three months ago after her engagement had been announced. He hadn't wasted time on niceties such as saying congratulations. He'd come straight to the point and said he was there to talk her out of marrying Burton. She'd told him the wedding would go ahead no matter what he had to say, and had very firmly asked him to leave, without hearing him out. She knew there was bad blood between him and Burton; she'd gotten the sense from what Burton had said that it had been some idiotic male rivalry over a woman. Whatever had happened, Raif had clearly carried a grudge, and she'd assumed that was what had motivated him to see her.

A deep and painful throbbing started behind her eyes. It was all too much to think about. Right now she felt as if she could simply crawl under the covers of the bed in the room next door and go to sleep for a week. Instead, she forced herself to move and put on a pair of socks and the shoes Cathleen had left behind.

When Shanal looked up into the mirror, her reflection was that of a stranger. She never usually wore this much makeup—hadn't really wanted to, even today—but Burton had insisted she allow him to send along a makeup artist during her preparations on the morning of their *special* day. She'd acquiesced, thinking it didn't matter, but as each layer of cosmetics had been applied she'd felt as if her true self was being hidden.

As if pieces of her were being pushed further and further into obscurity.

Was that what it would be like being married to Burton? His decisions overriding hers and suffocating everything that defined her until her very identity was buried beneath what *he* wanted? She bent over the bathroom basin and scrubbed her face clean, desperate to grab that part of herself back again.

A knock at the door turned her mind willingly away from questions she couldn't face and didn't want to answer.

"You okay?" she heard Raif ask through the door.

No, she was not okay. Not right now. But she had to hope she would be. "You can come in," she answered.

He did, and she noticed he'd changed into a pair of well-worn jeans that hugged his hips, and a navy sweater. The fisherman's rib knit clung to his broad shoulders, making him look impossibly strong and masculine. As if he could take on the weight of the world and barely notice the strain. She certainly hoped that was the case, because at this moment she felt even closer to fracturing apart than she had half an hour ago.

"We should hit the road. I've loaded up a bag in the Jeep with some things for you. Clothes of mine you can borrow—y'know, track pants, sweaters and a thicker jacket than that one of Cathleen's. They'll be far too big for you, but at least you'll be warm. We can stop somewhere and get you some underwear, toiletries and anything else you think of, on the way through."

She nodded. It was such a relief to simply hand over her care to him. To have someone else do all the thinking for a change. Shanal followed him out of the room, not even sparing a glance for the mound of tulle that still lay on the bathroom floor.

"I need to call my parents," she said as they reached the door to the garage. "To let them know I'm okay."

"Already done," Raif answered smoothly. "They send their love."

Did they? Or did they send their recriminations, their fears for the future now that she'd dashed their only hope for a secure retirement? The financial settlement Burton had agreed to pay her on their marriage would never happen now—in fact, she probably wouldn't even have a job after this.

"Are…are they all right?"

"They're worried about you, but I assured them you're being cared for."

She swallowed a sob and murmured a response, but something in her tone made Raif whip his head around and study her carefully.

"It'll be okay, Shanal. You did the right thing."

But had she? Or had she simply destroyed not only her parents' future, but her own, as well? Raif opened the passenger door of the Jeep for her to climb up before he walked around to the other side.

"Mac is stocking the houseboat with everything you'll need for a week, at least," Raif said as he settled in the driver's seat and hit the remote for the garage door.

"I'll pay you back, Raif. I promise," she said brokenly.

"Don't worry about that right now," he replied. "Why don't you put your seat back a bit and close your eyes. You look done in. Try and get a little sleep, huh?"

She did as he suggested, but found her mind was too active to sleep. Instead she listened as he called his younger brother, Cade, and arranged for him to collect the car that Raif had left parked near the church. Guilt sliced deep as she considered everything he had done for her so far today. And now he was going out of his way to drive her all the way to Mannum so she could take time out.

For someone she'd never exactly treated well, he seemed to be prepared to go to great lengths for her. Maybe it was just a measure of the man he was, she thought, as she heard him laughingly warn his sibling not to drive the Maserati too fast through the Adelaide hills on the way to his property. A man who, she had to admit to herself, she didn't know very well at all. When he ended the call he turned on the radio, tuned to a classical-music station. She was surprised, thinking him more likely to be into popular music or rock than anything resembling culture.

But then again, what did she really know about him aside from the fact that he was her best friend's cousin? Sure, he'd always been there when Ethan had invited her to attend family functions at The Masters. But Raif was three years younger than her and back when she'd met him, that three-year age gap between him at fifteen and her at eighteen going on nineteen had seemed huge. She'd mentally filed him away as a child, and had barely given him a second thought.

She'd recognized he had a crush on her early on, but had ignored it—and him, too, for the most part. He had been easy enough to ignore at first, especially since their paths didn't cross all that often. When she thought of him even now, she tended to think of the child he had been. Shanal hadn't really noticed when he'd left childhood behind for good.

Until now.

Until she'd realized the boy had most definitely

grown into a man. A man she could depend upon when it seemed she had no other options available to her.

She opened her eyes and watched him as he drove, his concentration on the road ahead, his hands capable and sure on the wheel. He was a bit more leanly built than Ethan, but aside from that the family resemblance was strong. Just over six feet tall, with dark hair brushed back off his forehead and blue eyes that always seemed to notice far too much, Raif, like the rest of the Masters family had more than his fair share of good-looking DNA. Added to that was the perpetual tan he wore, a byproduct of his work outdoors on the vines that grew in the various vineyards run by The Masters. But even so, the differences were there if you looked hard enough. There was a suppressed energy about Raif, whereas his cousin was calm and measured in everything he did. Raif projected a more physical and active air.

There was no doubt he was a man who thrived on action and on thinking on his feet. His spontaneity was one of the reasons it had been so easy to continue thinking of him as the child he'd once been—impulsive and thoughtless, never considering the consequences. Today had been a perfect example of that. What was it that Ethan often said about Raif? Ah, yes, he was the kind of guy to always leap before he looked. Well, today she was truly thankful for that. Not at any stage had he asked her why she'd run from her wedding. He'd simply taken her away when she'd begged to be taken.

If it weren't for him, she had no idea where she'd be or what she'd be doing. She was *not* the impulsive type, and never had been. Every choice was always meticulously planned and carefully considered. Until today. When she'd run out of that cathedral, she'd had no plan in mind, no destination in her sights. She'd just wanted to get *away*, with no thought for what would come next. Thank goodness Raif had run after her when he did. He might not be someone she thought of as a white knight, but he'd certainly come to her rescue. And the certainty that he had the situation in hand for the time being was enough to let her relax. For now, at least.

A steady rain began to fall and Raif switched on the windshield wipers. The rhythmic *clack-swish* of the blades across the glass was soothing and Shanal let her eyes close again, barely even aware that she was drifting off into sleep. When she awoke she found she was alone in the car. She struggled upright and rubbed her neck to ease the kinks out. Looking around, Shanal couldn't identify exactly where they were, but she spotted Raif exiting a small grocery store across the road. As he got back in the car he tossed a plastic bag in her direction.

"I didn't want to wake you so I guessed your size."

She opened the sack and spied a six-pack of multi-colored cotton panties and some ladies' toiletries inside. A blush bloomed in her cheeks at the thought of him choosing her underwear, but she pushed it aside. She should be grateful he was being practical about things.

"Thanks, it looks like you guessed right. And thank you again for helping me today. I—I don't know what I'd have done without you."

Emotion threatened to swamp her, and she felt his warm strong fingers close over one of her hands. A surprising tingle of response made her pull away. He gave her a sharp look.

"No problem," he said steadily. "Are you hungry yet?"

She should be enjoying the sumptuous repast that

had been booked at the reception center. Her stomach twisted. She couldn't think of anything less appealing.

"I'm okay for now. How about you?"

"I can wait," he said calmly as he started up the Jeep and swung back onto the road.

"Are we far from the river?" she asked.

"About ten minutes."

True to his word, they pulled up at a small marina a short while later. The rain had stopped, but there was a cool wind blowing, and Shanal wrapped her arms around herself as they got out of the vehicle. She should have grabbed that jacket of Cathleen's back at the house.

"Here, put this on."

She caught the down-filled jacket Raif tossed toward her from the back of the Jeep, and gratefully slid her arms inside. Instantly, she began to feel the warmth, almost as if he'd closed his arms around her and given her the comfort she so desperately craved today. She followed him in silence to the pier where a man waited for them.

"Mac, this is my friend Shanal."

Mac nodded a grizzled head in her direction. "Come aboard, I'll show you around."

Shanal was surprised by the luxury of the fittings on board. The boat, apparently one of Mac's smallest, boasted three bedrooms and was more spacious than the compact town house she'd rented back in Adelaide before having to move home to help her parents. In fact, the layout was similar, the only major differences being the helm positioned near the dining area of the boat's large main entertainment cabin, and the fact they were floating on the river.

"You driven one of these before?" Mac asked.

"No, but I'm sure Raif will show me."

"Better you get Mac to show you now," Raif said. "You'll need to know what to do when you're out on the water."

She noticed he didn't make mention of "we." Shanal turned troubled eyes to him and fresh panic clawed at her throat. "You're not coming with me?"

"Give us a minute," Raif said to Mac, before drawing Shanal onto the deck at the front of the boat.

He was shocked to feel her trembling beneath his touch. She'd appeared calmer after that nap she'd taken in the car, and some of the shell-shocked look in her eyes had faded, but it was back again now, with interest.

"Here," he said, pulling out one of the iron chairs that matched the glass-topped dining table on the deck. "Sit down."

He squatted in front of her, taking both her hands and chafing them between his. He was worried at how icy cold she felt to his touch.

"I thought you'd be coming, too. You're not going to leave me, are you?" she whispered.

Raif studied her, taking in the blatant plea in her beautiful green eyes and the worried frown that pulled between her brows. He hadn't planned to go with her. Honestly, it had never occurred to him that she'd want him there with her. All he'd done today was remove her from a bad situation and organize the escape she had wanted. He hadn't imagined she'd have any use for him beyond that.

And yet everything he knew about who she was—how strong and intelligent, how confident and admired—seemed to crumble before his eyes as he looked at her now. He'd thought the houseboat would be the ideal opportunity for her to get away and to think—to get things straight in her mind again before she went back to face the music. Why would she want him there for that? Why would she want any man around her when she'd just left her intended groom at the altar?

Though this was a woman who, in his experience at least, had no qualms about publicly humiliating men. Witness his own embarrassment when, in front of his entire family, she'd laughingly spurned his attempts to ask her to his high school graduation dance all those years ago. The sting of embarrassment had hurt far more than he'd ever admitted. Granted, it wasn't on par with what she'd done to Burton, but her method of making clear she wasn't interested had a way of staying with a guy.

"I'm sorry," she said, interrupting his thoughts. "I'm asking for more when you've already done so much for me. It's just..." She worried at her lower lip with her teeth and her gaze slipped out over the river that stretched before them.

"It's just?" he prompted.

"I don't want to be alone," she whispered, her words so quietly spoken.

The sudden vulnerability in her voice, hell, in her entire body, hit him fair and square in the solar plexus. Her slender fingers closed around his.

"You've already packed a bag," she said in a lame attempt at humor before becoming all serious again. "Raif, please? I know this is a big favor for me to ask, but I really need to be with someone I can trust right now. Just while I work things out."

She trusted him? Well, he wished he could say the feeling was mutual, but he certainly didn't trust her. During the drive here he'd had more time to think. When he'd talked to her after her engagement, she'd been so adamant that the wedding would go ahead. He doubted that anything *he'd* tried to say back then had been the trigger to change her mind. She'd certainly never before given his thoughts or feelings any weight in the choices she'd made. So what had changed things for her? She had to be holding something back, perhaps the very something that had put the haunted look in her eyes.

He considered her plea, turning it over in his mind. He wasn't prepared for this. Still, what harm would it do? Working the viticulture side of the family business certainly had its advantages come wintertime in that things definitely slowed down for him once he'd finished winter cane pruning on the vineyard. There was no other pressing business holding him at The Masters, nothing to prevent him from taking a week off work, if that's the time it took for Shanal to ready herself to face the world again. Besides, there were three bedrooms on the boat.

Movement in the cabin caught his attention. Mac was getting fidgety, casting them a curious glance every now and then. Raif had to make a decision. Leave her to her own devices, or go with her. He knew what Ethan would do. More importantly, what Ethan would expect *him* to do.

Sometimes family honor was a bitch.

"Fine," he said with a huff of breath. "I'll come with you."

# Three

Relief swamped her and she put out her hands to grasp his.

"Thank you. I owe you so much already—"

Raif pulled away from her and stood up. "You don't owe me anything."

She felt his withdrawal as if it was a slap. She lifted a hand to her throat as she watched him go back inside the main cabin. God, she'd made such a mess of all this. Did he regret rescuing her today? She wouldn't blame him if he did. It was one thing to whisk her away from the scene of her shattered future, quite another to continue on the journey with her. She was asking such a lot from him. And it wasn't as if they'd ever been close.

Aware of his crush on her, she'd always made a point of keeping her distance, never doing anything to lead him on. She'd felt that in the long run, that was the kinder choice—though admittedly, that had been as much for her sake as for his. Ever since he'd transitioned from schoolboy to young man, there had been something about Raif that had made the hairs on the back of her neck stand to attention. Something indefinable that always put her on edge when he was around, and that made her uncomfortably aware of herself and her body's reactions to him.

She'd told herself way back then that it was ridiculous. She had her whole life planned out, and someone like Raif had no place in it. He already had that devil-may-care attitude to life, while she was always quieter, more considered in her decisions. They'd had nothing in common whatsoever aside from Ethan as a link.

But that had been nearly a decade ago. A lot had changed, for both of them, since then. He'd become fully a man, and was now even more confident, more self-assured, with that air of entitlement and power that all the Masters men effortlessly exuded. And she? Well, she was still that nerd with her nose in her research, and she was no less discomfited by his presence than she'd ever been.

That moment back at his house, when his fingertips had touched her spine, had felt electric. All her nerve endings had jittered with the shock of it—and now the two of them would be confined together for the better part of the next few days. She started to wonder if she'd made a mistake in asking him to stay.

From inside, she could hear Raif's deep voice as he talked to Mac. Soon after, the two men hugged briefly and Mac debarked. Raif assumed his position at the helm and started up the engine. Mac cast them off from the pier with a wave. As the boat eased into the murky river waters, swollen with recent winter rain, Shanal felt a little of the tension that gripped her body begin to ease. She rose from the chair and went inside.

"I guess this has put a spanner in everything for you," she said, as Raif met her gaze.

His broad shoulders lifted in a nonchalant shrug. "It's not a problem. I'll let the family know I'll be away for a few days, and besides, I have nothing more important to deal with right now."

She felt the slight in his words—the implication that she was no more than a minor irritation to be dealt with—and stifled a sigh. "You're probably wondering why I ran away."

Again, that casual lift of his shoulders. "Not my business."

She struggled to find the words to begin to tell him. To explain her sudden overwhelming sense of suffocation and irrational fear. Standing at the altar—was it only a couple of hours ago?—and listening to the priest had forced her to see the rest of her life stretching out before her. None of it being as she'd planned.

Sure, as Burton's wife she'd still be heavily involved in her research—finding refuge in facts and figures and analysis—and she'd finally hold the position she'd craved for years. When it had come to negotiating their prenuptial agreement—a clinical document designed to appoint Shanal as head of research within the facility and to outline the terms of the large monetary settlement to be made to her upon their marriage—she'd had one thing only on her mind. Security. Not happiness. Not love—well, except for the love she bore for her parents, and her desire to lift the strain and sorrow from her father's frail shoulders for the life he had left.

While everything had been under discussion and was being fine-tuned by their legal counsel, it had seemed to be a reasonable trade-off. Financial security for her parents and job security for herself in exchange for marriage to a handsome, wealthy, charming man who she simply didn't happen to love. But perhaps love would come later, she had thought at the time.

Burton had made no secret of his attraction to her from the day she'd started working at the research facility that bore his name. They'd had the occasional date now and then. Nothing serious—or so she'd thought. But then he'd surprised her with his proposal of marriage. Shanal had avoided giving him an answer straightaway, certain that she'd have to tell him no, but wary of what her refusal might do for her chances of advancement within Burton International. But then her mother had taken her aside one day and disclosed the dire position that she and Shanal's father were in.

Shanal knew that the medical-negligence claim against her dad about five years back had cost him heavily. A proud man, proud in particular of his skill and sterling reputation as a physician, he'd hidden the early symptoms of motor neuron disease, to his cost and, even worse, to the cost of the life of one of his patients. After that dreadful episode, he'd been forced to give up his cardiovascular practice. No one wanted a surgeon whose muscles were systematically wasting away, leading to unexpected twitching. And certainly no one wanted a man who'd let his pride stand in the way of someone's life.

His malpractice insurance had covered some of the costs of the suit that had been brought against him. But bowed by guilt, and with his funds tied up in long-term investments that were time-consuming and expensive to convert into cash, her father had taken out a short-term loan to make a large private financial settlement on the family of his deceased patient. Using his home as security had seemed a good idea at the time, and he'd had every intention of paying the loan back out of investment income. Until the truth about his investments had been revealed.

He'd trusted his old school friend who ran a financial-planning company. A friend who had, unfortunately, turned out to be running an intricate Ponzi scheme. Shanal's parents had lost every last dollar. Shanal had given up her rental and moved back home immediately to help them out.

While she earned a good salary and had some savings, she knew it wouldn't support the three of them forever. For the time being, they were able to afford the loan payments and living expenses, but those expenses would soon rise beyond what she could handle, especially as her father's disease took greater hold on his body and he grew more dependent upon assistance. It struck Shanal as cruelly ironic that while her father had paid dearly to buy security for his patient's family, everyone in his own was now paying for it.

In a weak moment she'd shared her worries with Burton, who'd immediately proposed marriage again, saying he'd planned to make her his wife all along and that the timing was perfect now, since as her husband, he'd be able to help her and her family. For starters, he'd insisted on taking over her parents' mortgage and offering a financial settlement to relieve her and her parents' stress when they married. She had honestly believed she could go through with it.

The reality, however, had been an unwelcome shock. Once she'd agreed to become his wife, Burton had shown himself to be intent on taking over much more than just her parents' mortgage. The overwhelming sense of loss of self that had struck her when she'd been standing at the altar still lingered like cold, bony fingers plucking at her heart—at her mind. She closed her eyes briefly and shook her head to try and rid herself of the sensation.

When she opened them, Raif was looking at her again with those piercing blue eyes. She felt as if he looked right through her, but at the same time couldn't *see* what twisted and tormented her inside. She wanted to break free of that gaze—to do something, anything, to keep herself busy, even if only for a couple minutes.

"I'll make us some coffee, shall I?" she said, her voice artificially bright.

"Sure. Black for me."

Of course his coffee would be black. Deceptively simple, like the man himself, yet with hidden depths and nuances at the same time. Shanal familiarized herself with the well-appointed kitchen, finding the coffeemaker and mugs tucked neatly away.

"How long have you known Mac?" she asked, determined to fill the silence that spread out between them.

"About five years."

She waited for him to be more forthcoming, but may as well have been waiting for the polar caps to melt.

"How did you meet?" she persisted.

"We did some skydiving together, some canyoneering."

Shanal was well aware of Raif's interest in adventure sports. For a while it had seemed he was always hurling himself off some high peak or out some airplane, or kayaking down a wild river. The activities seemed a perfect match for the man he was—physical, daring and impulsive. But Raif's interest in such activities had waned suddenly after the death of his girlfriend, Laurel, in a canyoneering accident a few years ago.

"Did he know Laurel?" Shanal blurted, without really thinking.

"She was his daughter."

"Oh." Her hands shook as she went to put her standard spoonful of sugar in her mug, and the white granules scattered over the kitchen counter. "I'm sorry. I didn't mean to bring that up."

"It's okay," he replied, his voice gruff. "I don't mind talking about her."

Shanal flicked him a glance, noted the way his hands had tightened on the wheel, his knuckles whitening. "That's the hard thing about losing someone, isn't it? People often don't know what to say, so they say nothing at all."

Raif grunted a noncommittal response. Shanal finished making the coffee, thinking about what she'd said. She'd discovered the same thing applied when people suffered other tragedies—like illness. No one really wanted to face the issue, and conversation usually skirted around things. At least that's what she'd found with her father. As the motor neuron disease ravaged his body, piece by piece, he'd lost his independence and ability. Their friends, not knowing what to do or how to help, had slowly withdrawn.

It hadn't helped that her dad was such a proud and private man. He'd hated being forced into retirement because of his illness—still hated every lost ability, every task that he could no longer complete on his own that forced him to depend on the care of others. He had always taken such pride in his independence, his abilities. His work as a surgeon had saved lives and allowed him to provide handsomely for his family in a way that gave him a sense of purpose and meaning. Losing all that had been devastating. He'd become reclusive, despising himself for his growing dependency on others.

And then there was the financial situation.

Shanal slammed the door on her thoughts before guilt could overwhelm her. She had, literally, run away from the answer to her parents' financial problems. She didn't want to go down that road right now. She just couldn't. Maybe in a few days a solution would present itself to her—and maybe vines would one day grow grapes of solid gold, she thought, deriding herself.

She handed Raif his coffee and sat down beside him as he negotiated the boat up the river.

"How far do you plan to go today?"

"Not far," he replied, before taking a sip. "The sun will be setting in a couple of hours. We can pick a spot along the river, tie off for the night and then make an early start tomorrow if you feel like it."

"Sounds good to me."

"Here," he said. "Do you want to have a turn at the wheel?"

"Is that safe? I've never done this before."

"Gotta start somewhere," he replied. "Besides, we're not doing more than seven kilometers an hour. I don't think even you could get us into trouble at this speed."

"You're referring to the time I crashed one of the vineyard tractors into the side of a shed, aren't you?"

His lips quirked.

"In my defense, no one told me where the brake was on that thing."

"Point taken. Which brings us to your first lesson today."

He briefly explained the controls in front of them and then let her take the wheel. Once she got the hang of it, Shanal found it surprisingly relaxing as she gently guided the boat along the river.

The sun was getting low in the sky, sending the last of its watery golden rays through the trees silhouetted on the riverbank, when Raif suggested they pull in at a tiny beach on the river's edge. After they'd nosed in, and he'd set up the small gangplank, he went ashore to tie ropes to a couple of large tree stumps. Shanal shut down the motor, as instructed, and walked out onto the front deck.

"I know this is crazy," she said. "But I feel as if we're the only people on the river right now."

"I know what you mean. You get a sense of isolation very quickly out here. It's good in its way."

"Thank you. I really did need this."

He dipped his head in acknowledgment and went inside. After a few minutes she followed. Raif was opening a bottle of wine at the kitchen counter.

"Want some?" he asked, holding up an empty glass.

"Yes, please."

She watched as he poured the white wine, and accepted the glass when he handed it to her.

"Yours?" she asked.

"Of course. My grapes, Ethan's brilliance."

She smiled. "You make a good pair."

"Just like our dads did before us."

"Is your dad still hands-on in the vineyard?"

Raif took a sip of the wine and made a sound of appreciation. "Yeah, although he's pulling back more these days. He and Mum are planning a tour of Alsace and Bordeaux next year. He's been tied to the vineyard for most of his adult life. It'll be good for them to explore a bit more, and I know they'll love France."

Shanal took a sip of her wine, savoring the flavor

as it burst over her tongue. "This is from the vineyard by your house, isn't it? The one that partially survived the big fire?"

The Masters family had been devastated just over thirty years ago, when bush fires had destroyed the family residence, Masters Rise, and almost all their vineyards. It had taken years for them to recover. Years and many hours of hard work and determination from a family that had pulled together, growing closer and more unified in the face of the tragedy. Now, they were successful and strong again, but the ruins of the old house still stood sentinel over the family property—a solemn reminder that everything could be snatched away in the blink of an eye.

"Certainly is," Raif confirmed.

"Ethan was telling me that you've become a keen proponent of organic vineyard practices."

He smiled at that—the first real smile she'd seen from him all day—and seemed to relax a bit. "It's hard to break with the old ways, but I think in this case it's worthwhile. It's always been my aim to work toward making the vineyards as efficient as possible using sustainable processes."

"Well, if this vintage is any example, you're definitely on the right track."

He held his glass up in a silent acknowledgment of her compliment. "Shall we take these outside? You'll be warm enough if you put my jacket back on."

Shanal followed his suggestion, and after putting on the jacket she'd discarded on the couch earlier, walked out onto the front deck and sat in one of the wicker easy chairs positioned there. The sun gave a final burst of golden color before disappearing. Darkness spread, heightening the sense of isolation she'd mentioned earlier. And yet even with the night's noises beginning around them, she didn't feel anxious or afraid. Raif's solid presence beside her put paid to that, she realized. And no wonder she felt safe with him, given the way he'd helped and protected her today. She owed him, big time. Not many men would have done what he did.

She sighed and sipped her wine. The silence between them was companionable, but she felt compelled to say something about the way she'd absconded from her own wedding.

"I guess I owe you an explanation," she started, turning to face Raif, who stared out into the darkness beside her.

"Nope."

Raif had no need to know what had finally brought Shanal to her senses and sent her flying from the cathedral this morning. And frankly, the less time they spent talking about her would-be groom, the better Raif would feel.

"But I—"

"Look," he interrupted. "Burton Rogers and I might have been at school together. We might even have resembled friends once upon a time, but we're not now. To be honest, I've wondered more about your reasons for agreeing to marry him than I have about your reasons for running away. You don't need to explain a thing."

Shanal sat up a bit straighter in her chair. "You really don't like him, do you?"

"Don't like him, don't trust him."

"That's what you tried to talk to me about, back when we announced our engagement, wasn't it?"

He drained his glass. "Another?" he asked, standing up and putting out his empty hand.

"No, thanks, I'm okay. In fact, I think that glass has completely gone to my head. I was too nervous to eat this morning and—"

"I'll go warm up dinner. Mac left us a chicken casserole in the refrigerator. We'll have to cook our own meals from tomorrow."

He went inside before Shanal could realize he'd completely avoided answering her question. But he hadn't counted on her dogged determination to see things to an end. He should have known better. It was what made her a good research scientist, but not necessarily good company right now.

"What was it that you *didn't* say to me at the time, Raif? Why do you dislike him so much?"

"It doesn't matter now."

"I'd like to know."

He set the microwave to reheat and popped the covered casserole dish inside before straightening to face her.

"He killed Laurel," he said simply.

# Four

"Raif, that's not true! You know he was cleared of any responsibility in that accident," Shanal cried in response, her smooth brow creasing in disbelief.

"I figured you'd say that. That's why I didn't want to say it to you then, or now."

He turned away and hunted out cutlery and place mats for their meal, then walked past her to set the table.

"You still cold?" he asked, reaching for the switch to turn on the gas heater.

"I'm fine. What do you mean, you figured I'd say that?"

She had a bit more color in her cheeks right now than she'd had all day. Obviously she thrived on conflict and argument more than he'd realized.

"You were engaged to the man. Obviously you'd take his side. And let's face it—we've always been at loggerheads with one another, haven't we? You're hardly likely to believe what I say."

Raif crossed his arms in front of him and stood with his feet planted shoulder-width apart, daring her to contradict his last statement. As he watched her, she lost that air of bravado that had driven her to confront him just now. Her shoulders sagged and she seemed to shrink inside herself.

"I'm sorry you feel that way," she said softly, before lifting her eyes to meet his again. "And yet, despite your opinion of me and my choices, you were the only one who came to help me today."

How did he tell her that he hadn't done it for her as much as he'd done it to defy Burton? Hell, hadn't Raif vowed after Laurel's death that he'd do whatever it took to prevent Burton from hurting another woman, especially one he—?

Raif slammed the door on that thought before it could take wing, and busied himself with finding condiments to put on the table, and throwing the packaged salad he found in the refrigerator into a bowl.

Without actually saying in so many words that he believed the other man was a murderer, he'd tried his hardest to convince Shanal to question her reasons for marrying him. But she'd been adamant. Right up until that crucial moment this morning.

"Raif?" Shanal's voice gently prodded him to respond.

"You were upset and wanted to get away. I was there and I had the means to help you—what else could I have done? I wasn't going to just stand aside and let you be turned into a freak show."

"No, I guess that's bound to come when I return home again."

"It doesn't have to. You can make a statement to the

media and request privacy." He issued a bitter laugh. "Or you could not go home at all."

She shook her head. "It's not quite that simple."

"It can be, if you want it to be."

She averted her gaze, but not before he saw raw grief reflected in her eyes. There was more to this than she was letting on, he just knew it. But how to get it out of her? That was the question.

"Anyway," he continued, "I'm not in a hurry to head back, are you?"

A shudder racked her body. "No."

"Then let's not borrow trouble."

The microwave pinged and Raif retrieved the casserole and put it on the table.

"Come on. Take a seat and have some food."

He lifted the lid of the dish and the delicate aroma of apricot chicken filled the air. Raif ladled a generous portion onto a plate and put it in front of her.

"Help yourself to salad," he instructed, before serving himself.

They ate in silence, Shanal putting away more food than he thought she would, given the circumstances and how tightly she was wound. Halfway through the meal he retrieved their wineglasses and poured them each another serving.

"Trying to help me drown my sorrows?" she asked with a humorless smile.

"Are you sad?" he returned pointedly.

She held his gaze, her determined chin lifting a little, as if in defiance. "Not sad, exactly."

And then her eyes grew shuttered again. She gathered up her plate and cutlery.

"Leave that," Raif instructed. "I'll take care of it."

"I'm not a fragile ornament about to shatter apart,"

Shanal protested as he took the things from her and stacked them in the dishwasher.

"Go, get an early night, and then maybe you'll look less like one," he said firmly, even a little harshly.

There was a flash of hurt in her eyes, which made him realize he'd gone too far. But then he saw her spine stiffen, and a bit of the fire she'd shown earlier returned.

"Fine, then. Since you put it so nicely. I'll go to bed. Did you have a preference as to which room you want to use?"

"I put the bag of clothes in the end room for you. It's the biggest."

"But won't you need clothes now, too?"

"We can stop somewhere along the river and I'll get a few extra things. But I don't need anything else for tonight."

He slept in the nude, always, no matter the weather. Just because he'd rescued a runaway bride wouldn't change that, no matter how her cheeks suddenly flamed with color as she also came to the realization he'd be sleeping naked.

"G-good night, then, Raif."

She turned to go. He put out a hand to stop her, catching her slender fingers in his own. He felt her tremble at his touch, and silently cursed himself for being a boorish idiot.

"I'm sorry I was rude to you."

"No, you weren't," she protested.

"Yes, I was. And I apologize. I shouldn't have taken my frustration out on you. You've had a tough day and it's not you I'm mad at."

To his surprise, Shanal went up on tiptoes and lightly kissed his lips. "Thank you," she whispered.

She pulled her fingers free of his hold and went down

the passage to the bedrooms. He remained rooted to the spot until she closed her door. Half his life he'd waited for that kiss. Fifteen long and often painful years filled with the crazy adolescent yearnings of a first crush. As he grew older and more in control of his emotions, there had even been the occasional dream fantasy that always left him wondering whether they'd be as good together as he'd always imagined. This was the first faint taste he'd gotten in real life of what he'd imagined in such feverish detail.

Her touch had been as delicate as a butterfly's, yet he still felt the imprint on his lips. Still felt the surge of fire through his veins at her closeness. Still wanted her with an ache that put his teenage self to shame. This was going to be one hell of a week; he knew it right down to his bones. Just as he knew that the word *good* couldn't come anywhere near to describing what they'd be like together, should it come to that. In fact, even *incendiary* didn't come close.

In an effort to distract himself, Raif continued to tidy their things away, then poured himself another glass of wine. Maybe the alcohol would dull the allure of imagining Shanal asleep, in something of his, just down the hall. She was a tiny thing and would swim in his stuff. He groaned. This wasn't helping. Even so, the picture of her dainty figure swamped in one of his T-shirts wouldn't budge from his mind.

He went out onto the rear deck and into the cool night air. He stared, unseeing, into the ribbon of river, barely noticeable beyond the lights of the boat, as a cloudy sky obscured all possible star and moonlight. Had he done the right thing in agreeing to come along on this ride with Shanal? Probably not, he had to admit. He'd thought he had this unrelenting attraction he bore for her under control, and yet tonight all that restraint had melted under the merest touch of her lips.

It wasn't as if she'd been the only woman to occupy his mind through these past years. In fact, the reverse was more accurate. He'd had plenty of other relationships, even loved one woman enough to consider asking her to be his wife. But something had always held him back. His reluctance to commit to Laurel had seen her finding solace in Burton Roger's willing arms. And in the end, her life had been snatched away by one careless act.

Careless? Or deliberate? Only one man knew for certain—possibly two, as they'd had a guide on that trip. All Raif knew for certain was that there'd been three people alive at the top of the waterfall that day, and one hadn't survived. It was supposed to have been a controlled descent, but somehow Laurel's rope had failed and she'd fallen horribly before drowning in the water hole at the base of the falls.

A faulty knot, Burton had said, laying the blame fully on Laurel for tampering with a rope he'd already set. And that had been the coroner's finding, too. But once Raif had pared away his grief and studied the incident, he'd felt there was more behind the death of his ex-girlfriend than anyone admitted. Burton had never been what Raif could have called a close friend, but after that incident there was no way Raif had been able to stand being in the same airspace as the guy. He didn't like him and he certainly didn't trust him.

Which brought him full circle back to Shanal. Another woman who needed protection from Burton. Raif would stand by her and keep her safe for as long as she would let him, the way he wished he'd been there to protect Laurel on the trip that day.

* * *

Raif was locked in a nightmare. One where he hovered between the top of the waterfall and the water hole beneath. He saw the terror and panic on her face as Laurel plummeted past him, bouncing off the rocks before hitting the water with a splash and sliding beneath the surface. She was visible through the crystal clear water, and he could see her hair floating out from under the edges of her helmet. He dived into the pool, but no matter how hard he swam, he still couldn't reach her. And still her screams echoed, over and over, "No! No!"

He woke with a jolt, his heart racing and a cold sheen of sweat drenching his body. His chest burned with the breath he still held and he forced himself to let it go, and to try and release the horror of the nightmare.

"No!"

It took him a moment or two to realize he was actually hearing a woman's cry—apparently that part of the dream had been real rather than a figment of his tortured mind. He moved from the bed, reaching for his jeans and skimming them up his bare legs. It took only seconds to swing his door open and follow the passageway to Shanal's room. As he entered he could see her twisted in the sheets, her movements jerky and confined by the cocoon of bedcovers wrapped around her. She moaned in protest and he quickly moved to her side.

"Shanal, wake up, it's just a dream."

Her head thrashed from side to side and he spoke again, more firmly this time, his words a command rather than a suggestion.

In the filtered moonlight from outside he saw her eyelids flicker and open. She stared at him in surprise, her cheeks wet with tears.

"It's okay, you're all right," he assured her.

"I couldn't get away this time," she said in a shaky voice. "He wouldn't let me go."

Raif tugged at the covers that surrounded her. "You probably dreamed that because you've got yourself all caught up in the bedsheets. Here, let me get you free again."

Shanal pushed herself to a sitting position the moment she was free. Her hand shook as she raked it through her hair. "God, that was awful. It felt so real."

"Dreams can be like that," Raif answered, sitting on the bed beside her. His own nightmare continued to leave tendrils of horror clinging to the corners of his mind. "Want to talk about it?"

"I... He... No, not really," she said, wrapping her arms around her torso and giving a little shiver. "Thank you for waking me."

"No problem. I'll leave you to get back to sleep."

He was at the door before she spoke.

"Raif?"

There was a slight wobble to her voice.

"Uh-huh?"

"I know this is probably inappropriate..." Her voice trailed off.

"What is it?"

"Could you stay here with me tonight? I really don't want to be alone."

Stay here? Was she crazy? Hell, was he? He sighed softly in the semidark. Obviously he was.

"Sure."

He waited until she'd settled back down under her covers, and then lay on top of them beside her.

"Thank you. I feel ridiculous, but there's a part of me that's expecting Burton to come through that door any second."

"Not going to happen. He doesn't even know where we are."

"That's good," she answered, her breath a tiny puff of warmth against his bare shoulder. "Um, won't you be cold on top of the covers like that?"

Hardly likely, he thought, given the amount of blood pumping through his system. Did the woman have no idea how alluring she was with her hair all tumbled and dressed only in a thin T-shirt—*his* T-shirt—that did next to nothing to hide the fullness of her breasts or the shape of her nipples through the well-washed cotton?

"I'll be fine. G'night."

He determinedly closed his eyes, even though he could still feel her looking at him, and forced his breathing into a slow and steady rhythm. It didn't take long before he heard her breathing fall into the same deep pattern. He opened his eyes and turned his head on the pillow so he could watch her as she slept.

Her black hair was an inky shadow across her white pillowcase, her eyelashes dark crescents sweeping her face. His gut clenched. Was it possible she was even more attractive asleep? Maybe it was because she seemed softer like this, more approachable. Touchable. He curled his hands into fists, determined not to reach out and touch that silky swathe of hair, or to trace the fine shadow of her cheekbones.

He closed his eyes again. It was going to be a long, long night.

# Five

Shanal woke with a deep feeling of contentment and an awareness that she was safe, secure and deliciously warm. Outside she could hear the soft patter of rain. A pair of strong arms, lightly dusted with dark hair, encircled her and she was snuggled up against a very strong, very warm and very bare chest.

A powerful ripple of pure feminine delight spread through her body. Even from between the sheets, she could feel the hard evidence of his arousal. Instinctively she flexed against his hardness, before she realized what she was doing, and with whom.

She pulled away slightly and looked up at Raif's face. Blue eyes, languid with slumber, looked back at her.

"Good morning," she said shyly.

She felt a pang of remorse for moving and waking him when he untangled his arms from around her. Raif sat up and rubbed at his face.

"Good morning to you, too. Did you sleep all right?"

"Like a baby, thank you."

"Good."

He was off the bed and heading for the door before she could protest. But then, what would she say? Would she beg him to stay and hold her again? She buried her face in her pillow. What kind of message was that to send anyone, anyway? Yesterday she'd been ready to marry another man and today she wanted *Raif* to stay and tangle the sheets some more with her? What was she thinking?

Shanal forced herself from the bed and quickly made it before heading to the bathroom. There, she had a hot shower and dressed again in Cathleen's jeans and T-shirt, topping it off with a thick sweater of Raif's she'd found in the bag he'd left in her room. The sweater was far too big for her, of course, reaching to the top of her thighs. She rolled up the sleeves and considered her image in the bathroom mirror. Not too ridiculous, but then again she wasn't here for a fashion show, was she? No, she was supposed to be getting her head straight and figuring out how on earth she was going to solve her family's financial woes, and what she would do if she had no job.

It was ridiculous to think that Burton would still let her keep her position as head of viticulture research and development at the lab. A man like him didn't take kindly to public humiliation. Although, having seen him work the media on more than one occasion, Shanal figured he'd have spun something suitable to ensure he didn't lose face. But spinning the situation undoubtedly meant blaming someone—and that someone would have to be her. So no, she wouldn't have a job anymore.

She loved her work with a passion that didn't extend

to any other part of her life. It was her everything. While she'd always hoped to find love of the kind her parents shared, and which she'd watched bloom between Ethan and Isobel, in the absence of it she'd always been happy to focus solely on her research. While it didn't bring physical reward, it did emotional rewards of a sort, not to mention the recognition and accolades that came along with a job well done.

But if she didn't have her job, she'd have to look for work elsewhere. That could mean leaving Adelaide, leaving her parents. The thought of doing so as her father's illness progressed sent a chill through her. With no extended family in Australia, they were all each other had. She had to hope that Burton would be charitable about her reneging on their agreement to marry, and refrain from blacklisting her with other Australian facilities, even if he didn't allow her to keep her job at Burton International.

A knock on her bathroom door jolted her from her thoughts.

"You okay in there?"

Raif, checking up on her again. What did he think she was going to do? Drown herself in the plug hole? She reached for the door and opened it.

"I'm fine, thanks. Hungry, though. Shall I put our breakfast together?"

"If you'd like. I can cast off and we can start heading upriver while you get it ready."

"Sure," she agreed, pleased to have something to do. Anything, really, to take her mind off the confusion of her thoughts.

In the kitchen, Shanal rummaged through the refrigerator and the pantry.

"How does French toast and bacon sound?" she called to Raif, who manned the helm.

"Better than cereal, that's for sure," he said with a smile that all but took her breath away.

She stood there like an idiot, captured by his male beauty for far longer than was acceptable for people who were merely acquaintances—even if they had shared a bed last night. Shanal forced herself to the business at hand. What was it again? Breakfast. That's right. She flicked a glance back Raif's way. His focus was wholly on the river ahead, which was just as it should be, she told herself sternly.

So what if she had felt a tingle run from head to foot when he'd smiled at her? It didn't mean anything. He was a good-looking guy, and was well aware of his charms—nor was he afraid to use them to his advantage. She'd seen the evidence of that at many a Masters family gathering, when Raif had brought one girl after another. The only girlfriend of his that she'd seen more than once had been Laurel. And, Shanal realized, since the other woman's death, Raif had either been scarce at family do's or had come alone.

Shanal put a pan on the stove to heat for the bacon, and then broke eggs in a shallow bowl and whipped them with a little milk, nutmeg and cinnamon, adding a tiny dash of vanilla extract to the mixture. The cabin soon filled with the scent of frying bacon, and by the time she popped the strips onto a plate in the oven to keep, and added the egg-mixture-soaked bread slices to the pan, her stomach had begun to growl.

"Smells good," Raif commented from his vantage point.

"It's about the only thing I know how to cook well," Shanal said with a laugh. "So I do hope it tastes okay."

"How is that?" Raif asked, turning in his chair to look at her.

"How is what?"

"That you can only cook one thing."

Shanal had the grace to look a bit ashamed. "Even after I left home my mum still cooked for three every night. Before I moved back in with them, she would put meals in her freezer for me and I'd gather them up, a load at a time, when I came over to visit. So I never really had to think about cooking when I got home from work."

Raif laughed out loud and she felt that tingle all over again. Even when he was serious, the man was gorgeous, but laughing? Well, it made something deep inside her clench tight. To avoid examining that odd sensation any further, Shanal quickly turned the bread, then set the table.

"Did you want coffee or tea with breakfast?" she asked, realizing that for all she'd known him half his life, she knew very little about him.

But she wanted to.

Her breath caught on a gasp as she burned herself on the side of the frying pan. Where on earth had that thought come from?

And why now?

"Coffee, please," Raif responded, blissfully unaware of the turmoil she was going through.

"Coming right up."

Ignoring the sting of the burn, she quickly set the coffeemaker to go and added the next batch of bread to the frying pan. In no time the pieces were golden and she plated them up. But with her thoughts still in a whirl, she realized that she wasn't so hungry anymore.

"Breakfast is ready," she said.

"Great, just give me a minute to pull in over there."

He gestured to a small indentation in the riverbank, then nosed the boat in and cut the engine.

"Don't we need to tie off?" Shanal asked.

"We should be okay here while we eat, since we're out of the current. If there's a problem I'll just start her up again."

Shanal poured their coffee and took the mugs to the table. As she did so, Raif's eyes suddenly narrowed.

"Is that a burn?" he asked, grabbing her hand and turning it so he could inspect the redness more closely.

Shanal tried to tug free. "It's nothing."

"It doesn't look like nothing to me. You need to run some cold water over that."

"Seriously, Raif, it's nothing."

He ignored her and led her to the kitchen sink, where he held her hand under the cold tap. The entire time, she was aware of his closeness, of the latent power in his male body, of the gentleness in his touch as he cradled her hand in his. The water might have been cold, but she felt anything but. In fact, heat simmered inside her in a way she'd never experienced before. Heat... and something else.

"How's it feeling now?" Raif asked.

"Fine."

Her voice sounded husky. Embarrassed by her reaction to him, she pulled her hand free and reached for a towel.

"Here, let me." Raif took it from her before she could protest and gently patted her skin dry. "I saw some aloe gel in here before... Ah, here it is," he said, as he poked through a small first-aid box she hadn't noticed on top of the refrigerator.

Raif squeezed a small amount on her hand, his touch light as a feather as he smoothed it over the burn.

"You should be good as new in no time. Any more pain?"

She shook her head. "Thanks, it's good now. Seems I'm always finding reasons to thank you lately," she said, feeling ridiculously shy all of a sudden.

She stepped away from him and reached for the oven door.

"Let me. You go sit down."

"I'm not helpless, you know," she muttered in frustration.

"I know. Tell you what. You can wait on me for the whole rest of the trip. How's that?"

She laughed, her irritation dissolving just as quickly as it had arisen, which was what he'd obviously intended all along. "Fine, I'll do that. But you might be sorry."

"Oh, yeah, that's right. You don't cook. Well, let's see about teaching you, hmm?"

He put their plates on the table and sat down with her.

"This is good," he said, after tasting the toast. "There's something different about it."

"Could be the vanilla essence," she said, accepting his compliment with a buzz of satisfaction.

"Interesting addition."

"It's something my mum does. I learned it from her."

"But not anything else?" he questioned.

"No, not anything else. What about you? Do you cook?"

"Mum made me learn before I went to uni. It was pretty useful when it came to impressing the girls, so I expanded my repertoire pretty quickly."

She rolled her eyes. "Yes, I would have expected that of you."

He shot her a cheeky smile and applied himself to the rest of his breakfast. When they'd finished, he suggested that he get the boat back en route upriver and leave her to guide it while he tidied up.

For the next few hours they lazily cruised along the Murray, taking turns at the helm and admiring the riverbanks as they went along. It was incredibly peaceful, with the exception of the occasional speedboat that went whizzing past, often with a wetsuit-clad wakeboarder hanging off a rope on the back even on a cold day like today.

It was past midday when they reached a small town. The rain had stopped a couple hours earlier and Shanal had been sitting out on the front deck, admiring the ocher-colored cliffs that rose from the river.

"What do you say about a walk?" Raif called to her through the open cabin door.

Shanal started to say yes, but then a memory from the bad dream she'd had last night tickled the back of her mind. She could still recall the all-encompassing fear she'd felt in the dream when Burton had forced her to remain at the altar. She knew it was ridiculous, that her ex-fiancé couldn't possibly have tracked her down yet—and even if he did, he was hardly the violent type—but nevertheless she shook her head. "I'm happy to stay on the boat. But you go on if you want to."

"He's not going to find you here, Shanal. And even if he does, you don't have to go with him."

She closed her eyes and counted slowly to ten. How was it that Raif could read her so easily?

"Okay, I'd like to take a walk with you."

They moored near a ferry landing and then followed the road up the hill and around a sharp bend. It was good to get out of the boat and really stretch her legs, she found, and she enjoyed the view once they made it to the lookout. From there they had a great panorama of the river. Beneath them the ferry plied back and forth, and other houseboats were moored near the terminal on the other side.

"Our boat looks tiny from up here, doesn't it?" she commented.

"It does. I always think a view like this helps remind me to keep things in perspective. When we're on the boat, that's pretty much all we see—aside from the river around us, obviously. Sometimes you just need a bit of distance to rebalance your perceptions. There's so much else that's out there. It makes what we are, what we're going through, seem insignificant sometimes."

"I guess," she agreed, but held the safety railing in front of her in a viselike grip. She wished her problems could fade away into insignificance with just a little distance, but she'd have to return to face them sooner or later. "So, where are we heading from here?"

Raif pointed upriver. "I thought we could keep motoring up toward Swan Reach. Or maybe stop near Big Bend for the night and get to Swan Reach in the morning."

She nodded in agreement and they started the walk back to the boat. As they strolled together, Shanal mulled his words over in her mind. Perspective. That's what he was giving her here by taking her away like this. Time to make her problems seem less insurmountable than they'd begun to be. A tightness invaded her chest as she thought of what might lay ahead. So far, for her at least, the concept of perspective wasn't working all that well. Right now, avoidance was her preference.

She staggered a little as Raif gave her a playful shove.

"You're thinking too hard—I can see smoke pouring from your ears. Come on, I'll race you back to the boat. Last one there makes lunch!"

Her mind latched onto the challenge. With his long legs and strength she had no doubt that he'd beat her, so she took advantage of the fact he was still talking, and started to run.

"You're on!" she shouted over one shoulder.

Rapid heavy footsteps gained steadily from behind, making her squeal.

"I never took you for a cheat," Raif goaded her, from far too close.

"You have to take the advantage where you can!" she laughed, and pushed herself just that little bit harder.

She was out of condition. With helping at home and all the palaver in the lead up to the wedding, combined with her heavy workload, she'd struggled to find time to even do so much as go for a walk each day. She couldn't remember the last time she'd spent any time at the gym. A stitch began to develop in her side but she was nothing if not determined. She would win this race.

Shanal had one foot on the gangplank to the boat, then another, and was about to turn and relish her success when a pair of strong arms wrapped around her and lifted her clean off her feet. She squealed again, this time in surprise, as Raif spun her a full 180 degrees.

"I win!" he crowed as he set foot on the deck and slowly lowered her down, laughing in the face of her frustration.

"And you say *I* cheated?" Shanal said through gasps of air, turning to him in disgust.

"Hey, you forget. I've seen how you can run," he teased, obviously alluding to her bolt from the church yesterday. "I had to use every advantage I had. Besides, I like to win."

"That's not fair," she protested. Was it only a day ago? It felt like forever. Or did she just wish it was?

"All's fair in love and war." He smiled back cheekily.

"You may live to regret that statement," she warned. "Remember, I can't cook."

Raif shrugged. "I also like to live dangerously, don't you?"

She looked at him and felt a tug that pulled from her core. It had nothing to do with her labored breathing and everything to do with the fact that he still had her in the circle of his arms. Her heart was already pumping hard, her senses heightened, and all she could think of was how snugly she fit against him, how close his lips were to hers. How, if she just flexed her hips a little, she'd be nestled in the cradle of his pelvis.

But did she dare?

She did.

Shanal lifted her hands to his head and tugged it down toward her. "I haven't had much cause to live dangerously so far, but I'm willing to give it a try."

And then she kissed him.

# Six

She felt the shock roll through his body as her lips touched his. He was unresponsive for a second, then two. She began to wonder if she'd been foolish to do this, to act on the impulse that had overridden her usually careful and considered way of approaching things.

But then his lips began to move over hers, and his arms tightened, pulling her even closer against his body, against his solid strength. Her fingers furrowed through his short dark hair, holding him in place. Not wanting to let him go for a second, because if she did, she'd have to face the questions that would no doubt be in his eyes. Questions she didn't know the answer to herself.

All she knew was that she suddenly realized just how deeply she longed for this. For this man, for his kiss. She slid her tongue softly along his lower lip, felt the shudder that racked his body, felt him harden against her.

This was how it was meant to be between a man and

a woman. Need, desire, want. Not a cold clinical agreement. Not the feeling of being a possession, to be shaped and molded to someone else's taste. Just the need to possess and be possessed in return. She moaned as Raif's tongue touched hers, as a flame of heat speared through her body. She pressed against him, aching for him to fill that emptiness that echoed inside her. Desperate for him to ease the pounding demand that throbbed through her veins.

His hands slid under the sweater she was wearing—his sweater—and the heat of his touch burned through the thin T-shirt that acted as a barrier between his skin and hers. She wanted more. She wanted Raif. Her fingers clenched in his hair and she kissed him more fiercely, her tongue now dueling with his. Advance, retreat, advance again. The taste of him was intoxicating, another sensation to fill her mind and overwhelm her senses.

She felt her nipples tighten into aching buds, and she pressed against him, the movement sending tiny shafts of pleasure to rocket through her body. She'd never felt anything quite like this before. This level of total abandonment, this depth of need.

The sound of the ferry horn echoed across the water—a stark and sudden reminder of where they were, of what they were doing. Shanal let her hands drop to Raif's shoulders as she pulled back. Her entire body thrummed with energy and anticipation, but as she came back to awareness of her surroundings once more, the strength leached from her body, leaving her feeling empty, limp.

"I—" she started.

Raif pressed a short and all-too-sweet kiss to her lips. "Don't say a word. It's okay. To the winner, the spoils, right?"

He bent and lifted the gangplank, stowing it away before he released the ropes that secured the boat to the pier, then he went inside, shrugging off his jacket as he went.

How could he be so nonchalant? As if what they'd just done had meant nothing to him at all? Shanal spun around and gripped the rail that surrounded the deck, desperate to ground herself on something, anything that had substance. Anything that wasn't the emptiness that roared to fill the giant hollow cavern swelling deep inside.

Unexpected tears burned in her eyes and she blinked them back fiercely. What on earth had come over her? She was a rational woman. Not one prone to obeying instinct. Not one who literally flung herself at a man and kissed him until every logical part of her brain was burned into an oblivion of physical awareness.

He'd talked about perspective when they were up on the bluff. She'd never needed it more than she did right now. This was the time for rational thought—for her usual careful deliberation. And yet her body continued to make its demands felt, insisting that she do what felt right without a thought to the consequences. She fought for the equanimity that was her signature in every single thing she did, until every beat of her heart, every breath she took, returned her to a state of lucidity once more. Then and only then would she be ready to face the man inside. At least she hoped she would.

Raif went through the motions, sending the boat back upriver, but he couldn't take his eyes off the woman in front of him. A sheet of glass was all that separated, but it may as well have been a five-foot-thick wall of lead for all the good it did him. Shanal had taken him by surprise, kissing him like that. He should have been a gentleman, should have stepped back right away. Should even have let her win their stupid race instead of grabbing her into his arms as he had. But then he'd always lived life on the wild side—always relished provocation, stimulation. And boy, was he ever stimulated right now.

The fact that he hadn't simply dragged her through to the nearest bedroom and acted on the incredible conflagration that had ignited between them was a testament to his upbringing. His mother would have been proud. Well, except for the kiss, maybe. That, she probably wouldn't have approved of, especially not when the situation between Shanal and Burton was still so murky. Sure, Shanal had removed her ring and run away from their wedding, but Raif had the sense that somehow she was still intrinsically linked to the other man. Whatever was between her and Burton, it wasn't over yet. And Raif didn't like it. Not one bit.

He studied Shanal as she stood on the front deck, staring into the water as if she could somehow find the answer to the meaning of life out there. He wished it was that simple. He'd done his fair share of empty gazing, but all it had taught him was that most often the answers you sought lay within a person, not outside. And sometimes those answers weren't exactly what you wanted to see, either.

"Hey," he called through the door. "You still owe me lunch, remember."

Maybe if he could goad her, as he always had in the past, she'd fire back to life again. He counted several beats before he saw her relinquish the stranglehold she had on the railing and straighten her shoulders once more. She came inside the main cabin, wearing that same fragile, shell-shocked look she'd had yesterday when he'd rescued her in the park. It hit him hard in the gut. He'd put that look on her face by letting their kiss become more than it should have.

"Think you're up to making a sandwich and a pot of coffee?" he prodded.

A faint flare of color brushed her cheeks and a tiny spark of life came back into her pale green eyes.

"I believe I can do that without giving either of us food poisoning," she answered, with her cute little nose up in the air and a haughty expression on her face.

He couldn't help it; he had to smile. It only served to make a frown pull between those perfectly arched brows of hers.

"Life's not a joke, you know," she said in her Miss Prim voice that he already knew so very well.

"No one said it had to be all hard work, either."

He transferred his attention back to the river, but even so he could feel her staring at him. Eventually she gave a small sniff and a few seconds later he heard her rummaging around in the kitchen. Not long after that, a small hand carrying a plate bearing a sandwich appeared in his peripheral vision.

"Thanks," he said, taking it from her. He let his eyes drift over her face, checking to see if the strain of earlier had gone. A sense of relief filled him as she looked back at him steadily. "You okay now?"

She nodded and shifted her attention outside. "I'm not in the habit of kissing just anyone."

"I know," he confirmed.

He was childishly tempted to ask how the kiss they'd shared compared to Burton's, but then pushed the thought from his mind. He didn't want to think of Burton anywhere near Shanal. Not now, not ever.

"It won't happen again," she continued.

"If you say so," he conceded.

"I mean it, Raif. It can't happen again."

There was a thread of panic in Shanal's voice that gave him pause. What had her so scared?

"Shanal, you're safe with me. I'm not going to make you do anything you don't want to do, I promise. But remember, we only get to live this life once. I don't know about you, but I already have enough regrets on my conscience. I don't plan to live the rest of my days with any more."

He had a gutful of regret when it came to Laurel. He'd told her he had concerns about her still being too much of a novice to tackle that waterfall trip. Telling her had been part of what had led to the argument that had eventually seen them break up. He'd never have believed that it would ultimately lead to her death. Regret left a bitter echo in his heart. He didn't want to add to that with Shanal.

Outside, it started to drizzle, then rain more heavily, making visibility on the river difficult. Since they weren't on any timetable but their own, Raif decided to moor the boat along the bank, getting muddy and soaked to the skin as he jumped ashore to tie off the lines. He was chilled right down to his bones by the time he came back on board.

"Why don't you look through the DVDs on the shelf under the TV and see if you can find us something to watch this afternoon," he suggested. "I'm going to grab a quick shower and a change of clothes."

By the time he came back to the main cabin, dressed in an old comfy pair of track pants and a sweatshirt Shanal had handed him from the bag of clothes he'd originally packed for her, she had a couple DVDs on the coffee table. He picked one up.

"You like sci-fi?" he asked.

She nodded.

"Huh, I would have picked you for something else."

"Like what?" Shanal sounded irritated. "Chick flicks?"

He gestured to the Jane Austen boxed set on one side of the shelf. "More that kind of thing."

She shrugged. "I like that, too, but I like this better." She suddenly looked insecure. "Don't you like sci-fi? We can choose something else if you'd rather."

"No, it's okay. I'm a huge Sigourney fan."

"Really? I prefer the alien myself. Such a misunderstood bio-form."

He laughed, plucked the DVD case from her hand and selected the first disc of the set to put in the player. To Raif's surprise, he discovered that not only did Shanal love sci-fi movies, but she also had a very bloodthirsty streak. By the time they were onto their second movie in the trilogy he found himself adjusting a few of his preconceptions about her. Sure, she was incredibly intelligent, but she had a fun side that he'd never seen before. As the alien creature took out a few more good men, she laughed and cheered, all tension from earlier now gone.

He found he really liked her laughter. It wasn't something he'd heard a lot of from her, but when it came it was a joyful gurgling sound that made him laugh right along with her. He found himself ridiculously desperate to hear her laugh some more. And when the movie got really tense and it looked as if all hope was lost for the hero, her dainty hand crept into Raif's for comfort. Squeezing tighter and tighter as the tension rose.

They took a break from movie watching to cook dinner together. Raif supervised as Shanal did most of the

work. And he basked in her pleasure as the pasta dish
came out better than she'd expected. They ate in front
of the TV, watching the last movie in the trilogy, and
as the credits began to roll on the screen, Raif caught
her yawning.

"Why don't you go on to bed? I'll sort things out
in here."

"Are you sure? I don't know why I'm so tired. We've
hardly done anything today but watch TV. It must be
the rain," she said, getting up from the couch.

Raif missed her presence immediately. He'd grown
all too comfortable with her small figure perched next
to his on the couch.

"Don't knock it. There's nothing else for you to do
right now but sleep, if that's what you want to do," he
said, getting to his feet.

The words no sooner left his mouth than a picture of
the two of them doing something else in a bed, something that had nothing to do with sleep, imprinted on his
mind. His body responded immediately, sending curls
of arousal to flick around his all-too-willing flesh. As
if her thoughts had taken the same direction, Shanal
paused and looked at him—her eyes wide, the pupils
dilated. Her hair, worn loose today, was slightly curly
and disheveled, making her look younger and more approachable than the tightly buttoned-down and sleek
appearance she normally favored.

He decided he liked this side of Shanal Peat just a
little too much. It would take very little effort on his
part to lean forward and brush his lips against hers. Just
a small kiss good-night, that's all it would be.

*Liar*, a voice sneered in the back of his mind.

"Go on," he said, his voice a little rough. "You head
off. I'll see you in the morning."

She bade him good-night and went to her room, leaving him standing there like a starstruck idiot watching his first crush walk away. Then again, she *was* his first crush. There was no doubt about it. But to still feel this way? It was ridiculous. They were both adults now—adults with nothing in common. Except for a love of gory sci-fi flicks and possibly much more.

He shook his head and focused on straightening up the cabin before going to bed himself. There'd be none of that "much more," not after the way she'd reacted after their kiss this afternoon. No matter how much he wanted it. No matter how much he ached for it. But even so, Raif went to bed that night with his door open—just in case she had a nightmare again, he assured himself.

Shanal woke the next morning to the sound of the boat motor running. She rubbed her face and stared at the bedside clock, shocked to realize it was nearly 9:00 a.m. She'd slept almost twelve hours, which was unheard of for her. She shot into her bathroom for a brief shower then quickly dressed and joined Raif.

"Sorry I slept in," she said, as he turned to greet her with one of those killer smiles he specialized in.

"No problem. You must have needed it."

She helped herself to some cereal and a cup of coffee and perched on the seat next to him as he steered the boat upriver. As with everything he did, his hands were strong and competent at the wheel. In fact, she'd never seen Raif Masters at a physical disadvantage with anything. Whether it was operating a post-hole borer to erect uprights for new vine trellises or training the canes along the wires, he approached everything with a surety she sometimes envied. In her line of work, developing new strains of vines, outcomes were not always guaranteed and she often found herself hooked up on data and forgetting that what she was actually doing was creating or improving a living thing. Raif's work was hands-on, all the way. Her gaze lingered on his long broad fingers. Those very same fingers that had caressed her back yesterday as they'd kissed.

A shudder ran through her.

"You cold?" Raif asked.

"No, I'm okay," she said, getting up from her seat and taking her bowl to the kitchen.

But she wasn't okay. She felt disturbed. That kiss yesterday had been all too revealing to her. With it, she'd answered unspoken questions that had plagued her for years. As much as she'd tried to pigeonhole Raif as that cheeky schoolboy she'd met half his lifetime ago, she could no longer do that now. He was very much a man. A man she desired. There. She'd admitted it.

She turned the thought around in her mind, over and over, until she felt almost dizzy with it. During all these years of exchanging verbal barbs with Raif, it had become habit, one designed to create a wall between them. But instead it had created an intangible link. A link that yesterday had become more tangible than not.

It had shaken her to her core, but from the way he'd walked away from her without a second glance, clearly he hadn't had anywhere the same kind of reaction. Why would he? He was a man well used to women throwing themselves at him. In fact, he'd probably found her kiss boring.

Still, there'd been nothing boring about the erection that had pressed against her. He'd been aroused, of that there had been no doubt. And yet he'd later acted as if nothing had happened between them. Shanal tried to tell herself it was a relief that he'd responded that way and had backed off the instant she'd hesitated. But she was female enough to feel piqued that he'd brushed the whole incident off as nothing special.

"We'll be at Swan Reach before lunchtime," Raif said over his shoulder. "We can take a walk around and then have lunch at the pub."

"That sounds great," she answered.

It would be good to be away from the cozy confines of the boat. As comfortable as it was, being out and around other people would hopefully provide some relief from this uncomfortable awareness she'd woken with. And even more hopefully, it would steer her mind clear of the completely inappropriate thoughts she was having toward Raif.

After mooring the boat they strolled to the local museum and spent a surprisingly companionable few hours poring over the displays and documented social history of the area.

"I always love to see these little museums, don't you?" she commented as they headed to the pub overlooking the river for lunch.

"It certainly gives you an insight into how tough people had it and how determined they were to carve out a living with what they had. Makes you realize how lucky we are."

"True, but your family, particularly, have worked very hard to be that *lucky*. You lost everything, and now look at you all."

"Giving up doesn't come easily to a Masters, that's for sure."

Because the sun continued to shine, at the pub they chose to sit outside at one of the picnic tables on a cobbled courtyard. The waitress was quick to bring them each a drink and menus. Shanal was completely relaxed and laughing at some comment Raif had made when she felt her neck prickle uncomfortably with awareness. She turned around, catching a glimpse of a tall man leaving the courtyard and going through the large glass doors that led into the main dining area.

"Someone you know?" Raif asked.

"I don't know anyone here," she said, turning back to face him.

But even so, she couldn't quite shake the uncomfortable feeling that told her the man had been watching her. She was oddly relieved when they returned to the boat and cast off again. She took control of the wheel for the next hour or so before Raif suggested they pull in on the riverside again. After tying off, he put some music on the stereo and challenged her to a game of backgammon. She'd never played before, but she was a quick study, soon grasping the strategy behind the game and beating him soundly several times. Several games in, she realized that Raif was spending more time watching her, and studying her expressions as she analyzed the board, than concentrating on the game. Eventually, he threw up his hands and cried uncle when she beat him once again.

"Remind me not to be such an awesome tutor next time," he grumbled good-naturedly as she packed up the counters and board.

"Oh dear, was that a blow to your masculinity?" she teased back with mock sympathy.

"Ha, it'd take more than that to knock me down. Now, if you want to challenge me to an arm wrestling match…?"

She laughed aloud. "I think I'll pass on that. I know where my strengths lie."

"You hungry?"

She looked at the time and realized how long they'd been playing backgammon. "I could eat," she admitted, surprised to find it true, even though it hadn't been all that long since lunch.

But then again, she'd ended up only picking at her lunch after that unsettling feeling she'd had of being watched. It had left a shadow lingering in the back of her mind that even now had a presence. She forced herself to ignore it again.

"Come on then. Time for cooking lesson number two."

Shanal followed Raif to the kitchen, where he selected a series of ingredients from the vegetable crisper in the fridge and extracted a couple packets she couldn't identify. Raif began to chop vegetables with an ease that spoke of much practice.

"Now, the key," he said, chopping swiftly, "to impressing your dinner partner is to deliver food to the table that looks as though you slaved over it all day, when in actual fact it only takes a few minutes to throw together."

"Is that so?" Shanal leaned against the counter and watched him, mesmerized by the movement of his hands and how he managed to keep his fingers clear of the flashing blade. "And you've impressed a lot of dinner partners, I take it?"

"I suppose I've dazzled my share," he replied with false modesty, making her laugh again.

"What are you cooking tonight?"

"Me? I'm just doing the grunt work. You're doing the cooking and it'll be a seafood stir-fry, okay?"

She nodded. "I love seafood."

He winked in return. "Me, too."

He showed her how to prepare the squid and left her to it while he poured them each a glass of wine.

"Life doesn't get any better than this," he commented, before handing her wine to her and raising his glass. "To a good life."

Shanal wiped her hands and took the glass, clinking it against his. "A good life," she repeated, then took a sip.

The words were so simple, so easy to say, but while she had it good here and now, she had some serious decisions to make soon. She couldn't keep running away forever, no matter how much she wanted to. It wouldn't be fair to her parents, after she'd already let them down so badly. Yet Shanal looked up at Raif and realized that she'd happily run away with him forever.

She sighed. This was ridiculous. She couldn't feel that way about someone she'd actively avoided for so long it had become second nature. But then life wasn't simple, was it? She'd never have believed in a million years that her normally astute father would have put all his eggs in one very broken financial basket, either. Or that he'd have done something as stupid as risk a life out of pride. But he had, and his mistakes had left him and her mother so terribly weak—financially, physically and emotionally.

Was that what this was for her? A mistake? By running away from Burton as she'd done, she'd acted very irrationally indeed. But as hard as she tried, she couldn't regret it. And as hard as she tried, she could no longer ignore her attraction to Raif. His good looks were undeniable, but it was the man beneath all that male beauty that drew her like a magnet. That made her dream stupid dreams and hope ridiculous things for the future.

Shanal resolutely turned her mind back to the meal

she was preparing under Raif's excellent and patient tutelage, and tried to ignore the ember of warmth that glowed a little brighter every time their hands brushed, or whenever he accidentally bumped into her as they worked side by side in the small kitchen. She drank a little more liberally of her wine than she would normally, enjoying the delicious lassitude that spread through her veins, and taking pleasure in the moment.

Her life was usually so structured, so detail oriented, that it felt positively sinful to be so relaxed. She'd make the most of it while she could. The meal, when she plated it up, was delicious, and when Raif opened another bottle of wine she didn't object, instead holding her glass to him for a refill. It was a clear night, although cold, and they took a couple throw blankets outside with them to watch the stars as they enjoyed their after-dinner drink.

It felt completely natural to curl up next to Raif on the wicker two-seater sofa on the front deck, and with the cabin lights off behind them, to enjoy the reflection of the moon and stars on the gently rippling river. Soft drifts of classical music filtered on the night air from inside, and when Raif lifted his arm to drape it behind Shanal's shoulders, she didn't object, nor did she pull away.

"Look," he murmured, "a shooting star."

"Probably just space junk," Shanal commented with a tiny spark of her usual levelheadedness.

"Where's your sense of romance?" Raif chided gently. "Go on, make a wish."

She thought about where she was and what she had yet to face. A wish? Why not? It was a simple thing, after all, and who knew what lay around the bend? She closed her eyes and wished with all her heart.

"Did you make one?"

"I did," she replied.

"What was it?"

"Isn't it supposed to mean a wish doesn't come true if you tell someone?"

"Are you telling me you've overcome your scientific nature and become a believer in wishes now?" he retorted, but without a sting in his voice.

She hesitated a moment, then put her glass down on the deck before turning to face him in the darkness. "I wished for you."

# Seven

For the first time in his life that he could remember, Raif didn't know what to say. His breath caught in his chest, leaving it tight and aching. Much like another part of his anatomy. The silence stretched out between them.

"To be precise," Shanal eventually said in a small voice, "I wished for you to make love to me."

Every cell in his body urged him to seize the moment and take her up on her wish, but an unwelcome voice of reason whispered in the back of his mind. Why now? Was she looking for rebound sex? They hadn't even touched on her reasons for leaving Burton at the altar, mainly because of Raif's own reticence about hearing them. But whatever those reasons were, did he really want to be her rebound guy?

His hesitation must have communicated itself to Shanal because she suddenly ducked her head and drew away from him.

"I'm sorry. I'm being ridiculous. Probably too much wine. Don't mind me."

She started to get up from the couch, but his arm shot out, his hand clasping hers and pulling her back. He caught her chin between his fingers and lifted her face to his.

"Are you sure, Shanal? Is that what you really want?"

What the hell was he doing, asking her? She'd already said what she wanted and his body was certainly eager and willing to make her wish come true. A little too willing, if the current fit of his jeans was any indicator. He wasn't going to let his hormones take over. If he—if *they*—did this, it would be for the right reasons. And why was he even considering this? Was it to assuage all those pent-up, lustful teenage dreams he'd suffered for so long, or did it have more to do with getting back at Burton Rogers? He thrust the idea of the other man to the recesses of his mind. Burton was not going to intrude on whatever this evening turned out to be. Shanal deserved better than that and hell, so did Raif. He'd wanted her for what seemed like forever and he was more than ready, but she had to be certain. She had to come to him freely, unreservedly, or not at all.

Time crawled to a halt as he waited for her response.

He barely heard her answer when it came, but the softly spoken "yes" was all he needed. He bent his head and caught her lips with his. What he'd planned to be a sensitive and careful caress turned molten as she kissed him back. Her arms snaked around his waist and she pressed her body up against his as if he was a refuge from all the fears she held deep inside. Maybe that's all he was to her right now, but he'd take that, and more.

She was perfection in his arms. Her small frame fitted neatly against his. The softness of her curves melted into him as if the two of them had been carved from one piece. She moaned as he deepened their kiss, as his tongue met hers, as he caressed the roof of her mouth. Her hands found their way under his sweatshirt, tugging at his T-shirt until she touched his flesh.

It was everything he'd ever anticipated and yet not enough at the same time. They were too restricted here, and there was so much he wanted to do with her. So very much. He scooped her into his arms.

"Inside," he growled. "I want to see you. All of you."

"Yes," she whispered in return, her hands reaching for his face and drawing him to her to kiss again.

She was heat and hunger and everything he'd always dreamed she'd be. The kiss they'd shared yesterday had been only a prelude to this moment—the denouement of years of fighting his feelings for her, of subjugating his desire for her. He made their way to his room in the dark, but once there, he laid her down on the bed and reached to switch on the bedside lamps, bathing the room in a warm golden glow. He didn't want to miss seeing a single second of this.

He reached for her, guiding her clothing from her body, exposing her natural beauty to him and relishing the sensation as his palms and fingers caressed her skin and absorbed her heat, letting it mingle with his own. He skimmed his hands up from her tiny waist and over her narrow rib cage, then filled his palms with her breasts before bending down to take her nipple in his mouth. He rolled the peaked flesh with his tongue, pulling softly, feeling a pulse of satisfaction at the moan of pleasure that fell from her swollen lips.

"You are so beautiful," he murmured against her skin.

The words may have been clichéd, but to him, at this

moment, there was nothing better to be said. She *was* beautiful, and right now she was his. He had waited years for this moment and he wasn't about to rush any part of it. He wanted to burn this night into his memory forever. And not just this one night, if he had any say about it. Every night from now on sounded just about perfect.

"You make me feel beautiful," she whispered in return, her voice tinged with wonder. "*You* make me *feel*."

The unspoken message in her words hung in the air between them. He made her feel? What did she mean by that? Had no one ever taken the time to make her feel beautiful, desirable before? Not even the man she had promised to marry? Raif found that hard to believe, but then again, he'd thought there had always been an untouchable air about Shanal. Maybe he needed to revise that thinking. Maybe she carried more of an air of being untouched?

"Shanal? You're not—?"

"A virgin? No. But I don't have a great deal of experience. No one has ever...moved me the way I feel right now," she admitted shyly.

Whoever she'd been with and whatever the circumstances, Raif would make sure that this time, with him, she felt everything that lovemaking could be between two people. She would be as engaged in what they did together as a person could possibly be.

With that in mind, he transferred his attention to her other breast, sucking and pulling gently at her dark brown nipple until it, too, was as taut as its twin. He shifted so he could kiss her lips again, his hands never leaving her breasts, his fingers rolling and tugging at their tips until she began to squirm beneath him.

She kissed him back with a ferocity that made his

blood burn in his veins, scorching him until his entire body was aflame. He'd thought to keep the barrier of his clothing to remind him not to rush things, but found he could no longer wait to feel her body against his, skin on skin, heat on heat, hardness on softness. Her hands were there to help him as he sat up and pulled his sweat-shirt and T-shirt off in one sweep, his skin prickling in tiny goose bumps as her fingertips swept over his torso.

He felt ridiculously clumsy as he fought with the button fly of his jeans and finally shimmied out of the restrictive denim. His briefs, too, came off in haste. He almost groaned in relief as his straining erection was finally free of constraint, but the sense of freedom was short-lived as Shanal's fingers closed around him like a velvet glove.

His eyes slid closed and Raif clenched his jaw with the strain it took not to thrust against her gentle ca-ress, not to give in to the base need that threatened to overwhelm him. Her touch was tentative, exploratory—though she was clearly gaining confidence with each stroke, each featherlight touch. When she reached the aching head of his penis a shudder ran through his body. He opened his eyes and caught the smile of satisfaction on her face.

"You're driving me over the edge," Raif warned, his voice low and tight with need.

"I love that I can do this to you," she answered, her eyes glowing with need. "You're always so confident, so sure of yourself, but like this? In this moment you're vulnerable, and I can't help but wonder at the fact that it's because of me."

Did the woman have no idea of the allure she'd held for him all these years? Clearly, she hadn't the faintest clue that from the first day he'd met her he'd alternated between teenage angst and fighting some crazy hormonal response to her nearness every time they'd been in the same room. She'd always had this effect on him, long before tonight. Hell, even thinking about her had given him a raging hard-on—then and now.

"I'm at your disposal. All yours," he said. "Do what you want with me."

There, he'd handed over the reins to her, to let her act rather than be acted upon. She gestured for him to lie on the bed beside her, and kissed him the moment his head hit the pillow. Her mouth was hot and wet and demanding; her teeth gently abraded his lower lip before she began her exploration of his body.

"I've wondered what you felt like, what you tasted like," she said, positioning herself over him and rising onto her knees.

Her hands were spread like small fans over his chest, her fingertips tracing the shape of his nipples. Raif found himself ultrasensitive to her touch, not to mention the heat of her lower body as she settled over his groin. Shanal leaned down to mimic the movements of her fingers with the tip of her tongue, and he felt her touch all the way to the soles of his feet, his body attuned to her every movement, her every caress.

"Mmm," she murmured, "I like the way you taste."

Her mouth closed over his nipple and she bit gently on the sensitive skin, sending another bolt of sensation plummeting through him. Her long hair slid over him like a drift of silk. He didn't know how much longer he could take this and not lose control, but he reminded himself to stay strong, to let her take the lead the way he'd promised she could.

Somehow he found the strength to hold back, to allow her to continue her voyage of discovery as she followed the contours of his ribs, his abdomen, his belly. But when she began to slide farther down, he knew it was time to take charge again, or it would be all over before it truly began.

Raif flipped her so she lay on her back, her glossy black hair a wave of darkness across the pristine white pillow, her eyes glazed with desire for him. A smile curved those beautiful, sweet lips of hers as she looked up.

"So, I can do to you what you do to me." She said it as a statement, as if she'd discovered some incredible phenomenon.

"And what is that, exactly?" he asked, bending his head to nip at the lushness of her smile.

"Drive you crazy."

"Completely and utterly over the edge."

Even as he spoke, his hands were busy, one supporting most of his weight, the other sliding inexorably down to the apex of her thighs. He felt her heat, her wetness, and groaned.

"You're so ready."

"Then take me," she urged, pressing her mound against the palm of his hand. "Make me feel some more."

"You want me?"

He circled her center with the pad of his thumb, his fingers cupping her moist entrance.

"Yes, oh yes."

Shanal's breath came in short sharp gasps as he increased the pressure of his thumb, incrementally nearing that point of pleasure, taking delight in the uninhibited yearning that spread across her face. He eased one finger inside her, felt her instant response as she clenched tight around him.

"You like that?" he asked, brushing his lips over hers again.

"More, give me more, please," she begged.

Her hands cupped his face and held him to her. Her lips, her tongue, responded to his in feverish delight. He eased a second finger inside her welcoming sheath, and increased the tempo of his thumb, his tongue now mimicking the movement of his fingers as he dipped and dived into the cavern of her mouth in tandem with the center of her core. He felt the moment she tipped over the edge as her body went rigid and strained against him, her fingers now curled tight in his hair, tugging against his scalp as, with a keening cry, she fell into the abyss of orgasm. Her body shook and trembled beneath him and he ached to follow her into that moment of bliss, barely managing to hold himself back. Slowly, gently, he quieted his movements.

After a few moments Shanal moved beneath him. "So that's what everyone raves about? I had no idea. I mean, I've enjoyed sex before but…wow, not like that."

He couldn't help but feel an inordinate amount of pleasure that he should be the one to shatter her past experience into oblivion.

"That's just the beginning," he said. "We've got all night long."

"Thank goodness," she said with a small laugh. "Because I really want to do that again."

"I've created a monster," he groaned theatrically.

"Then I suggest you do something to soothe the beast," Shanal responded, her hands back at his erection. "Because there was something missing in that last effort."

"Missing?"

"Yes, you."

"Well, let's see about correcting that, shall we?"

\* \* \*

Shanal laughed softly, still amazed at the level of response this incredible man had coaxed from her body, and how, instead of leaving her sated, it had left her wanting more. More of him. And the laughter. She'd never laughed in such intimate circumstances with anyone before, yet with Raif everything was okay—natural. She shifted again so she was astride him, and positioned herself over his straining flesh.

"Shanal, wait, we don't have—" Raif started.

But then she lowered herself onto him, taking him into her body, into her heart.

"Shanal," he said again. "We—"

Again his voice cut off as she clenched his length with her inner muscles, the movement sending off ripples of exquisite sensation to spiral through her body. It was as if, having reached that miraculous height he'd brought her to just a little while before, her body now knew exactly what it wanted and exactly how to get it. It was liberating, and he'd done this for her. She moved, rocking and allowing him to withdraw slightly, before plunging down and rocking forward again and again and again, until she lost track of reason and time and could feel only pleasure as it built and built within.

Raif's hands were at her hips, her breasts, everywhere. She felt her body straining toward completion and then it began—that starburst of intense joy, that sense of complete rightness. She looked down, lost in her voyage of discovery, her gaze locked with Raif's. His hips pumped in unison with the movements of her body, his hands now clenched on her hips as he strained upward as if he wanted to lose himself in her forever. And then he hit his peak, his hips jerking, his arms closing around her to pull her down over him, crushing her against his chest as their bodies pulsed in unison.

It felt like eons later that Raif's hands drifted to her back, to caress the length of her spine, to cup her buttocks. Her head rested on his chest, and beneath her ear she could hear his heart still pounding, as hers no doubt did, too. She felt him withdraw from her and made a sound of objection.

"Shanal," Raif said, lifting a hand to brush her hair off her face.

"That was incredible," she sighed against the warmth of his skin, before pressing a kiss right there.

"It was, but sweetheart, we didn't use protection. Are you on the pill?"

"Yes, of course."

She was on a low-dose contraceptive. Anything else created unpleasant side effects for her.

"But you don't have your pills with you."

"True," she acknowledged, and while the scientist in her told her she'd been all kinds of crazy to have sex with Raif unprotected, the woman inside her told her that everything would be fine. "I'll be okay, I'm sure."

"From here on in, we use condoms."

"You brought some with you?" she asked, lifting her head and raising an eyebrow in surprise.

"No, silly." He gave her a gentle slap on her behind. "There are some in the bathroom."

"Then what are we waiting for?" she teased, sliding off him. "They're no good to us in there."

# Eight

Shanal eased from the bed as daylight began to trickle through the windows. Her body felt well used and she could barely keep the smile from her face as she made her way to the bathroom. After relieving herself, she studied her body in the mirror. She should look different after the transformative experience she'd shared with Raif last night, and yet she was still the same old Shanal. Short, neat figure—nothing spectacular. And yet in his arms she'd felt like one in a million—a rare prize to be cherished. No one had ever made her feel this way or taken her to such heights before in her life. In fact, she never wanted to even think about making love with anyone other than Raif after last night.

Locked in the band of intimacy they'd created, Shanal had come to realize some truths in the night. The first being an understanding of why she'd always kept Raif at arm's length for the whole time they'd known one another. She'd instinctively sensed, somehow, just how shattering an effect he would have on her.

How would she have met her educational goals if she'd succumbed to him before she'd completed her doctoral degree? Where would she be right now? Having tasted the glory he offered, she had no doubt that he would have clouded her mind so much that she would have been happy to sacrifice the personal goals she'd always used to drive herself. No, their time and place had not been back then, in the past. But it was here and it was most definitely now.

Raif appeared in the doorway behind her, closing the short distance between them and wrapping her in his arms. He rested his chin on top of her head and met her eyes in the mirror.

"You okay?"

"Never better." She smiled.

"No regrets?"

"None."

"Then come back to bed."

She could already feel his arousal pressing against her, and in that short sweet moment she felt her body react in kind. In the mirror she saw her nipples bead into taut points and a flush of warmth spread over her chest. He did this to her—no, she thought, he did this *for* her. She turned in his arms and lifted her face for his kiss.

They were both starving when they eventually woke again. After a leisurely shower together they made breakfast and ate it on the rear deck of the boat, looking out over the river. Shanal felt tired but invigorated at the same time. And for the first time in the past several weeks she felt as if she could tackle all the worries in her life head-on. A solution to her father's problems had to be able to be found, in a way that would preserve his dignity and still allow for both her parents to enjoy the years they had left together—without requiring Shanal to sacrifice her own life.

"Where are we headed to next?" she asked as they cleaned up the kitchen after breakfast.

"We'll get through Lock 1 and stop at Blanchetown if you like. We could do the historical walk around town or go a little ways out and visit the conservation park."

"Both sound good. Let's play it by ear, shall we?"

They continued up the river. Raif gave three long blasts on the boat's air horn to signal the lock attendant as they approached. Shanal watched with interest as a red flashing light on top of the control box let Raif know a chamber was being prepared for them. Once it was filled with water, they were given a green flashing light to proceed. The whole process went incredibly smoothly and before long they'd passed under the Sturt Highway bridge and were tied up at a new mooring.

Shanal and Raif got off the boat and, arms linked and laughing, headed toward town. She hadn't felt this carefree in forever, she thought, or cared less about how well she was groomed. She was dressed today in one of Raif's long-sleeved T-shirts, topped by a voluminous checkered bushman's shirt, which she'd tied in a clumsy knot at the waist of his sister's jeans. No designer fashion underneath a prim white lab coat for her today, and she'd never felt happier.

As they walked under the bridge, a movement caught her eye, drawing it to a familiar BMW parked near the massive struts that supported the structure. Suddenly she understood that odd sensation she'd experienced yesterday back at the pub where they'd stopped for lunch. That sensation of being watched. Somehow, Burton had tracked them down. He must have had his spies out all along the river, on the lookout for them. After all, it wouldn't have been too hard to have found Raif's Jeep parked back at the marina in Mannum, and worked out the rest from there. Finding her location today had simply been a matter of continuing on the route from yesterday. A sick feeling of dread filled Shanal and she tightened her fingers on Raif's arm.

"What—?" he started to say, then stopped as he realized where she was looking.

She felt him stiffen, and didn't object when he broadened his stance and pulled her behind him. Despite knowing he wanted to protect her, she found the nerves in the pit of her stomach knotting as the driver's door of the car opened. For the briefest second she wondered if she was wrong, if she'd mistaken the make and model of car for someone else's, but then the driver unfolded from inside the vehicle.

Tall, with dark blond hair and a slim build, Burton was impeccably polished as usual. She saw his eyebrows rise slightly as he walked toward them and took in her appearance.

"Slumming it, Shanal?" he said silkily. "That's not like you."

"What are you doing here, Burton?" Raif demanded, before she could respond.

"Why, I'm here for my bride, of course."

"She's not your bride and she's not your possession."

"Well, we'll see about that, won't we," Burton replied, with a smile that held all the warmth of a glacier. "Shanal, could we talk? In private please."

Shanal suppressed a shudder at the saccharine tone in his voice. She wanted nothing more than to grab Raif's hand and run away—get on the boat and out on the river and never look back. And she could still do that. She knew without a doubt that if she asked him, that's exactly what Raif would do. But realistically, she knew she couldn't run away forever. She didn't just have herself to consider. The weight of her father's problems returned to lie across her shoulders like a cape of lead.

"You don't have to do anything you don't want to do," Raif said to her as she started to move out from behind him.

"It's okay. I knew I'd have to talk to him sometime. It may as well be now."

Raif hooked one arm around her and pulled her to him, kissing her fiercely before letting her go. "I'll be waiting right here for you."

She lifted one hand to stroke his cheek with her fingertips. "I know," she breathed softly. "That means everything to me."

"How touching," Burton commented. "I suppose you think you're one up on me now, Masters?"

"I'm always up on you, Burton."

Shanal could hear the loathing in Raif's voice as he answered his old nemesis.

"Funny, I don't believe Laurel felt the same way. As I recall, she chose me over you."

"Don't you dare bring her into this." Raif started to move forward, his hands clenched into fists, but stopped when Shanal put a hand on his chest to halt him.

"Don't, Raif. He's just baiting you," she pleaded.

"Don't dare? Or what?" Burton jeered. "You'll take my fiancée from me again? I don't think so. You'll remember that Laurel left you for me. I don't suppose you told many people that, did you? That she was with me because you weren't enough for her anymore. While you secreted Shanal away in your love nest on the water over there, did you share that piece of information with her?

Does she realize that these past few days have probably been little more than a childish tit for tat? You attempting to get back at me for Laurel choosing me over you."

"Laurel would never have been happy with you. Don't kid yourself into believing differently," Raif growled.

"Oh, really. Perhaps it was more accurate that she would never have been happy with you. She saw that you wouldn't, or perhaps more accurately *couldn't*, offer her what she needed, the way I did. The way I'm doing for Shanal now.

"Shanal, are you coming?" Burton changed tack, his voice once again sickly sweet. "Don't let him trick you any longer, darling. I'll forgive you for this episode if you come with me now. Trust me, this was more about his need to poke at me than any real desire for you. I'm prepared to overlook that and forget all about this if you'll come back where you belong."

Shanal threw Raif a silent plea to refute those poisonous words. What he'd suggested, that Raif had taken her away only to get back at Burton, was nothing but spite on the part of a man thwarted in his goals, surely. When Raif said nothing, she had to ask him.

"Revenge, Raif? Seriously? Was that what all this was about?"

He stood stoic and strong, his eyes not budging from Burton, as if he didn't trust the man one inch. "No."

"But you thought of it, didn't you?" she asked, desperate to know the truth.

"Far as I know, a man can't be condemned for his thoughts."

But he could be condemned for his actions. Had everything about these past couple days been a lie? Had their night of loving been no more to him than a means to an end, driven by rivalry with Burton rather than real feelings for her? Shanal didn't want to believe it was true, but Raif said nothing to tell her differently. He seemed more determined to continue the now silent standoff between the men than to assure her he hadn't been using her.

"Shanal, come with me," Burton instructed. "I promise you, if you come now, everything will be as it was before. I have a message for you, too. From your father. He's counting on you."

Shanal almost got whiplash from the speed at which she spun her head to look at him. The threat implied in his words was clearer than anything he'd ever said before.

"What's he talking about?" Raif asked.

"Nothing," Shanal said automatically, so used to keeping her father's shameful secret that she couldn't bring it out into the open now. The time for confidences in Raif was gone. She cast one more look at him, silently begging him to contradict Burton's accusations—to be someone she could trust again. But even if he did, she was still caught between a rock and a hard place. A helpless sense of the inevitable seeped like a dark fog into her mind.

"Remember just how much you have hanging on this," Burton reminded her in an undertone. "Your job, the roof over your parents' heads. And if you think your father's still worried about his reputation, I can only imagine how he'd feel to see yours raked through the muck along with his."

Shanal bit the inside of her mouth to hold back the cry of protest that instinctively rose. The writing was on the wall. If she didn't go back with Burton, she wouldn't have a job or a reputation left. It would be no hardship for him to use his extensive network and power to ensure that she didn't find work again in Australia. Possibly even overseas, as well. Anyway, seeking work overseas was a moot point with her parents needing her so much and her father's illness progressively getting worse. But without the income from her job, how would she be able to take care of her parents?

"I'm losing patience," Burton said with an ugly twist to his mouth. "Figure out what you want, *darling*. You are running out of time."

It was what he left unsaid that drove her to her decision. She knew he wouldn't hesitate to act. To make both hers and her parents' lives hell. There was only one thing left she could do.

"I'm coming, but let me say goodbye to Raif— alone," she added, when Burton made no move to get back into his car.

"Two minutes, no more," he conceded.

The second his car door was closed Raif caught her by her arms. "You don't have to do this," he said urgently.

She looked into his eyes and knew this was the end of what they'd shared together. "Yes, I do. Look, whatever your reasons for helping me, I am grateful at least for the fact you got me away from a situation I wasn't comfortable with."

"What about us?"

"Good question." She dived on his words. "What Burton said about you wanting to hurt him, that was true, wasn't it?"

"I can't lie, Shanal. Not to you. There's bad blood between us and yes, it did cross my mind and give me a certain amount of pleasure to know that spiriting you away would drive him crazy."

She felt Raif's words as if they were tiny cuts across her heart. "Then that's all I needed to know."

"But that's not all," he persisted. "It might have started that way—back in the park, at the very beginning—but it isn't how I feel now. Not about you, Shanal."

"How can I believe you?" she asked desperately, tears filling her eyes and obscuring her vision. "Let's be honest, Raif. For years we've been sparring with one another. We've never seen eye to eye and it's not as if we were ever friends. I'm the fool. I should have questioned your willingness to help me in the first place."

And really, what did it matter whether she believed him or not? Staying with him wasn't an option, even if he truly wanted her to. She had only one choice available to her: she had to go back with Burton. That crushing sense of how inescapable her situation was now consumed her. She pulled away.

"I have to go. He won't wait forever."

"Let him leave then."

"I can't."

She forced herself to turn away from Raif and walk toward the car. Burton got out as she approached and strode around to the passenger side to hold the door open for her.

"Looks like history repeats itself," he taunted. "And yet again, I win the girl."

# Nine

Raif watched as the BMW drove away, his body a mass of bunched muscle still tensed in shock. He couldn't believe what had just happened. That Shanal had chosen Burton over him. Burton's parting jeer echoed in his head, and a red film of rage crossed Raif's vision. The man was toxic. He'd twisted the truth of what had happened in the past—surely Shanal had to see that.

So why had she chosen to return to him? There had to be more to it. She was an intelligent woman and she had to see that things didn't add up with Burton. The man always had an agenda, always had to be on top— by fair means or foul.

Even when they'd been at private school together he'd been competitive, but that had been nothing compared to how competitive Burton had become as they'd grown into adulthood. Nothing was sacred anymore. Burton had crossed the bridge between good-natured rivalry and the out and out need to win at any cost long before they'd finished high school. Raif had felt the rifts in their camaraderie—for they had never truly been friends—years ahead of the issue with Laurel.

But none of that meant anything right now, he thought as he watched the taillights on the BMW flick once before it turned and disappeared from view. All that mattered was that the woman who'd blown his mind and his body into new realms had walked away from him for good.

Raif strode back to the houseboat. There was nothing keeping him here now. He needed to get back downriver and home. As he shoved off and headed back toward the lock he considered everything that had happened in the past four days. It had been such a short time and yet it felt like so much longer.

After passing through the lock and setting his course, Raif let his mind mull over the final confrontation. Though he hadn't heard everything they'd said to each other, there'd been an undercurrent between Shanal and Burton. He'd felt it as if it was a tangible thing. Their body language had not been that of lovers, that was for sure. In fact, when he thought back to the church—to before that moment when Shanal had dropped her bouquet, given Burton back his ring and headed for the door—Raif had noticed already the sense of triumph in Burton's posture. As if Shanal was a prize he'd won, rather than the woman he loved and wanted to spend the rest of his life with.

Raif knew Shanal deserved more than that in her life partner. In fact, he'd always believed she wanted more than that, too. Even Ethan had said the same after that botched business when he'd asked Shanal to marry him, as part of his misguided efforts to avoid admitting his own feelings about Isobel a couple years back. If Shanal was the kind of woman who was just after what money could bring her, or even if she simply wanted a marriage that brought practical benefits and made logical sense, she'd have accepted Ethan's offer with alacrity, not laughingly but lovingly turned him down. And Ethan was her best friend—someone she always looked at with warmth and affection, even if there was no heated passion between them. There had been no warmth or affection in her expression when Shanal looked at Burton.

Raif thought about the niggle he'd had a day or so ago, suspecting there was way more to this than met the eye. His instincts hadn't let him down before and he had no reason not to trust in them now. And even if he was wrong about Shanal and what she really wanted, he needed to know the truth, for his own sake. If he was right, and he fully expected to be, somehow he'd convince her to walk, hell, *run* away from Burton again. And this time, he'd hold on to her and keep her safe forever.

Traveling back on his own had been harder than Raif had anticipated. First there was the physical evidence of their passionate lovemaking to contend with. Second was the physical memory of expecting her to be by his side when he worked in the kitchen or even here, at the helm of the boat. The houseboat was not large and yet it felt echoingly empty without Shanal there beside him. He couldn't get away from it fast enough. What had taken them a leisurely few days to travel upriver, he accomplished in half the time, heading back down.

Mac was at the marina to greet him.

"Everything handle okay?" the older man said.

"Like a breeze," Raif replied, tossing him the rope to tie off.

"Where's your little lady?"

"Gone home with her fiancé," he answered, unable to keep the bitterness from his voice.

"Her what?"

"Yeah, Burton Rogers. You remember him?"

"Remember him, sure. Ever want to see him again? No. I couldn't understand it when Laurel left you for him. I thought I'd raised her to have better judgment than that. But I think she was swayed more by what he could offer her than by who he was. I've always like to think that if she'd lived, she'd have eventually figured him out and left him."

Raif just grunted in response. After all, what could he say? That he'd stood by and not fought back when she'd given him an ultimatum about marriage or breaking up? He hadn't been ready for that commitment. But he certainly hadn't been ready to lose her altogether, either. And the thought that his choice had driven her into Burton's arms and from there to her death... No, he wouldn't let himself think about that.

"What happened?" Mac asked.

Raif gave him a brief rundown once he was off the boat.

"And you let her go?" There was censure in the older man's voice.

Raif wanted to vehemently deny it, but he couldn't. "She was never mine to hold on to."

Mac stared out at the slow-moving river. "You know, I never held with that saying about letting love go free. I've always thought that if you really want something, you gotta hunt it down and fight to keep it."

"My thoughts exactly," Raif concurred, picking up his bag. "And that's just what I'm going to do."

"That's my boy." Mac slapped him approvingly on the shoulder.

Raif drove back to his home in the Adelaide Hills in heavy rain, which meant he had to keep his concentration very firmly on the road ahead and not on his plans to get back Shanal, where he wanted it to be. But the minute he walked through his front door he was reminded of the last time he'd returned home, and who he'd had with him.

There was a note from his cleaner on the hall table:

> I have hung the wedding dress that was on the floor in the guest room en suite on a hanger in the guest room wardrobe. Please inform me if you need the garment sent to the dry cleaner.
> —H.

Raif cracked a wry smile. It would have been worth it to see the expression on his cranky cleaner's face when she came across that little surprise. He went to the spare room to see the dress in question.

It hung in all its subdued glittering splendor on the rail, the layers of froth at the bottom almost filling the generous space of the wardrobe. Off Shanal's body it lacked the power and substance it had carried when she'd worn it into the church last Saturday. It was nothing more than a pretty dress with maybe a few too many sparkles attached. He wondered if she wanted it back, and the dainty shoes set beneath it on the shoe rack.

A swell of impotent rage filled him, making him want to drag the gown from its hangar and cast it back on the floor where Shanal had left it. He swallowed against the urge to roar in disgust at the whole situation. The relief would be only temporary and yelling would do nothing whatsoever toward solving the problem. Shanal had chosen to go with Burton. Sure, there had been disturbing undercurrents between her and her fiancé—it didn't take an honors student to figure that out. What they hadn't said in front of him was certainly more interesting than what they had.

But how to get to the bottom of it, that was the question. Burton had to have some kind of leverage over Shanal. He just had to. Or did he? Maybe it was just that Raif preferred to believe that, since otherwise he'd be forced to conclude that Shanal had used him simply to make a point with her fiancé. He shoved the idea ruthlessly from his mind before it could bloom into anything else.

She was not like that. At least, she'd never been like that in all the years he'd known her. Besides, Ethan was a great judge of character and he certainly wouldn't call someone his best friend if she was the type of person to use another, to go so far as to sleep with him, simply to further her own agenda. And there'd been that sense of innocence about Shanal when they'd kissed and when they'd made love for the first time. That wasn't something you could fake.

Raif slammed the door of the wardrobe and strode from the room. He'd get to the bottom of this somehow.

Shanal shoved a pen behind her ear and rubbed at her eyes. Working late at the laboratory, going over and over the test results from their latest genetic experiment to increase the yield of a particular strain of vinafera hybrid, had done nothing to calm her mind or relieve the ever tightening noose of strain that trapped her. She pushed her chair back from her desk and stared out the window of her office into the darkness that lay beyond. How symbolic it was of her life at the moment, at least of her future, she thought with a shiver of foreboding.

When Burton had delivered her to her parents' home on Tuesday night last week, she'd felt exhausted and unwilling to talk. But sometime in the night she'd heard her mother up and moving about in the house, and she'd gone to her. Shanal still couldn't quite rid herself of the dreadful and overwhelming sense of guilt she'd felt as she'd seen her mother—her shoulders bowed, her skin gray with worry and her mouth a grim line as she'd paced back and forth. It was Shanal's fault her mom was unable to sleep even though she was exhausted from caring for her husband all day. All their problems could be solved if she'd just do one thing—marry Burton Rogers.

And she had a second chance now to put things right, even if doing so would probably kill every last dream and hope she'd ever had. She had to go through with it, though, for her father and for her mother. They'd done everything for her, given her every opportunity. Oh, sure, she knew that's what parents did for their beloved children. Yes, with love came sacrifice. But what of her love for them? If she could do anything, anything at all, to make her father's remaining time—whether it be months or years—as trouble free and comfortable as he'd worked to make her life from the day she was born, she would do it. It was that simple.

And that hard.

Burton had been civil since he'd brought her home—that was about the only term she could use to describe the cool politeness with which he greeted her each day as she'd arrived at work. She caught his reflection behind hers in the window now. It was as if thinking about him had helped him to materialize here in her office. She turned, ready to face him.

"You've been home a week now," he said calmly, but she could see the vein pulsing high on his forehead, at the edge of his hairline. She'd learned that was the marker that he was less than pleased. "I thought you might have made some effort to discuss our wedding by now."

"I…" Her voice trailed away. There was nothing to say.

"I've been more than reasonable, Shanal—I've given you a week to pull yourself together after your unfortunate behavior. But I think you can appreciate that I will not wait forever. I want you as my wife. Set a date."

There was a grim note of determination to his voice that sent a shiver down her spine. She held back a sigh and swiveled her chair around to face him.

"Twelfth of September," she said, as firmly as she could. She pulled her calendar up on her phone and scrolled through the dates. "But no fuss this time. Just something small."

He nodded. "Excellent. I'll make the arrangements. I'm glad to see you've come to your senses. The twelfth is perfect timing. I'll be back by then."

"Back? From where?" He hadn't mentioned anything about having to go away anywhere in the lead-up to their original wedding day.

"I'm needed at our facility in California. An urgent and unexpected matter. I leave tomorrow."

Shanal fought to hide her relief. Not having his oppressive presence around would be small compensation for the next few weeks, at least.

"A problem?" she asked.

"Nothing I can't handle," he replied smoothly.

He stepped forward and raised a hand to grip her chin and tilt her face upward, then bent down to kiss her. His lips were cold and smooth, so very much like the man himself. Despite his coaxing, she kept her mouth firmly closed. This was nothing like the warmth and slow burning need she'd shared with Raif. In fact, if two men could be polar opposites, then Burton and Raif were that. Instead of desire gently unfurling within her, she felt the sting of distaste. Instead of anticipation, she felt only dread.

She would submit when it was time, but right now, with the memory of Raif's kisses still so sweet and fresh in her mind, this embrace of Burton's was nothing but a travesty. She jerked back slightly as he suddenly released her and straightened, looking down upon her once more, his face impassive.

"See if you can't drum up a little enthusiasm for my touch while I'm gone, hmm? And I expect I don't have to tell you this, but stay away from Raif Masters."

And with that parting shot he was gone. He didn't need to verbalize a threat. She knew what would happen if she saw Raif again and Burton found out. All bets would be off the table and he'd follow through on his threats against her. As much as Burton Rogers coveted her, he wouldn't share her with anyone else—certainly not a second time.

He was not a man who liked to be thwarted. She knew her appeal to him had grown out of his need to surround himself with rare and beautiful things. The way he looked at her, as if she were a priceless artifact, made her feel more objectified than if he'd wolf-whistled every time he saw her. Her intelligence only served to make her more appealing to him, she knew for a fact. And as his wife, she'd never leave his employ. All of that played into his original reasons for proposing. And now, ever since the wedding day that wasn't, she got the sense that his competitiveness with Raif just made him more determined to "win" her away from his rival and lock her into marriage vows once and for all.

Despite the way everything inside her railed against Burton's dictates, she wouldn't be making any effort to see Raif again. He'd used her—he hadn't even attempted to deny it. And even more galling, she'd been his willing partner in that. The man had swamped her with feeling, with emotion. He had cut past all the clinical and careful ways she'd lived her life to date, and made her aware of everything with a clarity that had taken her breath away. And it had all happened so darn fast.

How could she trust it? She was the kind of person who measured everything twice, examined every minute detail over and over. Who took the greatest care before committing to a decision, whether it be work or social or even what shoes to wear with her outfit each morning.

Raif was the antithesis of that. He was impulsive and daring. Physical and creative. Her body burned anew as she remembered just *how* creative he could be. They'd spent only one intimate night together, and one equally intimate morning, learning one another's bodies as if they were maps to a pirate's bountiful treasure, but the memories they'd created burned with perpetual ferocity, making her nights ever since barren and empty by comparison.

Shanal let go of the breath she'd been holding. She'd thought the idea of marrying Burton before was impossible. Marrying him now was going to be a great deal more difficult than she had ever imagined. But she'd do it. She had no other choice.

# Ten

Raif pulled up outside Shanal's parents' home. Shanal hadn't taken his calls last Friday at work, nor would she come to the phone over the weekend. An attempt to see her at Burton International had led to being escorted from the building by security—whether by Burton's dictate or Shanal's, he couldn't be sure.

There was nothing left but to try and catch her here, at home. Raif knew Mr. and Mrs. Peat were out because he'd just passed them in their specially modified car, heading the other way. He drummed his fingers on the steering wheel for a minute before grabbing the garbage sack he'd stowed on the seat beside him, and getting out the car. Bringing the Maserati probably hadn't been the best idea, but he'd realized that only after he'd shoved and squeezed the bag full of the foaming concoction of material that was Shanal's wedding dress into the trash bag and put it in the passenger seat beside him. And once he'd gotten it into the car, there was no way he was dealing with hauling it back out until it was time to pass it over once and for all.

Shanal's car was nowhere to be seen, but he knocked on the front door of the house anyway, and counted slowly under his breath, waiting for an answer. Nothing. Seconds later, he noticed her little hatchback slowing outside the house. From his vantage point on the front porch he saw the moment she recognized his car parked out front.

She pulled into the driveway and looked toward the front door, her face pale and her beautiful eyes huge as she saw him standing there. For a second he thought that she'd shove the car into Reverse and back out of there and away from him as fast as she could. Instead she appeared to hasten to get out the car. She all but ran the short distance to the front door.

A waft of her scent, that combination of spice and flowers that he would never again be able to smell without thinking of her, tantalized him. She looked tired. He'd bet good money that Burton was responsible for that, too. It made Raif want to physically remove Shanal from the man's noxious sphere. But, he reminded himself grimly, she'd made her choice and that choice had not been him.

"What are you doing here?" she asked in a fierce undertone, looking over her shoulder at the road—almost as if she was afraid she was being watched.

"I had to return this. I imagine you'll be needing it again soon?" He deliberately let the jibe fall from his lips.

She flinched as if the words had held more sting than he'd intended. "Thank you," she said stiffly, raising her eyebrows a little at the receptacle he'd chosen to return the dress in. She took the bag from him and then stood to one side as if, dress delivered and accepted, she now expected him to leave.

"And we need to talk," he continued.

"There's nothing to talk about. Please leave."

"Not until you answer at least one question."

"Fine," she huffed, her eyes drifting up and down the street before returning to his face. "Spit it out."

"Why are you marrying him?"

"Because I have to. You've asked your question. I've answered it. You can go now. If Burton knew you were here—"

"What?" he interrupted. "What would he do?"

"Please, Raif, just leave," she begged.

A sour taste filled Raif's mouth when he recognized the fear behind her words. "What? Can't you do anything without his approval? And you're telling me you want to *marry* him? Is he really the kind of man you want to be bound to for the rest of your life?"

"I've asked myself a lot of things, Raif, but it all comes back to the same thing. He's the man I'm going to marry."

Raif shoved a hand through his hair. "I just don't get it. Why him? You don't love him, I know that for a fact. A woman like you... Well, I doubt you'd have shared yourself with me the way you did if you actually had feelings for him. Unless...unless *you* were using *me*. Playing me off against him for some crazy reason. Was that what it was?"

If anything, her face paled even more. The garbage sack fell from her fingers and her eyes filled with tears. "Is that what you think? That I'd do something like that?"

"Is it true?"

She shook her head vehemently. "No, it's not. Now, I've answered more than one question. Consider the extras a bonus and please leave."

Shanal reached into her handbag and pulled out a house key. Her hand was shaking as she fitted it to the lock. Raif reached to take the key from her and finish the job, but she pulled away so quickly when his fingers brushed hers that the key fell to the floor. He bent to pick it up, and shoved it into the lock, giving it a sharp turn and pushing the door open. He extracted the key and made a show of handing it back to her carefully so that they didn't need to touch at all this time.

"I'm not going to let this go, Shanal. You ran away from him once."

"That was a mistake. Finding out you used me to get back at Burton helped me to realize what I need to do," she said breathlessly, and pushed past him to get inside the house.

"Shanal, really? Do you honestly think that what we shared together was about revenge?"

She sighed deeply. "No," she admitted with a huff of air, and started to close the door.

"I'm still here for you. Confused as hell about why you're doing this, but here for you. Do you understand me?"

"I don't need you, Raif. I have Burton. Goodbye."

The door shut in his face. He considered knocking on it, demanding she explain further, but he knew it would be futile. He went back to his car, and all the way home replayed her words over and over in his mind. Not once had she mentioned caring for Burton or, heaven forbid, loving him. So why the hell was she going through with this again?

Love was, or at the very least *should* be, the only

reason one person married another. Marriage was a lifetime commitment. It was the blending of two people to make a better whole. A combination of personalities that knitted together with one thread. It was the root stock of a family, the basis for generations to come. What sense was there in starting a relationship like that without a strong foundation of love in the place first?

As he pushed the Maserati the winding miles back to his home, Raif realized that, more than anything, he wanted a real, loving marriage—and he wanted it with Shanal. His foot eased a little on the accelerator as a new revelation filled him. He loved her, and probably had since he was a teenager. All those little barbs they'd flung at one another, on his side at least, had masked deeper feelings. Feelings he'd hidden after the embarrassment of her rejection all those years ago. But deep down, underneath it all, he loved her and, subconsciously at least, he hadn't been able to settle for anyone else. He'd been prepared to wait.

Accepting the knowledge brought a strange sense of peace, easing the turmoil of his thoughts. It was right. Maybe the timing hadn't been the best for them in the past, and by the looks of things, it certainly wasn't now, but Raif wasn't about to let her go. Initial failure had never discouraged him from striving to reach his goals before, and he wasn't about to let it knock him back now. Whether she knew it or not, the waiting was over.

Shanal Peat was his. He had only to convince her of that, to gain her full trust. Then and only then would she let him know the true reason why she was thinking about marrying Burton. She hadn't even been able to lie about her reason for marrying him. If she'd have said she loved him then maybe, just maybe, Raif might have stepped back.

He chewed the thought over in his mind and then barked a cynical laugh. Who was he kidding? There was no way on this earth he would accept that a woman as sensitive and vulnerable as Shanal could love a man like Burton Rogers. But could she love Raif? He certainly hoped so, because suddenly the idea of a life without her in it loomed very emptily ahead.

Shanal lifted her head in shock at the doctor's words. *"Pregnant?"*

A roaring sound filled her ears. She couldn't be pregnant. It just wasn't possible. She knew the doctor continued to talk to her, and somehow she must have responded, but she failed to grasp his words. She'd come to the surgery, on her mother's insistence, for a general checkup, because she'd been feeling off-color and over-tired these past few weeks. While Shanal was ready to blame her general malaise on the stress she was feeling with her wedding in only two weeks' time, not to mention her current workload, she was not prepared for this.

And then there were the daily calls from Burton, checking up on her even though she had a very strong suspicion he also had people watching her every movement. He'd dropped a bombshell last night, telling her he'd wrapped up his business early and would be home tomorrow. She'd hung up from the call and felt so ill with nerves at the prospect of seeing him again that she'd been forced to head straight for the bathroom as her stomach rejected its contents. She'd put it down to anxiety, but it seemed the cause was something far more alarming.

This morning, her mother had been insistent that she see her doctor, and Shanal had been lucky enough to fit into his schedule, thanks to a cancelation. Now this. Her hand automatically fluttered to her lower belly, to where a child was forming. Her baby—and Raif's.

This was unarguably the worst thing that could happen to her right now. There had been only the one time without protection. She'd been off the pill for just three days. She'd believed the odds of her becoming pregnant to be so remote as to be unsustainable, and yet here she was. Her head swam as she tried to adjust to the news. She was going to be a mother.

Fear and exhilaration battled with equal strength inside her. What on earth was she to do? She certainly couldn't marry one man while she was pregnant with another man's child. How was she going to tell either of them?

By the time she was outside the doctor's office and back in her car she was no clearer on what to do. She'd shoved the fistful of brochures the nurse had given her into her handbag without even looking at them. She couldn't push more information into her brain just yet. She was still struggling to accept the fact that her life was on the cusp of massive change at a level she'd never imagined.

"Your fiancé will be excited, I'm sure," the nurse had said with a cheerful smile and a knowing look at the ring Shanal had been forced to wear again.

*Excited* was not the word she would use, mainly because given the fact they'd barely done more than share several lukewarm kisses, Burton would know there was no chance the baby was his. He hadn't pressured her into anything more, saying he was happy to wait until their wedding night. The wedding night that had never happened. Her stomach clenched on that thought. The nurse was looking at her brightly, expecting a reply. Shanal could only murmur an indistinct sound in response. She dreaded the thought of his actual reaction. The last thing she wanted was to give the manipulative man beneath the courteous veneer another reason to tighten the leash he already had her on.

Shanal started the car and pointed it in the direction of her parents' home. Somehow she'd get through today. And then tomorrow, when Burton returned; she'd get through that, as well. She didn't want to think past that point because the variables were far too many and most of them too awful to even consider. One step at a time. That's what took her through her research and that's what would get her through the next twenty-four hours, too.

On Saturday, Shanal drove to Burton's inner-city apartment when she received his call to say he was home. He'd sounded pleased when she'd said she needed to see him, but she doubted he'd sound that way for long once he heard what she had to say. All the way up in the elevator, she twisted the strap of her handbag round and round, letting it go to unravel, then she'd start all over again. It was much like her stomach felt right now, she thought. Caught up in a coil of tension that would release momentarily, then wind back up. Each time tighter than before.

The door to Burton's apartment swung open before she could so much as raise her hand to press the bell.

"Come in," he said, leaning forward to kiss her, his expression of welcome freezing just a little when she averted her head so his lips grazed her cheek and not their intended target. "I've missed you, darling. Did you miss me, too?"

Oh, she had. She absolutely had. But not in the way he obviously hoped—more like how someone missed an aching tooth once it had been pulled. "It's been quiet without you," she said in a weak compromise.

He laughed, the sound forced and artificial in the soullessly beautiful, magazine-spread-style perfection that was his apartment. It had never bothered her before, but somehow now it felt empty of personality. More like a stage than a home and nothing at all like Raif's house, which, although modern, was furnished in a warm and comfortable manner. What she'd seen of it during her short time there, anyway.

"I'm flattered that you were in such a hurry to see me. Come, let me get you something. A cup of tea? Coffee?"

Her stomach lurched. "Maybe a glass of water."

He cast her an assessing glance. "Are you feeling well, Shanal? You're a little pale."

And here it was. Her opening. But she couldn't quite find the words. How did you tell your fiancé you were expecting another man's baby? And not just any man's, but the baby of the man he hated above all others. She'd realized that fact the day on the riverbank.

"I've been feeling a little unwell recently," she admitted, taking the glass of water he gave her and having a small sip.

"Nothing serious, I hope? Have you been to the doctor?"

He was all concern, on the surface at least. But she could see the hard glint in his eyes as he studied her, looking for signs of imperfection.

"No, it isn't serious—well, not in a life-threatening way at least," she said with a wry quirk to her lips. "And, yes, I've seen a doctor. He gave me some surprising news."

"News?" Burton dropped all pretense of civility. "Cut to the chase, Shanal. What's wrong with you?"

"Actually, nothing is *wrong*, per se. I'm just pregnant, that's all."

# Eleven

Burton's face went pale, then suffused with vivid color as he digested her words. *"Pregnant?"*

"I know, it came as a surprise to me, too."

"A surprise. That's rich. We both know it's not my child. You haven't let me touch you."

"We agreed on that, Burton." She felt she had to point it out in her defense.

"Yes, but not because I thought you would let your passions overwhelm you and drive you to sleep with Raif Masters!" he spat in return.

Shanal flinched. Burton had never shown anger like this before. Sure, she understood he had to be very angry indeed at this news. It was a very unexpected wrinkle in the fabric of his plans. But it had happened. Now they needed to deal with it.

"You'll get rid of it, of course," he stated flatly.

"I beg your pardon?" Shanal couldn't quite believe what he'd said.

"I have chosen to accept the fact that you've slept with Raif Masters, however ill-advised it was, and move on. I will not, however, accept his bastard as a cuckoo in my nest. You *will* get rid of it," he ordered, his voice seething with revulsion, "and before the wedding."

"Rid of it? You mean—?"

"Yes, of course I mean an abortion. Let me be very clear, Shanal. I won't tolerate you continuing this pregnancy for a moment longer than necessary. Remember what you have at stake here. If you insist on going through with this pregnancy you can forget about the money you need so very much to help your parents, and you can forget about your position with Burton International. And let's not forget your restraint clause. I will invoke that if I have to. And you can be certain that once those two years are up, I will make sure you never get work in this field again into the bargain.

"Ask yourself, what do you really want? Hmm? The choice is yours. But if you choose me, then you do so without that man's brat inside you."

Fine tremors rocked her body. She couldn't believe what Burton was asking of her. Every particle within her vehemently rejected his ultimatum, but what other choice did she have? Her father couldn't work anymore. Her mother was now his full-time caregiver, and besides, she'd never worked outside the home. Even if she could find a job it would be unskilled and the pay would hardly make a dent in their living costs. For her entire married life her sole focus had been her husband and Shanal. If they could sell their home, sure, their debts would be cleared, but where would they live? What would they do to cover their living expenses? It was likely a moot point, anyway, with the mortgage that Burton now held over the property. They'd never be able to sell it with his interests registered against it.

Burton's stipulation was an all-or-nothing deal. If she married him, she continued with her work and provided the necessary security for her family, but that meant she'd have to give up the child of a man who'd done everything she'd asked of him without question, but who could do nothing to save her now.

"What's it to be, Shanal?" Burton pressed relentlessly.

Could she do what he asked? She swallowed against the lump in her throat and lifted her head to look at this man she'd agreed—not once, but twice—to marry.

In a voice that sounded foreign to her ears she replied, "I'll marry you."

A smile stretched across Burton's face and Shanal watched in horror, wondering how she'd ever thought him handsome.

"Don't you worry about the details, darling," he said with that crocodile smile. "I'll arrange everything. Besides, we can't have a baby ruining that pretty little figure of yours, can we?"

His words sent a chill through her. She could understand he wouldn't want Raif's child, but from what he'd just said, he didn't ever want to see her pregnant. "Burton, are you saying you don't want children at all?"

"When we're ready we can use a surrogate. I don't want anything to mar the perfection of you, Shanal. Not now, not ever. I remember the first time I saw you. I knew you had to be mine. I couldn't believe my luck when you interviewed for the position at the lab eighteen months ago. There was no way I was letting you go. Ours will be the perfect marriage and together we'll make Burton International the number-one research facility in the world."

Two things locked into her mind. First, that he'd planned to marry her all this time. And second, that she'd earned her role in the lab based on her looks rather than her qualifications. She'd never felt more trivialized in her life. The knowledge heightened her loathing of him.

Oblivious to her distress, Burton continued. "So, tell me, you are going to wear that exquisite gown again for our wedding, aren't you? I can't wait to see you in it once more."

By the time Shanal left his apartment she felt bruised inside. Through everything they'd discussed, she couldn't help feeling she was making the worst mistake of her life. Raif had tried to warn her months ago and she hadn't been prepared to listen. But then again, she had never seen the side of Burton that she'd seen today.

It was as if he were two distinct people—the charming, urbane, smiling gentleman boss on the one hand, and a calculating, controlling despot on the other. And she was linking herself to him, in marriage, forever. He didn't even really see her as a person, but more of an asset. This wasn't what she'd mentally signed up for when she'd first agreed to marry him. Although maybe, somewhere along the line, she'd subconsciously realized who Burton Rogers really was when she'd chosen to run away from the cathedral that day. If only that instinct had taken over before she'd agreed to his proposal in the first place.

How could she go through with this?

She thought about her parents, of her father wilting away in his wheelchair. Of her mother, burdened with his care.

How could she not?

\* \* \*

On Monday morning, at work, she got a call to see Burton in his office. She smoothed her white coat with trembling hands and knocked on the door to his inner sanctuary.

"Come in," he answered, his muted voice sending a shiver down her spine.

"You asked to see me?" she said, as she stepped inside.

Burton had his back to her, surveying the impeccably landscaped grounds outside. Slowly he turned. Shanal looked at him and felt her skin crawl. Her hands curled into balls and she shoved them into the deep pockets of her white coat. Maybe if she could just focus on the pain of her fingernails embedding into her palms, she could fight back the swell of nausea assailing her that had absolutely nothing to do with her pregnancy.

"How are you today, darling?" he said with a smile that she noticed didn't touch his eyes.

"Busy." Her response was clipped and to the point. And it was true, she was incredibly busy in the lab. An intern had inadvertently corrupted important data on her most recent study and she'd been cross-referencing her notes all morning.

"Glad to see you're still taking your responsibilities to your work so seriously. Which leaves the other matter." Burton's mouth pulled into a frown of distaste.

She stared at him, refusing to acknowledge "the matter" in the same terms as he had couched them. Logically, she'd known that Burton wouldn't be happy with the news about the baby, but her mind emphatically rejected the idea that he could so clinically dismiss the child that even now formed within her.

"You'll be pleased to know I've been able to have

you scheduled at a private clinic the day after tomorrow. That gives you ten days to recover before our wedding."

"Wednesday? So soon?" she blurted.

"It doesn't pay to allow these things to linger," he said, all pretense of amiability now gone. "I'll pick you up in the morning and take you myself."

No doubt to ensure that she went through with it, she thought, nodding to indicate that she had heard.

"Is that all?" she said, now desperate to leave the oppression his presence had become.

"For now," Burton said, turning back to the view outside, dismissing her as if she was no longer of consequence now he'd made his dictate clear.

A phrase he'd mentioned on Saturday, about not wanting anything to mar the perfection of her, echoed in her mind. Was that all she was to Burton? An image of his idea of perfection? Something to be admired and brought out and displayed at will? She'd honestly thought, even though she didn't love him, that they could possibly make a go of marriage. If she hadn't believed that from the very start she would never have agreed to marry him. But now, that looked less and less likely. And yet how on earth was she to extricate herself from this dreadful mess? He held all the cards and he'd made no bones about playing them to punish her if she thwarted him in any way.

She entered her office and closed the door firmly behind her before sinking into her chair and staring with blind eyes at the data displayed on her computer screen. Sure, she could tell Raif—in fact she *should* tell Raif— about the baby. She knew without doubt that she and the child would be gathered up in the embrace of his family in an instant. But what of her parents? What of her career? If she didn't do as Burton said, she'd save a potential life but destroy every other person and thing in her world that mattered.

What the hell was she going to do?

Shanal woke with a dreadful sense of loss on Wednesday morning. She'd barely slept and she felt weak and vulnerable as she prepared herself for the visit to the clinic. Burton would be here any moment and she had to be ready, but she struggled to find the motivation to wash and dress and gather her few things together. Doggedly, she pushed on, hoping she could be gone before her parents rose for the day. She had no wish to face them before the procedure. She couldn't bear to tell them any of it—about the pregnancy, or the abortion—because it would only expand the guilt her father already wore like a heavy yoke around his neck. It was better that they knew nothing about this.

The flash of Burton's lights as he turned into the driveway propelled her out the front door.

"All set?" he asked, as she got into his BMW.

She nodded, unable to speak. This was wrong, so wrong.

He reached across and patted her on the knee. "Don't worry, Shanal. Everything will be okay once it's over."

But would it? She'd still be tied to a man who was more ruthless than she'd ever expected. A man who lived to his own agenda without a thought or a care for others. A man who had blackmailed her into staying with him. Raif had tried to warn her, but she hadn't listened, hadn't seen what he'd been talking about. And now an innocent life would be lost because of it.

How many people had Burton hurt in his quest for perfection? Shanal had always admired how he didn't waver on the level of his standards. In fact, she'd been proud to work for a man who never accepted less than the best. It was how she'd worked her entire life. Always reaching to set the bar higher, to ensure that her marks were that much better, the results of her research unquestionable. They hadn't been so different, had they?

Nonetheless, there was an edge to Burton that she'd completely misunderstood. She'd thought it was a sign of his quest for excellence, but now it only seemed to be indicative of his quest to dominate.

They completed the journey in silence. Burton escorted her from the car to the admitting area and bent to kiss her on the cheek before he left.

"Call me when you're done and I'll come back for you," he said. "You're doing the right thing. Our life is going to be perfect together, Shanal. Trust me on this."

Perfect? She swallowed back the bitterness that rose in her throat. Perfect was lazy days on a houseboat on the Murray River. Perfect was a passionate night in the arms of Raif Masters. Her eyes filmed with unshed tears as she turned to confirm her details with the nurse waiting to admit her. She felt Burton leave, the air around her lightening in his absence.

The nurse was compassionate and professional, briskly showing Shanal through to the room where she'd change into her hospital gown, and discussing what would happen next. After some minor tests, an examination and a brief scan, she would be third on the list that morning. The procedure itself would be short, her recovery would include up to two hours under observation afterward, and then she could go home and rest.

It wasn't until the scanning equipment was brought in and Shanal bared her stomach that she knew for certain she couldn't go through with this. While her baby was no more than a blueberry-size bundle of multiplying cells at this point, he or she was still *her* baby and, she realized with increasing certainty, she wanted this baby with all her heart.

"No!" she said, pushing the sonographer's hand away. "I'm not doing it. I'm keeping my baby."

"Are you certain, Miss Peat? It's not unusual for you to feel undecided about this," the nurse said, her face a mask of compassion.

"I've never been more certain of anything," she answered. She sat up and wiped the gel from her stomach with her hospital gown. "I'm going home and I'm keeping my baby."

When the taxi deposited her back on the driveway at her house Shanal could feel only relief. She'd deal with Burton later. First, she had to tell her mum and dad about the baby.

Her parents were at the kitchen table when she let herself inside.

"You're back from work early, *pyaari beti*. Is everything okay?"

Beloved daughter. Shanal smiled fleetingly at her mother's endearment. While her mum had embraced her new Australian lifestyle over thirty years ago with the same love and commitment she showed to her Australian husband, she was at heart still Indian and often peppered her conversation with an odd mix of Hindi and English that left many people scratching their heads.

"I need to speak with you both. Do you have time?"

She sat at the table and accepted the cup of tea her mother had automatically poured for her.

"What…else would…we be doing?" her father asked in his stilted speech. "We're here…for you. What's… wrong?"

His struggle to form words seemed worse than usual and Shanal exchanged a look with her mother. Yet another advancement in the illness that was, inch by inch, taking her father's life away. Even so, there was nothing wrong with his mind and she needed to talk to them both. Initially, she didn't know where to begin, but eventually she took a deep breath and started with the day she'd run from her wedding. Her parents, to their credit, said very little during her recitation. But she felt her mother's cry of dismay as if it was a physical thing when she mentioned Burton's insistence on the termination.

"So you see, I couldn't go through with it. Which leaves me in a very difficult position."

"Do you love Raif?" her mother asked.

Shanal felt her breath hitch as she allowed the idea to expand in her mind. Love him? She knew she was deeply attracted to him. It was something she'd fought for so many years it had become second nature. Right up until he'd become her knight in shining armor and whisked her away from a marriage she hadn't wanted, to a retreat where she could hide from her problems. The urge to kiss him had come from a place deep inside her. Their lovemaking had brought the kind of fulfillment she'd always sought in her life, and the kind that had been lacking in her few relationships so far. So, did she love Raif? The tightness in her chest loosened and warmth swelled and filled its place.

"I don't know," she said. If she acknowledged how she felt about him that would only make marrying Burton all the more difficult and all the more hopeless. And it would leave her all the more susceptible to being hurt if he didn't share her feelings, too. "I think I might."

"Then marry Raif," her mother said bluntly. "He does know about the baby, doesn't he?"

"It's not that simple," Shanal replied, her voice soft and her eyes now fixed on her father. "I can't rely on him, Mum. He used me to get back at Burton."

"Did he really?" her mother asked, getting up to brew another pot of tea. "From what you've said, it seems to me that the thought might have crossed his mind initially, but it certainly didn't stay there."

"That's what he said," Shanal admitted.

"Then I see no reason for you not to believe him. Did he lie to you? Did he hide the truth from you when you asked him?"

"No, he didn't, but there are other things to consider. If I don't marry Burton, I will lose my position with Burton International. And there's a restraint clause in my contract. If I leave Burton International, I am legally unable to work in the same field anywhere in Australia for at least two years. It was stupid of me not to realize the long-term implications of that."

Understanding filled her father's eyes as he digested the message hidden in her words. Understanding that was swiftly followed by remorse. She was not about to put it in so many words, but the three of them knew that without her income they'd all be destitute.

"I just don't know what to do anymore."

Shanal stood up and took her cup of tea through to her childhood bedroom. There, surrounded by so many reminders of her past, she tried to digest the truth about her feelings for Raif. Theoretically, it should be so simple. She could just tell Burton the truth, that she planned to keep her baby and that she wouldn't be marrying him. How hard could that be?

But then the look on her father's face came back to

haunt her. He'd been through hell since the medical-negligence compensation claim. He hadn't fought it, instead taking full responsibility for the damage he'd done—for the death he'd caused by trying to soldier through his illness without telling his peers. Her dad's shame and sorrow were a heavy burden for them both. He was a man used to being larger than life and a powerful force in the health field, along with supporting his family. The physical and mental toll the whole incident had taken was huge, accelerating the symptoms of his illness.

She looked up as she heard his wheelchair at her door.

"Will…you be…okay?" he asked, forming his words carefully.

Shanal looked at her father, his eyes still bright with intelligence and shining with the love he bore for her.

"Yes, Dad, I'll be okay." *Somehow.* "We'll *all* be okay, I promise."

Her father looked up at her. He laughed, a dry crackling sound that held little warmth. "Your mother reckons…she's going…to get a job."

Shanal shook her head. "No, she can't. You need her here at home."

When Shanal had learned about her father's illness, they'd realized that there would come a point when he'd need full-time nursing care. Her mother had been adamant that if anyone was to care for her husband, it would be her for as long as she could manage. Shanal had used some of her own savings to make alterations to the house so her father could remain at home and maneuver safely in his wheelchair.

Shanal's mum appeared in the doorway, resting her hands on her husband's shoulders and giving them a squeeze. Her features were drawn into a tight mask and her jaw was set with determination.

"Either way, *pyaari beti,* you can't carry our responsibilities on your own, not with a baby now to consider, as well. We don't want you to put yourself through hardship for us."

"We...love you," her father added. "You must...do... what's right for...you."

Shanal watched as her parents left her room, marveling at the way their love for one another was still as rock solid as it had ever been. She wanted that for herself now more than ever—that kind of love that endured through good times and bad, through sickness and in health. She wouldn't have that with Burton. She knew that. Could she honestly let herself live without it?

Her hand rested against her lower belly. She had responsibilities here—to her unborn babe and to her parents. She had to go ahead with her marriage to Burton. She simply had no other choice. And when he discovered that she hadn't gone through with the termination, well, she'd just have to cross that bridge when she reached it.

# Twelve

Raif paced the tasting room at The Masters vineyard, oblivious to the expression of amusement on his cousin Ethan's face.

"Of course I love her. Do you think for a second that I'd be this wound up if I didn't?" Raif raged.

"Well, why don't you do something about it," Ethan drawled, as he leaned back in his chair and twirled the stem of a glass of Shiraz between his fingers.

"Like what? She refuses to see me, she won't answer my calls, I'm banned from Burton International—"

"Seriously?" Ethan choked on a laugh. "Banned from her workplace?"

Raif clenched his teeth together as he struggled to get his frustration under control. "It's no laughing matter."

Ethan sobered, all humor gone as he sat up straighter in his chair. "Then you have to find a way. If she's that important to you, then you have to go get her. You spirited her away once, and I have to say I commend you for that. You can do it again, surely. I still can't believe it, though. You and Shanal."

"Why is that so strange?"

"You've always been at one another. If she said black, you'd say white. If you said organic, she'd just about write a treatise on why the use of chemicals was vital for strong healthy growth."

Raif had to admit it, on the surface it had looked as if they couldn't bear one another. But when they'd been alone together on the boat, the animosity and bickering had vanished. They'd been happy together—the happiest he'd ever been. And he knew, to his soul, that she felt something for him. Love? Well, he could only hope. He just knew that she was marrying Burton for all the wrong reasons, whatever they were. She'd had reasons for running from the wedding last time, too. Reasons that, while she hadn't shared them with him, had made her desperate to leave the cathedral behind. Reasons that had given her nightmares that first night on the boat. Whatever she felt for Burton, it certainly wasn't love. If anything, it looked more like fear.

"What if you get her over here for lunch with you and Isobel, and then leave us to it. Would you do that for me?" Raif asked, latching on to the suggestion like a drowning man.

"Are you asking if I'm prepared to damage a friendship of fifteen years by tricking her into seeing you?"

Raif pinched the bridge of his nose and closed his eyes for a minute. It was asking too much of his cousin to do this. It was unfair. But then again, this whole situation was unfair. And beneath it all he still had the feeling that something about the whole thing was twisted. As if Burton was manipulating them all. There was only one answer to Ethan's question. Raif opened his eyes, let his hand drop back to his side.

"Yes," he said.

His cousin nodded in acknowledgment and sighed. "Fine, I'll do it. But don't blame me if it all blows up in your face."

"I won't," Raif assured him, even though deep down he had no such confidence.

Without saying another word, Ethan reached for his mobile phone and keyed in Shanal's number. After some idle chatter he got to the point, inviting her to lunch on the coming Sunday—one day shy of a week before her new wedding date.

"It's done," Ethan said. "She'll be here at midday. I suggest you come about an hour after that."

"I'll be here," Raif promised.

Sunday came, delivering one of those perfect early spring days filled with sunshine and a top temperature in the low sixties. Even so, Raif felt chilled as he got out of his car and walked toward the main house, where Ethan and Isobel were entertaining Shanal. She wouldn't be pleased, he knew that. No doubt she thought she'd effectively seen the last of him that day he'd returned her wedding dress, but if that was the case she'd failed to factor in the Masters family's resilience and determination to reach their goals.

He walked around to the back veranda of the house, which accommodated most of his family in its widespread wings to the sheltered spot where Ethan had texted him earlier to find them. Raif could hear the delicate sound of Shanal's laughter as he drew nearer. Laughter that cut short as she saw him step up onto the covered wooden deck.

"Ethan?" she asked, turning to his cousin.

"He needed to see you, Shanal. I'm sorry."

Isobel looked from one to the other and back again. "Is there something I'm missing here?"

"No, nothing," Shanal insisted, but Ethan spoke over her.

"I'll tell you, inside," he said to his wife, rising from his chair and offering her his hand.

With another sharp look at Raif and then Shanal, Isobel took her husband's hand. Raif waited until they were both inside and the door had closed behind them.

"I don't know what you hope to achieve by this, Raif. I told you, I can't see you anymore. We have nothing to say to each other."

"Can't see me? Or don't want to see me? They're two very different things, don't you think?" he said, lowering himself to sit beside her at the beautifully laid table. "I don't understand why you have to marry Burton."

"It's none of your business, Raif. Please, just leave me alone."

"Oh, Shanal, that's where you're so very wrong. It's entirely my business."

Her eyes flicked up to meet his, a tormented expression clearly evident. Raif's heart squeezed painfully that he had to be the one putting her through this.

"If you're going to marry anyone, it should be me. I love you, Shanal, and I believe, if you're honest with yourself, you love me, too."

She shook her head sadly. "No, don't do this to me, Raif. It's not fair."

"Not fair? Isn't denying yourself the truth unfair, too? I think it is. Especially when that truth is what we mean to one another."

Shanal drew herself upright in her chair. "You're

mistaken. We had a fling. A very *brief* fling," she re-iterated. "That's all."

Raif held back a sigh. She was going to fight him on this to the bitter end, wasn't she? Well, if she thought he'd tuck his tail and run she had another think coming. He'd waited this long, he wasn't going to wait any longer. He loved and respected her too much for that. "We both know that's a lie. You're not that kind of woman and it was way more than a fling."

She smiled. "You think not? Well, I have news for you. You don't know me as well as you think you do. I'm tired of playing games and of being some kind of toy to be fought over between you and Burton. I know you don't like him. How do I know you're not saying you love me just to get back at him again? You two were always competitive, even back in your school days, from what I've been told. Clearly that hasn't changed."

"It's more than that. Way more. He's not the right man for you."

"Like he wasn't for Laurel, either? And yet she chose him."

Raif felt the barb strike home, but it only served to make him even more determined. "And look what happened to her, Shanal."

"It was an accident."

"It was carelessness. Burton's deliberate carelessness, I'm sure. It couldn't have been anything else."

"The inquest found otherwise. He was exonerated," she persisted.

"He lied. That's the way he operates, can't you see that? He'll say whatever he needs to, and pay whoever he needs to, to get what he wants."

Didn't she *want* to understand? Raif fought the urge to strangle something, or someone—preferably

Rogers—and dragged his focus back to the woman in front of him. Everything he said was the truth, but still she fought back.

Shanal huffed a derisive snort. "Of course you'd say something like that. But then, you're not all that different, are you?"

"Burton is all about the chase, Shanal. He likes the hunt, the capture. The win. Do you really think he loves you? He doesn't. He loves the *idea* of you."

Shanal pushed her chair away from the table. "I think I've heard enough. Either you go or I do."

Raif put out a hand to stop her from getting up. "Shanal, please reconsider. It's not too late."

She looked down at his hand on her arm, then raised her eyes to his again. "I've made my decision, Raif. You have to live with that."

Knowing that anything else he said now would be a waste of time, Raif loosened his hold on her. "Don't get up. I'll go. But I'm not giving up on you, Shanal. Not for a second. Whether you believe me or not, I love you. What I want more than anything is for you to be happy—and since I know you'd never find happiness with Burton, I'm not going to stop trying to put an end to this wedding."

"Raif, you're wasting your time."

"That's for me to decide," he said, and he turned to go.

He couldn't quite remember when he'd made the decision to drive into the city, but he knew exactly why when he pulled the Maserati up outside Burton's apartment block.

"We need to talk," he said into the intercom in the foyer, after buzzing Burton's apartment.

"By all means," replied the silky smooth voice of the man he'd grown to detest more than any other.

Inside Burton's apartment, Raif found himself holding on to his rage by a thread.

"So, to what do I owe the pleasure of your visit?" Burton said, after leading him into a sitting room that was more a testament to his ability to collect beautiful things than it was a place to relax.

"Let her go."

"I beg your pardon. I'm not sure I understand what you're talking about."

Raif wanted nothing more than to wipe the smug look off Burton's face. "You know full well that I mean Shanal. Let her go."

"She comes to me of her own free will," Burton replied. "If she wanted to stay with you, surely she wouldn't have terminated your baby just this week."

Bile rose, hot and sharp, in Raif's throat. "My baby?"

"Yes," Burton drawled. "I took her to the clinic last Wednesday myself. Such an unfortunate side effect of your little dalliance together, but easily dispensed with. It's a good thing I'm a forgiving man. Now that little mess is tidied up, Shanal and I can move forward. We'll make quite the dynamic duo, don't you think?"

*Little mess?* It took every ounce of Raif's considerable control not to take Burton by the throat and choke him for his lies. But was it a lie? Only one person could tell him that and she wasn't willing to talk to him again. She'd told him there was nothing left to say. Did that mean she really had gone through with it?

Why hadn't she told him about the baby? She had to know he'd stand by her, didn't she? Goodness only knew Raif had tried to make that clear to her often enough. Rage suffused him. At Burton for being the supercilious grasping spawn he was, at Shanal for refusing to see the real person behind the smiling fiancé she planned to pledge her life to, and for the unborn child he hadn't even had the chance to know about and would now never have the chance to meet.

He could barely speak. Burton Rogers had now effectively destroyed the lives of two people, Laurel and now Raif's baby, who should have been able to count on him for anything. Two people he'd loved, or would have loved if given half a chance. He spun on his heel and stalked to the door of the apartment.

"What? Not stopping for a drink, old friend?" Burton taunted from behind him.

But he wasn't listening anymore. He had let this happen and he had to admit the worst of his rage was for himself. For his inability to prevent Burton from destroying yet another life. Well, he'd failed, twice now. There was no way he'd fail again. Whatever it took, whatever he had to do, Shanal would not marry Burton Rogers next Saturday.

Raif forced himself to drive slowly back to his house. He had to get control of this fury that held him tight in its grip. He had to deconstruct what Burton had told him, to take it apart piece by piece and examine it carefully. Now, more than ever, it was vital he not rush at things like a bull at a gate. He'd done that with Shanal and met only resistance. There had to be more beneath all this.

As he sat in an easy chair staring out at the vineyard, *his* vineyard, he mulled over everything that had happened in the past few weeks. Trying to peer beneath the layers to find the truth at the core. Through it all, he could only see the woman Shanal was. Focused, dedicated and loyal to a fault.

Was that where the problem lay? Her loyalty? To Burton, maybe? He was her boss. Even as the idea bloomed in his mind he cast it aside. No, he had seen no indication of loyalty in Shanal's behavior when Burton had come to take her away. Loyalty to her family, maybe? Raif had been shocked to see her father accompany her down the aisle in a wheelchair. Someone had whispered something about his illness, motor neuron disease, in hushed tones as they'd gone past. Raif had had no idea Curtis Peat was in such bad shape.

Was it desperation to be married before her father died? Was that what drove her? Surely she knew Raif would offer marriage himself if they had a baby on the way. Ideas tumbled around in his head until he was almost dizzy with them. Perhaps it was her parents who had loyalty to Burton, who had chosen him as Shanal's suitor? But while Mrs. Peat was traditional in some ways, Raif couldn't believe she'd push her daughter into an arranged marriage. Not when it was well known that the Peats themselves had been a love match.

Yet Raif couldn't help thinking that her parents were the key to understanding the situation in some way. Shanal was close to her parents, there was no question of that. But what would be so important to their happiness that she'd sacrifice her own to ensure it? It couldn't be money. The Peats were an affluent family. Before her father's early retirement he'd had a very successful private practice as a cardiovascular surgeon.

So what the hell was it?

It was growing dark when he finally moved and got himself something to eat from the kitchen. But food did little to fill the aching sense of loss at the idea of a child gone before he could know about it. He scraped off his plate into the garbage, most of his meal uneaten, and shoved the plate in the dishwasher before heading to bed.

There, he lay in the dark of a starless night, lost in the many variables and possibilities that presented themselves. Vignettes from his and Shanal's time on the river rose in his thoughts again and again, to torment him. Her trust in him from the start, her asking him to stay. The night they'd spent together locked in passion so deep, so everlasting—at least he'd thought so at the time—that it had left an indelible imprint on his heart.

He loved her. It was pure and simple. And he wanted her in his life, forever. She could be clinical and almost scarily intelligent, but then on the flip side she was warm and compassionate, as well. No matter how he viewed the woman he'd known for half his life, he couldn't see her doing what Burton had suggested.

Which meant that possibly, hopefully, she hadn't gone through with it. Maybe Burton had it wrong. Maybe she still carried his child. There was only one person who could tell him, and he'd make certain she did as soon as he could see her again.

# Thirteen

Shanal took her time getting ready to go out to The Masters for dinner. She'd initially turned the invitation down. It was a weeknight, she'd protested when Isobel had phoned to ask her to come over, and she was very busy at work. But Isobel had cut straight through her objections and to the heart of why she didn't want to go, and had told her that while Raif would be there, he'd been warned to be on his best behavior and not leave her in the same state she'd been last Saturday when he'd gone.

She lifted a hand to apply her eyeliner, having to pause and take a breath when her fingers shook slightly at the prospect of seeing him again. Could she do it? Deep down, she craved the sight of him, but every time she saw him made it that much more unpalatable to think about going through with her marriage to Burton. But surely she'd be able to keep her distance from Raif for just one night. The whole Masters family would be at the gathering. She knew them all well, and as Ethan's friend, had been a part of these types of gatherings for years. How difficult could it be? she reasoned with herself. Either way, Raif could hardly abduct her from his family home in front of his relatives.

Last Saturday, he'd said he wouldn't let her go. What exactly had he meant by that? If he intended to try and change her mind again, he was definitely running out of time. Her rescheduled wedding was in only three days' time.

Her tummy did that all too familiar flip at the thought, warning her that she was going to be sick. She fought back the nausea, gripping the bathroom basin until her fingers ached—their pain distracting her from the roiling sensation deep inside.

She heard the whir of her father's chair as it passed the bathroom.

"You all…right?" he asked from the doorway, enunciating his words with care.

"Sure, Dad. Just getting ready to go to The Masters for dinner."

"That's…nice. You work too…hard. You…deserve a break."

And so did he, she reminded herself in the mirror as he wheeled away again. He deserved a break from the guilt that plagued him every day over the medical error that had killed his patient, and from the ill-fated decisions he'd made about his investments. He deserved a break from the illness that took away his control over his life one piece at a time. And most of all, he deserved a break from the relentless fear that they'd lose the house over their head if she didn't go through with her marriage to Burton. Of all the horrors that her dad faced as his disease slowly claimed what was left of his body, this was the one thing that she could help with. She could make that single fear go away. And she would.

With that thought clear in her mind, Shanal finished applying her makeup and twisted her hair up into a loose chignon. There, she was ready for anything, she thought as she eyed her reflection. No one needed to know about the turmoil that alternately slithered and coiled in the pit of her stomach, every waking hour. She could only hope the tension wasn't harming her baby. She placed a hand over her still-flat tummy as a surge of protectiveness shot through her. She would allow *nothing* to hurt her child, no matter what Burton said or did.

She was the last to arrive at the gathering. She smiled her hello to Ethan's aunt Cynthia, who presided like some matriarchal queen over these evenings, and kissed Ethan on the cheek as he came forward to welcome her. Raif's parents must still be overseas, Shanal thought as she scanned the room, her eyes skimming over the man himself quickly. She knew the second he was aware of her presence there, and from the corner of her eye noted his movement as he excused himself from talking to Isobel.

"Do you want to talk with Raif," Ethan asked at her side, "or would you rather I head him off?"

"No, it's okay," Shanal responded, her heart beating like a trapped bird in her chest. "We need to be able to be civil with one another."

"Civil?" Ethan huffed a quiet laugh. "He doesn't look as if he has civil on his mind." But respecting her wishes, he stepped back. "I'll be just over there if you need me."

"Thank you," she said, swallowing hard. "But I'm sure I'll be fine."

She had mere seconds to shore up her defenses and then Raif was right there in front of her.

"I'm glad you came tonight," he said simply.

"I wasn't going to let the thought of you scare me away."

She knew her response was blunt, offensive even, but she also knew that if she was to get through this evening she needed to maintain the upper hand.

"Like I said," Raif said, with a smile that made his eyes glitter dangerously. "I'm glad you came. We need to talk."

She sighed in exasperation. "Raif, we've said all there needs to be said. Can't you just accept defeat? I'm marrying Burton on Saturday and that's final."

"Sweetheart, we can do this in front of my family or we can do this in private. Your choice."

There was something in his tone that made her spine stiffen. "Look," she started, "I told Ethan I'd be fine with you here, that we could be civil. If I thought for one minute that you'd be anything else, I wouldn't have come."

"Oh, I'm being civil." His voice was clipped, as if he'd clenched his jaw and was biting his words out in tiny chunks. "More civil than you realize. So, tell me about the baby."

A chill ran the full length of her spine. "B-baby?" she gasped.

"Yes, *our* baby, if I'm to believe your fiancé."

Shanal looked at Raif in horror. Burton had told him about the baby? If that was the case, he would have told Raif about the abortion, as well. That would go a long way toward explaining the anger that vibrated off him right now.

She shuddered. She hadn't wanted it to come to this, but now it seemed she had no choice. Could she maybe let him go on believing the baby was gone? No, she knew she couldn't. It was not only unfair to him, but grossly unfair to the child she carried. Raif deserved to know. Her mind fractured into a hundred scattered thoughts. If he knew that she was still pregnant, though, what would he do? Would he tell Burton that she hadn't gone through with the abortion, after all? Would she lose that final chance to save her parents from homelessness, and keep her own job? She had to find out.

"Is there somewhere private—?"

"Come with me," he said, taking her by the elbow and leading her from the salon where they'd gathered for predinner drinks.

Ethan looked up and started toward them when he saw Raif begin to lead her away, but she mouthed, "It's okay," and he halted in his tracks. A look of concern was still on his face as Raif closed the door behind them.

He led her a few doors down the wide, wood-paneled corridor into a room she recognized as the library. She'd always loved it in here. The high ceiling looked as though it was held up by all the knowledge and stories held in the books that lined the tall shelves on all walls. A padded window seat beckoned the avid reader, who had the choice of reading there or in one of the comfortable, deep armchairs that flanked the large fireplace.

"Private enough for you?" he asked, as he closed the heavy door behind them with a thud.

"Thank you," she answered, wrapping her arms about her as if she could somehow protect herself from what she had to say.

"Is it true?" he asked.

"Is what true?"

"Don't play games with me, Shanal. You're better than that. You know how I feel about family. How important it is to me. Were you or were you not pregnant with my child?"

She couldn't find the words to tell him the exact truth, and instead just nodded. The instant she did Raif paled, and a look of grief so raw, so painful it tore at her heart, crossed his face.

"Raif, no!" she cried, rushing to him and reaching up to cup his face with her hands. "It's not what you think."

He pulled away roughly. "Don't. Just don't. You can't console me on this, Shanal. You made a decision about something that affected both of us without telling me anything. If I hadn't brought it up tonight, I never would have known, would I? You had no right to do that."

"But I didn't do it. Please, you have to believe me. I didn't go through with the procedure. Burton doesn't know. I'm still pregnant with your baby."

"What are you saying? That you didn't have the… the…" His voice trailed away, as if he couldn't quite bring himself to even say the word.

"I couldn't do it." She couldn't help shuddering a little at her next thought. "Burton will be furious when he finds out."

"Burton has nothing to do with this."

"But he does!" she cried out. "I'm marrying him on Saturday. He doesn't want your baby in our marriage, and can you blame him for that? Would you want his if the situation was reversed?"

"You're kidding me, right? You're comparing me to him?" Raif shook his head. "You really don't know me at all, do you? If you were marrying me and carrying his baby, I would still do my very best by that child because, no matter what, it would be a part of *you* first. A child can't choose its parents, but parents can make all the difference in the life of a child."

Shanal felt her entire body sag at his words. She had misjudged him and she owed him an apology for that.

"Raif, I'm sorry. I shouldn't have spoken to you like that."

"Too right you shouldn't. But that's got nothing to do with this situation, with us. You can't marry him, can't you see that? This baby, *our* baby," he said with a wealth of emotion in his voice. "It changes everything."

She shook her head. She was so dreadfully trapped. She'd promised her father she'd make everything right for him and her mum. She couldn't let them down now. She couldn't abandon them.

"I have to marry him, Raif."

"*Have* to?"

"You don't understand," she cried, her voice breaking as the pressure and responsibility threatened to swamp her like a mud slide rapaciously consuming everything before it.

"Then explain it to me. Tell me why," he demanded, frustration and anger creeping into his voice.

She wrapped her arms tighter around her body and shook her head, her eyes blurring with tears. She closed them, not wanting to see the confusion and hurt on Raif's face a second longer. Not wanting to see the questions in his eyes that only she could answer. But they weren't her answers to give. They were her father's, and she knew his pride couldn't take any more. With his health so precarious now, another blow would merely hasten his inevitable death. She couldn't bear to have that on her conscience.

Strong arms wrapped around her from behind and the warmth of Raif's body filtered through her clothing to her skin. She hadn't realized how cold she was until she felt his heat and his comforting touch.

"It'll be okay, Shanal. I'll make it okay for you, but you have to let me in. I'm working in the dark here until you tell me what kind of hold Burton has on you."

His words penetrated the sorrow in her mind. What kind of hold Burton had on her? What would make him ask a question like that? She asked him.

Raif's sigh was deep and she felt it all the way through to her bones. He turned her around in his arms so she was facing him.

"Burton Rogers is the kind of guy who gets what he wants. By fair means or by foul. I'm guessing he's gotten you by foul, am I right?"

She didn't so much as blink.

"Shanal," Raif coaxed. "I meant what I said last Sunday. I love you. I want to make everything right for you, but you have to tell me what's wrong so I can fix it. I want there to be an *us*. A future with you and our baby."

The authenticity in his words, in his delivery of them, pierced the shell around her, making her want to dream that he could be right. But Burton held all the cards in this particular game. If Shanal could have seen a way clear to leave him for good by now, she would have.

"It's impossible," she said, her voice so quiet that Raif had to bend his head closer to hear her. "He controls everything, Raif. You know what he's like. He doesn't make mistakes, not when it comes to getting something he wants. There's no way out of this for me."

"There's always a way out," Raif said, determination clear in every syllable. "Tell me, why does he have such a hold over you?"

She had to tell him. The burden of bearing it all on her own for so long was simply too much. Slowly, she began, going back five years to her father's motor neuron diagnosis, to his negligence, to his guilt and shame.

"I don't mean to sound callous," Raif said when she paused. "But didn't your father have insurance for that?"

"He did, and the settlement at the time was a generous one. But how do you make up for taking a life—a man's future? It tormented Dad. If he hadn't operated that day—if he'd told another consultant about his illness and admitted that he shouldn't be operating anymore—that patient might still be alive. He'd still be a loved and valued, contributing member of his family. Dad felt he owed it to the man's wife and kids to make sure they had monetary stability at the very least—that there would be money available for the children if they wanted to attend university, that his widow would have no financial concerns about loan repayments or being forced back to work just to provide for her kids. So he took out a loan using his home as security—a very large loan, thinking he could pay it back when his investment portfolio matured."

Understanding lit in Raif's eyes. "And he was one of the affected parties in that Ponzi scheme that made the headlines a couple of years ago, wasn't he? Did he lose everything?"

She nodded. "They had some funds aside, separate from the investment accounts, which they used to meet their loan repayments for a while, and to live on. I gave up my apartment and moved back home to help them out financially, and to give my mum some assistance with Dad's care."

"Could your mum and dad not sell the house? Move somewhere smaller, maybe?"

"We considered it, but we'd already done alterations

to the house to accommodate Dad's mobility issues. Besides, he's lost so much already, Raif. I promised him he'd be able to stay in his home right up until the end, and that I'd look after him and Mum. He's counting on me."

"So where does Burton come into this?" Raif asked.

"One night, when I was working late, Burton caught me at a weak moment. I broke down and told him about our financial troubles. He offered to make everything all right. He'd personally take over the mortgage on my parents' house, repay their loan to the bank and provide a living allowance for them, on one condition."

"That you marry him."

She nodded.

"And what will he do if you don't marry him?"

"He will expose my father's negligence case to the media. The settlement was private and the facts of the case were never brought into the public eye. Also, Burton said he'd evict them from their home. Raif, the private shame of that case is already driving Dad into an early grave. I know he did wrong, making the decision to continue to operate that day, but he's done everything he possibly can to make amends. He stopped practicing, stopped everything that gave him purpose in his life. That error of judgment aside, his reputation, the *good* work he'd done up until his retirement, is all he has left.

"And there's something else. Burton made it clear to me that if I don't marry him, I will lose my position with Burton International. And aside from my two-year restraint clause, he assured me that I would never be able to find work here in Australia again—or anywhere else his reach extends. Dad needs specialized care for the rest of his life, and it won't be long before Mum can't cope on her own anymore, even with me helping where I can. If I can't support my parents financially, Raif, what am I to do?"

# Fourteen

Raif held her close. He was still trying to assimilate the news that she hadn't gotten rid of their baby, along with the information she'd just given him. She was trembling now—with emotion, with fear and with helplessness. He understood it all. Had gone through it all himself when Burton had flung his cruel gibes in Raif's direction. But there was one thing Burton hadn't counted on: that Raif would do anything for his family, no matter what. Family always came first—including his unborn child and that baby's mother.

He eased her away slightly and tilted her face up to his. "Shanal, answer one thing. Do you trust me?"

Her lips quivered and she drew in a sharp breath. Her irises were all but consumed by the pupils of her eyes as she stared up into his face. "Yes, I do. I trust you."

"Then believe me when I say I will help you, if you'll just let me. Get me a copy of the loan agreement your father had with the bank. I'll ensure that the debt he owes Burton disappears. And trust me when I say that I can more than adequately provide for your parents, Shanal. And for you and our baby, too."

"But what about my work?" she protested. "Burton doesn't make idle threats. He'll spread out his tentacles and make it impossible for me to work anywhere."

Anyone else might have thought her concern about her work a selfish one, but Raif *knew* Shanal. She was, at heart, a geek. A lovable, intense, scarily clever geek. Her work meant so much to her, and she took justifiable pride in her professional accomplishments. Without her job she would feel as though she had no definition in life. It was as much a part of her as those perfectly arched eyebrows or the delectable texture and taste of her skin. And she had a fair share of her father's pride, as well. He knew, without question, that if Burton destroyed her reputation—which he was more than capable of doing—he might as well just grind her into the ground along with it.

It was up to Raif to make sure that didn't happen.

"I don't want you to worry about that. It's not going to be your problem. Just leave it with me."

"Raif, that's a lot of trust you're asking me to give. It's already Wednesday. We get married on Saturday afternoon."

"No, it won't get that far."

"But how on earth can you prevent it?"

"I just need you to trust me, Shanal. Can you continue to act as if you're going along with his plans?"

"Of course I can. I've managed to get this far."

He pressed a kiss to her lips. "That's my girl," he said approvingly. "I will fix this. I promise. Your parents will be okay and your job will be safe."

"But how—?"

"Trust me. Everything will be okay."

A knock at the door prevented Shanal from asking any more questions. As they acknowledged Ethan's presence and his summons to join the rest of the guests at the table for dinner, Raif quietly vowed that there was no way he would ever allow Burton to have any more power over Shanal or her family. Or anyone else, if he had any say in the matter.

By Thursday afternoon Raif was climbing the walls with frustration. The private-investigation company he'd retained to look into Burton's affairs had come highly recommended, but given the tiny window of time they had to work in, would they be able to dig up enough dirt on Rogers soon enough to make a difference?

Shanal had emailed a scanned copy of her parents' original loan agreement. The sum was staggering, but not impossible to meet out of his private resources. Raif was already in talks with his bank and financial planners to liquidate the necessary funds to ensure that sum Rogers had paid through a company facade, together with the appropriate market rate of interest, would be available to be settled, and the mortgage, also registered in that company's name, discharged. But the information he needed to nail Burton's ass to the wall, and ensure it stayed there—information necessary to keep Shanal from losing her job and her professional reputation—still eluded him.

He thought back through what he knew of the man. Always competitive at school, Burton had never excelled purely for the pleasure of it—no, he'd excelled because he felt he *had* to be the best, the fastest, the brightest. If another student's marks beat his in one exam, it hadn't been long before that student began to slide back in his work, or—even more sinisterly—was found with a copy of an exam paper, or alcohol, or even worse things, in his locker.

It wasn't that Rogers wasn't a clever man—he most definitely was, which made him all the more powerful an adversary. But there was a clinical air about him. As if he was detached from the world he lived in, choosing to lord it above everyone, and carefully selecting the things and people he wanted in his realm. And he'd chosen Shanal.

It was easy to see why. Intelligent, good at her work and incredibly beautiful into the bargain, she would have appeared to him like a prized exotic flower to be collected by an avid botanist. Raif had no doubt that Burton had bided his time before approaching Shanal. That was part of his modus operandi. He liked to stalk for a while, to savor his victory before pouncing.

It was how Burton had seduced Laurel away from Raif, striking when she was at a low moment. A month before the canyoneering trip, they'd argued, after Raif had once again avoided discussing the future of their relationship. The weekend they'd broken up, he'd used that dreadful adage, the one that usually struck fear into the heart of any person in a long-term relationship— he had told her that he "just needed a bit of space." So she'd given it to him.

Raif had loved Laurel, but not in the way he now knew he loved Shanal—and maybe, deep down, she'd sensed that, too. Maybe she'd known, on some level, that his dedication to her hadn't been as deep as hers for him. He'd certainly enjoyed their relationship, had even believed they were on the same page when it came to their time together—and, yes, maybe in time his feelings would have deepened and they would have married. But it hadn't happened fast enough for Laurel, and she had begun to ask for more from their relationship. Things including a commitment he hadn't been prepared, at that stage, to give to her or to anyone.

Either way, Raif still blamed himself for her death that awful day. He should have known she'd continue with the expedition without him. And if he'd been there for her as he should have been, Raif knew she wouldn't have died. He might have a reputation as a bit of a daredevil, but he never underestimated danger and always double-checked—no, *triple*-checked—everything when it came to equipment and environment in the pursuit of adventure sports.

Remembering Laurel made Raif wonder again if there should have been more to the reports that had been submitted to the coroner after her death. Was it possible that some vital information had been withheld? There were only two survivors from that day. One was Burton, the other was the guide. Raif picked up his phone and punched in the number for the investigator who had been assigned to him. After a brief conversation, directing the man to explore deeper into the circumstances of Laurel's death, and to talk directly with the guide who'd been with them that day, he hung up his phone.

Could the guide be the key? The man had sworn he'd checked the ropes and carabiner that had connected them. He had no reason to lie about that, or did he?

It was Friday evening when Raif got a call from the private investigator. He'd tracked down the guide, who'd said he would speak only to Raif. The investigator gave him the details of where to meet the man.

Raif fired a quick text message off to Shanal: Trust me!

It took him a while to find the address the investigator had given him, but Raif was persistent, eventually spotting the overgrown driveway on the hill road. He parked his car and walked toward the house. The front door opened as he approached. He recognized the guide immediately; Raif and Laurel had used him several times before her fatal expedition.

"Noah, good to see you," Raif said, stepping forward and offering his hand.

"Good to see you, too," the other man replied.

But he didn't meet his eyes as they shook hands ,and Raif had to admit to some shock at Noah's appearance. Was he sick? Always lean, the guy was almost skeletal in appearance now. And even though Noah was a good five years younger than Raif, right now he looked at least ten or fifteen years older.

Raif followed him inside and sat down in the living room. There was a layer of dust on every surface, and although the room held quality furnishings, an air of neglect hung over everything.

"Can I get you anything?" Noah offered, looking out from a face that was more gray than tan.

"No, I'm good, mate. You know why I'm here. Let's cut to the chase, huh? I don't have a lot of time."

Noah huffed a breath. "Yeah, time. I seem to have all too much of it."

"You're not guiding anymore?"

"I did a few trips after that day, but to be honest, since then…" His voice petered out and he shook his head.

Noah reached for a packet of cigarettes on the table. His hand shook as he tapped one out and raised it to his lips to light it. He drew deeply on the cigarette, taking his time to blow out the smoke before talking again. It was a habit Raif had never seen the man indulge in before. He'd always thought Noah was like him, testing himself against nature and the elements. Taking his highs from the thrill of living, not through stimulants like tobacco.

"He paid me."

Raif sat up a little straighter. "Burton?"

"Yeah." Noah took another long drag on his cigarette. "I'm so sorry, mate... I accepted the money. I said I wouldn't tell what really happened that day. He was so forceful. I could see her—lying there, at the bottom of the water hole, and he was arguing with me, physically holding me back from getting down to her. He told me he'd send me over the edge, too. He was actually holding me right there on the lip, with my back to the falls, telling me how much money he'd pay me if I just kept my mouth shut. In the end I said yes so he'd let me go...so I could attempt to retrieve Laurel...but I was too late. Once I realized she was gone, I guess I figured it didn't matter what I said, one way or another. The truth wasn't going to bring her back."

Conflicting emotions swelled and ebbed inside Raif. Noah had lied to save his own life, that much was clear. As much as it went against Raif's sense of honor, he could accept that, under the circumstances, Noah had felt as though he had no other choice.

"You said Burton held you back from checking on her. Did you think she might have still been alive at that point?"

"I couldn't be certain. She hit her head pretty hard on the way down, but there was still a chance. If I could have just gotten her out of the pool, I could have at least tried to save her. We were all trained for that kind of rescue. You know the saying. Train for the worst, expect the best. I lived by that, mate. And he wouldn't even let me try."

Raif considered Noah's words. "Tell me how she fell. You checked the equipment, right?"

Noah nodded. "I did. In fact she had been laughing at me, teasing me a bit for being so cautious—you know what she was like. Kind of flirty and fun, even when she was about to drop off a cliff face. I guess Burton didn't like that too much. He took her aside before she went over. I couldn't hear exactly what he was saying, but he didn't sound pleased. I did hear her reply, though. She told him to stop acting like a jealous child and to lighten up. I could see that made him mad.

"She'd already set her own anchors, Raif, three of them. He said he'd check them and her rope, and then she went over."

"It was the rope that came undone, wasn't it?"

"The knot slipped, yeah."

"Did you see him touch it?" A sick feeling gripped Raif's gut. "Or loosen it?"

Noah stubbed out his cigarette, lit another. "Yeah. I didn't realize it at the time or I'd have done something. You have to believe me on that."

Raif barely heard him, though. He couldn't quite come to terms with the shocking truth. Burton had knowingly tampered with Laurel's equipment. His actions had directly led to her death—a death he had further ensured by making certain Noah was unable to rescue or revive her. The ramifications were huge.

Raif rubbed his eyes and leaned back in the chair. He'd always known Burton was driven, dangerous even, but this was an entirely new level, even for him.

"He told me he'd just wanted to teach her a lesson.

Give her a fright, you know. He didn't expect the knot to fail completely."

Raif had to swallow down his anger and frustration. A beautiful life lost, and for what? One man's ego? It was beyond comprehension.

"Are you willing to swear to this, Noah?"

The younger man nodded. "Look at me, man. I can't live with myself any longer. Yes, he gave me money and I spent it, but since that day I haven't slept a full night or been able to work. Every time I tried to guide a group I'd have a panic attack and relive that day all over again. I'm done with that. I lied to the police and I'll take the rap for what I did, but he has to be held to justice, too. For Laurel's sake."

"Oh, he will be, I promise you that. And I'll get you help, Noah."

"Nah, man, I'm done. I made my choices that day—they were wrong, but I made them. I need to take responsibility for that and then maybe I can learn to live with it, and myself."

Raif made a mental note to ensure that Noah received the psychological and legal help he'd need. Sure, he'd done wrong, but he needed support now that he was trying to do the right thing. "Noah, you were a victim, too."

"I may have been, but I didn't pay the ultimate price like Laurel did. You have to stop him, Raif. The guy's dangerous."

"I will, rest assured. Are you prepared to come with me to the police station to make a statement?"

Noah looked around him, then back at Raif. "Money's not all it's cracked up to be, is it? Not if you can't live with yourself."

Raif stood up and looked down at the shell of the man who'd once been a vibrant, fit and happy person.

"That's true, but you're doing the right thing, Noah. And I meant what I said about helping you."

Noah stood, too, and shook his head. "I don't deserve it, but thank you."

It was a simple matter to head to the nearest police station and for Noah to make his statement. Raif was mindful of how late it was getting, but this situation wasn't something that could be rushed.

By the time Noah was finished, he was exhausted, but Raif could see how a weight had lifted from the man's shoulders. Maybe there'd be hope for him yet, Raif thought, as they shook hands and parted ways.

# Fifteen

"Are you sure you want to do this, *meri pyaari beti*?"

"It will be okay," Shanal replied, as her mother finished dressing her once again in the much-loathed bridal gown. Shanal frowned in distaste at the reflection in the full-length mirror in her parents' bedroom. The dress was a symbol of everything Burton was. Show and glamor with very little substance.

She felt sick with nerves, which was not much of a change from the nausea that usually assailed her upon waking each morning. What would she do if Raif didn't show up in time to call a halt to the wedding? He'd asked her to trust him, and she did, but that didn't stop fear from creeping up from the shadows in her mind.

Burton had exposed a side of himself that she'd never thought possible. If anyone had told her back when they first got engaged that he could be cruel and manipulative like that she would not have believed it. Now,

of course, was a different story. She couldn't believe
she'd been so oblivious to his true nature. Granted, she'd
never been all that attracted to him—certainly not in
the way that Raif set her blood pumping and her heart
skittering.

To think she'd even initially felt guilty about using
Burton to solve her problems. It was enough to make
her doubt her own judgment. If she'd made a mistake
like that, was she making an even worse one by trusting
Raif to make her problems go away? Surely she should
be capable of doing that herself?

She looked up in the mirror and studied her reflection again, and that of her mother as she fussed and
tweaked with the fall of the new veil until it was just
so. Shanal reminded herself she was a capable woman.
She'd gained a doctorate in her field. She'd written respected papers. She ran the lab at Burton International
without fault or flaw. She wasn't weak or incapable—
she was just in over her head. And in those circumstances, it showed how intelligent she was that she was
willing to let someone else lend a hand. Despite all the
things she could do on her own, she needed help now.

Her mother's eyes met hers in the mirror, a question
behind them. *What if Raif doesn't show?*

"It will be all right, you'll see," Shanal said, inject-
ing as much enthusiasm into her voice as she could.
"Everything will be all right."

Her parents had chosen not to come to the church
this time. Her mother had argued that it had been hard
enough last time to get her father out of the house and
to the cathedral, where he'd felt the eyes of everyone
around them as he'd accompanied Shanal in his wheelchair. Shanal had agreed. Besides, it wasn't as if this
wedding was going to go ahead. At least she fervently

hoped not. Her hand strayed to her belly, where Raif's child nestled safe and secure inside her.

She had to do this. She had to go through the motions for her child and for Raif. He'd promised he'd find a solution to her problems and she had to believe he would. He was, she thought with a private smile, a Masters, after all. They were not the type of people to ever quit. Knowing that gave her the inner strength she needed, and she straightened her posture and squared her shoulders.

The car Burton had arranged to collect her and to take her to the church would be here any minute now. After one final check in the mirror, she turned away. Her father was in his chair in the sitting room, staring out the window. She bent before him and took his limp hands in hers. Hands that had supported her as a baby and held hers as she'd balanced on walls and jumped waves at the beach. Hands that had saved so many lives over so many years. Hands that had taken one.

"It will be all right, Dad. I don't want you to worry anymore. It's all going to work itself out." She leaned forward and kissed him, gently squeezing his hands in reassurance before repeating, "Like I just told Mum, everything is going to be okay."

The words continued to echo like a mantra, over and over in her mind, as the car took her to the cathedral from where, only seven weeks ago, she'd fled. From where Raif had rescued her. Would he get here in time to do it again? She had to believe he would. She just had to, because the alternative was not worth considering.

As the driver opened her door and offered her a hand to help her alight, she caught a glimpse of the crystal encrusted satin pumps she wore. Perhaps running shoes would have been a better choice, she thought cynically.

But then, she had no more need to run. Not with Raif at her back.

She ascended the stairs to the cathedral and was greeted by the priest, who took a few minutes with her.

"Is everything okay today, my dear?" he asked, concern drawing his bushy white brows together. "You're certain about this?"

She nodded, unable to enunciate the words that he sought from her. It would be a lie if she said she was sure. She had never been more uncertain about anything. With every second that ticked past she came that much closer to having to go through with marrying Burton.

"Shall we start?" she asked, with as much of a smile as she could muster.

"Certainly. I'll bring Burton out to you."

"B-Burton?"

"Yes, he said that given what happened last time, he wanted to escort you in himself. No need for nerves this time around."

The priest opened the door and made a small gesture with his hand. Shanal was forced to swallow against the bitter taste in her mouth as Burton joined her. As soon as they were alone his eyes swept her from head to toe.

"You look beautiful," he said, as if that was all that mattered. And to him, it probably was. "Are you ready?"

She inclined her head and Burton took her hand and placed it on his forearm.

"Good, we look perfect together. I so look forward to dancing with you at our reception."

With any luck there would be no reception, she thought fervently. Music began inside the church and she and Burton started to walk down the aisle. She was surprised at the number of people there. She'd asked for

this wedding to be simpler and smaller, but she'd left
those details to Burton to arrange, and clearly he'd chosen to ignore her preferences. Anyway, she supposed
that none of it mattered anymore. Burton had never
taken her wishes into account before, so it shouldn't
surprise her that he wouldn't have over this. The sight
of so many friends and colleagues made her all the more
uncomfortable in the overdone confection of fabric and
diamantes that he'd insisted she wear again. But, she
made a mental reminder, she would stand here today
as *herself*, not as Burton Roger's puppet bride. At least
she wouldn't be if Raif got here in time. Where was he?

She scanned the many faces turned to them as they
walked down the aisle, searching for Raif's dark head,
his square shoulders. He was nowhere to be seen. Fear
tightened its screws on her already tightly strung nerves.
He wasn't going to make it!

At the altar the priest gave a brief welcome before
launching into the service.

"We are gathered here today..." he began, with a
wink at the bride and groom before him.

Struck by a near overwhelming sense of déjà vu,
Shanal flung a frightened look toward the door. Still
no sign of Raif. Firm, almost painful pressure on her
hands made her look up into Burton's eyes, where the
hard gleam of satisfaction reflected back at her. He was
getting what he wanted and she could do nothing to
stop it. The feeling of powerlessness was terrifying,
but nowhere near as frightening as the cruel smile that
curved Burton's lips.

How had she ever thought that marrying him would
be a good idea? How had she allowed him to gain so
much control over her? She knew all too well that the
fault lay with her. She'd gone into this with two objec-

tives: her parents' financial security and the head research position at Burton International. She hadn't ever believed she could lose her soul in exchange for those things. She should have known better than to try and strike a deal with the devil.

"If anyone here has just cause why Burton and Shanal may not be lawfully joined together, let them speak now or forever hold their peace."

Burton fired a seething glare at the priest. "I thought I told you to take that out of the service."

"It's a requirement, dear boy, but don't worry. Everything will be all ri—"

His words were cut off as the front doors to the cathedral clanged open and a loud male voice rang out.

"Stop the wedding. I object!"

Shanal sagged in relief as she saw Raif stride toward the altar, a look of grim determination on his face.

"Oh, not again," the priest groaned, his face paling.

"Keep going," Burton insisted, his own face suffusing with ugly, angry color.

"We can't," the cleric whispered back. "He has to state his objection."

"There's nothing he can say that can stop this wedding, trust me."

"Let's find out, shall we?"

The priest looked at Raif. Everyone looked at him, including Shanal, who had never seen a more welcome sight in all her life. Her eyes raked over him, taking in his disheveled hair and the determined light burning in those beautiful blue eyes of his. He stood there, tall and proud, dressed in a casual windbreaker and worn jeans and boots, and to her, he'd never looked more appealing.

"Young man, please state your objection," the priest directed.

"Before I do, I need to know one thing."

"What is that?"

Raif looked directly at Shanal, his expression intense and sure. "Shanal, do you love me?"

There was a collective gasp around the cathedral.

"Don't answer him!" Burton interrupted, stepping forward, his hands clenched.

Shanal moved swiftly to insert herself between the two men. The air between them seethed with testosterone. She turned her back to Burton and faced Raif, her eyes meeting his. Love him? She hadn't wanted to think about that through all of this, but now, with him here before her, she knew the truth without doubt.

She breathed for him. Her heart beat for him. Her body yearned for him.

"I do. I love you, Raif Masters, with all my heart and with everything I am."

Raif's lips quirked in a half smile that made her want to stretch up and kiss him with all the devotion and passion that dwelled inside her.

"That's perfect, then. Because you know I love you, too."

Two policemen appeared in the doorway to the cathedral, drawing everyone's attention.

"Good, thank goodness. Finally someone with some sense," Burton blustered. "Please, come and arrest this man. He's disrupting my wedding and being a public nuisance."

"I don't think so, Burt," Raif replied, his smile widening as he did so.

Shanal saw Burton bristle at the loathed shortening of his name.

"This is preposterous. Get this man out of here," he directed the two officers, who'd drawn level with Raif.

"No, Burton, they're not here for me. They're here for you, and this time you're not getting off without the blame that's been due to you for far too long."

"Don't be ridiculous. I don't know what you're talking about."

Burton stood even more upright, as if by doing so he could convince everyone what a model citizen he was. But Shanal knew better. She knew the darkness that lurked beneath the surface of his smooth facade. She understood the latent danger he kept well hidden under that apparently charming and debonair exterior.

Raif caught the priest's attention. "Father, I object to this marriage on the grounds that this man is a criminal. His deliberate, spiteful actions led to the death of an innocent woman three years ago, after which he deliberately withheld the truth from a police investigation and perverted the course of justice by bribing others to hide the truth."

Burton paled, his eyes narrowing at Raif as he directed the full force of his hatred toward him. "You're lying. It's all lies," he said, his voice cold and deadly as finely honed steel. "You will regret this, Masters."

"I don't think so," Raif replied just as smoothly. "You won't get away with it this time. The police have a full statement from Noah. It seems he couldn't live with hiding the truth."

The officers stepped forward, one on either side of Burton. "Sir, you need to come with us."

Burton launched himself toward Raif, a feral expression on his face. "You think you've won? You haven't— you can't win. *I'm* the winner. I remember how you mooned about her when we were at school. How love-lorn you were when you thought no one was looking. When she came to work for me I knew there was nothing that would stop me from getting her. I had had Laurel, now I have Shanal. She's mine, I tell you!"

The police grabbed Burton's arms and pulled him back before he could do more than unleash his diatribe.

"Take him away." Raif nodded to the officers, but Burton, it seemed, hadn't said quite enough.

"I waited a long time to lord it over you the way you did over me at school. You think it didn't hurt when we were growing up, when you excelled at everything—the way you thought you were so superior because you always won at sports, with your grades or with girls? I vowed a long time ago I would beat you, and I did. Shanal is mine."

The look in Burton's eyes held a hint of mania that sent a thread of fear winding through Raif's heart. The man was dangerous, and far less stable than Raif had realized. Had he truly done all this—manipulated everyone so cruelly—because of some petty school yard grudge?

"She's her own person," Raif said quietly. "She makes her own choices."

One of the policemen recited the charges against Burton and then read him his rights before they escorted him, still struggling, from the cathedral. Raif and Shanal watched in silence. Around them, the silence changed to a loud hum of excited murmurs.

Raif looked at Shanal and offered her his hand. "Shall we go?"

"Please."

His strong fingers closed around hers and together they walked outside. Raif's Maserati was parked at the curb and he held the door open for her, then made sure her dress was completely tucked inside before closing the door. Shanal sat in the comfortable leather seat and let relief wash over her in drenching waves. Burton's hold on her was over.

Raif settled in the seat beside her. His face was more serious than she'd ever seen it.

"You're safe now," he said firmly. "Safe from him, safe to do what you choose. He can't control you anymore."

"What will happen now?"

"He'll be formally charged and questioned. Given it's the weekend, it might be a while before he comes up before the court. I don't imagine he'll be happy about cooling his heels in jail so his lawyer will try and have him released on bail. The police assure me that, due to his easy access to unlimited funds, they consider him a flight risk and will do everything in their power to ensure he remains behind bars."

Shanal sighed in relief, then looked deep into Raif's eyes. "And us? What will happen with us?"

"That's entirely up to you. Would you like me to take you to your parents' place?"

She shook her head. "No, I'd like to call them, let them know I'm all right—that this business with Burton is over—but I want to be with you. I want to be wherever you are."

His eyes darkened at her words and he leaned forward, pressing his lips all too briefly against hers. "If that's what the lady wants, then that's what the lady will get."

He started the car and drove away from the cathedral. Shanal briefly looked back at the people now spilling from the church doors and down the steps. She shuddered at the thought of how different it all could have been if Raif hadn't made it on time, if he hadn't discovered the information that had put a stop to Burton's manipulation. She turned her head to look forward again, to her future. A future that, hopefully, would include the man next to her, for a long time to come.

When they pulled in through the gates that led to Raif's home, Shanal knew she was in the right place. He stopped at the front door and came around to help her from the low-slung car. When he led her inside she couldn't help feeling how different this was than the last time she'd been here. Then, she'd been filled with anxiety. Now, nothing could be further from her mind.

Raif gestured to his office. "Use the phone in there to call your mum and dad. I'll go pour us a drink."

She smiled in thanks and went into the room. Her mother answered on the first ring.

"Mum, it's okay. It's all over. The police have Burton now."

"What—? The police?"

"I'll explain it all to you and Dad later. I promise."

"What about the mortgage and the loan?"

"Raif said he'd take care of everything. I believe him, Mum. You can, too." And she meant every word. After what Raif had done today she would trust him with her life.

"Oh, thank God for that. When are you coming home?"

"Soon. I'm with Raif now. He's where I belong." As she said the words, she knew she'd never belong anywhere else—with anyone else—more than she did with him.

"Then that is good. Have you talked yet? About the baby?"

"Not properly. But Mum, don't worry, and tell Dad everything will be all right now."

By the time she hung up, Shanal felt drained. Even

so, the weight of responsibility that had so burdened her these past months had lifted. Yes, there was a great deal to sort out and work through, but she could see an end in sight. A happier end. One that began with the man waiting for her across the hall.

Raif was struck anew by Shanal's beauty and grace as she walked toward him, the overblown fussiness of her gown serving to accentuate the classical beauty of the darkness of her hair and the burnished bronze of her skin. He handed her the glass of mineral water he'd poured for her, and lifted his wine in a toast.

"To us," he said.

"Yes, to us."

Shanal clinked her glass against his and took a sip.

"You okay?" Raif studied her, sensing that she was in a state of turmoil.

"Just thinking, wondering what's going to happen next with Burton International, with my parents' home, with you and me."

"Let me put your mind at rest about the first two," Raif said, leading her over to the sofa and sitting down next to her. He stretched one arm along the back of the couch and brushed her cheek with his fingertips. "The board will step in at Burton International and keep things running. He'll be removed as CEO and a provisional one will be installed in his place."

"How do you know all this?" she asked.

He smiled in return. It hadn't been easy and it had taken the better part of the morning to meet with the movers and shakers who would take control of the company. But they hadn't needed much convincing when he'd explained that Burton would be arrested on a manslaughter charge, at the very least, before the wedding.

More importantly, he'd done it in time to save Shanal from committing herself to a man who treated people as if they were no more than accessories designed to make him look all the more powerful or appealing.

"I know some people," he said, keeping the details to a minimum. There'd be time enough to go into the specifics of how things would pan out.

"And my parents? The mortgage Burton held over their house?"

"All sorted out. He didn't hold that personally. It was done through a company run by some of the same people on the Burton International board. The mortgage will be discharged in full on Monday, as soon as business opens."

Tears brightened the pale green of Shanal's eyes. Raif took her glass from her and put it with his on the table in front of them. He then turned to pull her into his arms.

"I can't believe it's over," she whispered against his chest.

"It's only just begun," he murmured in response.

He put a finger under her chin and lifted her face to his, capturing her lips in a kiss that conveyed all the promise and hope he had for the future, their future. She was quick to respond. Her hands reached up to cup his face, to hold him to her as if she would never let him go. And he didn't want her to. He'd waited a long time for this woman. He planned to hold on to her for the rest of their lives.

She protested when he broke their kiss, but came willingly when he stood and took her hands. He led her down the hall toward his master suite, to the place where he could show her, by words and by deed, exactly what she meant to him.

"Raif?"

"Hmm?"

"I meant what I said in the cathedral. I do love you. Not just because you rescued me, again. Not just because you promised to make everything right for me and my parents. But because you make me happier than I've ever been. And what makes me happiest of all is the thought of a future with you and our child."

An incredible swell of joy filled him. She'd put into words the most astounding gift of all.

"Thank you. You humble me," he replied, resting his forehead against hers and hooking his arms around her waist. "I would move heaven and earth for you and our child. I want you to know that. All you ever need to do is ask."

"Just love me back. That's all I'll ever want or need."

"I do. Let me show you exactly how much."

He took his time undressing her, in undoing the row of crystal buttons down her back until her exquisite beauty was revealed without adornment. As he did so, he traced the lines of her body with his fingers, with his tongue, with his lips. She trembled beneath his touch—not with fear or discomfort, but with need and want that was a mirror to his own. And when he lifted her into his arms and laid her gently on his bed, he knew he could explore her every day and never tire of her.

Shanal watched him from under hooded lids as he stripped away his own clothing with far less finesse than he'd undressed her. His erection jutted from his body, his flesh aching to find surcease within her. When he joined her on the bed her hands were quick to find him, to stroke his length, to cup his balls, to squeeze gently, making him close his eyes and give himself over to trust. Trust in her the way she'd trusted him.

They kissed, their lips fusing. First soft and gentle,

then with increasing heat until Raif felt as though his entire body was aflame with want for her. His tongue probed the moist recess of her mouth, stroking her tongue as it met his, teasing the roof of her mouth in a kiss that was hot and wet and deep. Shanal arched her back, pressing her breasts against his chest. He tore his mouth from hers, then kissed a trail across her jawline, down her throat and farther, until he caught one nipple between his lips.

His teeth grazed the taut bud and he felt her shake beneath him, her fingers digging into his back, her nails tiny points of pleasure-pain as he drew the hardened tip deeper into his mouth and pulled with his teeth and his tongue.

"I love you, Shanal, and I'm going to show you just how much," he growled against her skin, pressing kisses lower and lower down her body.

She moaned in delight as his hands spread her thighs, as he nuzzled her neatly trimmed thatch of dark hair. Her hips bowed upward as he licked the curve of her groin. His mouth found her center, his tongue flicking against the bead of nerve endings he knew would tip her completely over the edge. Again and again he stroked that tiny pearl. Beneath his hands he felt the muscles in her legs grow tense, then begin to tremble as a wave rode through her body, then another and another until she collapsed against the bed, gasping.

Her fingers tangled lazily in his hair, traced tiny circles against his scalp. Raif rose over her again, fitting his body against hers. When he looked down at her face he felt a deep sense of pride that he'd finally chased away her shadows—that this beautiful creature was his as much as he was hers, and that he'd made her as happy as she deserved to be.

He fitted himself between her legs, nudging his arousal against her hot, wet center. He groaned as his tip slid into her body.

"Yes," she whispered to him, her hands at his hips, pulling him, urging him to go all the way. "Be mine."

"Always," he answered, kissing her and allowing his length to slide deep inside her.

She was heat and velvet, all in one. Her inner muscles tightened around him, drawing him deeper. The act of joining with another human being had never felt so perfect or so right. He pulled back and then slid home again, slow and sure—taking every second, every sensation, and savoring it as the extraordinary gift it was.

"I love you, Raif," Shanal cried, holding him tight.

This was the ultimate in life, he thought fleetingly. This was perfection. And then he let instinct take over, and the moment became a blur of unique pleasure, of giving and receiving, and finally, of completion as they climaxed together in a kaleidoscope of sensual gratification.

When his heart rate had returned to something approximating normal, Raif rolled to his side, holding Shanal in his arms as if she was the most precious thing in his world. She was and, God willing, always would be. Only one thing more would make this moment perfect.

He pulled away slightly so he could see her face, then drew in a long breath.

"Shanal, I want you to know that I will always be here for you and—" he pressed his hand across her lower belly "—our baby. I know you are most probably sick of weddings by now, but when you're ready, would you do me the utmost honor of becoming my wife?"

Her perfectly formed lips pulled into a smile. "I think

I can find it in me to walk down the aisle once more, as long as you're the one waiting for me at the other end. But it will definitely be the last time," she teased, tracing the line of his nose with a fingertip. Then her expression grew serious and she nodded. "I would love to be your wife, Raif. It would be my greatest privilege to spend the rest of my life with you and to raise our children together."

"I'm glad to hear it," he answered with a smile. "Because if you'd said no, I might have had to whisk you away on a houseboat once again, and this time never let you go."

She shook her head. "You don't ever need to worry about that. I'm yours, for always. As you are mine."

# Epilogue

Raif turned to watch his family as they took their seats in the marquee on the lawn at The Masters, his infant son, dressed in a baby tuxedo, cradled in his arms. In the background, the vineyard stretched out over the hillside, and farther in the distance, the dark silhouette of the old family mansion stood sentinel on top of the hill. The setting had a permanence and sense of history that he'd always enjoyed. It was good to know that some things never changed. But as he looked around at everyone gathered here at the family home to celebrate the birth of his and Shanal's first child, and their wedding, it was also good to see the future shaping and changing with each new member of the family.

"Here, you better give me that baby," his mother said, bustling over to his side. "You're spoiling him rotten, you know. He needs his grandmother's firm hand."

Raif relinquished his son with a laugh. "Mum, you

know you're the family softie. Besides, haven't you always said you can never spoil a baby?"

"Very true. But I have a feeling your hands are going to be all too full very shortly. Don't you have a wedding to enjoy?"

"I do," he said with a wide smile. "And I'm looking forward to it."

"Well, you've both waited long enough. It's a shame Shanal's dad didn't live long enough to see her happily married."

"Yeah, but at least he found peace before he went. He saw her happy, and that's the main thing, right? And he knew we'd be naming our little guy Curtis, after him."

Marianne Masters patted her eldest son lovingly on one cheek. "You're a good man, Raif Masters. I'm so proud of you."

"I love you, Mum."

Ethan arrived beside him, dressed in a dinner suit and with a boutonniere affixed to his lapel. He raised the one he held in his hand. "Your turn," he said, pinning the flower to his cousin's suit jacket. "And we need to go line up. Apparently, your bride is ready."

"Then what are we waiting for?" Raif asked.

Together they walked toward the temporary altar that had been set up beneath the decorated marquee on the grounds. The June weather had been kind so far and the predicted rain had held off.

"What's the latest on Burton Rogers?" Ethan asked. "The case against him still hasn't gone to court yet, has it?"

"I'm told his lawyers are dragging it out—fighting to have him declared mentally unfit to stand trial. Either way, he'll be put away for a long time and he won't be able to hurt the people I love ever again."

"They should lock people like him up forever," Ethan said emphatically.

"I couldn't agree more."

Raif and Ethan joined Raif's brother, Cade, and the celebrant who stood waiting. Raif turned to face the aisle that Shanal would be coming down. As he listened for the music that would cue her arrival, he studied the faces before him. His parents sat in front, looking exceptionally proud and happy. Their trip to France had whetted their appetite for more travel and they had a trip to Tuscany planned for the European autumn. Whether his father succeeded in taking Marianne away from baby Curtis for more than a month would be the test, though, Raif thought.

His cousins Judd Wilson and Nicole Jackson were also there with their respective spouses, Anna and Nate. Anna bore a delicate bump, announcing her early pregnancy. Ethan's sister, Tamsyn, sat a row back with her husband, Finn Gallagher, who was propping their sleeping five-month-old daughter on one shoulder. Beside Tamsyn was her half sister, Alexis, who together with her husband, Raoul, was busy reining in their twin boys. The toddlers were charming and delightful, but also well-skilled at keeping their parents on their toes. The boys' half sister, Ruby, a month shy of her third birthday, was to be Shanal's flower girl, and Raif had heard that she'd been delighted when she was shown the miniature sari she would wear today.

And then the sound of delicate notes wrought from violin strings dragged his attention back to the house, to where his bride now appeared on the back veranda, together with her mother and Ruby. She was a resplendent vision in red and gold, eschewing a white bridal gown for her mother's traditions, and to Raif she'd never looked more beautiful. His eyes never left her as, with her mother by her side, she followed Ruby down the aisle. Shanal grinned at him in return. They turned together to face the celebrant, who smiled at them both, then began.

"We are gathered here today…"

"No running away this time," Raif whispered to his bride as the celebrant intoned in the background.

"Never again," Shanal answered. "I have everything I want right here, with you."

\* \* \* \* \*

# "I'll not have you calling me Your Highness in bed.

"Call me Gabriel."

"Gabriel," she echoed, her soft voice low and intimate in a way that warmed his blood. "I promise to remember never to refer to you as Your Royal Highness or Prince Gabriel while we are making love."

Away from the public eye, Olivia was no longer the enigmatic, cultured woman he'd decided to marry. Impish humor sparkled in her eyes. Intelligence shone there, as well. Why had she hidden her sharp mind from him?

"All of a sudden, it occurs to me that I've never kissed you."

"You kissed me the day you proposed."

"In front of a dozen witnesses," he murmured. It had been a formality, really, not a true proposal. "And not the way I wanted to."

"How did you want to?"

"Like this."

\* \* \*

**Royal Heirs Required**
is part of the No.1 bestselling series from Mills & Boon® Desire™, Billionaires and Babies: Powerful men...wrapped around their babies' little fingers.

# ROYAL HEIRS REQUIRED

BY
CAT SCHIELD

All rights reserved including the right of reproduction in whole or in part in any form. This edition is published by arrangement with Harlequin Books S.A.

This is a work of fiction. Names, characters, places, locations and incidents are purely fictional and bear no relationship to any real life individuals, living or dead, or to any actual places, business establishments, locations, events or incidents. Any resemblance is entirely coincidental.

This book is sold subject to the condition that it shall not, by way of trade or otherwise, be lent, resold, hired out or otherwise circulated without the prior consent of the publisher in any form of binding or cover other than that in which it is published and without a similar condition including this condition being imposed on the subsequent purchaser.

® and ™ are trademarks owned and used by the trademark owner and/or its licensee. Trademarks marked with ® are registered with the United Kingdom Patent Office and/or the Office for Harmonisation in the Internal Market and in other countries.

Published in Great Britain 2015
by Mills & Boon, an imprint of Harlequin (UK) Limited,
Eton House, 18-24 Paradise Road, Richmond, Surrey, TW9 1SR

© 2015 Catherine Schield

ISBN: 978-0-263-25254-5

51-0315

Harlequin (UK) Limited's policy is to use papers that are natural, renewable and recyclable products and made from wood grown in sustainable forests. The logging and manufacturing processes conform to the legal environmental regulations of the country of origin.

Printed and bound in Spain
by CPI, Barcelona

**Cat Schield** has been reading and writing romance since high school. Although she graduated from college with a BA in business, her idea of a perfect career was writing books for Mills & Boon. And now, after winning the Romance Writers of America 2010 Golden Heart® Award for series contemporary romance, that dream has come true. Cat lives in Minnesota with her daughter, Emily, and their Burmese cat. When she's not writing sexy, romantic stories for Mills & Boon® Desire™, she can be found sailing with friends on the St Croix River, or in more exotic locales, like the Caribbean and Europe. She loves to hear from readers. Find her at www.catschield.com. Follow her on Twitter: @catschield.

For Delores and Jerry Slawik.
Thank you for making me feel like part of your family.

# One

"She's the perfect choice for you," Gabriel Alessandro's brother joked, nudging his shoulder.

The two princes were standing at the edge of the dance floor watching their father, the king, sweep Gabriel's future bride through a series of elegant turns while their mother concentrated on keeping her toes from beneath the prime minister's clumsy feet.

Gabriel released an audible sigh. With his future bride's father building a high-tech manufacturing plant just outside the capital, Sherdana's economy would receive the boost it badly needed. "Of course she is."

Lady Olivia Darcy, daughter of a wealthy British earl, was just a little too perfect. While she exuded poise and warmth in public, in private she never relaxed, never let down her guard. This hadn't bothered him at all in the days leading up to their engagement. From the moment he'd begun looking for a wife he'd decided to listen to his head and not his heart. Past experience had demonstrated losing himself in passion led to nothing but heartache and disappointment.

"Then why are you looking so grim?"

Why indeed? Even though Gabriel didn't have to pretend to be besotted with his fiancée in front of his brother, he wasn't about to admit his regret that his personal life would have less passion and drama once he was married.

Until the wedding planning had begun in earnest, he'd considered himself well and thoroughly lucky to have found a woman who wouldn't drive him mad with her theatrics and demands. It was in sharp contrast to his affair with Marissa, which had been a tempestuous four-year romance with no future.

Gabriel was not a world-famous musician or a dashing Hollywood actor or even a wealthy playboy. He was the heir apparent of a small European country with strict laws that dictated his wife must be either an aristocrat or a citizen of Sherdana. Marissa had been neither.

"How happy would you be if you were marrying a virtual stranger?" Gabriel kept his voice soft, but there was no hiding his bitterness.

Christian's grin was positively wicked. "The best part about being the youngest is that I don't have to worry about getting married at all."

Gabriel muttered an expletive. He was well aware that neither of his brothers envied him. In many ways that was a relief. In centuries past Sherdana had seen its fair share of plots against the crown both from without and within. It would have been awful if either of his brothers had schemed to keep him off the throne. But that was highly unlikely. Nic lived in the US, building rocket ships that might someday carry regular—wealthy—citizens into space while Christian was very happy buying and selling companies.

"...hot."

"Hot?" Gabriel caught the final word his brother had spoken. "What's hot?"

"Not what." Christian shot him a wry glance. "Who. Your future bride. I was just remarking that you should spend some time getting to know her. It might be more enjoyable than you think. She's hot."

Lady Olivia Darcy was many things, but Gabriel wouldn't label her as hot. A gorgeous package of stylish sophistication, she had the fashion designers competing to dress her. Her features were delicate and feminine, her skin pale and unblemished. She was slender, but not boyish, with long legs, graceful arms and an elegant neck. There was a serene expression in her keen blue gaze.

And it wasn't as if she was a frivolous socialite, spending her days shopping and her nights in clubs. She worked tirelessly for almost a dozen charities all focused on children's causes. The perfect future queen of Sherdana.

Gabriel shot his brother a narrow look. "You just referred to your future sister-in-law and queen as hot. Do you think Mother would approve?"

"I'm her baby boy." The youngest of the triplets, Christian had played the birth-order card all his life. "She approves of everything I do."

"She doesn't approve of your antics, she simply feels bad for all those times she had to leave you to the nanny because she could only carry Nic and me."

Ignoring his brother's gibe, Christian nodded toward the queen. "She's hot, too, you know. She'd have to be to keep Father interested all these years."

Gabriel had no interest in discussing his parents' love life. "What has you so determined to stir up trouble tonight?"

Christian's expression settled into severe lines. "Now that Mother has you all settled, she going to turn her sights to Nic and me."

"Nic is more interested in fuel systems than women," Gabriel said. "And you've made it clear you have no intention of giving up your bachelor ways."

In the five years since his car accident, Christian had become guarded and pessimistic when it came to his personal life. Although the burn scars that spread down his neck and over his shoulder, chest and upper arm on the right side were hidden beneath the high collar of his formal blue tunic, the worst of Christian's hurts were below the skin, deep in his soul where no healing reached. The damage was visible in those rare moments when he drank too much or thought no one was watching.

Gabriel continued, "I don't think either of our parents hold out any hope that the two of you will settle down anytime soon."

"You know Mother is a romantic," Christian said.

"She's also pragmatic."

But Christian didn't look convinced. "If that was true, she'd accept that you will father all the heirs Sherdana could ever want or need and leave Nic and me alone. That's not the impression she gave me earlier this evening."

A knot of discomfort formed in Gabriel's chest as he thought of his future bride. Once again his gaze slid to Olivia, who was now dancing with the prime minister. Although her smile was lovely, the reserve in her blue eyes made her seem untouchable.

His days with Marissa had been sensual, wild and all-consuming. They'd awaken before dawn in her Paris apartment and make love in the quiet hush of the early morning. After which they'd sit by the window, gorge themselves with pastries washed down with strong coffee and watch the sun paint the rooftops with golden light.

"Your Royal Highness."

Gabriel turned to his private secretary, who'd appeared out of nowhere. Usually Stewart Barnes was the calm eye in the middle of the hurricane. At the moment, sweat shone on his forehead.

The hairs on the back of Gabriel's neck rose. "Problem?"

Stewart's approach had caught Christian's attention, as well. "I'll deal with it," he said, stepping away from his brother's side.

"No, sir." The private secretary moved to block Christian. He gave a small shake of his head and met Gabriel's hard gaze with a look that conveyed the seriousness of the issue. "I know the timing is bad, but a lawyer has arrived with an urgent message for you."

"A lawyer?"

"How did he get into the palace?" Christian snapped, eyes blazing.

Gabriel barely registered Christian's words. "What could possibly be so important?"

"Did Captain Poulin give you a reason for granting this man entrance at such an inappropriate hour?"

"Can't it wait until after the party?"

Stewart's attention bounced between the two men as they fired questions at him. "He wouldn't tell me what it's about, Highness, only the name of his client." Stewart's tone was low and urgent. "I think you'd better speak to him."

Unable to imagine what could have rattled his unflappable private secretary, Gabriel shared a glance with Christian. "Who is his client?"

"Marissa Somme."

Hearing his former lover's name aroused a hundred emotions Gabriel would have preferred not to feel. He was a little surprised that Marissa had waited so long to contact him. He'd expected her to pull a stunt five months ago when he'd announced his engagement. To say she had a flare for the dramatic was like describing the Himalayas as tall hills.

"What mischief is she up to?" Gabriel demanded.

Christian cursed beneath his breath. "Something newsworthy, no doubt."

"I can't afford anything to interfere with the wedding." Sherdana's future was riding on the deal he'd struck with Lord Darcy. A deal that wouldn't be sealed until Olivia became a princess.

Gabriel glanced around to see if anyone had noticed their exchange and met Olivia's level gaze. She was beautiful, his future wife. But he'd chosen her for more than her appearance. She had a purity of spirit he knew would charm the Sherdanian people and her efficient, calm way of handling problems would see her through the hectic days ahead.

Beside her his father was laughing at whatever story she was telling him, looking years younger. Recent economic difficulties had taken their toll on the king. Once vibrant and strong, he'd begun to tire faster in recent months. It was why Gabriel had taken on more and more of the day-to-day running of the country.

Although she returned her attention to the king, the slightest lift of her delicate eyebrows let Gabriel know her curiosity had been aroused by his exchange with Christian and Stewart. Awareness surged through him. It was the first time that they'd connected at a level deeper than politeness. Anticipation sparked. Perhaps they would be able to share something more than a bed.

"Please, Your Highness."

Glancing toward Christian, he said, "Will you go entertain my fiancée while I discover what's going on?"

"Don't you mean distract?" Christian countered, his expression sour.

"Just make excuses for me until I can get back."

And then he was slipping through the multitude attending the ball honoring Sherdana's independence from France back in 1664, smiling and greeting the guests as if nothing in the world was wrong. All the while two words pounded in his head: *Marissa Somme*. What could this be about?

Since it first declared itself a principality, Sherdana had survived as an agrarian economy. But Gabriel wanted his country to do more than survive, he wanted it to thrive.

Tucked between France and Italy on a verdant plane resplendent with grapevines and fertile fields, Sherdana
needed an active technological culture to move the economy into the twenty-first century and beyond. Olivia's father, Lord Edwin Darcy, held the match that would light
the fuse. Nothing must interfere with that.

Entering the green salon, Gabriel strode over to greet
the man who'd barged in unannounced. The lawyer wore
his gray hair short, making no attempt to hide the bald
patch that caught the light from the wall sconces behind
him. His clear gray eyes had few lines at the corners. This
was not a man who smiled often. Dressed in a navy suit
and black overcoat, the only spark of color about him was
a thin line of yellow in his striped tie.

"Good evening, Your Royal Highness," the gentleman
said, bowing respectfully. "Forgive me for interrupting,
but I'm afraid the matter is quite urgent."

"What mischief is Marissa up to now?"

"Mischief?" The man looked dismayed at Gabriel's
harshness. "You misunderstand the reason I'm here."

"Then enlighten me. I have guests waiting. If you have
a message from Marissa, then deliver it."

The man straightened his shoulders and tugged at his
coat lapel. "It's a little more complicated than a message."

"My patience is wearing thin."

"Marissa Somme is dead."

Dead? Gabriel felt as if he'd been clobbered with a
poker. For a second he couldn't process the man's words.
Brilliant, beautiful, vivacious Marissa dead? His gut
twisted.

"How?"

The older gentleman nodded in sympathy. "Cancer."

Even though he hadn't spoken with her in a very long
time, the news rocked him. Marissa had been the first
woman he'd ever loved. The only one. Their breakup three

years before had been one of the most painful experiences of his life. But nothing compared to knowing she was gone for good. Wounds he'd thought healed were reopened, the pain as fresh as it had ever been. Never would he see her again. Hear her laugh.

Why hadn't she called him? He would have helped her out.

"You came all this way to deliver the news of her death to me?" Had she still cared about him? Despite her final angry words? Impossible. She'd never once tried to contact him.

"And to bring you something she said you should have."

"What?" Gabriel demanded. Had she returned the diamond heart pendant he'd given her for their first anniversary? He'd been a romantic fool in those days. Young. Rebellious. Caught up in a passionate affair that had no future. And a fool. "What did you bring me?"

"Your daughters."

"Daughters?" *As in more than one?* Gabriel wondered if he'd heard the man properly.

"Twins."

"Marissa and I had no children together."

"I'm afraid that's not true."

The man pulled out two birth certificates and extended them. Gabriel gestured to Stewart to take them and watched as his private secretary scanned the documents. Stewart's blue eyes were awash with concern as he glanced up and met Gabriel's gaze.

"They bear Marissa's last name, but she listed you as the father," Stewart said.

"They can't be mine," Gabriel insisted. "We were careful." Perhaps not careful enough. "How old are they?"

"They will turn two in a month."

Gabriel quickly did the math. They'd been conceived in the week he'd been in Venice shortly after their breakup.

Marissa had come and thrown herself at him in one last attempt to make him abandon his duty. They'd made love all night, their kisses frantic, embraces feverish. When she'd awakened to find him departing the room before dawn, she'd lashed out, claiming that he'd led her on, accusing him of indifference. Despite her antagonism, regret had stuck with him for months afterward.

They'd had no future. His duty was to his country. She couldn't accept that and he'd let the relationship go on too long. She'd begun to hope he would give up everything for her and he'd enjoyed shirking his responsibilities. But it couldn't last. Sherdana always came first.

What would he have done if he'd known she was pregnant? Set her up in a villa nearby where he could visit? She would never have put up with that. She'd have demanded his complete and total devotion. It was what had torn them apart. He belonged to the people of Sherdana.

"This could all be a huge hoax," Stewart said.

"Marissa might have loved drama, but pulling a stunt like this goes beyond anything she'd do."

"We'll know for sure after a DNA test," Stewart said.

"And in the meantime? What am I to do with the girls?" the lawyer asked impertinently.

"Where are they?" Gabriel demanded. He crackled with impatience to see them.

"Back at my hotel with their nanny."

He didn't hesitate to ponder the consequences. "Get them."

"Think of your upcoming wedding, Highness," Stewart cautioned. "You can't have them brought here. The palace is crawling with media."

Gabriel aimed a disgusted look at his secretary. "Are you telling me you're not clever enough to transport two toddlers here without being seen?"

Stewart's spine snapped straight as Gabriel knew it

would. "I will see that they are brought to the palace immediately."

"Good."

"In the meantime," Stewart said, "I suggest you return to the gala before you're missed. I'm sure the king and queen will wish to discuss the best way to handle things."

Gabriel hated every bit of Stewart's sensible advice and the need to play host when his attention was shackled to reckless urges. He didn't want to wait to see the girls. His instinct demanded he go to the lawyer's hotel immediately. As if by taking one look at the toddlers he could tell if they were his. Ridiculous.

"Find me as soon as they're settled," he told Stewart.

And with those parting words, he exited the room.

Knowing he should return immediately to the party but with his mind racing, Gabriel strode into the library. He needed a few minutes to catch his breath and calm his thoughts.

Twins. His heart jerked. Did they have their mother's clear green eyes and luxurious brown hair? Had she told them about him? Was he insane to bring them into the palace?

A scandal could jeopardize his plans for stabilizing Sherdana's economy. Would the earl still allow Olivia to marry him if word got out that Gabriel had illegitimate twin daughters? And what if Olivia wasn't willing to accept that her children wouldn't be his only ones?

Gabriel left the library, burdened by a whole new set of worries, determined to make sure his future bride found him irresistible.

From her place of honor beside the king of Sherdana, Olivia watched her future husband slip through the guests assembled in the golden ballroom and wondered what was so important that he had to leave the Independence Day gala in such a hurry.

It continued to bother her that in less than four weeks, she was going to become a princess, Gabriel's princess, and she had very little insight into the man she was marrying. Theirs was not a love match the likes of which Kate had found with William. Olivia and Gabriel were marrying to raise her father's social position and improve Sherdana's economic situation.

While that was great for everyone else, Olivia's London friends wondered what was motivating her. She'd never told anyone about the dream conceived by her three-year-old self that one day she'd become a princess. It had been a child's fancy and as she'd grown up, reality replaced the fairy tale. As a teenager she'd stopped imagining herself living in a palace and dancing through the night with a handsome prince. Her plans for the future involved practical things like children's charities and someday a husband and children of her own. But some dreams had deep roots that lay dormant until the time was ripe.

Before Olivia considered her actions, she turned to the king. "Excuse me."

"Of course," the handsome monarch replied, his smile cordial.

Released, she left the king and headed in the direction her fiancé had gone. Perhaps she could catch Gabriel before he returned to the ballroom and they could spend some time talking, just the two of them. She hadn't gone more than a dozen steps before Christian Alessandro appeared in her path.

His gold eyes, shadowed and wary around most people, warmed as he smiled down at her. "Are you enjoying the party?"

"Of course," she replied, bottling up a sigh as the youngest Alessandro prince foiled her plan to speak to his brother alone.

She'd encountered Christian several times in London over the years. As the wildest Alessandro brother, in his university days, Christian had spent more time partying than studying and had barely graduated from Oxford. He'd earned a reputation as a playboy, but had always treated her with respect. Maybe because Olivia had recognized the clever mind he hid beneath his cavalier charm.

"I noticed Prince Gabriel left the party in a hurry," she murmured, unable to conquer the curiosity that loosened her tongue. "I hope nothing is wrong."

Christian had an impressive poker face. "Just some old business he had to take care of. Nothing important."

"He looked a bit shaken up." She stared at her future brother-in-law and saw the tiniest twitch at the corner of his eye. He was keeping something important about Gabriel from her. Olivia's pulse skipped. Seemed she wasn't the only one with secrets.

Since Gabriel had opened negotiations with her father a year ago, Olivia hadn't had much opportunity to get to know the man she would marry. The situation hadn't improved since she'd arrived in Sherdana a week ago. With the wedding only a month away and parliament in session, they'd barely spent an hour alone together and most of that had been divided up into one- to five-minute snippets.

A stroll in the garden the day after she'd arrived, cut short when they'd met the queen's very muddy vizsla. Gabriel had commended Olivia's nimbleness in dodging the dog and retreated to the palace to change his trousers.

A moment in the carriage before the parade yesterday. He'd complimented her hat.

A whole five minutes during the waltz this evening. He'd told her she looked lovely.

Their exchanges were polite and cordial. At all times

he'd been the perfect prince. Courteous. Gallant. Cultured. And she'd been seized by the absurd desire to muss his hair and shock him with outrageous remarks. Of course, she would never do that. The daughter of an earl, she was acutely conscious of her image and position.

Christian refocused her attention on the crowd around them and began filling her ear with all sorts of salacious gossip about the local nobility. Normally she'd be amused by his outrageous slander of Sherdana's wealthy and powerful, but with each new dance the air in the ballroom grew stuffier and she wanted to spend time getting to know her fiancé.

What did Gabriel expect from her? A political partner? Or an attractive figurehead that he could trot out for state occasions? She hoped it was the former.

Firstborn, he'd won the right to inherit the throne by a mere forty minutes. But there was no question in anyone's mind that he was utterly and completely suited to the role.

His commitment to Sherdana was absolute and apparent to all. He'd been educated here and rarely left, except on official business. While in contrast, his two younger brothers had both chosen to spend as little time in their native country as possible.

Drawn by a magnetic pull too great to resist, her attention returned to the ballroom doors that Gabriel had passed through. What could have taken him away in the middle of the party? As if her thoughts had summoned him, she spied the prince coming through the crowd toward her.

Her gaze traced the sculpted breadth of his shoulders, the way his white jacket stretched across his broad chest, providing an abundance of room for the medals pinned there. A blue sash cut diagonally from shoulder to hip.

"Forgive me for neglecting you," he said as he came to a stop before her. "I hope my brother has kept you sufficiently entertained."

"Christian has been filling me in on your guests."

For the first time in her company, Gabriel's courteous mask slipped. He shot his brother a hard look. "What have you been telling her?"

"Things most people, including you, wouldn't. If she's going to be Sherdana's princess, she needs to know where the bodies are buried or she'll be no help to you at all."

Gabriel shook his head. "She doesn't need to know all the ins and outs of our politics to help out the country or me."

Olivia's heart sank. Now she knew what he expected from her. There would be no partnership, no working together. She would attend ceremonies and support charities while he ran the country and dealt with its problems alone.

"She's smarter than you're giving her credit for, Gabriel. You should use her to your best political advantage."

"Thank you for your opinion, brother." And his tone said that was the end of the conversation.

With a mocking bow, Christian retreated. While part of Olivia regretted his departure, she was glad for a moment alone with Gabriel. Or she was until he began to speak.

"I know you haven't seen much of Sherdana since your arrival," he said, his polite formality pushing her to greater impatience. "But maybe that can change in the next week or so."

"That would be lovely." She bit back her thoughts on how unlikely it was. With the wedding only a month away she would scarcely have the opportunity to sleep, much less take a tour of the countryside. "I'm eager to visit the wine country."

"Sherdana takes pride in its wine as you well know."

"As it should," she murmured, her boredom coming through in her tone. "I'm glad you were able to get your business resolved so you could return to the party so quickly."

"Business?" There wasn't the least suggestion of understanding in his manner.

"I saw your private secretary approach you with some news. It seemed to be something unpleasant. And then you left. Christian explained it was old business you needed to take care of."

"Ah, yes. Just a misunderstanding with Stewart. It was nothing."

"I'm glad." But her mind was busy cataloging all the nuances of his tone and expression. Her future husband was skilled at deflection.

"Would you care to dance?" he asked, his deep voice rumbling through her like distant thunder.

Not really. She was tired and her shoes pinched. But she smiled. "Of course."

A waltz began to play as Gabriel took her hand and led her onto the dance floor. Keeping her expression pleasant and neutral was torture as his palm slid against her back. The gown she wore had a modest cut, showing no cleavage or bare shoulders, but the material was silk and the heat of Gabriel's hand burned through the fabric and set her on fire.

"Are you feeling compelled to marry because your father wishes it?"

The abruptness of his question was so unexpected, she almost laughed. "Why would I need to be compelled by my father? You're rich, handsome and going to be king one day. What girl wouldn't wish to be queen?"

"You didn't answer my question."

"I'm not being forced to marry you. I have been given an opportunity many would envy." She assessed his expression, curious where this line of questioning originated. "Are you worried that down the road I'll regret my choice?" She cocked her head and regarded him intently. "Or are you looking for an excuse to break our engagement?"

"Nothing like that. I am just wondering if perhaps you'd have preferred a different life."

"I'm sure many people wish every day that they'd done something different. Mostly, we must play the hand life deals us. For some, it's struggling with poverty. For others raising a child on their own or dedicating themselves to their career and forgoing a family." She pitched her voice into sympathetic tones for the next example. "For you it's ensuring your kingdom's economic security. I get to marry a prince and someday become a queen."

For some inexplicable reason, he grew short with her. "But is that what you want?"

"To marry you and become a queen?" She let her surprise show. "Of course."

Gabriel didn't appear convinced. "We haven't had much time to get to know each other," he said. "I hope that will change over the next month."

"Perhaps we could begin now. What is it you'd like to know?"

"Let's begin simply. How do you come to speak French and Italian so fluently?"

"I had a whole army of tutors from the time I was small."

"Your accent is quite good."

"I've been told I have an aptitude for languages. I speak quite a few."

"How many?"

"Six, but I understand three more."

"That will come in handy when dignitaries visit us."

Once again it hit her that she would never return to her home in England for anything more than a short visit. As princess, she would be expected to spend most, if not all, of her time in Sherdana. At least she would see her father frequently because he would want to keep an eye on his investment.

"You don't smile much, do you?" His question was more reflective than directly aimed at her.

His observation caught her off guard.

"I smile all the time."

Gabriel's gaze slipped intently over her features, arousing a frantic thrumming in her chest. "Polite smiles. Political smiles, but I'm not sure I've once seen you smile because you're happy."

"I assure you, I'm quite happy."

"Stop telling me what you think I want to hear. That's not what Sherdana needs of its princess and definitely not what I expect from my wife."

The intensity of his tone and the nuances of his observation did not belong to the man she'd known up to this point. His frank speech loosened her tongue.

"Are you giving me permission to argue with Your Highness?"

He made a face. "Gabriel."

"Of course."

"Olivia." Tone commanding, he somehow managed to caress her name in a way that vibrated through her. "It would make me very happy if you would start thinking of me as a man and not a prince."

His demand sent a ripple of excitement up her spine. She decided to speak her mind.

"I will if you stop thinking of me in terms of economic gain or financial dealings and realize I'm a woman who knows exactly what she wants."

At her words, Gabriel blinked. Surprise quickly became curiosity as he regarded her. For the first time she believed he was seeing her as a person instead of the clause in the contract he needed to satisfy so her father would build a plant in Sherdana and create technical jobs to bolster the economy.

"I'm beginning to think there's more to you than I realize," Gabriel remarked, executing a turn in the dance that left her breathless.

"Thank goodness." It was an effort to get out more than those two words.

Perhaps marriage might hold more of an adventure than she'd first thought. She hadn't expected her husband to excite her. Even seeing how handsome Gabriel was, he was always so in control. She never imagined passion. And growing up sheltered from the experiences an ordinary girl would have with boys such as dating or even just hanging out, she'd never experienced desire. Until this moment, she wasn't sure she could.

Relief made her giddy. Tonight she'd glimpsed a very important and unexpected benefit this marriage would have for her and for the first time in months, she faced her future with a light heart.

# Two

Olivia lay on the blue velvet chaise in the bedroom she'd been assigned at the palace, a heating pad taking away the discomfort of cramps. She stared up at the touches of gold leaf on the ceiling's ornate plasterwork twenty feet above her. From the tall, narrow mirrors between the wide cream silk-draped windows to the elegant chandeliers, it was a stunning, yet surprisingly warm, space.

It was a little after two in the morning. She'd felt the first twinge of pain not long after the king and queen left the gala and had taken the opportunity to slip away. The attack had been blessedly mild. A year ago, she would have taken a pain pill and retreated to bed. Thank goodness those days were behind her. A princess couldn't avoid public appearances because she wasn't feeling well. She must have a spine of steel and prove her value was more than the economic boost her father's new technology company would provide.

As if to mock her optimism, a fresh ache began. She'd first started suffering with sharp cramps and strong periods when she was fifteen. Frightened by the amount of blood she lost each month, Olivia had gone to see a doctor. She'd been diagnosed with endometriosis and had begun taking oral contraceptives to reduce the pain and shorten her periods. Yoga, massage and acupuncture had also helped her cope with her symptoms, but none of these could correct the problem.

She'd needed surgery for that.

Olivia couldn't explain why she'd been so reluctant to have the growths removed when the pain grew progressively worse in her early twenties. She couldn't share her fears with her mother—who'd died giving birth to her—so she'd hidden the severity of the problem from everyone, including her father. Only Libby, her private secretary, knew how debilitating the pain could get. Libby had helped Olivia keep her doctor visits out of the press and made excuses when she had bad days. Olivia wasn't sure what she'd have done these past eight years without Libby's help.

It wasn't until a year ago, when she'd confronted the connection between endometriosis and infertility, that she began to rethink her plans for coping with the disease. If she was marrying a wealthy businessman, a politician or even one of her own country's nobles, she could discuss this issue with him and together they could decide what to do about her potential barrenness. But she was marrying the future king of Sherdana and would be expected to produce an heir.

So, she'd had the surgery and had been living pain free for almost twelve months.

With a sudden surge of impatience, Olivia set aside the heating pad and got to her feet. Brooding over her medical condition was the quickest way to doubt herself and that wasn't the way she faced things. Despite the late hour, the luxurious king-size bed held no appeal. She needed some fresh air and exercise. Perhaps a walk in the garden.

Although she'd removed her ball gown upon returning to her room, she'd not yet dressed for bed. Slipping off her robe, Olivia pulled on a sleeveless jersey dress and found a pair of ballet flats that would allow her to move soundlessly through the sleeping palace.

The room she'd been given was in the opposite wing of the palace from the royal family's apartments and used for housing dignitaries and visitors. Her father slept next door, his room as expansive and substantially furnished as hers. Olivia tiptoed past his door, aiming for the stairs at the far end of the hall that would deposit her close to the pink receiving room and the side gardens beyond. With her limited time in the palace, Olivia hadn't had a great deal of time to explore, but she'd taken this route her second day to meet with the queen.

When she got to the end of the hallway, the high-pitched shriek of an unhappy child caught Olivia's attention. The sound was muffled and it came from somewhere above her. She reached the stairs and paused to listen. She waited no more than a heartbeat before the cry came again, only this time there were two voices.

In an instant Olivia's destination changed. Instead of going down to the ground level, she headed up to the third floor, following the increasingly frantic exclamations of the children and the no less agitated voice of an adult trying to quiet them.

At the top of the stairs, Olivia spied two shadows racing toward her down the darkened hallway. Curious as to what was going on, she'd taken several steps in their direction when a voice cut through the shadows.

"Karina. Bethany. Come back here this instant." The shrill command provoked the children to faster flight.

Worried that at the speed they were going, they might pitch down the stairs, Olivia knelt and spread her arms wide. With their path blocked, the children stopped abruptly. With eyes wide, arms around each other for comfort, they stared at Olivia.

"Hello." She offered them her gentlest smile. "Where are you two going so late?"

"You girls are nothing but trouble."

The scolding woman hadn't spied Olivia in the dimness or she wouldn't have spoken so rudely. The two little girls shrank away from their pursuer, obviously afraid, and sidestepped in Olivia's direction. Now that they were closer, Olivia could see them better. She blinked, wondering if she might be seeing double.

The two little girls, two frightened little girls, were mirror images of each other with long brown hair and large dark eyes in their pale faces. They were dressed in identical dresses and tears streaked their matching cheeks.

Olivia wanted to snatch them into her arms, but feared upsetting them still more. Although her childhood had lacked a loving mother, Olivia had developed a strong maternal instinct. Being warned by the doctor that unless she had surgery she might never have her own children had been a sharp knife in her heart.

"You'd better learn to behave and fast or the people who live here will kick you out and you'll have nowhere else to go."

Having heard enough, Olivia surged to her feet to confront the woman and was surprised when the girls raced to stand behind her. They gripped her dress with strength born of fear, and protectiveness surged through her.

"Stop speaking this instant," Olivia commanded without raising her voice. "No one deserves to be threatened like that, especially not children."

The nanny stopped dead in her tracks and sneered. "You don't know what they're like."

"Whom do you work for?"

The woman looked wary. "I take care of these two."

"Yes, yes." Olivia put one hand on each of the toddlers' heads. The hair was silky beneath her fingers and she longed to give the girls her full attention, but this woman must be dealt with first. "But who are their parents?"

"Their mother is dead."

Olivia sucked in a short breath at the woman's lack of compassion. "That's awful."

The woman didn't respond.

"In heaven," the child on her left said.

Olivia liked the girls' nanny less and less. Had the woman no heart? Did the father know how badly his daughters were being cared for? "Perhaps I should speak to their father. What is his name?"

"A lawyer hired me a week ago to take care of them." The woman stared at Olivia in hostile defensiveness.

"Well, you're not doing a very good job."

"They're terribly spoiled and very difficult. And right now they need to be in bed." Eyes on the children, the nanny shifted her weight forward and her arms left her sides as if she intended to snatch the little girls away from Olivia.

The little girl on her right shrank back. Her sister, emboldened by Olivia's defense, fought back.

"Hate you." She hung on Olivia's skirt. "Wanna go home."

Although she'd been too young to know the shock of losing her mother, Olivia remembered her lonely childhood and ached for the sadness yet to come for these girls. She wanted to wrap her arms around the toddlers and support them through this difficult time, but these were not her children and she shouldn't get attached.

With a heavy sigh, Olivia knew it was time to extricate herself from the situation. She would summon a maid to get the girls settled and return to her room. In the morning she would find out to whom they belonged and fill him in on his employee.

"If I make this mean lady go away," Olivia began, gazing down at the dark heads. "Would you go back to your room and go to sleep?"

"No." Only one of the pair seemed to be verbal. The

other merely gave her head a vehement shake. "Stay with you."

*Oh, dear.* Obviously she'd defended the girls a little too well. But maybe it wouldn't hurt for them to spend one night with her. There was plenty of room in her big bed and in the morning she could sort them out.

"Would you like to come to my room to sleep tonight?"

In unison, the two dark heads bobbed. Olivia smiled.

"You can't do this," the nanny protested.

"I most certainly can. I suggest you return to your room and pack. I will send someone to escort you out shortly." Olivia extended a hand to each girl and drew the children toward the stairs. Once they were settled in her room, she would send a maid up for their nightgowns and things.

It took time to descend to the second floor. The toddlers' short legs made slow work of the steps, giving Olivia time to wonder who in the palace would raise a cry that they'd gone missing. She looked forward to having a conversation with their father in the near future about the sort of person he'd employed to take care of his children.

When Olivia entered her room, she was surprised to find it occupied by a maid. The girl looked up in surprise from the desk items she was straightening as the trio entered. Although the palace had provided Olivia with maids to tidy up and assist with whatever she needed, she hadn't expected to find one in her room during the middle of the night. And from the expression on the woman's face, she wasn't expecting to be caught at it.

"Lady Darcy, I was just tidying some things up for you."

"At two in the morning?"

"I saw your light on and thought you might be needing something."

Not wanting to make a huge scene in front of the little girls, Olivia scanned the maid's face, confident she'd be able to recognize her again from the hundred or so servants that maintained the palace. She had a small scar just below her left eye.

"Could you run down to the kitchen and get glasses of warm milk for these two?"

"Hate milk," the talkative one said. "Ice cream."

Recalling the nanny's assessment that the girls were spoiled, Olivia hesitated a moment before giving a mental shrug. Again she reminded herself they weren't her responsibility. She could indulge them to her heart's content. "With chocolate sauce?"

"Yeah!"

Olivia nodded. "Please fetch two bowls of ice cream with chocolate sauce."

"Of course, Lady Darcy."

The maid scooted past her, eyeing the odd group before disappearing through the doorway.

Olivia half sat, half collapsed on the sofa near the fireplace and gestured to the girls. "Let's get acquainted, shall we? My name is Olivia."

They hesitated for a moment before coming toward her. Olivia kept her warmest smile fixed on her face and patted the seat beside her.

"Please sit down. The ice cream will take a little while. The palace is very big."

The girls held hands and stared about the enormous room in wide-eyed silence. Now that she could see them better, Olivia noticed the Alessandro family resemblance. In fact, they looked like the pictures she'd seen of Gabriel's sister, Ariana, at a similar age. Were they cousins? She frowned. Her extensive research on Sherdana had included all the royal family. She recalled no mention of young cousins.

"I've only been here a few days and I've gotten lost a dozen times already," she continued, her voice a soothing monotone. "I was very scared when that happened. But I also discovered some wonderful places. There's a library downstairs full of books. Do you like stories?"

They nodded at her, their movements identical as if choreographed.

"So do I. My favorite stories when I was a little girl were about princesses. Would you like to hear one?" She took their smiles as assent. "Once upon a time there were two princesses and their names were Karina and Bethany."

"That's us."

Gabriel paced his office, impatient for Stewart to arrive with news that the twins had been settled into the palace. In his hand was the single photo he'd kept of Marissa after they'd broken up. He'd sealed it in an envelope and shoved it in the back of a drawer. Why he'd kept it was a question he was brooding over now.

After a long, unproductive strategy session with Christian regarding Marissa's daughters, he'd sent his brother home. Although he had rooms for his use in the palace, Christian liked his privacy and only rarely stayed in them. Sometimes Gabriel suspected that if either of his brothers had a choice they would give up their titles and any claim to Sherdana's throne. As it was they spent almost no time in Sherdana. Nic had gone to university in the US where he'd met his business partner and only returned when he absolutely had to, while Christian spent most of the year out of the country pursuing his business interests.

As close as the triplets had been growing up, the distance between them these days bothered Gabriel. While he'd known, as eldest son, that he'd be in charge of running the country someday, he'd never expected that his brothers wouldn't be around to help.

Stewart appeared as Gabriel was returning Marissa's photo to the envelope. Glancing at the clock he saw it was almost three in the morning. He'd sent his private secretary to check on Marissa's daughters half an hour earlier.

"Well?" he demanded, pushing to his feet.

"They arrived at the palace a couple hours ago and I arranged to have them escorted to the nursery in the north wing." It had seemed prudent to squirrel them away at the opposite end of the palace, far from where the royal family was housed.

"Have you seen them?" He wanted to know if the girls bore any resemblance to him, and could scarcely restrain himself from asking the question outright. Christian had cautioned that a DNA test would have to be performed before Gabriel let himself get emotionally involved. It was good advice, but easier agreed to than acted upon.

"Not yet."

Gabriel's temper flared. "What have you been doing?"

The private secretary wasn't fazed by his employer's impatience. "I went to the nursery, but they appear to be missing."

"Missing?" He couldn't imagine how that had happened. "Didn't the lawyer say they had a nanny? Did you ask her where they are?"

"She's gone. Apparently she was escorted from the palace by one of the guards an hour ago."

"Escorted…? On whose authority?"

"Lady Darcy's private secretary."

Unable to fathom how she'd gotten involved, Gabriel stabbed his fingers through his hair. This business with Marissa's daughters was fast spiraling out of control. "Have you spoken with her?"

"It's three in the morning, sir."

And if two little girls weren't missing, he might be inclined to leave his questions until morning. "Tell her I want to speak to her."

"Right away."

His private secretary wasn't gone more than five minutes. "Apparently she's in Lady Darcy's room, sir." Stewart paused. "With the girls."

Dismay shouldered aside irritation as Gabriel headed for the wing that housed his future bride. An encounter between Olivia and Marissa's daughters was a problem he hadn't anticipated. No doubt she would have questions about them. She was proving more troublesome than he'd expected based on their limited interaction before he'd proposed. Christian had warned him there was more to Olivia than a pretty face and polished manners, but she'd done an excellent job keeping her agenda hidden. The question was why.

Gabriel knocked on the door of Olivia's suite, agitation adding sharpness to the blows. His summons was answered more quickly than he expected by a pretty woman in her early thirties, wearing a classic blue dress and a frown. Her eyes widened as she spied him standing in the hall.

"I'm here looking for two little girls who've gone missing from the nursery," Gabriel said, his tone courteous despite the urge to push past her. "I understand they are here. May I come in?"

"Of course, Your Highness." She stepped back and gestured him in. "Lady Darcy, Prince Gabriel is here to see you."

"If you'll excuse us," Gabriel said, gesturing her out before entering the dimly lit suite and closing the door behind him.

His gaze swept the room in search of his fiancée. He spied her by the fireplace. She looked serene in a simple cotton dress, her hair in the same updo she'd worn to the gala. So she hadn't yet gone to bed. This thought made his attention shift to the large bed where he spied a lump beneath the covers.

"Sorry for the late visit," he told her. "But two children have gone missing."

"Bethany and Karina."

She knew their names. What else had she found out?

"What are they doing here?" he asked the question more sharply than he'd intended and saw her eyes narrow.

"They each had a bowl of ice cream and fell asleep." Her sweet smile had a bit of an edge. "They were terrified of that horrible woman who'd been hired to look after them and refused to sleep in their own beds. So I brought them here."

"And plied them with ice cream?"

"Their mother just died a few days ago. Strangers tore them from the only home they'd ever known and brought them to this big, scary place. Do you have any idea how traumatic all that was for them?"

"The nursery is not scary."

"It was for them. And so was that awful woman who was taking care of them."

"Is that why you had her escorted out of the palace tonight?"

Olivia's eyes flashed. "I suppose you're going to tell me it wasn't my place to fire her, but she reminded me of the villain in every children's story I've ever read."

Her outrage was charming and Gabriel found his annoyance melting away. "How did you come to meet them?"

"I couldn't sleep so I thought I'd go for a walk. When I got to the stairs I could hear their cries and the nanny's scolding. They were running down the hall away from that woman and the things she said to them." Olivia's lips tightened. "I would like to speak to their father about her. First thing tomorrow morning if at all possible."

"The situation with them is a little complicated," Gabriel told her, his gaze once again drawn to the lump in the center of the mattress.

"Then explain it to me."

This was what Gabriel had been wrestling with all evening. What he was going to tell the world about Marissa's daughters was a small issue compared to how he would explain things to his parents and the woman he would soon marry.

"Some matters need to be cleared up first."

Olivia's hard stare searched his expression for a long silent moment before she spoke. "What sort of matters?"

He couldn't tell her that the girls were none of her business when she'd already taken their care upon herself. At the same time, he didn't want to claim the girls before the matter of their heritage was cleared up.

"Perhaps you're referring to a DNA test." She laughed at his surprise. "They look like your sister when she was young."

"They do?"

"Didn't you notice?"

"They only just arrived. I haven't seen them yet."

Heart thumping hard against his ribs, Gabriel moved toward the bed. Since finding out about the twins, he'd been impatient to see them, but abruptly his feet felt encased in concrete. Caught between dread and hope that the girls belonged to him, Gabriel stared down at matching faces, peaceful and so innocent in sleep.

The breath he'd taken lodged in his chest as recognition flared. Marissa hadn't lied. They were his. He traced each of the children's delicate cheeks with his finger and his muscles slackened as relief washed over him.

"They're yours, aren't they?" Olivia's voice swelled with emotion, but when he glanced at her, her expression was as serene as if they were discussing the weather. "I had hoped they belonged to Christian."

"I just learned about them tonight."

"Their mother never told you?" Olivia sighed. "And now she's dead."

"Things ended badly between us." He couldn't face Olivia with his emotions this raw, so he kept his gaze on his daughters. "I didn't know she was ill." For a moment he was consumed by despair. He pressed his lips into a tight line. Then, feeling her watching him, he settled his features into an impassive mask.

"You loved her."

He and Olivia had never spoken of love. Their marriage was about politics, not romance. But if she suspected he'd given away his heart to another woman, she might not be so happy.

"We were together a long time ago."

"Karina and Bethany aren't even two. It wasn't that long ago."

Despite her neutral tone, Gabriel suspected she wasn't thrilled to have his past thrown so fully in her face. If the truth about the twins got out the press would speculate and create drama and controversy where there was none. Olivia would become the unwitting victim of their desire for ratings.

"This has to remain a secret," he told her.

"Impossible. The minute you brought them to the palace you risked word getting out."

"Perhaps, but I'd like to postpone that as long as possible so we can strategize how we're going to control the damage."

"If you're worried about my father's reaction, don't be. He's committed to opening a plant here."

"And you?"

"They're two precious little girls. I'll support whatever decision you make, but I think you should proudly claim them as yours."

Her eyes were clear of hesitation or deceit. Did she

realize this would make her a stepmother to his former lover's children? Would another woman have been so understanding?

"I can't figure you out."

"Your Highness?"

"Gabriel," he growled, amused rather than annoyed. "I'll not have you calling me Your Highness in bed."

The underlying heat in his voice reached her. Her cheeks flared pink.

"Gabriel," she echoed, her soft voice low and intimate in a way that warmed his blood. "I promise to remember never to refer to you as Your Royal Highness, or Prince Gabriel, while we're making love."

For the first time he glimpsed the Olivia beneath the enigmatic, cultured woman he'd decided to marry. Impish humor sparkled in her eyes. Intelligence shone there, as well. Why had she hidden her sharp mind from him? Gabriel considered how little time they they'd spent together and shouldered the blame. If he'd gotten to know her better, he'd have seen the truth much sooner.

"All of a sudden, it occurs to me that I've never kissed you." He took her hand and dusted a kiss over her knuckles.

"You kissed me the day you proposed."

"In front of a dozen witnesses," he murmured. He had asked her to marry him in front of her father and close relations. It had been a formality, really, not a true proposal. "And not the way I wanted to."

"How did you want to?"

She'd never flirted with him before and he discovered he liked the challenge in her gaze. Anticipation lit up the room as he set his finger beneath her chin and tilted her head, bringing her lips to a perfect angle to align with his. He watched her long lashes drift downward.

Her breath caught as he stopped just shy of brushing Olivia's lips. The disturbed rush of air awakened his senses with fierce urgency. He longed to crush her against him and feast on her soft mouth. Instead, he concentrated on the scent of her, a delicious floral that reminded him of a spring evening when the roses were in full bloom, while he reined his urges back under control.

What was happening to him? Her body's tension communicated across the short distance between them, the trembling of her muscles, a siren call that demanded he claim her. He was a little startled how compelling that desire was.

Ever since they'd danced, he'd been preoccupied with investigating the chemistry that had sparked between them. He hadn't expected to find passion in his marriage. But now that the sexual chemistry had flared, he couldn't wait to explore her every sigh and moan.

From the start she'd intrigued him. Every time they shared the same room, she'd claimed and held his attention. But he'd chosen her because of what her father's investment could mean for Sherdana rather than for any emotional connection between them. And then tonight she'd revealed that her tranquil exterior camouflaged a quick mind and determined nature.

"This might not be the best place for our first kiss," he told her, his voice raw and husky. Body aching in protest, Gabriel stepped back.

"I understand." She glanced toward his sleeping daughters.

But he doubted that she did because he barely understood his own actions.

No woman before or after Marissa had made him feel like losing all control, and it was logical to assume that no one ever would. Earlier he'd thought of Olivia as cool and untouchable. He'd been very wrong.

This abrupt and overwhelming craving to make love to her long into the night until she lay sated in his arms wasn't part of the plan. He needed a woman who would grace his side in public and warm his bed at night.

The operative word being *warm*.

Not set it on fire.

"I think they should stay here tonight," Olivia murmured, her words wresting him back to the other complication in his life. "In the morning, we can get them settled upstairs." She must have seen a protest building because she shook her head. "They're staying put. They've been through enough for one night. I want to make certain someone familiar is with them when they wake."

Gabriel's eyebrows rose at her adamant tone. "And you're that someone familiar?"

"I fed them ice cream," Olivia said, her expression lightening. "They'll be glad to see a friendly face."

"You certainly have that." He glanced toward the sleeping girls. "And a very beautiful one, as well."

# Three

Olivia didn't sleep well on the couch. But she wasn't sure she'd have slept any better in her bed alone. She kept running through her evening. Rescuing the twins, discovering they were Gabriel's illegitimate children and finally, the kiss that had almost happened.

Why had he hesitated? Had she imagined the desire in his eyes as they'd danced earlier that night?

Doubts had begun to plague her as soon as Gabriel left. Her experience with men wasn't extensive. Indulging in lighthearted affairs wasn't something she'd ever done. Her friends accused her of being overly conscientious about her reputation, but in fact, she hadn't been attracted to the men in her social circles. She might have worried about her inability to feel physical desire if she hadn't experienced something magical her first year of university.

She'd attended a masquerade party with one of her friends. The event's host was one of London's most notorious bachelors, and it was the last place she should have shown her face. Fortunately, the costumes and masks had enabled her to remain anonymous. The crowd had been racier than she was used to. Drinking and drugs had led to some boisterous behavior and Olivia had made the mistake of getting cornered.

The man had used his size and strength to pin her against the wall and run his hands beneath her skirt. She'd struggled against the hateful press of his moist lips against her throat, but couldn't free herself. And then it had been over and he'd ended up sprawled on the floor some distance away, the hands he cupped over his bloody nose muffling the obscenities he launched at the tall stranger who'd stepped in.

The hallway was too dark for her to see her rescuer clearly and she was still shaken up by the violence of the encounter, but she managed a grateful smile. "Thank you for helping me."

"You don't belong here," the stranger had told her, his English lightly accented. "It isn't safe for someone as young as you are."

Her cheeks had grown hot at his words because he was right and she had felt foolish. "When is it safe for any woman when a man won't stop when she says no?" She peered through the guests, searching for her friend. "Next time I will carry a stun gun instead of lipstick in my purse."

He'd smiled. "Please don't let there be a next time."

"You're right. This isn't my crowd." She had spotted her friend halfway across the room and decided it was time to leave. "It was nice to meet you," she had told him. "I wish the circumstances had been different." Impulsively she rose up on tiptoe and touched her lips to his cheek, before whispering, "My hero."

Before she moved away, he had cupped her cheek and dropped his lips to hers. The touch electrified her and she swayed into his solid strength. His fingers flexed against her skin, pulling her closer. The kiss had been masterful. Demanding enough to be thrilling, but without the roughness that would make her afraid.

Magic, she remembered thinking, as she'd indulged in a moment of reckless daring.

Olivia released a long slow exhale at the memory. Seven

years later it continued to be the most amazing kiss she'd ever had. And she'd never even known his name. Maybe that's why it dwelled so vividly in her memory.

Lying with her forearm across her eyes, Olivia pushed aside the emotions stirred by that singular event. No good would come from dwelling on a romantic moment. The man who rescued her was probably as vile as the rest of the guests and had merely suffered a momentary crisis of conscience. She was marrying an honest, good man and needed to stay focused on the here and now.

As the room began to lighten, Olivia gave up on sleep and pulled out her laptop. During her research into Gabriel and his family, she'd focused on all things Sherdanian. Now she searched for his past romance and discovered a couple articles that mentioned him and Marissa Somme, a half American, half French model he'd dated for several years.

Olivia scanned the news stories. A few mentioned rumors that Gabriel had been considering abdicating the throne to one of his younger brothers, but ultimately, the affair ended instead.

Awash in concern, Olivia went looking for images of the couple. What she saw wasn't reassuring. The news outlets had gotten it right. The couple had been very much in love. Olivia stared at Gabriel's broad grin and Marissa's blinding smile and guessed if she hadn't been a commoner and an unsuitable candidate to give birth to the future king of Sherdana, they would have married and lived happily ever after.

Obviously Gabriel had chosen his country over his heart. And Marissa had vanished.

Hearing soft whispers coming from the bed, Olivia rose from the sofa. Sure enough, the twins were awake. They'd pulled the fluffy cream comforter over their heads, encasing themselves in a cozy cocoon.

For a moment, Olivia envied them each other. An only child, she'd always longed for a sister to share secrets with. If her mother had lived, she could have had a second child and Olivia might not have grown up so isolated from other children. Because her world had been filled with adults—nannies and various tutors—she'd never had a best friend her own age to play with. In fact, playing wasn't something she'd been given much freedom to do.

Multiples obviously ran in the Alessandro family. Did that mean she could expect a set or two of her own to be running around the palace in the years to come?

Olivia tugged on the comforter, pulling it down little by little to reveal the twins. They lay with noses touching, intent on their communication. Their first reaction as the comforter slid away was fear. Olivia saw their hands come together, as they took and received reassurance from each other.

Then, they recognized her and smiled.

"Someone's been sleeping in my bed," she teased, her words bringing forth giggles. "And they're still here."

Then she growled like a big bad bear and reached down to tickle them. Squeals and laughter erupted from the girls, a vast improvement over last night's terrified protests.

Olivia sat down on the bed. The prince would be back soon and the girls needed to be prepared to meet him. No doubt he'd informed the king and queen and they would be interested in meeting their grandchildren. It would be an overwhelming day for the girls and Olivia wanted to prepare them.

"Today you are going to meet many new people," she told them. "I know you might be scared, but you don't need to be."

"A party?"

"Sort of." If that was what it took to keep the twins from being afraid, then so be it.

"A birthday party?"

"No."

"Mommy said."

Bethany's mention of their mother reminded the girls that she was dead. Olivia saw Karina's lip quiver and rushed to distract them.

"Are you this old?" She held up two fingers and was rewarded with head shakes.

"We're this old." Bethany held up one finger.

"But you're too big to be one. I'll bet you have a birthday coming up soon."

"Get pony," Bethany said with a definitive nod.

Olivia rather doubted that, but clever of her to try to sound convincing. "I'm not sure you're old enough for a pony."

Karina spoke for the first time. "Puppy."

That seemed more doable.

"Pony," Bethany repeated. "Mommy said."

"There might be a pony in the stables," Olivia said, aware she was already caving to their demands. She hadn't pictured herself the sort of mother to give in to her child's every whim.

Bethany nodded in satisfaction. "Let's go."

"No." Karina shook her head. "Puppy."

"Oh, no. It's too early to go to the stables. We have to get dressed and have breakfast. Then we have to get you settled in your own room."

"No." Karina's large green eyes brimmed with anxiety.

Immediately Olivia realized what was wrong. "It's okay," she assured them. "The mean lady is gone. You will have really nice people taking care of you."

"Stay here." Bethany had an imperious tone well suited to a princess.

"I'm afraid you can't do that."

"Why not?"

"This is my bed and you two take up way too much room."

"Slept with Mommy."

Somehow they'd circled back to Marissa again. Olivia held her breath as she watched for some sign that they would get sad again, but the girls had discovered the mattress had great springs and they started bouncing and laughing.

Olivia watched them, amusement taking the edge off her exasperation. The challenges confronting her were coming faster than she'd expected. She wasn't just going to become a wife and a princess, but now she was going to take on the role of mother, as well. Not that she couldn't handle all of it. Maybe it was just her sleepless night and her anxiety about marrying a man who might not be over his dead former lover.

While the girls jumped off the bed and raced around the room, looking out the window and exploring the attached bathroom, Olivia heard a soft knock. Assuming it was Libby, she opened the door. To her intense surprise, Gabriel stood there, looking handsome and elegant in a charcoal pinstripe suit, white shirt and burgundy tie.

"I hope it's not too early," he said, entering the room. His gaze slid over her hair and silk-clad body.

Several maids followed, one pushing a cart loaded down with covered plates. Delicious smells wafted in their wake.

Olivia smoothed her hair, acutely aware of her makeup-free face, knowing she wasn't looking her best after such a rough night. She hadn't even brushed her teeth yet.

"No, of course not. You're eager to meet the girls."

"I am." His gaze went past her shoulder, golden eyes intense and a little wary.

Olivia's heart gave a little start as she realized he must be thinking about their mother. Chest tight, she shifted her attention to the twins. "Bethany. Karina. Come meet..." She wasn't sure how to introduce the prince.

Gabriel supplied the description. "Your father."

Beside him, Gabriel felt Olivia tense in surprise. In the hours since leaving her room, he'd contemplated what the best political move would be regarding his daughters and decided he didn't give a damn about the fallout. He intended to claim them.

Olivia held out her hands to the girls and they went toward her. She introduced them one by one, starting with the little girl on her right. "This is Bethany. And this is Karina."

Gabriel could discern no difference between their features. "How can you tell?"

"Bethany is the talkative one."

Neither one was verbal at the moment. They stood side by side wearing matching nightgowns and identical blank stares.

Deciding he would appear less intimidating if he was at their eye level, Gabriel knelt. "Nice to meet you." As much as he longed to snatch them into his arms and hug the breath from their bodies, he kept his hands to himself and gave them his gentlest smile.

The one Olivia had introduced as Bethany eyed him suspiciously for a moment before declaring, "We're hungry." Her imperious tone made her sound like his mother.

"What would you like for breakfast?" he asked them. "We have eggs, pancakes, French toast."

"Ice cream."

"Not for breakfast," he countered.

Olivia made no effort to hide her amusement. Her grin and the laughter brimming in her blue eyes transformed her from an elegant beauty to a vivacious woman. Gabriel felt his eyebrows go up as her charisma lit up the room.

"Wit' chocolate."

Bethany's demands forced Gabriel to refocus his attention. "Maybe after lunch." He'd met some tough negotiators in his time, but none had shown the sort of determination exhibited by his daughters. "If you eat everything on your plate."

"Want ice cream."

"How about waffles with syrup?" He tried softening his words with a smile. The twins weren't moved.

"Olivia." Bethany's plaintive, wheedling tone was charming, and Gabriel found himself struggling to restrain a grin.

"No." Olivia shook her head. "You listen to your father. He knows what's best." She gently propelled the girls toward the table the maid had set for breakfast and got them into chairs. "There aren't any booster chairs so you'll have to kneel. Can you do that?"

The twins nodded and Gabriel pulled out the chair between them, gesturing for Olivia to join them, but she shook her head.

"You should spend some time alone with them. I'm going to shower and get dressed." With one last smile for the twins, she headed toward the bathroom.

As the door shut behind her, Gabriel turned his full attention to the toddlers. "Have you decided what you want to eat?"

Their green eyes steady on him, they watched and waited for some sign that he was weakening. Gabriel crossed his arms over his chest and stared back. He was not going to be outmaneuvered by a pair of toddlers.

"Pancakes."

The word broke the standoff and Gabriel gestured the maid forward to serve pancakes. Having little appetite, he sipped coffee and watched them eat, seeing Marissa in their gestures and sassy attitude.

The girls ate two large pancakes before showing signs of slowing down and Gabriel was marveling at their appetite when the bathroom door opened and Olivia emerged. Her long blond hair framed her oval face in soft waves and she'd played up her blue eyes with mascara and brown eye shadow. She wore a simple wrap dress in seafoam that accentuated her tiny waist and the subtle curves of her breasts and hips. Nude pumps added four inches to her five-foot-six-inch frame and emphasized the sculpted leanness of her calves.

Gabriel felt the kick to his solar plexus and momentarily couldn't breathe. Her beauty blindsided him. Desire raged in his gut. He hadn't expected to feel like this when he proposed. She'd been elegant, poised and cool, inspiring his admiration and appreciation.

In a month she would be legally his. But he was no longer content to wait until his wedding night to claim her. Such had been the heat of his desire for her last night that if the twins hadn't occupied her bed, he would have made love to her.

The strength of his desire gave him a moment's pause. Wasn't this feeling what he'd hoped to avoid when he chose her? Craving something beyond reason was what had gotten him into trouble with Marissa. But desire wasn't love and didn't have to become obsession. He should feel a healthy desire for his future wife. Surely, he could prevent himself from getting in too deep with her and repeating his past mistakes.

He'd sunk into a black depression after his breakup with Marissa. Knowing they couldn't have a future together hadn't prevented him from letting himself be lured into love. He'd come through the other side of losing Marissa, but the fight to come back from that dark place wasn't something he wanted to go through ever again.

"Coffee?" he asked, shoving aside his grim reflections.

He just needed to be certain that he kept a handle on his growing fascination with her. He'd lost his head over Marissa and look what it got him. Two beautiful, but illegitimate, daughters.

"Yes." she gave a little laugh, seeming more relaxed with him than ever before. "I'm afraid I'm in desperate need of the caffeine this morning."

"Rough night?"

"The couch is not as comfortable as it is beautiful."

"Did you get any sleep?"

"Maybe an hour or so." She dished up scrambled eggs, fruit and a croissant. She caught him watching her and gave him a wry smile. "Your pastry chef is sublime. I will need plenty of exercise to avoid becoming fat."

"Perhaps after we speak to my parents about the girls we could take a walk in the garden."

"That would be nice, but I don't think there's time. My schedule is packed with wedding preparations."

"Surely if I can let the country run without my help for half an hour you can delegate some of the wedding preparations to your private secretary. We haven't really had a chance to get acquainted, and with our wedding less than a month away, I thought we should spend some time alone together."

"Is that a command, Your Highness?"

He arched an eyebrow at her playful tone. "Do you need it to be?"

"Your mother is the one who determined my schedule."

Suspecting his fiancée needed no help standing up to the queen, he realized she was chiding him for his neglect during her first week in Sherdana. "I'll handle my mother."

"A walk sounds lovely."

"Go see pony," Bethany declared, shattering the rapport developing between the adults.

"Pony?" Gabriel echoed, looking to Olivia for an explanation.

"Apparently Bethany wants a pony for her birthday. I told her she was too young, but I thought maybe there was a pony in the stables they could visit."

"None that I know of." He saw the bright expectation in their faces vanish and couldn't believe how much he wanted to see them smile again. "But I could be wrong."

He made a mental note to have Stewart see about getting a pair of ponies for the girls. He and all his siblings had all started riding as soon as they could sit up. Ariana was the only one who still rode consistently, but Gabriel enjoyed an occasional gallop to clear his mind after a particularly taxing session of cabinet.

"Do you ride?" he asked Olivia.

"When I visit our country house."

A knock sounded on the door. Olivia's private secretary appeared, Stewart following on her heels. They wore duplicate expressions of concern and Gabriel knew the morning's tranquillity was about to end.

"Excuse me a moment." He crossed the room and pulled Stewart into the hall. "Well?"

"The king and queen are on their way here."

He'd hoped to be the one to break the news to his parents. "How did they find out?"

"The arrival of two little girls in the middle of the night didn't go unnoticed," Stewart told him. "When your mother couldn't find you she summoned me."

"So, you felt the need to spill the whole story."

"The king asked me a direct question," Stewart explained, not the least bit intimidated by Gabriel's low growl. "And he outranks you."

"Gabriel, there you are. I demand to see my granddaughters at once." The queen sailed down the hallway in his direction, her husband at her side. Lines of tension bracketed the king's mouth. After nearly forty years as a queen, nothing disturbed her outward calm. But discovering her son had fathered two illegitimate girls was more stress than even she could graciously handle.

"They've been through a lot in the last few days," Gabriel told her, thinking she would upset the twins in her current state of agitation.

"Have you told Olivia?"

"Last night." He held up a hand when his mother's eyes widened in outrage. "They spent the night with her after she stumbled upon them fleeing their nanny."

The king's light brown eyes had a hard look as they settled on his son. "And how does your future bride feel about it?"

As diplomatic as his parents were with the outside world, when it came to family, they were blunt. It wasn't like them to dance around a question. Of course, they'd never come up against something this enormous before.

"What you want to know is if she intends to marry me despite my having fathered two children I knew nothing about."

"Does she?"

The king's deep frown made Gabriel rein in his frustration. As much as he disliked having his carelessness pointed out, he had let passion overwhelm him to the exclusion of common sense. Marissa had made him wild. She was like no other woman he'd ever met. And because of that their relationship had made his parents unhappy.

Gabriel exhaled harshly. "So far it appears that way."

"Does her father know?" the king asked.

"Not yet. But the girls are living in the house. It won't be long before the truth comes out."

His mother looked grim. "Will Lord Darcy back out on the deal?"

"Olivia doesn't think so. He wants his daughter married to royalty."

"Have you figured out what we're going to say to the press?"

"That they're my daughters," Gabriel said. "We'll send out a press release. Anything else would be a mistake. Olivia noticed the resemblance immediately. They look exactly like Ariana did at that age. Coming clean is a good offensive and hopefully by doing so we can minimize the scandal."

"And if we can't?"

"I'll ride it out."

"We'll ride it out," the king said.

"Have you considered that Olivia might not want to raise Marissa's children?"

Gabriel had already entertained those doubts, but after what he'd seen of Olivia, he'd discovered layers that might surprise everyone. "I don't think that will be an issue. She's already very protective of them and they trust her."

The queen sighed and shook her head. "It *will* be wonderful having children in the palace again. Let's go see your girls."

# Four

Olivia was standing with her hands relaxed at her sides as the door opened to admit the king and queen. Libby had warned her they were coming and she'd made sure the girls' hands and faces were clean. The arrival of more unfamiliar people had revived the toddlers' shyness and they hid behind Olivia.

"This is your father's mother," Olivia explained to them, using gentle pressure to nudge them into the open. "She's come to meet you."

Karina shook her head, but Bethany peered at her grandmother. The queen stopped dead at the sight of the girl and reached out a hand to her husband.

"Gabriel, you were right. They look exactly like your sister at that age." She took a seat nearby and gestured Bethany toward her. "What is your name?"

To Olivia's delight Bethany went to the queen.

She stopped just out of arm's reach and studied the queen. "I'm Bethany."

"It's nice to meet you." The queen looked toward her sister. "And what is your name?"

Bethany answered again. "Karina."

"How old are they?" the king asked.

"They'll be two in a few weeks," Gabriel answered.

"Puppy." Karina had finally spoken.

"I have a puppy you can meet. Would you like that?"

The queen smiled as Karina nodded. "Mary," the queen said to the maid who'd brought the twins' clothes from upstairs. "Go get Rosie." The Cavalier King Charles spaniel loved people, especially children, and was a great deal calmer than the queen's vizsla.

In five minutes the maid was back with the dog and both twins were laughing as Rosie licked their cheeks. "Gabriel, why don't you and Olivia make yourself scarce for a while. I'll see the girls are settled."

Recognizing an order when she heard one, Olivia let Gabriel draw her from the bedroom and down the stairs.

"Let's get out of here while we can," he murmured, escorting her through a side door and into the garden.

The late May morning had a slight edge of coolness, but when he offered to send someone upstairs for a sweater, Olivia shook her head.

"Let's walk in the sunshine. I'll warm up fast enough."

He took her hand and tucked it into the crook of his arm. Olivia gave herself up to the pleasure of his strong body brushing against her side as they strolled along the crushed granite pathways.

"Thank you for all you've done with the girls," he said.

"It breaks my heart that they'll grow up without their mother, but I'm glad they have you."

"You never knew yours, did you? She died when you were born?"

She'd never told him that. "I guess we both did our research."

"I've treated our engagement like a business arrangement. For that I'm sorry."

"Don't be. I knew what I was getting into." She heard a touch of cynicism in her tone and countered it with a wry smile.

Gabriel didn't smile back. "I don't think you have any idea what you're getting into."

"That sounds intriguing." Olivia waited for more, but the prince didn't elaborate.

"Starting now I intend to learn everything there is to know about you."

While she was sure he meant to flatter her with the declaration, Olivia froze in momentary panic. What if he found out she hadn't come clean about her past fertility issues? Even with the problem solved, he might be angry that she hadn't disclosed such an important fact.

"A girl needs to keep a little mystery about herself," she countered, gazing up at him from beneath her lashes. "What if you lost interest once you discovered all my secrets?"

"It never occurred to me that you'd have secrets," he murmured, half to himself.

"What woman doesn't?"

"I'd prefer it if we didn't keep secrets from each other."

"After the surprise you received last night, I understand why. So, what would you like to tell me?"

"Me?"

Olivia congratulated herself on turning the conversation back on him. "Getting to know each other was your idea. I thought you'd like to show me how it's done."

Gabriel's eyes gleamed with appreciation. "What would you like to know?"

"Why did you pick me?"

"Your passion for issues relating to children and your tireless determination to make their lives better." Gabriel stopped and turned her to face him. "I knew you would be exactly the sort of queen my country would love."

As his words sank in she stared at the pond, watching the ducks paddle across the still water. "Your country."

At times like this it amused her to think of how many girls longed to be her. If they knew what her life was like, would they still want that? Marriage to a prince might seem like a fairy tale come true, but did they understand the sacrifices to her privacy or the responsibility she would bear?

But marriage into Sherdana's royal family would offer her the opportunity to focus on things near and dear to her heart and to advocate for those who needed help, but who had no one to turn to. Earlier in the week she'd had an opportunity to speak with a local hospital administrator about the need for a more child-friendly space to treat the younger patients. The woman had a lot of ideas how to change the children's ward to make a hospital stay easier on the children as well as their families.

Olivia was excited about the opportunities to help. Sherdana would find her an enthusiastic promoter of solutions for at-risk and underprivileged children. She was proud of the money she'd raised in London and loved the hours she'd spent visiting with children in the hospitals. Their courage in fighting their illnesses always inspired her. She intended to inspire others to help.

As Sherdana's princess and future queen, she would be in the perfect position to bring children's issues to the forefront of public awareness.

"I will do my best to never let your country down."

"I knew you'd say that."

Her knees trembled as he slid his hand beneath her hair, fingertips drawing evocative circles on her nape.

Cupping her cheek in his palm, Gabriel turned her head until their eyes met. Her heart skipped a beat. He wanted her. The expanding warmth in her midsection told her so and she basked in the certainty.

His gaze held her entranced until the second before his lips skimmed hers. Wrenched free of anticipation, relief rushed through her like a wildfire. A groan built in her chest as his tongue traced the seam of her lips. Welcoming the masterful stroke of his tongue into her mouth, she leaned into him, pressing her breasts against his chest, needing his hands to cup their weight and drive her mad.

A throat cleared somewhere behind them. "Excuse me, Your Highness."

Gabriel stiffened and tore his mouth free. Chest heaving, he drew his thumb across her lower lip. "We will continue this later," he promised, his voice a husky rasp against her sensitized nerve endings.

"I look forward to it."

She received the briefest of smiles before he turned to face his private secretary. Released from the compelling grip of his gaze, Olivia had a hard time maintaining her composure. The kiss, although cut short, had been everything a woman craved. Passionate. Masterful. A touch wicked. She locked her knees and moderated her breathing while she listened to Gabriel's conversation with his secretary.

Stewart cleared his throat again. "Sorry to interrupt, but the media found out about your daughters and Lord Darcy is meeting with your parents."

Distantly, she became aware that Stewart was filling in Gabriel rapid-fire style about what had been on the television this morning.

"How did they get wind of it so fast?" Gabriel demanded.

Not even the ice in his voice could banish the lingering warmth Olivia felt from his kiss.

Stewart came up with the most obvious source. "The lawyer might have gone to them."

"Unlikely. He had nothing to gain."

"Someone in the palace, then."

"Who knew last night?"

"The maids who were tasked with preparing the nursery," Stewart said. "But they've worked for the palace for over a decade."

Olivia considered the one who'd been straightening her room at two in the morning. The strangeness of it struck her again, but surely the palace staff was carefully screened and the woman had merely been doing as she said.

"The nanny." Olivia knew with a sinking heart that this had to be the source of the leak. "The one I had escorted off the property."

Stewart considered this. "The lawyer assured me she'd been kept in the dark about the twins' parentage."

"But that was before they'd been brought to the palace," Gabriel said.

"I'm sorry," Olivia murmured, aware she'd committed her first huge mistake as Gabriel's fiancée. "I shouldn't have taken it upon myself to remove her."

"She was the wrong caretaker for the girls and you had their best interests at heart." Gabriel offered her a reassuring nod. "Besides, it was going to be impossible to keep the twins hidden for long."

Although she was accustomed to life in the public eye, she'd never been the focus of such frenzied interest on the part of the media, and the upcoming wedding had stirred them like a cane striking a wasp nest.

"If we present a united front," Olivia said, feeling like his partner for the first time, "I'm sure everything will blow over."

Gabriel took her hand and scorched a kiss across her knuckles. "Then that's exactly what we'll do."

Hand in hand, Olivia and Gabriel entered the salon most often used by the family for its proximity to the back garden and the views of the park beyond. They found Christian and Ariana there. Gabriel caught sight of the television and heard the reporter. The amount of information the news channel had gleaned about the twins' arrival late last night revealed that someone inside the house must have been feeding them information. Gabriel went cold as the reporter speculated on whether or not the powerful Sherdana royal family had paid Marissa to go away or if all along she'd hidden her daughters to keep them from being taken away from her.

"They may be painting us as the bad guys," Christian commented, "but at least they're not claiming we're weak."

Gabriel didn't reply to his brother's remark as Marissa's face came on the screen. As the narrator gave a rundown of her career, Olivia moved as if compelled by some irresistible force, stepping closer to the television. Dismay rose in Gabriel as one after another, the photographs of his former lover on the covers of *Vogue, Elle* and *Harper's Bazaar* flashed on the screen. Her legs looked impossibly long. Her face, incredibly beautiful.

Gabriel knew his daughters would be as exquisite. Would they follow in their mother's footsteps and pursue careers in fashion? Photographers would stand in line to take their picture. They'd make an incredible pair. But was that any way for an Alessandro to make a living?

The question forced Gabriel to consider his daughters' place in his household. They were illegitimate. With their mother's death, that situation could never be rectified. An ache built in his chest for Bethany and Karina. At their age they would retain few memories of their mother. They'd never again know her love.

When the television began showing images of Gabriel and Marissa together, laughing, arms around each other, looking happy and very young, he realized Olivia had gone still. Picture after picture flashed on the screen, and many of them weren't paparazzi shots. There were photos taken of them in private at friends' homes, even a couple when they'd vacationed on a private island in the Caribbean.

Gabriel's disquiet grew as Olivia's attention remained

glued to the news footage that recapped his turbulent years with Marissa. Naturally the reporters made their relationship sound more dramatic, the end more tragic than it actually had been.

While he watched, Olivia's private secretary approached her and spoke softly in her ear. She nodded and came to stand before Gabriel.

"My father wishes to speak to me."

"I'll walk with you."

"You should stay and discuss what is to be done now that the story is out."

Her suggestion made sense, but he wasn't sure it was good to let her leave without clearing the air. "I'd like a moment alone to speak with you."

"I have a fitting for my wedding dress at ten. I should be back a little before noon."

Once again their schedules were keeping them apart. "I have a lunch meeting with my education adviser."

"Perhaps Stewart and Libby can find us a moment to connect later this afternoon."

Gabriel wanted to proclaim they should make time, but had no idea what he was committed to for the rest of the afternoon.

"This shouldn't wait until later. Let's go to my office and discuss this situation in private."

"Whatever you wish."

Disliking the polite calm of her tone, he guided her from the room with a hand at the small of her back. Beneath his palm, her spine maintained a steady inflexibility that marked the change in her mood from their earlier interlude.

As pointless as it was to resent the timing of recent events, Gabriel couldn't stop himself from wishing he and Olivia had been given a month or two to form a personal connection before their relationship had been tested to this extent. But that wasn't the case and as he escorted her into his sanctuary and shut the door, he hoped they could weather this storm without sustaining permanent damage.

His office was on the first floor of the palace, not far from the formal reception room. Originally the space had been one of the numerous salons set aside for visiting guests. Five years ago, he'd appropriated it for his own use, tearing down the lavender wallpaper left over from the late 1970s and installing wood paneling and bookshelves that he'd filled with his favorite authors. The room was his sanctuary.

"You're upset."

"Just concerned about the twins." Her quiet voice and dignified demeanor were at odds with the passionate woman who'd melted in his arms a little while ago. Gabriel felt something tighten in his chest. "I think it might be a good idea to have them in the wedding. I thought I would talk to Noelle Dubone. She's creating my wedding dress and I'm sure she would be happy to design matching flower-girl dresses for Bethany and Karina to wear."

Gabriel leaned back so he could stare into her eyes. "Are you sure?"

"Completely. The world knows they're here. Hiding them would be a mistake."

"I agree. I'll speak with my parents about it." He could tell that Olivia's anxiety over the twins' welfare had been sincere, but surmised more than that was bothering her. "The news coverage about my relationship with Marissa—"

At his slight pause she jumped in. "You looked very happy together." She seemed to have more to say, but remained silent.

"We had our moments." Gabriel drew a deep breath. "But much of the time we fought."

"The paparazzi must not have caught any of those moments on film."

She sounded neutral enough, but Gabriel sensed she

wasn't as tranquil as she appeared. "We fought in private." And then made up in spectacular fashion.

His thoughts must have shown on his face because her eyebrows rose.

She moved toward the French doors and looked out. Gabriel stepped to her side. For a moment he wanted nothing more than to take her in his arms and relive the kisses from earlier. The compulsion to be near her tested his composure.

Her gaze slid in his direction. "Passion can be addictive."

How would she know that?

He knew of no serious romances in her life. Her private life was without even a whiff of scandal. No boyfriends. No lovers.

"Do you have firsthand knowledge of this fact?" Lord in heaven, he sounded suspicious. And yet, he couldn't stop himself from probing. "Have you…?" Realizing what he'd almost asked, he stopped speaking.

"Taken a lover?"

Damn the woman, she was laughing. Oh, not outwardly where he could see her mocking smile and take offense. But inwardly. Her eyes sparkled and her voice had developed a distinct lilt. Had his expression betrayed an unanticipated flare of unfounded jealousy? Or was she reacting to the revelation that for all his sources, he knew nothing about her?

Gabriel turned her to face him, but she wouldn't meet his gaze. "Have you?"

"No." She shook her head. "You'll be my first."

Desire exploded as she met his gaze. Wild with satisfaction that she would be completely his, Gabriel lost touch with his rational side. Surrendering to the need to kiss her senseless and show her just how addictive passion could be, he cupped her cheek in his palm, slid his other hand around her waist to hold her captive and brought his lips to hers.

He gave her just a taste of his passion, but even that was enough to weaken his restraint. Breathing heavily, he set his forehead against hers and searched her gaze.

"Your only." He growled the words.

"Of course."

Her matter-of-fact tone highlighted just how fast he'd let his control slip. His hands fell away, but his palms continued to burn with the heat of her skin. He rubbed them together, determined to banish the lingering sensation.

The need to spend some time alone with her had just grown more urgent. He was concerned that the media storm surrounding the arrival of the twins would make her father consider changing his mind about letting his daughter marry Gabriel. No wedding. No biotech plant on the outskirts of Caron, Sherdana's capital. Gabriel needed to hedge his bets with Olivia.

As long as she still wanted to marry him, everything would proceed as planned. He just needed to reassure her that marrying him was a good idea. And he knew the best way to convince a woman had nothing at all to do with logic.

Some private time should do the trick, just the two of them. A chance to present her with a small token of his affection. Thus far her engagement ring was the only jewelry he'd given her. He should have had a gift ready to present on her arrival in Sherdana, but he'd been preoccupied. And if he was honest with himself, he hadn't been thinking of Olivia as his future bride, but as a next step in Sherdana's economic renaissance.

"I'll arrange for us to have a private dinner in my suite."

"I'll look forward to it," Olivia said, her expression unreadable. Gabriel had chosen her partly because of her composure when dealing with reporters and her public persona. Now, he wasn't happy at not being able to read her.

Shortly after she departed, Gabriel summoned Stewart and had him reschedule his morning appointments so Gabriel could meet with his jeweler. Half an hour later, he entered the reception room where Mr. Sordi waited with two cases of sparkling gems. Despite the wide selection, Gabriel wondered if he'd have trouble selecting the perfect piece for his bride-to-be. In the end, he chose the first bracelet that caught his eye, believing the fanciful design of flowers rendered in diamonds and pink sapphires would please her.

Business concluded, he let Stewart show the jeweler out while Gabriel slipped the bracelet into his office safe. He dashed off a quick note to Olivia, inviting her to dinner, and got one of the maids to deliver it. Then he went off to his lunch meeting with his education adviser, but his thoughts were preoccupied with the evening to come.

After a short conversation with her father to assure him that she'd already known about the twins and was perfectly happy that they'd come to live with their father, Olivia went to change her clothes, but ended up standing on the stone terrace outside her room, staring at the garden below. The euphoria of those passionate moments in Gabriel's arms were misty memories.

Olivia's heart sank to her toes. Caught up in the romance of kissing Gabriel in the beautiful garden, she'd been on the verge of doing things in public she'd never even done in private. While on a subconscious level she'd begun to think in terms of love. In reality she was embarking on an arranged marriage.

Being told Gabriel had loved the mother of his children and being confronted by the hard truth of it were very different animals. The pictures playing across the television screen had complicated her emotions. She'd been besieged by thorny questions.

Had he been thinking of Marissa as he kissed her? Had he been wishing that the woman he'd loved wasn't dead? Or that her ancestry had permitted them to be married? Marissa had been every man's fantasy. Vivacious, sexy, breathtakingly beautiful. In her eyes danced promises she might or might not keep. A man could spend a lifetime wondering which way she would go. How could Olivia hope to compete?

She couldn't.

But she wasn't marrying Gabriel because he loved her. She was marrying him because as a princess her voice advocating for children would reach further and she could fulfill her dream of becoming a mother. Her children would be the next generation of Alessandros. Still, it hurt to see the way Gabriel had stared at the screen as his former lover's face was shown in photo after photo. Her heart had ached at the way his expression turn to stone while his eyes looked positively battered.

Suddenly Olivia wasn't sure she could do this. Sucking in a sharp breath, she glanced down at her engagement ring. Sunlight fell across her hand, lighting up the large center diamond like the fireworks at a centennial celebration. She'd come to Sherdana to marry a prince, not a man, but after tasting passion and realizing she wanted more, she didn't think she could settle for marrying a man with a past that still haunted him.

A man still in love with the mother of his illegitimate twin girls.

Maybe this marriage wasn't meant to be.

But so much was riding on it. So many people were counting on the jobs her father's company would bring to Sherdana. And the wedding was less than a month away. She had a fitting for her dress in less than an hour. Olivia stared at the slim gold watch on her arm, her mother's watch.

A short time later, Olivia stepped out of the car that had driven her and Libby to the small dress shop in Sherdana's historic city center. She'd pushed aside her heavy heart, averse to dwelling on something over which she had no control. She was her father's daughter. Raised as a pragmatist, she knew it was impractical to indulge in pretty dreams of falling in love with her prince and living happily ever after.

The shop door chimed as Olivia entered. Wide windows provided a great deal of light in the small but elegant reception room. The walls had been painted pale champagne to complement the marble floors. There was a gold damask-covered sofa flanked by matching chairs in the front room. The glass-topped coffee table held a portfolio of Noelle Dubone's previous work. Some of her more famous clients were not featured in the book, but on the walls. Stars, models, heiresses, all wearing Noelle's gorgeous gowns.

Almost before the door shut behind them, Noelle was on hand to greet her. The designer offered Olivia a warm smile and a firm handshake.

"Lady Darcy, how delightful to see you again."

Noelle had a lilting Italian accent. Although Sherdana shared borders with both France and Italy, it had chosen Italian as its official national language. With her dark hair and walnut-colored eyes, Noelle's lineage could have gone back to either country, but from earlier conversations Olivia knew the designer's ancestry could be traced back to the 1500s. Noelle might not be one of Sherdana's nobility, but the church kept excellent records.

"It's good to see you, as well," Olivia said, warming to the willowy designer all over again. Choosing to have a dress made by Noelle had been easy in so many ways. Although her London friends had counseled Olivia to go with a more famous designer and have an extravagant gown made, Olivia had decided she much preferred Noelle's artistry. Plus Noelle was Sherdanian. It made political sense for Olivia to show her support of the country where she would soon be a princess, especially taking into consideration how hard-hit Sherdana's economy had been in the past few years.

"I have your dress waiting in here." Noelle showed Olivia into a dressing room.

For her more famous clients, Noelle often traveled for fittings. She would have brought the dress to the palace if Olivia had requested. But Olivia liked the shop's cozy feel and wasn't eager to entertain anyone's opinion but her own.

The dress awaiting her was as beautiful as she remembered from the sketches. It had stood out among the half dozen Noelle had shown her six months ago; in fact, the rendering had taken her breath away.

With the help of Noelle's assistants, Olivia donned the dress. Facing the three-way mirror, she stared at her reflection, and was overcome with emotion. It was perfect.

From the bodice to her thighs, the dress hugged the lean curves of her body. Just above her knees it flared into a full skirt with a short train. Made of silk organza, embroidered with feathery scrolls over white silk, the gown's beauty lay in its play of simple lines and rich fabrics. Although Noelle had designed the dress to be strapless, Olivia had requested some sort of small sleeve and the designer had created the illusion of cap sleeves by placing two one-inch straps on either shoulder.

"What are planning to do for a veil?" Noelle asked.

"The queen is lending me the tiara she wore on her wedding day," Olivia said. "I'm not sure I want to use a veil with it."

"Good. When I designed the dress, I didn't picture it with a veil." Noelle stepped back to admire her handiwork.

"You have lost a little weight since we measured you. The waist needs to be taken in a little."

Olivia turned sideways to peer at the way the short train looked behind her. "I will try not to gain before the wedding."

For the next hour, Noelle and her staff worked on minor alterations to the fit. While Olivia thought the dress fit well enough that she could have worn it as is, Noelle was obviously a perfectionist.

"I have another project that I'd like to talk to you about," Olivia said as Noelle handed off the dress to her assistant.

Ever since arriving, she'd been thinking about including the twins in the wedding. While Gabriel seemed okay with the idea, she wasn't sure how his family would react, but after this morning's media coverage of the girls' arrival at the palace, hiding them from public scrutiny would be impossible and counterproductive.

"Come into my office," Noelle said. "Tell me what you have in mind."

Sipping the coffee Noelle's assistant had provided, Olivia contemplated the best way to begin, then decided to just dive in.

"Did you happen to see the news this morning?"

"About Prince Gabriel's daughters?" Noelle pressed her lips together. "The royal family hasn't given them much fodder for stories in the last few years. I'm afraid the level of coverage on this particular item so close to your wedding is just too huge for them to use restraint."

"Dealing with the media comes with the territory," Olivia said. "You'd know that."

Noelle looked startled for a second. "I only design for the stars," she demurred. "I'm not one of them myself."

"You are making a name for yourself. Don't be surprised when you become as big a story as your clients."

"I hope that doesn't happen. I like my quiet little life."

Noelle's gaze touched a silver frame on her desk. It held the photo of a small dark-haired boy. The angle didn't offer a very good view of his face, but Olivia could tell from Noelle's expression that he was very special to her.

"Is he your son?"

"Yes. Marc. He was two in that picture. The same age as the prince's daughters."

Olivia felt a clenching low in her abdomen. A cry from her empty womb. "He's beautiful. How old is he now?"

"Almost four."

Olivia didn't ask about the boy's father. She knew Noelle wasn't currently married and wasn't sure if the question would arouse difficult memories.

"I would like to include Prince Gabriel's daughters in the wedding and want you to make dresses for them."

"I'll work on some sketches and send them over to the palace. Did you have a color in mind?"

"White with pale yellow sashes. To match Princess Ariana's gown." The color suited the dark-haired princess and would her nieces, as well.

"I'll get to work immediately."

At the sound of a light knock, both women looked toward the door. Noelle's assistant hovered on the threshold.

"I just wanted to let you know that there are media outside."

Although the announcement of her engagement to Gabriel had briefly made Olivia newsworthy in England, the future princess of a small country hadn't interested the British press for long.

In Sherdana, however, it was a different story. She'd found the citizens were very curious about her. When she'd visited three months ago, she'd been besieged by requests for interviews and followed wherever she went. Numerous public appearances had filled her daily schedule from ribbon-cutting ceremonies to attending sessions of parliament.

But when Olivia emerged into Noelle's reception room, she understood the assistant's concern. At least a hundred people crowded the streets, most of them armed with cameras. Surely not all these people were reporters. David, her driver, and Antonio, the enormous man Gabriel had assigned to accompany her whenever she was out in public, had called in five others from palace security to create a corridor of safety between the front door of the wedding shop and the car.

Olivia shot Libby a look. "I think life as I knew it has come to an end." Then she turned to Noelle. "Thank you for everything. The dress is perfect."

"You're welcome."

Squaring her shoulders, Olivia put on her public face and stepped toward the front door. Noelle held it open for her with a whispered, *"Bon courage."*

"Olivia, how are you dealing with the discovery of the prince's illegitimate children?"

"Lady Darcy, can you tell us if the wedding is still on?"

"How do you feel about raising another woman's children?"

"Do you think the prince would have married Marissa if he'd been able?"

The questions rained down on Olivia as she headed for the car, smiling and waving as she walked, but responding to none. She slipped each query into its own special cubbyhole for later retrieval and didn't realize she was holding her breath until the car had pulled away from the curb. Libby watched her in concern.

"I'm fine."

"You look...unhappy."

"I'm just tired. The twins slept in my bed and I wasn't able to get comfortable on the couch. That's all."

The excuse pacified her secretary and gave Olivia the space to sort through the highs and lows of the last twenty-four hours. While she wasn't naive enough to think that Gabriel was marrying her for anything other than business, Olivia had hoped that he'd grow fond of her. But while they'd kissed in the garden, she'd let herself believe that their future could be filled with passion and romance.

The photos of him with Marissa that the media had broadcast this morning had been a wake-up call. That was love. Olivia stared out the window at the old town slipping past.

She needed time to adjust to sharing him with a ghost.

# Five

When Olivia returned to her room after the fitting, she discovered an invitation and a small, slender box wrapped in ribbon. Heart pounding, she opened the envelope and recognized Gabriel's strong handwriting.

A quiet dinner, just the two of them. In his suite. She clutched the stationery to her chest and breathed deep to calm her sudden attack of nerves. Except for the brief time last night and this morning, they hadn't been alone together. Did he intend to seduce her? Olivia certainly hoped so, but what did she wear to her deflowering? Something demure that matched her level of experience in all things sexual? Something that bared her skin and invited his touch?

Her fears that he didn't find her attractive had melted beneath the heat of this morning's kiss. But he was accustomed to women with far more experience than she possessed. Apprehension made her nerves buzz like a swarm of angry hornets.

Leaving her worries to sort themselves out, she tugged at the ribbon holding the box closed. The pale blue silk fell away. Her fingers brushed the hinged lid as she savored the anticipation of her first gift from Gabriel. From the box's shape, she knew it was a bracelet.

Olivia took a deep breath and opened the lid. Lying on a bed of black velvet was a stunning free-form emerald an inch and a half wide and almost two inches long that dominated the design. The rest of the band was diamonds, set in a diamond-shaped pattern. Bold and contemporary, it wasn't the sort of thing she'd wear, being a little too trendy, but she couldn't fault Gabriel's taste.

Ignoring a pang of disappointment that he'd chosen something so not her taste, she draped the wide cuff over her wrist. As she admired the sparkle, she couldn't shake a nagging sense of familiarity. It was a unique piece, something one-of-a-kind, yet she was certain she'd seen it before. But where? The answer eluded her and she set aside her musings as Libby arrived and helped Olivia decide on the perfect outfit to highlight Gabriel's extravagant gift.

Around midafternoon she went up to the nursery and found the twins eager to visit the stables. But she listened with only half her attention as Bethany chattered on the short walk to the stables. Olivia was having a hard time thinking about anything except her dinner with Gabriel and the hope that they could forget all about Marissa and begin their lives together. Comparing herself to Gabriel's former lover would only lead to trouble down the road. She'd be smarter to put that energy into keeping Gabriel's mind fixed on the present.

While a pair of grooms took Bethany and Karina to look at the ponies their father had ordered to be delivered to the stable, Olivia drifted along the barn's center aisle, stroking a soft nose here and there, lost in a pleasant daydream. The soothing sounds of the barn wrapped her in a cocoon of stillness that allowed her ample privacy to relive the moments in the garden that morning.

Her blood heated and slowed, flowing into the sensitive area between her thighs that Gabriel's fervent kiss had awakened earlier. She leaned her back against a stall and closed her eyes to better relive the delicious caress of his hands against her back and hips. Her breasts had ached for his possession. She'd never felt anything like the powerful craving his kiss aroused. She'd been seconds away from begging him to touch her everywhere. He'd been her master. Her teacher. And she, a very willing student.

The memories disturbed the smooth rhythm of her breathing. How was it possible that just thinking of Gabriel aroused her?

"Are you okay?"

Olivia's eyes snapped open. A groom peered at her, concern in his brown eyes.

She offered a weak smile, feeling heat in her cheeks, put there by her sensual daydreams. Had she really been standing in the middle of a barn, imagining how it would feel to have Gabriel's large, strong hands roaming over her bare skin?

"Fine." The word came out a little garbled. What magic had he wrought to make her forget her surroundings so completely? "I'm fine."

From outside came the twins' high-pitched voices lifted in childish delight. Olivia pushed away from the wall and went in search of them. In the stable yard, beneath the watchful eyes of the grooms who'd taken charge of them, they each stood on a mounting block in order to better acquaint themselves with their new pony.

Olivia fought anxiety as she watched the girls, but soon she calmed down. These ponies had obviously been chosen for their placid demeanor; otherwise the excited movements of the twins would have startled them. The geldings were well matched in size, color and markings. Bethany's had a long, narrow blaze that stretched from forehead to right between his nostrils. Karina's had a wider stripe of white that spread out as it reached the nose. Both ponies had two white front socks and one back.

Bethany was the first to notice Olivia. She threw her

arms around the pony's neck and said in an excited voice. "Look at my horse. Her name is Grady."

Olivia started to correct Bethany on the gender of her new pony, but Karina jumped in before she could speak.

"Peanut." The quieter twin looked so delighted that Olivia wondered if she would still demand a puppy for her birthday.

"They're lovely," Olivia said. "But I think they're both boys."

The girls were too excited to listen and went back to petting and chattering to their ponies. The head groom came over to where Olivia stood.

"They will make fine horsewomen."

"I believe you're right."

"Would you like to see the mount His Highness chose for you?"

It had never occurred to Olivia that she would receive a horse as well when she told Gabriel how she loved to ride whenever she spent time at Dansbrooke. The park around the palace wasn't as extensive as the lands surrounding her family's country estate, but she welcomed the opportunity to get whatever exercise she could.

"I'd love to see him." She laughed. "Or her."

"It's a mare. A Dutch Warmblood. I heard you've done some eventing. You'll find Arioso is a wonderful jumper and an eager athlete."

The beautiful chestnut had large, soft eyes and a gentle disposition, but before she had time to do more than stroke the mare's long neck, the twins had finished with their ponies and joined her at the stall.

Deciding they'd had enough for one day, Olivia gathered them together and bid the grooms goodbye. After depositing them with a pair of maids in the nursery, she returned to her room to bathe and dress.

Olivia took a long time preparing for the evening. She

played with hairstyles for an hour before settling on a softly disheveled updo that required only a couple of pins to keep it in place. The gown she'd chosen was a simple black sheath that bared her arms and appeared demure in the front but dipped low in the back.

Anticipation began to dissolve her calm as she zipped up the dress and fastened simple diamond dangles to her earlobes. Boldly eschewing panty hose, she slid her feet into elegant patent leather pumps.

She wanted everything about her to say "touch me."

And surveying her appearance in the full-length mirror, Olivia felt confident she'd done just that. That left only one more thing to do. Olivia popped the top on the jewelry box and laid the wide bracelet across her wrist. Libby helped by securing the clasp.

"Is this all for my brother's benefit?" Ariana had slipped into the room after a soft knock.

Olivia felt her cheeks heating. "Do you think he'll approve?"

Ariana smiled. "How could he not?" Her gaze slipped over Olivia, stopping at the diamond-and-emerald bracelet. She reached for Olivia's hand, as the color drained from her face. "Where did you get that?"

"Gabriel sent it to me." Concern rose in Olivia. Why was Ariana looking as if she'd seen a ghost? "Why? Do you recognize it?"

"Gabriel sent it?" Ariana echoed. She shook her head. "I don't understand."

"You recognize it?" Olivia felt her heart hit her toes. "It's cursed, isn't it?"

"You might say that."

"Tell me."

"It's none of my business."

There was no way she was letting Ariana get away

without an explanation. "If there's something wrong, I need to know."

"Really, I shouldn't have said anything." Ariana backed toward the bedroom door. "I'm sure everything is fine."

It wasn't like Ariana to hedge, especially when it came to things that distressed her. And seeing the bracelet had obviously upset the princess.

"What do you mean everything is fine? Why wouldn't it be? What aren't you telling me about the bracelet?"

Olivia caught Ariana's wrist in a tight grip. Startled, the brunette looked from the hand holding her, to the bracelet on Olivia's wrist and finally met her gaze.

"I don't want to upset you."

"And you think that's going to persuade me to let you walk out of here without spilling the truth?" Olivia tugged her future sister-in-law toward the wingback chairs flanking the fireplace. She didn't let go until Ariana sat down. "Tell me what about the bracelet upset you."

Releasing an audible sigh, the princess leveled her pale gold eyes on Olivia. "The last time I saw that bracelet was the night before Gabriel broke things off with Marissa."

Pain lanced through Olivia, sharper than anything she'd experienced this morning as she'd watched the pictures of Gabriel and Marissa on the television.

"He bought it for her."

"Yes. It was…for their second anniversary."

The cool platinum burned like acid against Olivia's skin. She clawed at the clasp, blood pounding in her ears. Her excitement over having dinner alone with Gabriel vanished, replaced by wrenching despair. The first gift he'd given her had been the bracelet he'd bought to celebrate two years with Marissa?

The clasp popped open beneath her nails. Olivia dropped it on the mantle and sat in the chair opposite

Ariana, unsure how much longer her shaky legs would support her.

"How did he get it back?"

"I don't know. Maybe she returned it when they broke up."

Olivia felt sick. It was bad enough that Gabriel had given her the trinket he'd bought for another woman, it was worse that it was a returned gift. "I thought I'd seen it before," she murmured.

Ariana leaned forward and placed her hand over Olivia's. "I'm sure this is all a huge misunderstanding. Maybe I'm thinking of a different bracelet."

Olivia drew comfort from Ariana for a moment, before sitting up straight and bracing her shoulders. "The only misunderstanding is mine. I thought tonight was supposed to be the beginning of something between us." She offered Ariana a bitter smile. "I forgot that our marriage is first and foremost a business arrangement."

"I don't believe that's true. I saw the way Gabriel watched you this morning. He was worried by how you reacted to the press coverage of the twins' arrival and all the scandal it stirred up."

"He's worried about losing the deal with my father."

"Yes, but there's more to it than that. He had other opportunities to secure Sherdana's economic future. He chose you."

Ariana's words rang with conviction, but Olivia shook her head. The sight of the bracelet made her long to hurl it into the deepest ocean. She felt betrayed and yet she had no right. She was marrying Gabriel because he was handsome and honorable and she would one day become a queen. Her reasons for choosing him were no more romantic than his.

"Ask him to tell you about the first time you met."

"The party at the French embassy?" Olivia recalled

his stiff formality and their brief, stilted conversation, so different from their exchange in the garden this morning.

"Before that."

Olivia shook her head. "We didn't meet before that."

"You did. You just don't remember."

How was that possible? Every time he drew near, her stomach pitched and her body yearned for his touch. His lips on hers turned her into an irrational creature of turbulent desires and rollicking emotions. If they'd met, she'd have recognized the signs.

"Your brother is very memorable," she argued. "I'm certain you are mistaken."

Ariana's eyes glowed. "Just ask him."

Abruptly filled with uncertainty, Olivia looked down at her gown and noticed the brush of cool air against her bare back and arms. She'd dressed to entice Gabriel. She'd wanted his hands to go places no man had ventured before. Even after learning that he'd given her a bracelet that once belonged to his former lover, she still wanted him. She ached with yearning. Burned with hungers unleashed by an hour in the bath tracing her naked skin with her fingertips, imagining Gabriel doing the same.

"Damn it." The curse shot out of her and startled Ariana.

"Oh, I've really done it," the princess muttered. "Please don't be mad at Gabriel. That was five years ago. I'll bet he doesn't even remember the bracelet."

Olivia's gaze sharpened into focus as she took in Ariana's miserable expression. "You remembered."

"I'm a woman. I have an artist's eye for detail." Ariana shook her head. "Gabriel is a man. They don't notice things like fashion. Now, if he'd given you a set of antlers off a buck he'd shot, that he'd recall."

Olivia recognized that Ariana was trying to lighten her mood, but the damage had been done. She wasn't half as angry with Gabriel as she was with herself. For being a fool. For not realizing that she never would have agreed to marry Gabriel unless she was already emotionally engaged.

But it was too late. She was already in too deep. The only thing she could do now was keep her wits about her and not allow herself to be disappointed again.

To his intense shock, Gabriel was second-guessing himself.

As he towel-dried his hair. As he shaved for the second time that day. As he dressed in gray slacks and a black collarless button-down shirt.

All he could think about was what a mistake he'd made with the bracelet he'd chosen for Olivia's first present. As beautiful as the item was, he couldn't help but think she'd appreciate something more romantic with a little history attached.

He was grimly amused with himself. Since when had he devoted this much time and energy to a gift for a woman? In Marissa's case, he'd always zeroed in on the most flamboyant piece available, the more expensive the better, and been richly rewarded for his generosity.

Gabriel slid a watch onto his wrist and checked the time. He had half an hour before Olivia was due to arrive if he wanted to fetch a particular piece from the vault. "I have a quick errand to run," he told Stewart. "If Lady Darcy arrives before I return, serve her a glass of champagne and assure her I won't be long."

With that, he exited his suite and headed to the vault, his mind on the perfect thing to present to his fiancée. It took him exactly ten minutes to find the necklace and return. Stewart was alone when Gabriel returned.

"Dinner is set to be served at eight."

"Perfect." Gabriel had no interest in rushing. At the

same time, he wanted plenty of the evening left over for getting to know Olivia thoroughly. "You ordered all her favorites?"

"Of course." Stewart's head turned at the light knock on the door. "That must be Lady Darcy. I'll let her in, then make myself scarce."

Gabriel grinned, glad she was as eager to begin their evening as he. Stewart went to answer the door. With his pulse kicked into overdrive, Gabriel found himself holding his breath in anticipation. Realizing what he was doing, he exhaled, wondering how long it had been since the idea of spending time alone with a woman had excited him. But Olivia wasn't just any woman.

She aroused him faster and more intensely than anyone since Marissa. To look at her, it made no sense. She was elegant, cool and poised. Not the sort of sultry, lush temptress that turned men's heads. But today he'd discovered an inner core of vibrant, sensual woman hiding within her. The little he'd sampled explained his craving for a more prolonged taste.

A tense conversation was taking place near the door. Gabriel frowned as he spied the petite woman standing in the hall. Not Olivia. Her private secretary. Although curious about the content of their discussion, Gabriel made no attempt to listen in. He would learn what it was about soon enough.

The exchange at the door came to an end. Stewart came toward him, wearing a frown.

"What's wrong?"

"Your Highness." Stewart looked as if an elephant had stepped on his toes. "Lady Darcy has declined your invitation."

Dumbstruck, Gabriel stared at his assistant. Declined his invitation? Outrageous.

He'd anticipated their evening alone and the chance to learn more about her. "Is she ill?"

Stewart hesitated. "I didn't...get that impression."

"What impression did you get?" he demanded, impatient at his secretary's caginess.

Stewart squared his shoulders. "That perhaps she was unhappy...with you."

"With me?" When they'd parted this morning she'd been all dreamy eyes and feminine wiles. What could have possibly happened in the past twelve hours?

Without another word to Stewart, Gabriel exited his suite. Long, determined strides carried him down the hall toward the rooms assigned to Olivia. He barely noticed the maid scurrying out of his way as he passed her. He did, however, notice Ariana stepping out of Olivia's suite.

"Gabriel, what are you doing here?"

"I'm here to collect Olivia for dinner."

Ariana's gold eyes widened. "Didn't you get the message? Olivia's not up to having dinner with you tonight."

He leaned down and pinned his sister with a steely glare, wondering what mischief she had been up to. "What's wrong with her?"

Ariana set her hand on her hip and regarded him with annoyance. "She's not feeling well."

"Then I'd be remiss in not checking on her," Gabriel intoned, sounding as suave as he could through gritted teeth. "Step aside."

But his sister didn't budge. "Leave it tonight, Gabriel," she coaxed. "Give her a little time."

"Time for what?"

"Honestly," his sister fumed. "You can be so insensitive sometimes."

What was he missing? "Enlighten me."

Ariana pressed her lips together, but Gabriel kept up his

unrelenting stare and she finally sighed. "She's had your affair with Marissa thrown in her face all day."

He remembered the expression on Olivia's face while the footage of him and Marissa had played on the television. But he thought they'd cleared the matter up in his office. Why was she letting the past bother her? Gabriel nudged his sister aside and reached for the door handle.

"Gabriel—"

"This is none of your concern. It's between me and my future bride."

"Fine." Ariana tossed up her hands. "But don't say I didn't warn you."

With her dire words ringing in his ears, Gabriel entered Olivia's suite. Some impulse prompted him to slip the lock before scanning the space. His fiancée was not in the bedroom. After his encounter with Ariana, he'd expected to find Olivia sulking over some perceived slight. Then he noticed a slight billowing of the sheer curtains over the French doors leading out onto the terrace.

Olivia stood near the terrace railing staring out over the pond and the park, her gaze on the path where they'd walked and kissed this morning. She wore a black dress that bared her back in a plunging V. She'd knotted her hair on top of her head, exposing the nape of her neck. The sight of all that bare skin did unruly things to his body. He'd always been a sucker for a woman's back, finding the combination of delicacy and strength an intoxicating combination.

Gabriel shoved aside desire and refocused on the reason he'd come here in the first place.

"We're supposed to be having dinner in my suite."

"I don't feel up to it," she replied in a cool tone, not bothering to turn around.

"Then you're not upset."

"Of course not."

He didn't believe her. For the briefest of moments he wondered if she was trying to manipulate him with some feminine trickery. He almost laughed at the notion. Marissa was the only other woman who'd tried to best him with her wiles. He'd quickly set her straight.

Time to set Olivia straight, as well. "I thought this morning you understood that whatever was between Marissa and me has been over for three years."

"What sort of evening did you have in mind for us tonight?" She turned around and faced him and he got his first glimpse of her expression. Genuine anger shimmered in her gaze. "Were we to sip champagne and become lovers or did you plan to educate me on Sherdana's upcoming social and economic challenges?"

What had gotten into her? This morning she'd been like warm honey in his arms. Tonight she'd become an ice sculpture. All this because a few reporters dredged up old news from three years ago?

"I'd hoped we'd spend some time getting to know each other tonight, but I had no intention of rushing you into bed." Tired of sparring with her, he stepped within touching distance. "I thought that we'd reached an understanding this morning."

"So did I," she murmured, the fire fading from her tone.

"Then what's wrong?"

"Our marriage is an arrangement."

"Yes." He grazed his fingertips up her sides from her hips, letting them coast along the side of her breasts. The hitch in her breath told him the fight was over. "But it doesn't have to be all business between us."

"And it isn't," she agreed. "It's just that I'm not really sure what's happening."

So, he wasn't the only one struggling to find his way. Ever since last night, he'd found himself drawn to her as never before, but he wasn't sure she felt it, too. And now that he knew she did, he wasn't about to let her run away from it.

"We have strong sexual chemistry," he told her, and then in a softer voice confessed, "I wasn't expecting that."

Her scent flowed around him, feminine and enticing. As desire began to assert itself, he noticed the details his anger had blinded him to. For a woman intent on denying him her company, she'd dressed with care. He dipped his head and drank in the feminine scent of her. She'd dabbed a light floral perfume behind her ears. His lips found the spot and made her shiver.

"Gabriel, please." Her hand on his chest wasn't going to deter him now that he'd gotten wind of her imminent surrender.

"Please, what?" he inquired. "Stop?"

Knowing it was what she had in mind, he tugged the pins from her hair and tossed them aside. The golden waves spilled around her face and shoulders.

"Yes." But the word lacked conviction.

"You're lying," he pressed. "And badly. This is what you wanted when you dressed tonight." He took her stiff body in his arms and immediately the fight began to drain from her muscles. "My hands on you." He dipped his head and drew his lips across her cheek, finishing his thought with his breath puffing against her ear. "My mouth tasting your skin."

Her body was limp against him now, all resistance abandoned.

"We're meant to be together." He was more convinced of that than ever. "You know it as well as I do."

She'd closed her eyes to hide from him, not realizing how futile her actions were. "Yes."

# Six

Without sight, all her other senses came to life. The unsteady rasp of Gabriel's breath told her he too was disturbed by the attraction between them. But was it enough? Hadn't she discovered less than an hour ago that she wanted more from him? So much more.

His fingertips grazed along the sensitive skin inside her arm, from the hollow behind her elbow to the pulse jerking frantically in her wrist. Gently he laced their fingers and began to pull her along the terrace. Her eyes flew open.

"Where?" Her gaze found his and she saw feverish hunger blazing in the bronze depths.

"To bed, of course," he teased, but there was nothing lighthearted about the determined set of his mouth or the tension that rode his muscles. Tension that communicated across the short distance between them.

"What about dinner?"

Inside the suite once more, he drew her close, sliding a hand over her hip to pull her against the hard jut of his erection, and bent to whisper in her ear. "You made me hungry for something besides food."

His lips dropped to hers, lingering at the corner of her mouth for too long. His unproductive nuzzling wasn't getting the job done. She wanted a kiss. A real, hard, deep kiss with no possibility of interruption. Growling low in her throat, she lifted on tiptoe and framed his face with her hands, holding him still while she pressed her mouth to his. Her tongue tested the seam of his lips as she flattened her breasts against Gabriel's broad chest, eager to convey her desire, letting her hunger shine through.

Gabriel captured handfuls of the dress near her shoulder blades and pulled the edges forward and down, baring her torso to the waist. Olivia gasped at the sudden rush of cool air over her breasts.

He slid his hands up over her rib cage until his fingers reached the undersides of her breasts. Smiling with male satisfaction, he cupped her and kneaded slightly.

She arched into the pressure of his hands, offering herself to him. Reaching behind, she found the dress's zipper and slid it down. With a determined stroke of her palms against her hips, the dress pooled at her feet, leaving her wearing nothing but her black pumps and a white lace thong.

He had tracked the progression of the dress to the floor, his gaze sliding over her legs as the falling black fabric bared her to him. Liking the way his nostrils flared at the sight of her nakedness, Olivia stepped out of the dress and kicked it aside.

Pressure built inside her as she hooked her fingers in the thong, determined to rid herself of it, as well. Gabriel's hands covered hers, halting her actions.

"This is your first time." His voice sank into rich, warm tones that did little to equalize her pulse or diminish her hunger. "I want to take this slow."

"I don't."

His lips moved into a predator's smile, slow and lazy. "You'll thank me later."

And with that, he swept her feet off the floor.

Placing her in the center of the big bed, Gabriel stepped back to rid himself of his clothes. Olivia raised herself on her elbows to better catch the unveiling of all that amazing bronze skin. From the little contact she'd had with his body, she knew he was lean and well-muscled, but nothing prepared her for the chiseled perfection of his torso as his shirt buttons gave way. She goggled at the sheer beauty of his broad shoulders and the sculptured magnificence of his chest.

He raised his eyebrows at her obvious curiosity, his hands going to the belt buckle. As he unfastened the top button, he kicked off his shoes. His pants hit the floor, followed by his socks.

He left on his boxers, but Olivia's eyes were drawn to the way they bulged in front. Her obvious curiosity and lack of concern turned him on and sped even more blood to his groin. Making this the most amazing night of her life might prove challenging. She certainly wasn't playing the part of nervous virgin.

He climbed onto the bed.

"What's this?" His finger grazed a black Chinese character in the hollow beside her hip bone and her stomach muscles twitched.

"A tattoo."

His elegant British fiancée had a tattoo? And in a very sexy spot, he might add. He frowned.

"What does it say?"

"Hope." She bent the leg opposite him and braced her foot on the mattress so she could cant her hips toward him. "I got it in college. My one wild act freshman year."

He imagined her baring her body for the needle, sliding down jeans and underwear. And the thought of another man touching her there made him want to roar in outrage.

His emotions must have shown on his face because she rushed to say, "It was done by a woman."

His shoulders relaxed at her words. She was his, or would be soon. And he wasn't the sort of man who cared to share. Living with two brothers had turned him into a possessive madman when anything encroached on what he believed was his.

"In that case, it's very sexy."

She grinned at how grudging his words sounded. It continued to both infuriate and delight him that she was not even remotely close to the type of woman he thought he'd chosen to make the next queen of Sherdana and his wife.

He hadn't anticipated surprises. He'd expected gracefulness and composure, not this wanton creature with her disheveled hair, bare breasts and body marked by the word *hope*. But now that he had her, she turned him inside out with wanting. She fired his imagination and his blood in the span of a heartbeat. Life would not be dull with her.

Which was the problem. He'd had passion once, crazy desire. It had consumed him and compelled him to think with every part of him but the one that mattered for the future king of Sherdana: his head. He didn't need a wife who made him feel out of control. He needed someone sensible, who kept him focused on matters of state.

Yet deep down he knew Olivia would do that.

And then, behind the closed doors of their private suite, she would make him forget everything but the sweet rush of carnal pleasure.

The best of both worlds.

What was there to worry about?

Taking her leg in his hand, he caressed upward from her knee to the place where her thighs came together.

"That's..." Her voice faltered as he slid one finger beneath the scrap of lace hiding her hot, wet center from him. She balled her fists into the coverlet, holding her breath as the tip of his finger grazed her warmth.

"You are incredibly wet," he said, delighted by the quickness of her arousal.

"Stop talking and touch me."

"Like this?" Stripping off her underwear, he did as she

asked, dipping between the folds that concealed her core and riding the river of wetness toward the knot of nerves. He circled it slowly, listening to her pant, smelling the waves of her arousal. Her hips rose off the mattress, pushing into his hand.

Gorgeous.

With her eyes closed, her knuckles whitening as she held on to the bed linens for dear life, she was as deep into the throes of sensual pleasure as any woman he'd ever known. She writhed against his hand, mindless in her pursuit of her ultimate goal. He watched her face, absorbing each tremble and jerk of her body as he carried her closer and closer to orgasm. Her brow knit as she concentrated. He picked up the pace and watched her mouth open, her back arch.

It was the sexiest thing he'd ever seen.

And it was his name that escaped her lips as she climaxed.

Panting, she opened her eyes. "That was incredible."

He grinned. "It gets better."

"Better?" She sounded doubtful. "I can't imagine that it could get better than that."

He loved a challenge. "Hold your opinion for another hour or so."

"An hour?" She stared at him, her eyes wide with uncertainty. "I don't think I could possibly survive that long."

He didn't think he would survive that long, either. But he was determined to try.

Forking his fingers into her hair, he brought his mouth to hers. Desire continued to claw at him, and tasting her eagerness only made it that much harder for him to maintain control.

He wanted to claim her, make her his. The notion that he was the first man to put his hands on her made him wild. The uncivilized part of him that had run wild with

Marissa roared within its cage, demanding to be free. Gabriel turned his back on those impulses.

Making this first time perfect for her was the only thing that mattered. And for him to do that, he must stay in control.

Her hands left the mattress and moved up his sides. Caresses like fire swept over his skin as she explored the contours of his shoulders and back.

His tongue delved between her parted lips, tasting her passion, capturing the soft cries she made as his fingers found her breasts, nails raking lightly over her taut nipples. Her legs tangled with his. Her wet curls dampened his boxers. He rocked against her heat and broke off the kiss to take her nipple in his mouth.

Her head fell back as he suckled her. Cupping her butt in his hand, he guided her undulating rhythm until they were in sync. A groan collected in his chest as her fingers speared beneath the waistband of his boxers and found him.

Olivia gasped at the first contact with Gabriel's erection. The silken feel of his skin. The steel beneath. The sheer size of him made her whimper with fear and excitement. How was she supposed to take all of him inside her?

"It's okay," he murmured, easing her fingers away. Somehow he'd understood what was in her mind. "I'll take it slow. You'll get the chance to get used to me little by little."

"But you aren't little, so little by little isn't how I see this happening," she retorted, twisting one hand free so she could touch him again.

A groan burst from him as she wrapped her hand fully around his length and measured him from tip to base.

He pulled her hand away and pinned it on the pillow by her ear. "It certainly isn't going to happen that way if you don't stop touching me."

"But I like touching you," she countered, lifting up to kiss his chin. She'd been aiming for his lips, but with his chest pressed against hers, she couldn't lift up that high. "Kissing you." She could barely gain the breath she needed for speech as his body slid down hers. "I've been waiting a long time for this."

"Then let's not delay."

Further conversation became impossible as Gabriel kicked off his boxers and slid between her thighs. Olivia felt his erection against her skin and wiggled her hips to entice him to bring their bodies together in the way they both wanted. Her entire focus consisted of this powerful man and the ache only he could satisfy. Despite her inexperience, she knew exactly what she wanted. Gabriel inside her. She needed to be connected to him on that elemental level and she needed it now.

"Gabriel, please," she murmured, her body shuddering as his mouth slipped over her skin, licking, nibbling, kissing. He seemed determined to investigate every inch of her when there was only one place she wanted his attention focused. "Take me."

Her voice broke on the plea. But it had its effect. He kissed her one last time on the hollow beside her hip bone and settled the tip of his shaft at the entrance to her core. The feel of him there was so amazing. She lifted her hips and took him a little way in.

"We'll get there," he murmured, framing her face with his hands.

Surrendering to the ride was part of the excitement. Forcing him to move faster would get her to satisfaction quicker but wasn't the journey worth some patience?

"You're extremely tight." Capturing her lips in a hot, sizzling kiss, Gabriel flexed his hips forward, sliding into her a little deeper. "It will go easier the first time if you relax."

She was a mass of anticipation and tension. How the hell was she supposed to relax? Olivia gripped his wrists and focused on his expression. His rigid facial muscles and intense concentration told her that this slow loving was taking its toll on him, as well.

"I have no idea how to do that." The heavy throb in her womb grew more powerful as she held her breath and waited for him to join with her completely.

His low chuckle sounded near her ear.

"Breathe."

"I can't." Her words were garbled, starved for air.

His teeth nipped her throat and she gasped. Then he was sucking on the spot where he'd administered the love bite, his tongue laving the tender area. Her mouth fell open as an electric charge shot from where he'd placed his mouth to the place where he was claiming her in the most elemental way possible. Her body stretched as he rocked against her again, his movement driving him a little deeper into her.

The sensation was incredible. She focused on the joy of being filled by him and her muscles unwound. Relief swept through her and she gave herself over to wonder with a murmur.

"Or maybe I can."

"That's it," he coaxed, withdrawing with the same deliberate motion only to move into her again.

The sensation was incredible. She loved the way he filled her.

It took a moment of concentration before she shifted her hips into sync with his slow rhythm. Which was too slow as it turned out. He might have all the patience in the world, but she didn't. His gentleness wasn't getting him where she needed him most. So, as he began his next measured, torturous thrust into her body, she arched her back, drove her hips forward and sunk her nails into his tight rear, accepting all of him. They cried out in unison. If she hadn't been so shattered by the feel of him so deeply buried in her, Olivia might have giggled. Utterly possessed, she had no breath to laugh or speak.

Gabriel licked his lips and slowly his gaze refocused. The transformation of his features from rigid concentration to outright shock magnified the pleasure inside her.

"What happened to slow?" he murmured, fingertips grazing her cheeks with reverent gentleness.

Olivia's body had adjusted to his. A contented purr rumbled in her chest. She ran the soles of her feet down his calves and drifted her hands along his spine.

"You were taking too long."

"It's your first time," he grumbled. "I was trying to be gentle."

"What happens now?" Her inner muscles flexed as he rocked his hips against hers.

"Watch and see."

With those cryptic words, Olivia turned herself over to the dazzling display of fireworks in Gabriel's eyes as he began to move against her, gauging her every response. Then he thrust back inside her and pleasure began to build once more.

He captured her hips in his hands and helped her find his rhythm. To her astonishment her body caught fire. Pleasure radiated outward from her core, spreading in waves of sensual hunger that climbed higher and higher, reaching outward with an intensity that made her feel as if she was on the verge of splintering into a million pieces.

And then it began, the breaking. Yet this time, unlike the last, she had Gabriel with her, climbing beside her. She held on to him, glorying in his strength and the power of the pleasure he gave her.

Her breath caught as the sun exploded behind her eyelids. Ecstasy blasted through her, detonating with all the power of a volcano. She cried out and clung to Gabriel as his movements increased. Everything went dark for a second, then she heard her name on Gabriel's lips and he thrust one last time, shaking with the power of his orgasm, before collapsing on her.

Olivia tunneled one hand through his hair while her other unlocked from his shoulder. His chest heaved against her, as he dragged air into his lungs in great gulps. Their hearts thundered in unison, as matched in the aftermath as they'd been during their loving.

She scrambled for words, but nothing could describe her emotions at the moment. Instead, she settled for silence and let her fingers talk for her. She ran them soothingly across his skin, conveying her profound thanks.

"Are you okay?" Gabriel asked, rousing himself enough to slide out of her and roll onto his side.

The loss of him from her body hit her like a sledgehammer. The connection they'd had, now severed, made her realize just how intimate the act of making love was. For those few minutes, she'd not just taken him into her body, into her womb, but into her heart, as well. He'd possessed her body and soul.

"Never better," she replied, unable to mask the smile in her voice.

He gathered her close and dropped a chaste kiss above her brow. Beneath her palm, his heartbeat returned to normal.

"That makes two of us." His thumb moved against her shoulder in an absent fashion as if his mind was somewhere besides the two of them naked in this bed. "You're sure that wasn't too rough?"

"Since I have nothing to compare it to, I'm going to say it was just rough enough."

He stopped staring at the canopy overhead and sliced a sharp look her way. His mouth tightened for a second until he realized she was teasing him.

"I had hoped to initiate you in a more civilized manner."

"There's a civilized way to make love?" Despite her best intentions, she giggled. "Do tell." Lifting onto her elbow, she walked her fingers down his stomach. "Better yet, why don't you show me?"

Gabriel growled and captured her fingers in a tight grip, placing their clasped hands on his chest. "Behave."

"Or what?" She had no idea what demon had possessed her but suddenly she felt more free and alive than any time in her life. Keeping her virginity intact all these years had obviously created a powder keg of trouble. Like a genie in a bottle, once released, her sexuality was ready to cause as much mischief as possible before she stuffed it back in and replaced the cork. "You'll spank me?"

Gabriel's eyes widened at her outrageous suggestion, but temptation danced in their bronze depths. His pupils widened, a sure sign of sexual arousal, and his erection flared to life again.

And shockingly enough, she felt herself awakening, as well. What did this man do to her?

"You led me to believe you were cool and composed," he complained as she wiggled around until she got a thigh on either side of his hips. His erection prodded her from behind. He looked pained as she extricated her hand from his grasp and raked her nails down his chest and over his abdomen, smiling as his muscles twitched beneath her touch. "What's gotten into you?"

She leaned forward to grin at him. "You."

His hands bracketed her hips as she poised herself over his shaft and slowly lowered herself downward. Taking him deep, adjusting the angle to give herself the most pleasure, she watched his face contort with delight and his eyes glaze over.

When she sat on him, savoring the feel of him buried inside her once more, she watched his gaze come back into focus. He reached up to capture her breasts in his hands, kneading gently, pulling at her nipples while she rose off him, mimicking the slow way he'd tortured her.

For a while he let her control the action, and she appreciated the chance to learn how the feel of him sliding in and out of her could be different if she leaned forward or backward. She liked taking him deep until the tip of him nudged against her womb.

But her education would not be complete without a little tutoring, and Gabriel's patience couldn't last forever. His fingers bit into her hips, changing her cadence. He began to move powerfully, driving himself into her. The bite of her nails created half-moons in his shoulders as his hand slid between their bodies and touched the knot of nerves hidden in her hot wet lips. Sparks exploded behind her eyes as her body began to pulse with ever stronger pleasure. She threw her head back and her mouth fell open in a keening cry as pleasure spun through her like a cyclone.

Gabriel thrust into her, his pace frantic, his own mouth open to expel a groan of acute pleasure. Olivia watched him climax, watched him become completely hers. Panting, she trembled in the aftershocks of her orgasm, her inner muscles clenching around his shaft as he poured his seed inside her and she welcomed this essence of him she could keep.

For the past two hours, Gabriel had lain beside Olivia and listened to her deep regular breathing while his thoughts retraced the evening. As morning light began to come in through the windows, he rolled out of bed, moving carefully to avoid waking Olivia. While he dressed he kept his eyes off her to avoid succumbing to the temptation to return to bed and wake her. Again. A full-fledged grin engaged every muscle in Gabriel's face. He couldn't help it.

Making love with Olivia had demonstrated his life would be spectacularly entertaining from here on out.

As he exited her room, he wondered if she'd done it on purpose. Picked a fight with him that ended in spectacular lovemaking. It was something Marissa had done often enough. Sex with her had been mind-blowing, hot, passionate, animalistic. She'd scratched long welts on his back and marked his shoulders with love bites. She'd possessed him as much as he'd possessed her.

But although their sex had been out of this world, it had many times left him feeling empty. And in typical male fashion, he'd ignored the emotional vacuum because what did he care if his carnal needs were satisfied.

Then, last night, he'd discovered what he'd been missing all those years. Spectacular sex and a deep emotional connection that left him more than a little rattled. With her curious innocence and startling sensuality, Olivia had slipped beneath his skin as if she'd been there all along. As if she was the answer to a prayer he hadn't even realized he'd breathed.

He hadn't liked the sexual power Marissa had held in her delicate hands. He liked Olivia's ability to influence his emotions even less.

Which was why he was heading for his suite of rooms rather than face her in the moments before dawn.

An hour later, Gabriel found Stewart in the office on the first floor. His private secretary had a cup of coffee at his elbow and wore a troubled frown.

"You're up early," Gabriel commented, settling himself behind the intricately carved cherry desk.

"I think you might be interested in seeing this." Stewart extended a jewelry box in Gabriel's direction.

He frowned at it. "What is that?"

Stewart nudged his chin at the box. "When Lady Darcy's secretary delivered her message that she wasn't joining you for dinner, she gave me this. You left before I had a chance to open it."

With an impatient snort, Gabriel cracked open the box. The hairs on the back of his neck lifted as he stared at the contents.

"Where the hell did this come from?" he growled, staring in shocked dismay at the bracelet he'd given Marissa for their second anniversary. "Why did Olivia have it?"

Stewart shook his head. "I spoke with her secretary this morning and apparently it was waiting in her room when she got back from her fitting."

"No wonder she was so angry." He closed the box with a snap. "Ariana must have told her I'd bought this for Marissa."

"Who would have done this?" Stewart asked, refocusing Gabriel on the real trouble spot.

"Whoever it was wanted to create trouble between Olivia and me." Gabriel sat back and steepled his fingers.

"Someone could have entered her suite and left it for her. Staff is coming and going all the time."

"That means someone in the palace is playing a dangerous game." Gabriel poked at the box with a pen. "Time to give Christian a call. This sort of intrigue is right up his alley."

# Seven

Finding Gabriel gone when she awoke didn't surprise Olivia. A quick glance at the clock told her it was past eight. He had probably been up for hours. She eased into a sitting position, taking inventory of every strained and aching part of her. Nothing a hot shower wouldn't cure.

When she stepped from the bathroom a short time later, she discovered a visitor. Gabriel sat beside a table laden with an array of breakfast offerings. With his long legs stretched out in front of him and his hands clasped around a steaming cup of coffee, he hadn't yet noticed her.

Olivia leaned her shoulder against the door frame and let her gaze drift over his strong features and muscular torso clad in a tailored midnight-blue suit, white shirt and shimmering burgundy silk tie. For the moment his powerful energy was banked. But Gabriel in a contemplative state was no less arresting than him fully engaged.

Some small sound, probably a dreamy sigh, alerted him to her presence. He straightened and came toward her, his movement fluid, and before she knew it, he'd wrapped her in a snug embrace and given her the lusty morning kiss she'd been hoping for when she'd first awakened.

Desire stirred at the firm press of his mouth against her. He tasted of coffee and raspberries. Olivia dipped her tongue in for a second taste, murmuring approval.

"Good morning," he said, breaking the kiss, but not

ceasing the slow advance of his hands up her spine. "I'm sorry I left without doing that earlier."

"Why didn't you wake me?" She snuggled her cheek against his chest, savoring the unsteady pace of his heart and the hoarse timbre of his voice.

"Because I would have wanted to pick up where we left off last night," he retorted, his voice soft and deep. "And the palace would have been fully awake by the time I left your room."

That wrenched a laugh out of her. "You don't think everyone knows what happened last night?" Her cheeks heated despite herself. She'd always known there would be no privacy for her in the palace, but facing his parents and siblings when she knew they'd be apprised of what had happened between them last night would take a little getting used to.

"Perhaps, but I'd prefer to at least give the appearance of propriety until we're married." Gabriel gave her a wry smile that enhanced the devilry in his eyes. "Are you hungry?"

Her hands snaked around his waist, to tug his crisp white shirt from his pants. "Starving."

With a deep, rumbling laugh he caught her wrists. "I meant for breakfast. We missed dinner last night."

She waited until he'd dusted a kiss across her knuckles before answering. "I'd quite forgotten about dinner."

His eyes glowed with fierce delight as he drew her toward the table and poured a cup of coffee. "I didn't know what you liked for breakfast so I ordered some of everything."

"Usually I have an egg-white omelet with mushrooms and spinach, but today I think I want pancakes with lots of syrup."

To her astonishment, Gabriel served her himself. Olivia found it quite difficult to concentrate on her delicious breakfast while he watched her through eyes that danced with fondness and desire.

"Aren't you eating?" she asked.

"I had something an hour ago." He glanced at his watch. "The girls are going for their first ride this morning. I thought we should go watch. I already checked with your secretary and she said you're available until ten."

Considering his busy schedule, Olivia was delighted that he'd made time for such an important event. "They'll be thrilled. I took them to the stables yesterday afternoon. They loved the ponies. I predict they'll be enthusiastic equestrians."

"I have something for you." He pulled a small box out of his pocket and set it on the table between them.

Olivia eyed the black velvet case on the crisp white linen and shook her head. "I don't want it." The memory of yesterday's gift had made her more blunt than polite.

Gabriel didn't look at all surprised or insulted by her refusal. "You don't know that until you open it."

More of his mistress's leftovers? Olivia heaved a sigh. "You really don't need to give me anything."

"I need to explain about the bracelet."

She did not want to hear about the wretched thing ever again. "There's nothing to explain. It was beautiful. It was rude of me not to accept something you put so much thought into."

Gabriel leaned back in his chair, his expression a mask. But his eyes glittered like sunlight on water. "I'm not certain whether to be appalled or delighted that you are such a skillful diplomat."

She kept her lashes down and her lips relaxed. All her life she'd been watched for any sign of reaction or weakness. She'd mastered her facial muscles well before her fourteenth birthday. And she'd needed to. Her stepmother had enjoyed poking her with emotional sticks. Any reaction was sure to displease Lord Darcy, who wanted nothing more than for his two girls to get on. He was fond of reminding the women that he loved them both. And wished with all his heart that they would get along.

"You are marrying me because of my diplomacy and public image."

"In part." Gabriel turned over her hand and set the box on her palm. "I'm also marrying you because of your impeccable breeding and the fact that ever since the day I met you, I haven't been able to stop thinking about you."

Stunned by his admission, she stared at Gabriel's gift, knowing no expensive bauble could compare to the gift of knowing he was smitten with her. "That's lovely of you to say."

"Now back to the bracelet. Do you know where it came from?"

His question confused her. "From you."

He shook his head. "This is what I selected for you."

"Then where did the bracelet come from?"

"That's what I'd like to know."

Relief swept through her. "Then you didn't give me Marissa's bracelet."

"No." He gave her a stern look. "And I'm a little bothered by the fact that you think I'd be so cruel."

Olivia opened her mouth but had no ready response. Since dancing with him at the Independence Day gala she'd become foolish and irrational where he was concerned. With her hormones overstimulated and her emotions swinging from one extreme to the other, she shouldn't be surprised her brain was producing nothing but gibberish.

"Someone in the palace with access to my room played a cruel joke on me."

"Whoever it is, I don't think they are playing. This is a very serious breach in security. One that I will address." The determination in his voice matched the steel in his expression. After a second his gaze softened. "Please open my gift."

Olivia did as she was told.

Unlike the previous evening's trendy, emerald bracelet, this necklace was exactly something she would have chosen for herself. Olivia touched her fingertip to the large teardrop-shaped aquamarine, set into a frame of diamond-lined branches and suspended from a chain of faceted aquamarine beads and diamond-encrusted platinum balls. Gabriel had picked out the perfect, unique gift.

"The necklace belonged to my great-aunt Ginnie. Her husband gave it to her as an engagement present. I believe it came from his mother who received it as her engagement present."

"I love it." And she did. More than any million-dollar diamond necklace he could have found in the treasury. It represented tradition and love. And it demonstrated a sentimental side she would never have guessed Gabriel possessed. Feeling bold, she picked up the necklace and sat down on her fiancé's lap. "Can you help me put it on?"

She lifted her hair off her neck and held still while his knuckles brushed her nape. The casual touch sent shivers spiraling along her nerve endings. As the drop settled against her skin, she turned and planted a sweet kiss on Gabriel's cheek.

"Is that the best you can do?" he questioned, laughter in his voice.

Veiling her eyes with her lashes, she peered at him. "If I do much better we run the risk of not leaving this room in time to take Bethany and Karina for their first ride."

His response was to capture her lips in a sizzling kiss. Olivia sagged against him, surrendering to the firestorm of desire that had not burned out even after last night's lovemaking. She groaned beneath his lips as his hand found her breast, thumb coaxing her nipple to a hard point.

With a low growl, he broke off the kiss. "Perhaps you were right to be cautious." And with that, he stood with her in his arms and carried her to the bed.

In the end, they were in time to watch the twins circle the ring on the docile, well-mannered ponies, each led by an attentive groom. Although both were equally delighted by the ride, their individual personalities shone through. Bethany chattered incessantly as she rode, her every thought voiced. Karina was more circumspect and her seat was more natural. Of the two, Gabriel suspected she'd be the better rider.

Soon the twins' first riding lesson was done, leaving Gabriel free to turn his thoughts to the woman beside him and all that had transpired in the past twelve hours.

Since discovering last night how swiftly Olivia became aroused, he'd taken full advantage of her ardent responses and made love to her with fierce passion. Already his lust for her was dangerously close to uncontrollable. Telling himself making love to Olivia was a novelty that would soon wear off wasn't cooling his ardor one bit. Even now, as he watched her smile as her gaze followed the twins, he felt heat rise in his blood.

It shocked him to realize that he'd happily forgo the rest of his appointments to spend the time alone with Olivia in her suite. This was how he'd been with Marissa. Preoccupied. Distracted. Obsessed.

Then again, it was early in their relationship. The time of exploration when all things were fascinating and new. Their lust would eventually burn itself out and they could settle into companionable monotony. But even as he entertained this possibility his instincts rejected it. More than his blood hummed when she was near. This was a feeling he'd never known before. Besides being beautiful, Olivia was intelligent and caring. He'd been right the first time he'd pronounced her perfect. But he'd underestimated how deep that flawlessness went.

"Gabriel?" Olivia said, returning him to the here and now. "I was just explaining to Bethany and Karina that we can't have dinner with them tonight."

"Because we are…" He had no idea what was scheduled that evening. How was that possible? He usually knew his itinerary backward and forward.

"Going to the ballet," Olivia prompted.

"That's it." He smiled at her.

"But perhaps we could visit before we leave to read you one quick bedtime story."

"That we can do."

The twins' chorus of happiness sent a bird winging off through the trees from a few feet away.

"I think it's time to head back to the palace," Olivia said, shaking her head as the girls began to protest. "Your father has work to do."

Gabriel was impressed how well she managed the toddlers. The twins were darling but rambunctious. Marissa had done a fine job of blending discipline with love for they seemed to take direction well and had none of the fits of temper he had grown accustomed to with their mother. Despite losing Marissa recently, they were adjusting nicely to life in the palace. Of course, they had each other, something he could relate to with two brothers of his own. Sometimes it had seemed as if it was him, Nic and Christian against the world when in truth it was probably more reasonable to say it had been the three of them against their parents.

After leaving the twins in the hands of two young maids, Gabriel walked Olivia to her meeting with the wedding planner and bussed her cheek in a chaste kiss goodbye. He had fifteen minutes before his first meeting of the day and went in search of Christian.

His brother was nowhere near the palace. Christian had an office in the city that he usually preferred to work out of, claiming fewer distractions. Gabriel suspected he liked working without the king's or queen's "subtle" influence. With two brothers ahead of him for the throne, Christian had always enjoyed a lot of freedom. So had Nic. The middle brother didn't even live in Sherdana. He'd gotten his education in the States and resided in California while he pursued his dream of privatizing space travel.

Gabriel envied them both.

And he wouldn't trade places with, either. He'd been born to rule and had never wished to do anything else. But being king came with a price. He belonged to the people of Sherdana and owed it to them to do what was best for the country, even at the expense of his own desires. Breaking off his relationship with Marissa was only one of many sacrifices he'd made for Sherdana, but it had been his hardest and most painful.

It was why he was marrying a woman he admired instead of one he loved. And yet, hadn't last night and this morning proved that life with Olivia at his side would be the furthest thing from hardship?

Grinning, Gabriel headed into his father's office where the energy minister had come for a briefing.


Olivia yawned behind her hand as she surveyed Noelle's drawings for the twins' dresses for the wedding. It was almost midnight. She'd just returned from another event, this one raising money for an arts program for underprivileged children.

She wasn't insensible to the irony that what she intended to pay for these two dresses could probably fund the program for a year.

Behind her the door to her suite opened and closed. Her skin prickled in anticipation as muted footsteps advanced toward her. The faint scent of Gabriel's aftershave tickled her nose a second before his hands soothed along her shoulders.

"Waiting up for me?"

Gabriel placed a kiss on her neck, his lips sliding into a particularly sensitive spot that made her tremble.

Was it possible that less than a week ago their every private encounter had been stilted and awkward? Now she spent her days as a tightly wound spring of sexual anticipation and her nights in Gabriel's arms soaring toward the stars.

"Of course," she answered, setting aside the sketches and getting to her feet. She'd already dressed for bed in her favorite silk pajamas. They covered her from neck to toe. Not exactly seductive, but Gabriel never seemed to care.

"I'm leaving early in the morning," he explained, pulling her into his arms and dropping a sweet kiss on her lips. "And I will be gone for four days. I wanted a private moment with you before I left."

Four long days. And nights. She'd gotten accustomed to cuddling against his side, her cheek on his bare chest, his heartbeat lulling her to sleep.

She adored his intensity—making love with Gabriel was like being consumed by the sun—but these moments of stillness had their own rewards.

"Just a moment?" She tipped her head to grant him better access to her neck and ran her nails along his nape the way he liked.

"Did I mention I'm leaving very early in the morning?" Tender mockery filled his voice. He nudged his hips into her, letting her feel his erection. She smiled, no less turned on despite wanting to do nothing more than stretch out on her mattress and sleep for twelve hours.

"Of course," she murmured. "I just thought that perhaps you could give me a few minutes to say goodbye properly."

"Just a few minutes?"

Olivia's bones turned to water as he drew his tongue along her lower lip, tasting, but not taking. With his hands warm and strong on her lower back, she leaned into his powerful chest and savored the tantalizing slide of his mouth against hers.

"Take as many as you need."

She'd grown accustomed to sharing her bed with him and hated the thought of sleeping alone these next four nights. Every morning, after he woke her with kisses and made love to her in the soft light before day, she fell back to sleep wondering if once they were married, once she became pregnant, if he would share her bed every night. She already knew that a suite of rooms was being prepared for them in the family wing. They would each have their own space. Their own beds after the wedding. That wasn't what she wanted.

Olivia wasn't surprised when Gabriel swept her off her feet and carried her to the bed. The chemistry between them had skyrocketed in the days since they'd first made love. With their clothes scattered across the mattress, Olivia clutched at Gabriel as he brought her to orgasm twice before sliding into her. Being filled by him was a pleasure all its own and Olivia wrapped her thighs around his hips and held him close while he thrust into her.

He stayed for several hours, his large hands moving with such gentleness up and down her spine. Snuggled against his chest, with their legs intertwined, Olivia let herself drift. When she awoke several hours later, Gabriel was gone and she was already lonely.

Exhausted, but restless, Olivia left the bed and slipped into a robe. Her suite faced the gardens behind the palace so she had no hope of catching a final glimpse of Gabriel, but she opened the French door that led to the terrace and wandered across to the railing. At night the garden was lit up like a magical fairy tale, but dawn was approaching and the garden had gone dark. A cool breeze carried the scent of roses to her. Olivia leaned her arms on the cool stone. Vivid in her thoughts was the night Gabriel had found her out here and demonstrated that resisting him was a pointless exercise.

And now she knew it had been all along. When she'd agreed to marry him, she'd fooled herself into believing that sexual desire and mild affection would make her happy. After several nights in his arms she'd completely fallen under his spell. It was as if all her life she'd been moving toward this man and this moment.

Recognizing that her motivation for marrying Gabriel had changed, she had to ask herself if she was no longer concerned whether one day she'd become a queen…what did she really want?

*Love.*

The thought made her knees weak. Olivia braced herself against the stone railing. Deflated, she stared at her hands. At the engagement ring sparkling on her finger.

She couldn't be falling in love with Gabriel. He certainly wasn't falling in love with her.

This was an arranged marriage. A practical union for the good of his country. A sensible bargain that would lead to stability and children. She hadn't expected to fall madly in love with her husband or be deliriously happy. She expected to be content. To feel fulfilled as a mother and someday as a queen.

Sexual satisfaction hadn't entered into her plans—not until Gabriel had kissed her.

Olivia turned away from the softly lit garden and returned to her suite. As she closed and locked the glass door, her gaze fell on her desk and the locked drawer where she'd placed copies of important paperwork, including a file with some of her medical information. Had those scratches always marred the lock's brass surface? The idea that someone in the palace could have tried to break into her desk was ridiculous. And then she recalled the night the twins arrived. There'd been a maid at her dresser in the middle of the night. When nothing was missing she'd seen no reason to pursue it.

A few hours later, when Libby entered the suite, Olivia was still seated at the desk. She'd opened the locked drawer and hadn't found anything disturbed, but with the twins' arrival at the palace having been leaked to the press and the mysterious appearance of Marissa's bracelet, Olivia had checked each page of her thick file to make sure it was intact.

"Why are you looking through your papers?"

"I might be mistaken, but I thought I spotted fresh scratches on the lock and wanted to make sure my medical file hadn't been rifled." Olivia glanced up when Libby didn't immediately comment. "What's wrong?"

"Prince Christian is systematically interviewing the staff about the leaks to the press."

A chill chased across Olivia's skin. "He thinks someone inside the palace is providing information?" She remembered the photos of Gabriel and Marissa. Those hadn't been paparazzi shots. They had been taken among friends.

Olivia touched the lock again, wishing she could determine if the scratches were recent. If someone had gotten their hands on her medical records it could have catastrophic results. "Keep me updated on the investigation," she said, "and see if you can find a more secure place for these."

Gabriel was having a hard time keeping his mind on today's biotech plant tour. For the past several days he'd been touring manufacturing plants in Switzerland and Belgium in search of other businesses that would be interested in moving their operations to Sherdana. He probably should have sent Christian to do this. His brother had made a significant amount of money investing in up-and-coming technology. Christian would have been interested in the product lines and the way the manufacturing facilities were organized. Gabriel was finding it as dry as overdone toast.

That's probably how both his brothers felt about what went into the running of the country. These days, they had little in common. It often amazed Gabriel that three people could share a womb for nine months, communicate among themselves in their own language until they were teenagers and participate in a thousand childhood adventures together yet be so completely different in their talents and interests as they entered their twenties.

Nevertheless, this trip couldn't have come at a better time. The past few nights with Olivia had been some of the most passion-filled of his life. She'd slipped effortlessly beneath his defenses with her eager sensuality and curious nature. He'd become obsessed with the soft drag of her lips across his skin and the wicked suggestions she whispered in his ear as he entered her.

His constant craving for her company warned him he was fast losing touch with why he was marrying her. Cool, sophisticated elegance and a warm heart. Not feverish kisses and blazing orgasms.

Gabriel cleared his throat and tugged at his collar as the head of the factory droned on. He definitely needed some space from her. Unfortunately, the distance wasn't having the effect he'd hoped for. Being apart was supposed to cool him off. That was what he'd anticipated, but that wasn't the result.

He daydreamed about her at the oddest moments. Him. Daydreaming. Like some infatuated fool. He'd never expected her to preoccupy him in this way. She was supposed to be a sensible mate, an able partner in governing the country, not a hellcat in bed.

*Hope.*

The tattoo drove him crazy. Its placement. Its message.

It awakened him to possibilities. He wanted to throw sensible out the window and take chances. Because of Olivia he wanted to shake up the established way of doing things. She'd awakened his restless spirit that he'd believed he'd conquered after ending things with Marissa.

Every day he was finding out that Olivia was more than he'd expected.

And he'd be a fool not to worry about the power she now had over him. Yet he was helpless to stop what was developing between them. The best he could hope for was to slow things down until he shaped the relationship into something he was comfortable with.

But was *comfortable* going to make him happy in the long run? Was he really going to shortchange his future all for the sake of feeling safe and in control?

A few days after Gabriel left on his trip, Olivia was scheduled to have a private lunch with the queen. Ten minutes before the appointment, she slipped pearl earrings into place and stepped in front of the mirror to assess her appearance. She'd chosen a sleeveless pink dress edged in white with a narrow white belt to highlight her waist, and accessorized with a pair of floral pumps. The feminine ensemble required a soft hairstyle so she'd left her hair down and coaxed out the natural wave with a light blowout.

This morning she'd awakened to some discomfort in her lower abdomen and wasn't feeling on top of her game, but wasn't about to cancel on the queen.

Drawing a fortifying breath, she entered the private dining room that only the immediate royal family used. Pale blue had been chosen for the chairs as well as the curtains framing the large windows. It was the only splash of color in a room otherwise dominated by white walls and lavish plasterwork painted gold. More intimate than many of the other rooms on the first floor, it nevertheless didn't allow her to forget that this was a palace.

"You look lovely," the queen said as she breezed into the room. She wore a classic suit of dusty lavender and a stunning choker of pale round Tahitian pearls. Noticing Olivia's interest, she touched the necklace. "An anniversary gift from the king," the queen explained, her smile both fond and sensual.

"It's beautiful."

"Matteo has exceptionally good taste."

The queen gestured toward the dining table, capable of seating twelve, but set for two. As the two women sat down, a maid set a glass of soda on the table before the queen.

"Diet cola," she, sipping the fizzy drink with pleasure. "I got a taste for it when we visited the States two decades ago. It's my indulgence."

Olivia nodded in understanding. She wasn't much of a soda drinker herself, but she understood how someone could come to crave a particular item. Like a tall, bronze-eyed prince for example.

The servers placed plates of salad in front of the two women and the queen launched a barrage of questions to determine what Olivia knew about Sherdana's current political climate and their economic issues. Although Olivia had been expecting to discuss the wedding preparations, she was just as happy to share what she knew about the country she would soon call her own.

"Does my son know how bright you are?" the queen asked, her expression thoughtful as the maids cleared the main course and served dessert. She frowned at the plate in front of her and sighed. "Oh, dear. The chef is experimenting again."

Olivia stared at the oddest fruit she'd ever seen. About

the size of her fist with a leathery hot-pink skin, it had been sliced in half to reveal white flesh dotted with tiny black seeds. A hollow had been carved out of the center and filled with yogurt and sliced strawberries.

"Dragon fruit," the queen explained. "And from what I understand quite delicious."

Olivia took her first bite and was surprised at the wonderfully sweet flavor. It had a texture like a kiwi with the seeds adding a little crunch to each bite.

"You look pale." The queen pointed at Olivia with her spoon. "I expect you'll get more rest with my son away."

Olivia's entire body flushed hot. The queen had just insinuated that she knew where Gabriel had been spending his nights.

"Oh, don't look so mortified," the queen continued. "You are to be married and my son was determined to have a short engagement. Besides, there are no secrets in the palace."

"No, I suppose there are not." Olivia knew better than to think her nights with Gabriel were something between just the two of them. She'd grown up surrounded by servants who knew most everything about her daily habits.

"How are the twins' dresses coming for the wedding?" The queen had taken a few days to approve the idea of Bethany and Karina being a part of the ceremony, but Gabriel had at last persuaded her.

"They should be finished later this week. The lace Noelle has chosen is beautiful. I think you'll be pleased."

"Noelle is very talented. You will all look beautiful." The queen nodded in satisfaction. "I must say, you've accepted this situation with Gabriel's children much better than most women would in your position."

"It's hard to imagine anyone not adoring those precious two," Olivia admitted, but she understood what the queen was getting at. "I love children. Helping to make their lives better is the foundation for all my charity work. I would be a wretched person and a hypocrite if I turned my back on Bethany and Karina because of who their mother was." And what Marissa had meant to Gabriel.

"They certainly have taken to you," the queen said. "And you seem to have everything it takes to be an excellent mother."

"Thank you."

The queen's praise should have allowed Olivia to relax, but the tick of her biological clock sounded loud in her ears.

# Eight

"How was the trip?" Christian asked as he and Gabriel crossed the tarmac toward the waiting limo. "I hope you brought me a present."

"Naturally." Gabriel hoisted his briefcase and deposited it in his brother's hands. "It's filled with all sort of things I'm sure you'll find vastly interesting."

"Unlike you?"

"Technology is more your and Nic's thing." Gabriel was aware that the trip had been less productive than he'd hoped. Mostly because he'd had a hard time concentrating. Thoughts of Olivia had intruded with a frequency he'd found troubling. "You probably should have gone instead of me, but it was something I needed to do. I want to encourage more technology firms to move to Sherdana. The best way for me to do that is to speak to companies that might be looking at expansion."

"I'll bet you hated it."

Gabriel shot Christian a quelling look. "I can't expect to enjoy every aspect of my position. Some things must be done no matter how painful. This was one of them."

"Is your future wife another?"

This time Christian laughed out loud at his brother's sharp look.

"How I feel about my future bride is none of your business."

"Come on, you've got to be a lot happier about having to get married these days. From what I hear, you two have been acting like a couple kids in love."

Gabriel growled in displeasure, but couldn't ignore the electric charge that surged through him at the mere thought of seeing Olivia again and feeling her soft lips yield beneath his. Each of the past four nights he'd gone to bed alone and found himself unable to sleep. Plagued by memories of Olivia's smiles and her sassy sensuality, he'd lain with his hands behind his head, staring up at the blank ceiling and doing his best to ignore his erection.

Cold showers had become his 2:00 a.m. ritual. How had she bewitched him in such a short time?

"Neither one of us is in love," Gabriel muttered. "But I won't deny we're compatible." He leveled a hard gaze at his brother, warning him to drop the matter.

"Not in love?" Christian cocked his head. "Maybe you're not. But are you sure about her?"

Christian's question roused a memory of the last evening before his trip. He'd almost succumbed to Olivia's plea to spend the night. She'd seemed so vulnerable, her characteristic confidence lacking. But that didn't mean she was in love with him.

"Ridiculous," he said. "We've only spent a couple weeks in each other's company."

"You don't believe in love at first sight?"

Gabriel regarded his brother's serious expression with curiosity. "Do you?"

"Absolutely."

"Is that why you do your best to chase every woman away who gets too close?" Gabriel wondered if his brother was taunting him or if he was offering Gabriel a rare glimpse into his psyche. "Have none of them made you feel as if you were clobbered by something beyond your understanding or control?"

Something flared in Christian's gaze but was quickly gone. His mocking smile returned. "Who wants to settle down with one woman when there's a banquet of lovelies to sample?"

"One of these days someone will appeal to your palate and you'll find that you can't get enough of that particular delicacy."

"Is that what happened to you?"

"I'm getting married because I have to." Gabriel was well aware that he'd dodged the question and not with any finesse.

Christian's eyes narrowed. "And if you didn't have to?"

"Since that's never been an option, I've never really thought about it."

And he didn't want to think about it now because it opened old wounds. Would he have stayed with Marissa if marriage to her had been possible? Had he loved her or had he inflated his feelings for her because circumstances made it impossible for them to have a future?

"Well, I certainly stirred you up," Christian taunted.

"Wasn't that your intention?" Gabriel countered, staring past the hedge that bordered the driveway to the palace. For a moment he glimpsed a pair of ponies and the two little girls riding them. Despite his tumultuous thoughts, he couldn't help but feel joy at the appearance of his daughters and feel sorry for Christian. His cynical attitude would undoubtedly prevent him from experiencing the wonder of holding his own children in his arms and feeling their enthusiastic kisses all over his cheek.

"God," Christian exclaimed, "you are smitten."

"I caught a glimpse of my angels out riding."

Christian snorted. "They're not exactly angels. In fact, they've been turning the palace upside down with their version of hide-and-seek, which entails them finding some tiny nook and not coming out until every servant is called upon to look for them. It's been worse these last few days with Olivia feeling unwell."

Gabriel frowned. "What did you say about Olivia? She's ill?"

"Didn't you know?"

"I spoke with her last night. She said nothing." Gabriel rubbed at the back of his neck. "How bad is it?"

"I don't know. She hasn't been out of her suite for the last two days."

"Has she been in bed that whole time?"

"I don't know," Christian sounded amused. "But if you'd hinted that you'd like me to check on your English flower in her bedroom, you should have said something."

Gabriel didn't even look at his brother as he exited the car and strode into the palace. Tension rode his shoulders as he entered the foyer, barely hearing the greetings from the staff on duty. Why hadn't Olivia told him she wasn't doing well? He took the stairs two at a time and turned in the direction of his fiancée's suite. His knock was answered by a maid.

"I'm here to see Lady Darcy," he told her, his scowl compelling the young woman to step back.

Three women occupied the room. Olivia sat on the couch with her feet up, her back to him while Ariana sat opposite her facing the door. Olivia's private secretary was by the desk. His sister's lilting laugh broke off as he entered.

"Good afternoon, ladies." He forced himself to approach Ariana first. His sister looked splendid as always in an evening-blue dress. The color flattered her golden skin and dark brown hair. She wore a simple gold bangle at her wrist and gold hoop earrings.

"Welcome back, Gabriel," she said, standing as he drew near and making her cheek available for a kiss.

"We missed you," Olivia echoed, turning to gaze up at

him. Her normally pale complexion lacked its customary healthy glow and there were shadows purpling the skin beneath her eyes.

Concern flared. He sat beside her on the sofa and touched her cheek with his fingertips. "Last night on the phone, why didn't you tell me you've been ill?"

"It's nothing."

"You're too pale. I demand to know what's wrong."

Olivia sighed and cast her gaze toward Ariana. Her eyes widened, causing Gabriel to turn his head. Ariana had vanished. The door to the bedroom was shut. They were alone.

Gabriel refocused on Olivia. "Answer me," he growled.

Red patches appeared on her formerly dull cheeks. "I've been having a particularly difficult period," she murmured.

Relief flooded him. She was embarrassed to discuss her body's natural process? Was that why she'd kept silent the night before? Amused, Gabriel dipped a finger beneath her chin and raised it.

"I'm going to be your husband. You better prepare to discuss all sorts of things like this with me."

"Be careful or you may live to regret those words," she muttered, but her lips were soft and eager beneath his. "Welcome home."

An endearment hung between them, unspoken. She'd promised not to call him Prince Gabriel or Your Highness as they made love, but she had yet to find a pet name for him. What would it be? Darling? Dearest? Sweetheart?

My love?

"Did you have a successful trip?" she asked.

"It was very long." He leaned forward and kissed her neck below her ear, smiling as she trembled. "And lonely."

She framed his face with her hands. "I missed you so much. In fact—"

A knock sounded on the door, interrupting her. Heaving

a weary sigh, Gabriel kissed Olivia on the nose and then raised his voice to be heard in the hall. "Come."

Stewart poked his head around the door. "The king wondered if you'd gotten lost on your way to the meeting with the prime minister."

Gabriel stood and bent over Olivia's hand. "Duty calls."

"Of course." The bright smile she gave him didn't quite reach her eyes. "Perhaps we can have dinner together?"

Regret pinched him. "I'm afraid I can't tonight. I already have an appointment."

"Of course."

He'd grown familiar with the micro expressions that belied her thoughts and could see she was disappointed. He hated being the one who robbed her eyes of their sparkle, and the intensity of his desire to see her smile caught him off guard. Falling in love with his fiancée wasn't what he'd had in mind when he decided to marry Olivia.

"I'll stop back to check on you later," he said.

Her gaze clung to his face. "I'll be waiting."

The morning after Gabriel returned from his business trip, Olivia caught herself smiling almost as often as she yawned. True to his word, he'd returned after his dinner to check on her and they'd snuggled on the sofa until almost three in the morning while Olivia filled him in on the twins and he spoke of what he'd seen in Switzerland and Belgium.

In addition to talking, there'd been a fair amount of kissing, as well. Lighthearted, romantic kisses that left Olivia breathless and giddy. He'd treated her with tender patience, not once letting passion get the better of him. Olivia had found his control both comforting and frustrating. Four days without him had aroused her appetite for his hands roaming over her skin and she cursed her cycle's timing.

On the other hand, there would be nothing to get in the

way of their magical wedding night. Unless there wasn't going to be a wedding.

This was her first period since discontinuing the birth control pills that regulated her cycle. At first she'd been down because as amazing as her nights with Gabriel had been, she hadn't gotten pregnant. Soon, however, she began to worry as old, familiar symptoms appeared. Assuring herself everything was going to be fine became harder each day as her period stretched out. For the past two days fear had begun to sink deep into bone and sinew. She began to confront the very real possibility that her surgery might not have cleared up her problem. She had to face that getting and staying pregnant might be more difficult than she'd assumed.

Then, after seeing Gabriel yesterday, it became clear what she had to do. She needed to tell him the truth. Despite the connection they shared, she wasn't sure how he was going to react to her news. She could only hope he would act like his father and work with her to solve any issues that came up.

"Olivia?"

A soft voice roused her. With the paparazzi hungry for their first glimpse of Gabriel's daughters, Olivia had requested that Noelle bring their flower-girl dresses to the palace to be fitted. Blinking, she refocused on the slim, dark-haired woman.

"Sorry, Noelle. With the wedding two weeks away my mind tends to jump around a great deal these days. What were you saying?"

"I asked if you wanted me to bring your dress here next week for the final fitting rather than have you come to my shop."

"It would help me if you brought the dress by. I'm drowning in wedding preparations and that would save me time."

"I'd be happy to."

A moment later the twins appeared in their new finery. They looked like angels in their matching sleeveless white dresses with full lace skirts and wide satin sashes in pale yellow. Noelle's assistant had pinned up their hair and attached wreaths wrapped in pale yellow ribbons.

"These are merely to demonstrate one possible look for the girls," Noelle explained. "If you like it, I'm sure the florist could create beautiful wreaths with yellow roses."

"The dresses are perfect," Olivia breathed. "Thank you so much for making them on such short notice."

"I'm happy you like them."

While Noelle and her assistant made little adjustments to the dresses, Olivia distracted Bethany and Karina by explaining to them what their role in the wedding would be. They seemed to understand the seriousness of the event because they listened to her with wide eyes and their full attention.

An hour later, Noelle had left, taking the dresses with her, and Olivia was reading the twins a story when the door to her suite swung open without warning. Startled, Olivia swiveled on the sofa to face a very unhappy Gabriel.

"What's wrong?"

"It's time for the twins to head back to the nursery," he answered, his voice level and cool as he gestured to the nanny who jumped to her feet. "I think it's time for their lunch."

Olivia set the book aside and got to her feet to urge the girls over to their father for a kiss and a hug. His manner softened for them, but a minute later they were gone and Gabriel was back to scowling.

"Is it true?" he demanded.

Her stomach twisted at the hard suspicion in his eyes. "Is what true?"

"That you're infertile?"

Of all the things that had raced through her mind, this was the last thing she'd expected. How had he found out? Libby was the only person who knew about her condition and Olivia knew her private secretary would never betray her.

"Where did you hear that?"

He stalked across the room toward the television and snatched up the remote. Dread filled Olivia as he cued the power button. She'd not imagined he could look so angry.

"Sources inside the palace confirm that the future princess has little to no chance of producing an heir for Sherdana's throne. With her medical condition you have to wonder what the prince was thinking to propose."

The words blaring from the television were so horrifying that Olivia would have crumpled to the floor at his feet if Gabriel hadn't seized her arms in a bruising grip.

His gaze bore into hers. "Tell me the truth."

"I had a condition," she began, and at his dark scowl, rushed on. "But I had surgery to correct the problem. I should be able to get pregnant." But after these past few days and the return of her old symptoms, her confidence had waned.

"Can you or can't you?"

"Six months ago when you proposed I thought I could. At this moment I honestly don't know."

"You should have told me." He set her free as if the touch of her was distasteful. "Did you think you could keep this a secret forever?"

"I really didn't think it was going to be a problem." Olivia clasped her hands to keep them from shaking and looked up at Sherdana's crown prince, who stood there like a granite statue. Little about his current demeanor encouraged hope that he might listen to her with a rational ear. "I would never have agreed to marry you if I believed I couldn't have children."

"But your doctor warned you the chances were slim." It wasn't a question.

She didn't ask him how he knew that. The reporter on the television was divulging her detailed medical records. Her privacy had been violated and yet she was being treated like a villain.

"He never said slim. He said there was a good chance I could get pregnant, but to do so I had to stop taking the pill and he wasn't sure how my body would react since I've been on it almost ten years."

"But you were a virgin. I can attest to that. Why were you on birth control?"

"I had severe cramps and bleeding. It helps control those problems." Olivia wrapped her arms around herself. "I quit taking the birth control before I left London. I wanted to get pregnant as soon as possible. Provide you with your heir. I knew that's what you all would expect."

Gabriel's expression didn't change, but his lips tightened briefly. "We expected you to be truthful, as well."

She flinched at his sharp words.

"I intended to tell you tonight. I haven't felt right these last few days and thought I needed to discuss the situation with you."

"I need an heir, Olivia." His harsh tone softened.

"I understand completely." Their marriage was an arrangement, an exchange of her hand in marriage for her father's business. But she was also expected to be a mother. "I never would've agreed to marry you knowing I might not be able to have children."

He needed to marry someone who could provide the next generation of Alessandros. At the moment she wasn't completely convinced she could do that.

A sharp pain lanced through her and she winced. Her cramps had been a dull ache all through the morning, but now they gained in strength.

"Are you okay?"

She shook her head. "It's been a hectic morning and I've done too much. I should probably take something and lie down for a while. Can we continue later this afternoon?"

She barely waited for his agreement before heading toward the bathroom and the bottle of pain medication she hadn't needed earlier in the day. She shut the bathroom door, hoping that Gabriel wouldn't come to check on her, and braced her hands on the vanity top. The woman in the mirror had dark circles beneath her eyes and white around her mouth.

The pain in her body was vivid and icy, very unlike her usual cramps. The difference scared her.

Forcing herself to take deep, even breaths, she fought back nausea and swallowed her medication. Within minutes, the sharp edges came off the ache in her pelvis and she was able to return to the bedroom. There she found Libby waiting for her with the queen. Helpless tears filled Olivia's eyes. She blinked them away.

"Have you tried pineapple juice?"

The queen's suggestion confused Olivia. "No."

"There's something in it that will help with your cramps."

Olivia clasped her hands as her stomach flipped sickeningly. Why was the queen being nice, given the news?

"Thank you. I'll try pineapple juice."

"You aren't the first woman in this palace to grapple with reproductive issues. I was young when I came to marry the king and eager to give him the heir he needed. Unlike Gabriel, Matteo had no male siblings to take over the throne if something happened to him."

"You had trouble getting pregnant?"

"There's a good reason why Gabriel has two brothers so close in age." The queen gave a fond smile. "I wasn't able to get pregnant without help. We did in vitro fertilization twice before the procedure was successful. Gabriel, Nicolas and Christian are the result."

"And Ariana?" The princess was six years younger than her brothers, close to Olivia's own age.

"My miracle baby."

Olivia liked the sound of that. She hoped her own miracle baby was on the horizon. Because the way she felt at the moment, a miracle might be exactly what she needed.

"Do you love my son?"

She rolled the engagement ring around and around on her finger. "Yes."

"Good, then you'll do what's best for him."

And leaving Olivia to ponder what that was, the queen took her leave.

When the door opened a short time later, Olivia looked up, expecting Libby, and saw a maid instead. "I really don't need anything right now. Perhaps you could check back in later this evening."

"I thought you'd like me to pack your things. I'm sure you'll be heading back to England now that the prince knows you can't have children."

The woman's snide tone wasn't at all what Olivia was expecting and she sat up straighter, adrenaline coursing through her veins. Of average height and appearance with brown hair and hazel eyes, the woman looked like any of a dozen palace maids. But there was a frantic energy to her movement that made Olivia apprehensive.

"Don't be ridiculous," she said, feeling at a disadvantage as the maid stalked toward her. "I'm not leaving."

Olivia pushed to her feet. The sudden movement sent pain stabbing through her. She swayed and caught the back of the chair. Her breath came in labored gasps. Something was very wrong.

"Of course you are." The woman's hazel eyes burned

with a crazy zeal. "The prince won't marry you now that he knows you're damaged."

"That's for him to decide." It was hard to keep her mind on the conversation when it felt as if hot pokers were being driven into her lower abdomen. "Get out."

"What makes you think you can order me around?" the woman spat. "Because you have a title and your father has money?"

Step by deliberate step, Olivia backed away from the maid's furious outburst. It was then that she recognized the woman's face. She'd been the one who'd been searching the desk the night the twins arrived.

"Who are you?" she asked.

"My sister was twice the woman you could ever hope to be."

The woman made as if to rush at her and Olivia stumbled backward.

"Marissa was your sister?" Impossible. This woman was as plain and dull as Marissa had been beautiful and vibrant.

"My younger sister. She was beautiful and full of life. Or she was until Prince Gabriel destroyed her."

"What do you mean?"

Olivia knew she had to keep the woman talking. Somewhere behind her was the bathroom with a solid door and a lock. She just needed to get there.

"In the months following her trip to visit him in Venice, she grew more and more depressed. She couldn't live with the fact that he wanted nothing more to do with her." The sister glared at Olivia as if she'd been the cause of Marissa's heartache.

"I'm sorry your sister was upset—"

"Upset?" The woman practically spat the word. "She wasn't upset. She was devastated. Devastated enough to try to kill herself. I was the one who found her bleeding to death. She'd slit her wrists. It was at the hospital that she found out she was pregnant. She loved her girls. They were everything to her."

Olivia reached her hand back and found the bathroom door frame. "Bethany and Karina are wonderful."

"He doesn't deserve them. He doesn't deserve to be happy. And now he won't because you can't have children. He won't want you anymore." Marissa's sister was shouting now, her voice rising in unbalanced hysteria.

Another wave of pain made Olivia double over. She backed into the bathroom and clawed at the door. Blackness pushed at the edges of her vision. By feel alone she shut the door and slid the lock into place. The door rattled as Marissa's sister beat against it in fury and Olivia staggered back.

With her strength failing, Olivia slid to the floor and set her back against the vanity, hoping that the door would hold. Hoping that someone would come find her. Hoping that Marissa's sister was wrong about Gabriel.

# Nine

Gabriel leaned forward in the saddle and urged his stallion to greater speed. Wind lashed at his face, and he focused on the thrum of hoofbeats filling his ears to slow his racing mind. He'd gone for a ride after leaving Olivia because he needed to sort through the conflict raging in him.

Although the powerful Warmblood had stamina enough for a longer run, Gabriel slowed him to a walk after only a mile. He passed the lake where he and his brothers had swum during the hot summers of their youth and wished he could go back to those innocent times.

Accusing Olivia of lying had been unfair. She wouldn't do that. If he'd learned anything about her, it was that she had a great deal of integrity.

What woman, when faced with the prospect of never becoming a mother, wouldn't deny the possibility? Especially someone who adored children the way Olivia did. He'd watched her with the twins. He'd seen how his daughters had bonded with Olivia. She'd won them over with her generous, kind heart. They'd been as helpless against her sweetness as he'd been.

By now his parents would be discussing damage control. And debating how to proceed. Olivia had understood the position this news report had put him in. They would advise him against marrying a woman whose fertility was in question. But he wouldn't make any decisions until he knew the extent of her problems.

And if she could never have children?

He would need to address the bargain he'd struck with her father. The deal with Lord Darcy was contingent on Olivia becoming Gabriel's wife.

Talk about being stuck between a rock and a hard place. No matter what decision he made, he would fail Sherdana.

Two hours later he entered the salon in the family section of the south wing and found everyone assembled.

His sister came forward to give him a hug. "Did you check on Olivia?"

"I went for a ride."

His father regarded him with a frown, his opinion clear. Gabriel ignored him and went to sit beside his mother. He'd come to a preliminary decision and knew it wouldn't meet with everyone's approval.

"I needed some time to think."

The king fixed Gabriel with a hard stare. "How do you intend to handle this?"

"Handle?" Gabriel hadn't considered how they should approach the press about this latest bombshell. "We could start by sending out a press release downplaying the serious nature of Olivia's problems, but I'm not sure with her doctor's records as proof, this is going to do us much good."

"I meant with Olivia," the king said, his voice a low rumble.

Gabriel became aware that his entire family was watching him and waiting for his answer. It was as if the occupants of the room had stopped breathing.

"What do you mean?" Gabriel asked, certain he knew where his father was going with the question, but needing to hear it asked out loud.

"You need a wife who can bear children."

In other words, he must break his engagement with Olivia and reexamine the dozen or so women he'd rejected when he chose her.

"And what am I to say to Lord Darcy? That his daughter's only value to me lies in her ability to produce heirs?" His father's glower told Gabriel he'd stepped into dangerous territory with his sarcasm. At the moment, Gabriel didn't care. What could his father do? For a moment, Gabriel reveled in rebellion. As a teenager, he'd been the best behaved of his siblings, getting into trouble rarely and then never with anything serious.

Nic had started a fire in his room at fifteen experimenting with rockets. Christian had "borrowed" their uncle's Ferrari when he was fourteen and gone joyriding. The expensive sports car had ended up half submerged in a ditch and Christian had been disciplined, but that had only temporarily slowed him down, not stopped him completely.

Gabriel had shouldered his future responsibility like a dutiful son and the newspapers had been filled with photos of him accompanying his mother on her visits to the hospital and various other charitable events and headlines about how lucky Sherdana was to have such a shining example of youth for their next monarch.

"I had fertility problems, as well," the queen reminded her husband, breaking the tension between father and son.

"But neither of us had any idea before we married," the king said, sending his wife a stern look.

"Yet despite your need for an heir, you didn't set me aside when my troubles came to light."

"We'd been married two years. How could I have let you go?"

Gabriel saw the unspoken communication that passed between his parents and felt a flare of envy. The emotion didn't surprise him. He'd felt twinges of it before when watching his parents in private. They were so in sync with each other. He'd hoped for just a little of that depth of intimacy in his own marriage and had begun to believe he'd find it with Olivia.

"Olivia and I will talk later this afternoon."

"You are intending to break off the engagement."

"I'm not sure that's necessary." He saw his father's brows come together. "She claims she had surgery to correct the problem. We need to discuss the situation in more depth and consult a doctor before I make such a radical decision."

The door flew open without a warning knock, catching everyone's attention. Stewart stood in the open doorway, his face stark with concern.

"Forgive my interruption," he said, bowing in apology. "Something has happened to Lady Darcy."

Gabriel's heart jumped in his chest. He surged to his feet and crossed the room in three strides. "What's wrong?"

"I don't know. Miss Marshall said she's locked herself in the bathroom and won't answer the door."

"What makes you think something has happened to her?"

"Her clothes are all over the suite and they've been shredded."

Cursing, Gabriel lunged past his secretary and raced down the hallway. Stewart's long legs usually made him a match for Gabriel, but he had to resort to jogging to keep up.

When Gabriel entered the suite, he registered the destruction in passing but didn't stop. He rushed over to join Olivia's private secretary, who was at the bathroom door, knocking and calling for her to answer. Shoving her aside, Gabriel kicked in the door.

When the door frame gave and the door shot open, the metallic tang of blood immediately hit him. Olivia lay on the cold tile, a large crimson patch on her pale blue skirt. Panic tore through him.

"Call an ambulance!" He dropped to his knees beside her and was relieved to see her chest rise and fall. "When did you enter the suite?" he demanded of her private secretary.

"Perhaps ten minutes ago. I called to her but she didn't open the door or answer. And from what had happened to her clothes I knew something had to be wrong."

How long had she been bleeding like this? Gabriel clenched his teeth and fought the fear rising inside him. She couldn't die. He wouldn't let that happen.

"Get me a blanket off the bed. We're going to take her to the hospital."

Libby did as she was told. "What about the ambulance?"

"There isn't time." Besides, he didn't think he could sit around and watch Olivia slowly bleed to death without going crazy. He'd always prided himself on thought before action, but right now, he was thinking of nothing but saving the woman he'd been yelling at no more than three hours earlier.

*Forget that. Focus on getting Olivia to the hospital.*

He wrapped her lower half in the blanket and scooped her into his arms. His family had arrived in the hallway just outside the suite. He brushed past his father and brother without answering their offers of help. Olivia was his fiancée. His responsibility.

And he blamed himself for her current crisis. Somehow he knew that if he'd been more approachable, if so much pressure hadn't been brought to bear on her, Olivia might have talked to him about her fertility problems and a safe solution might have been reached.

The limo was waiting at the bottom of the stairs. He settled her into the backseat and cradled her body in his lap. Only then did he become aware of the thundering of his heart. The painful pounding in his chest wasn't caused by carrying her through the palace, but by the sight of her utter stillness and pallor. As the car raced through the palace gates, it finally hit home just how bad this situation was.

"Faster," he growled to the driver as he hooked his finger around a strand of her blond hair and pulled it away from her lips.

The car's powerful engine roared as they sped through the city, but the fifteen-minute drive had never felt so long.

Gabriel brushed his lips across Olivia's forehead and silently pleaded with her to hang on and fight. *Like you fought for her?* Gabriel tried to tune out the mocking inner voice, but guilt sliced at him.

At the hospital's emergency entrance, five people in scrubs crowded the car as soon as it stopped. Stewart must have called ahead and warned them he was coming. They got Olivia situated on a stretcher and took her away before he had a chance to say a word. He rushed toward the glass doors in their wake, catching bits of medical jargon as they sped the unconscious woman inside.

He'd expected to be allowed into the treatment room with her, but a nurse blocked his way.

"Let the doctors work," she said, her voice kind but firm.

He might have ten inches and eighty pounds on her, but Gabriel sensed that the nurse could stop him if he tried to go past.

"How soon will I know something?"

"I'll make sure someone keeps you informed."

"She's lost a lot of blood," he said.

"We know."

She herded him into a private waiting room and offered coffee. Gabriel stared at her, unable to comprehend why this woman was behaving in such a mundane manner while Olivia was down the hall struggling for her life.

"No," he snapped, and then moderated his tone. "Thank you. All I need is information."

She nodded and headed off.

Left alone, Gabriel dropped his head into his hands and surrendered to despair. She couldn't die. She couldn't leave him. He wasn't sure how to step into the future, to become king without her by his side. They would figure a way around her infertility. He recalled his mother's words. She, too, had struggled to produce the heir her husband so desperately needed. When natural methods had failed, she'd gotten help from specialists. And now, she had four children to show for it.

He and Olivia would find specialists, as well. They would have children together.

"Gabriel?"

A hand touched his shoulder. He lifted his head and stared up into his sister's face. She touched his cheek and her fingertips came away with a trace of moisture.

"Is she?" Ariana gasped, seeing his expression.

He shook his head, guessing what conclusion she'd leaped to. "They're working on her now."

"Any word how she's doing?"

"No. The nurse said they'd keep me informed, but she hasn't been back." He glanced at his watch. "That was thirty minutes ago."

What had been happening while he'd been lost in thought? Anxiety flared that he'd had no news. How bad had things gone since she'd been taken away from him?

"She's going to be all right, Gabriel," Ariana said, moving toward him.

Standing, Gabriel wrapped his arms around his sister. She pushed her body against his to offer comfort.

"Your Majesties. Prince Gabriel. Princess Ariana." A

solemn man of average height in pale green scrubs stood five feet away from the royal pair. "I'm Dr. Warner."

Gabriel felt Ariana's tight embrace squeeze his ribs even harder and appreciated her support. "How's Olivia?"

"I won't sugarcoat it. Not good. She's lost a lot of blood." The doctor looked even grimmer as he delivered the next bit of news. "She's still hemorrhaging. We've sent her up to the OR."

A primal cry of denial gathered in Gabriel's chest. "What aren't you telling us?" he demanded.

"The only way to save her may be a hysterectomy. Naturally we will do everything possible to avoid such a drastic procedure."

"Do whatever it takes to save her life." Gabriel pinned the doctor with his gaze, making sure the man understood. "Whatever it takes."

# Ten

The first time Olivia opened her eyes, she was aware of nothing but pain. It stabbed at her like slivers of broken glass. Then, something changed. The hurt eased and she fell backward into darkness.

The next time she surfaced, she kept herself awake longer. But not by much. Voices reached her ears, but the speakers were too far away for her to catch individual words. And the pain was back. All she wanted to do was escape into numbness.

They said the third time's the charm. Olivia wasn't sure she agreed when next she regained consciousness. Her body ached. No. Not her body, her abdomen.

Breathless with fear, she stared around the hospital room. It was empty. She was alone.

She felt hollow. Like a balloon filled with air.

The last thing she recalled was fighting with Gabriel. Where was he? Did he know she was in the hospital? Did he even care? Her heart contracted.

"Good to see you awake," a nurse said as she entered the room. "How's your pain?"

"Manageable." Her mouth felt stuffed with cotton. "May I have some water?"

The nurse brought a cup close and placed the straw between Olivia's lips. She sipped gratefully, then sagged back against the pillow, exhausted by the simple movement.

"I feel so weak."

"You've been through a lot."

"What happened to me?"

"The doctor will be along in a little while to talk to you."

Without energy to argue, Olivia closed her eyes and let her mind drift. The silence pressed on her, heightening her tension. She fought to clear her head, sought her last memory. Her period had been heavier than ever before. And the cramping... She'd been afraid, depressed. Gingerly she sent her fingertips questing for the source of her discomfort. Pain shot through her as she pressed on her lower abdomen.

Just then, the door opened again and a handsome older man in scrubs came in. "Good afternoon. I'm Dr. Warner."

"I wish I could say it's nice to meet you."

"I understand. You've been through a tough time."

"What happened to me?" Her mind sharpened as anxiety filled her.

"You were hemorrhaging, and we had a difficult time stopping your blood loss." He plucked her chart out of a pocket attached to the foot of the bed and scrutinized it. "How's your pain?"

"About a six." She waited while he jotted something down on her chart before asking, "How did you stop the hemorrhaging?"

"Surgery." He met her gaze. "It was an extensive procedure."

He hadn't said anything specific, but his expression told her just how extensive the surgery had been.

"I'm never going to have children, am I?"

"I'm sorry. The only way we could stop the bleeding was to remove your uterus."

Olivia shut her eyes to escape the sympathy in the man's face. Denial exploded in her head. She clutched the bed rails, desperate for something to ground her as the world tipped sideways. A wail began in her chest. She clenched her teeth to contain it as a lifetime of discipline and order asserted itself. She would grieve later. In private.

"I know that this will be a difficult adjustment. You are very young to have undergone such a drastic change."

"Who knows?" she whispered.

He looked taken aback. "Your father. The royal family."

"The media?"

"Of course not." Dr. Warner looked appalled.

"Is my father here?"

"He's in the waiting room with Prince Gabriel. I spoke with him an hour ago."

"Could I see him, please? No one else, just my father."

"I'll have the nurse fetch him for you."

But the man who showed up next wasn't a sixty-year-old British earl with gray hair and a neat beard, but a tall, hollow-eyed man with a dark shadow blurring his knife-sharp jawline. Olivia's heartbeat accelerated as Gabriel advanced into the room, his clothes rumpled, his face a mask. He reached out to cover her hand with his, but she moved it away just in time.

"I'm sorry," she said, unable to lift her gaze higher than the open collar of his white shirt. "I should have told you about my medical issues. I just thought that everything was going to be okay."

"You gave us a scare." He pulled a chair beside her bed and lowered himself into it. This put him at eye level with her and made avoiding his fierce golden gaze that much harder. "When I found you on the floor of the bathroom unconscious." His tone made it hard for Olivia to breathe. "I thought…" He shook his head.

"I'm sorry. I had no idea that quitting the pill was going to cause this much…" To her dismay a sob popped out. Just like that. No warning. No chance to swallow it or choke on it. Then tears were streaming down her face and Gabriel was stroking her hair and squeezing her hand. His gentleness only made her feel worse.

"Olivia, I'm so sorry."

He placed her palm against his cheek. The warmth beneath her fingers spread up her arm and drifted through her entire body as she took in the aching sadness in his eyes.

"I'm going to be fine," she lied, hating how much she wanted to lean on him for support. Choking on her misery, she barreled on. "At least now there's no question whether I can have children. You'll never have to wonder if by marrying me you made a huge mistake."

"Marrying you would never have been a mistake."

But if she'd had difficulty getting pregnant, he couldn't help but blame her.

"That's a moot point." She willed herself to be strong and to make the break quick and final. "We can't marry now."

"I'm not giving up on us." He covered her hand with his and regarded her with somber eyes.

"There is no more us, Gabriel." She tugged her hand free. "You are going to be king of Sherdana one day. You need to put your country's needs first."

"I have two brothers—"

"Please." She couldn't bear to hear any more. Anything he said would encourage her to be optimistic and the last thing she needed to do was hope everything was going to be okay. "I'm really tired. And I'm in pain. I just want to see my father."

He looked as if he wanted to argue with her. She shook her head and closed her eyes. Another tear trickled down her cheek, but she ignored it.

"And I think it would be better if you don't visit me again."

"I can't accept that."

"Please, Gabriel."

He exhaled harshly. "I'll get your father."

She waited to open her eyes until his soft footfalls receded. Her fingers tingled from contact with Gabriel's cheek. It brought to mind all those times when her hands had roamed over him, exploring his masculine contours, learning all the delightful ways his body differed from hers.

Reaching toward a nearby box of tissues exhausted her. The weakness was frustrating. Before she had the chance to lose herself in the black cloud of misery that hovered nearby, her father entered the room. His embrace stirred up her emotions again and Olivia began to cry once more. This time, however, she didn't feel the need to hold back. His shirt was soaked by the time she ran out of tears.

"I want to go home," she told him, making use of the tissue box once again.

"The doctor wants to keep you in here for at least a week."

"Can't I be transferred to a hospital in London?"

"You are in no shape to travel." He patted her hand. "It's just a week. Then I'll take you home."

A week. It was too long. More than her body needed to heal and that wouldn't be possible until she was miles and miles from Sherdana and its prince.

Shortly after speaking with Olivia, Gabriel returned to the palace alone, his emotions in turmoil. Staff scattered as he crossed the expansive foyer, heading for his office. The way they disappeared he must have looked like the devil himself had come calling.

It had shocked him that after she'd survived her brush with death, her first act would be to end their engagement. She'd done it gracefully, shouldering the responsibility, leaving him free to move on with a clear conscience.

"Move on."

He spat out the words like the foulest curse. No matter how angry he'd been when he found out about her medical condition, he'd not really considered ending things. How could he ever replace Olivia in his life after making love with her? Watching her with his daughters? Seeing that damned tattoo. *Hope.* He could sure use some right now.

Entering his office, he flung himself into a chair near the cold fireplace. He'd been up all night. Exhaustion should be eating into his bones and muscles, but rage burned white-hot in his veins. He massaged his temples where a headache had begun the minute he'd walked out of Olivia's hospital room. Or perhaps it had been there all along. Up until that moment, he'd been completely focused on Olivia.

But after leaving her bedside, he realized that his role in her life was over. As was her role in his. From now on they would be nothing more than familiar strangers. He would probably not exchange a dozen words with her before she left for England and her old life.

God, his chest ached.

"Your Highness?" Gabriel's secretary had poked his head in the door.

"Not now, Stewart."

He needed some time to adjust. How much time, he didn't know. He'd never imagined having to live without Olivia and he wasn't going to pretend that he could just shake off this tragedy and continue on.

"Your Highness," Stewart persisted. "Your father, the king, wants to speak with you."

"I know my father is the king," Gabriel said, taking his annoyance out on his private secretary. He pushed out of the chair, deciding to face whatever his father had to say now rather that make the king wait until he'd showered and changed.

He found his father on the phone in his office and went

to pour himself a shot of scotch while he waited for him to conclude the call.

"A little early for that, isn't it?" the king demanded as he hung up.

"I think a man's entitled to a drink after his fiancée breaks up with him, don't you?"

The king shot him a hard glance as he rose to his feet and crossed to the tray with the coffeepot and cups. Pouring a cup, he plucked the crystal tumbler from Gabriel's finger and replaced it with bone china.

"I just got off the phone with Lord Darcy. He told me you and Olivia ended things."

Ah, so the old man was pulling his offer to set up a company since his daughter was no longer going to be Sherdana's queen. Gabriel shrugged. He didn't really blame the earl for changing his mind.

"She ended it," he said. "But don't worry. Christian will find us some other prospective investors." He sipped the coffee and regarded his father over the brim. "Perhaps one of them will even have an eligible daughter since apparently I'm back on the market."

The king let Gabriel's bitter comment pass unanswered. "Naturally, I would like to continue pursuing other companies, but the need isn't urgent. Darcy is going forward with his plans."

Gabriel's cup hit the saucer with a clatter. From his contact with Lord Darcy, he knew the man was a hardheaded businessman. Sherdana was a good choice for expansion, but not his only and not necessarily his best.

Olivia.

This was her doing.

The exhaustion he'd expected to feel earlier washed over him now. Gabriel wavered on his feet. "Olivia must have told him to honor the commitment. There's no other reason for Darcy to proceed."

"But if she knows you're not getting married, why would she persuade her father to honor his commitment to us?"

"Because that's the sort of woman she is," Gabriel said. "Honorable. The sort who doesn't go back on a promise. Unlike me," he finished in an undertone.

This time, his bitterness was too much for his father to ignore. "You are not reneging on a promise to Lady Darcy," the king said. "She understands she will never be able to give you an heir and has graciously ended your engagement."

That's when it hit him. He didn't want their engagement to end.

Olivia had promised to marry him. And if she was as honorable as he'd just described, she still would.

After six endless days in the hospital, with pain and grief her constant companions, Olivia was an empty shell in both body and soul. For the majority of her stay she'd lain with her eyes closed, floating on a tide of pain medication that dulled the ache in her lower abdomen but couldn't blunt the agony in her heart. With her ability to bear children ripped from her, she shrank from her future. Abandoned by optimism, tears filled her eyes and ran unheeded down her cheeks. Her losses were too much to bear.

On the third day of her incarceration, Libby had smuggled in her favorite chocolate. Olivia had put on a show of courage for her private secretary, but left alone once more, she'd retreated to the dark place where she contemplated what her life had become.

Then, this morning, twenty-four hours before she was scheduled for release, she instructed Libby to bring her files so she could compile a list of all the things she'd committed to in the past month.

"Are you sure you should be taxing yourself with this?" Libby protested, a dozen files clutched to her chest.

Olivia indicated that she wanted the files placed on the rolling tray positioned over her bed. "I've got to find something to keep my mind busy, or I'll go completely mad."

Libby did as she was told and then retreated to the guest chair with her laptop. "Prince Gabriel..." the private secretary began, breaking off when Olivia shook her head.

"How are Bethany and Karina?"

"They miss you." Libby opened the laptop and stared at the screen. "Everyone at the palace misses you."

Not wishing to go down that path, Olivia changed the subject. "Have they found Marissa's sister yet?"

"I'm afraid not."

The memory of the woman's attack had resurfaced a couple days after Olivia had woken up. It hadn't struck her as odd that no one asked about the incident because she'd assumed Marissa's sister had fled the palace with no one being the wiser.

When she'd shared the story with Libby, Olivia had learned what had happened after she'd passed out in the bathroom. She'd given herself a couple seconds to regret the loss of her wardrobe and then insisted on telling her story to palace security and the police.

"Her apartment in Milan is being watched," Libby continued, "but she hasn't returned there. From what I gather, she hasn't contacted her friends in six months. But I'm sure Prince Gabriel will not be satisfied until she's caught."

"I'll feel better when that happens," Olivia said, and opened the file sitting on top of the pile. It was a budget proposal for some improvements to a school she sponsored in Kenya.

The mundane work soothed her spirit. Nothing better for the soul than to worry about someone else's problems.

Ariana and Christian visited several times in the next

few days and brought regards from the king and queen as well as flowers. But Gabriel had been absent. She'd sent him away and asked Libby to make certain he understood that she wanted him to maintain his distance. Her grief was still too strong. She wasn't ready to face him. Not until she came to terms with the end of her engagement and her empty future.

"Prince Gabriel is desperately worried about you," Libby said.

As sweet as it was for Libby to say, Olivia doubted her use of the word *desperately.*

"I hope you've told him I'm recovering nicely."

"He might like to see that for himself."

Olivia's throat tightened and she shook her head. The words blurred on the sheet of paper she held in her hand and she blinked to clear her vision.

"He really cares for you. It's obvious." Libby sat forward, her eyes bright and intense. "I don't think I've ever seen a man so distraught as when we thought you might die. He commanded the doctor to do whatever it took to save you."

Joy dispelled Olivia's gloom for a moment as she let herself warm to Libby's interpretation of events. "Of course he cares," she agreed, wishing the situation was as simple as that. "We became...close these last few weeks. But he needs an heir. That's something I can't give him."

"But you love him. Surely that counts for more." Libby spoke quietly as if afraid of how Olivia would react to her audacity.

Olivia starting drawing circles on the notepad. She did love Gabriel, but he must never know. She didn't want to burden him with something like that. He already had enough guilt on his shoulders with Marissa. He didn't need to suffer even more regret because another woman entertained a desperate and impossible love for him.

"I love him, but please do not tell a soul," she rushed on as Libby's face lit up. "Prince Gabriel needs to find someone new to marry. I don't want him thinking of me at all as he goes about courting his future bride."

The thought of Gabriel with another woman made her heart ache, but she fought the pain.

Libby's delight became determination. "I really think he needs to know."

Olivia offered her friend a sad smile. "He can't. Sherdana deserves a queen who can have children."

"What about what you deserve?" Libby pushed. "Don't you deserve to be happy?"

"I will be," she assured her secretary. "My life isn't over. I'm just starting a new chapter. Not the one I expected to be starting, but how often do we get exactly what we expect?"

# Eleven

Staring at pictures of women he'd rejected six months ago wasn't stimulating Gabriel's appetite for lunch.

"What do you think of Reinette du Piney?" his mother asked, sliding an eight-by-ten head shot of a very beautiful brunette across the table toward him.

"She's pigeon-toed," he replied, slipping his spoon beneath a carrot and lifting it free of the broth. "What exactly is it I'm eating?"

"Creamy carrot soup with anise. The chef is experimenting again."

"You really must stop him from inflicting his culinary curiosity on us."

"Gabriel, you cannot reject du Piney because she's pigeon-toed."

He wasn't. He was rejecting her because the only woman he wanted to marry had made it clear she was going to do the right thing for Sherdana even if he wouldn't.

In the meantime, his mother had persisted in starting the search for his future wife all over again, despite Gabriel's refusal to contribute anything positive.

"I'm only thinking of our children," he countered, setting his spoon down and tossing his napkin over it. "Imagine how they'd be teased at school if they inherited their mother's unfortunate trait."

"Your children will not be teased at school because

they will be tutored at home the way you and your siblings were." His mother sifted through the pictures and pulled out another. "What about Amelia? You liked her."

"She was pleasant enough. But I think her husband would take umbrage with me for poaching his wife."

"Bother."

Gabriel might have felt like smiling at his mother's equivalent of a curse if he wasn't feeling so damned surly. Olivia had left the hospital a few days ago and was staying at the Royal Caron Hotel until her surgeon cleared her for travel. By bribing the man with an enormous donation toward updating the hospital with digital radiology, Gabriel had succeeded in keeping her in Sherdana longer than necessary. He'd hoped she would let him apologize to her in person, but she adamantly refused to see him.

"Gabriel, are you listening to me?"

"I'm not going to marry any of these women."

His mother sat back and stared at him, her eyes narrowed and searching. "Have you decided on someone else?"

"Yes. The same person I've wanted all along."

"Olivia."

"You don't sound surprised."

"You take after your father. He's a romantic devil, too." Her eyes sparkled at Gabriel's doubtful expression. "Oh, not that anyone other than me would know it, but he wouldn't consider divorcing me when I couldn't get pregnant. Even after I left him and made him think that I'd fallen in love with another man."

"What?" This was a tale he'd never heard. "You fell in love with someone while you were married to Father?"

His mother laughed gaily. "Of course not. But I certainly convinced your father I did." A faraway look entered her eyes. "But he chased after me and discovered there was no other man. I finally admitted that the doctor told me I couldn't get pregnant the old-fashioned way and together we figured out a solution."

That sounded familiar. Except for the part where a solution was found together.

"I'm surprised," Gabriel admitted.

"Because your father counseled you to break your engagement with Olivia even before the hysterectomy? You need to understand how difficult those days were for us. The doubt, the worry. It was hard on us. Hard on our marriage. And we were deeply in love."

Her last words struck a nerve. "And Olivia and I are not." His mother's assumption annoyed him more than it should.

Given that he'd only just begun to get acquainted with the woman he had been planning to marry, it made sense that he couldn't possibly love her.

And if not love, then what emotion was at the root of his miserable existence without Olivia?

"He just wants to spare you." She reached across the table and laid her hand over his. "We both do."

Gabriel captured her gaze. "Would you change anything about the decision you made? Knowing the trials and heartbreak you suffered, would you walk away from the man you love and never look back?"

His mother withdrew her hand and sat back. Her expression was determined and sad at the same time. "No."

"Thank you."

He stood and circled the table to kiss her cheek. Expecting her to ask what he was up to, she surprised him again by staying silent.

Leaving his mother, he headed upstairs to await Olivia's arrival. She'd made arrangements through his mother to visit Bethany and Karina and bring them a special birthday present. Gabriel knew it was cheating to use his daughters to secure time with Olivia, but he was feeling a little desperate. If his daughters had taught him anything it was how to exist in the moment. There was no past or future with them. They lived for hugs, treats, mischief and pony rides. Every second in their company reminded him that wonderful things came out of less than ideal situations.

The twins weren't in the nursery. He'd arranged for them to have a picnic in the garden. In half an hour they would arrive for their nap. He hoped that gave him enough time with Olivia. While he waited, he sat on Bethany's bed and picked up the photo of Marissa on the girls' nightstand. A scrapbook had been among the twins' possessions. Olivia had chosen this particular picture to frame and place between the girls so they would remember their mother.

Marissa was pregnant in the picture. Not full-term, perhaps seven months, yet still huge. Had she known she was carrying twins? He traced her smile with his fingertips. She looked older than he remembered, aged by experience, not years, yet luminescent in motherhood.

Why hadn't she contacted him when she knew she was pregnant? Had she not wished to burden him? Had she feared his rejection yet again? He couldn't have married her. Wouldn't have married her. Even if Sherdana's laws hadn't dictated his bride needed to be a citizen of the country or of noble birth for his offspring to be able to inherit the crown, where Gabriel and Marissa had been most compatible was between the sheets, which was where they'd spent half of their time together.

Out of bed, her passionate nature had revealed itself in turbulent emotions and insecurity. He knew the latter had been his fault. He couldn't offer her a future and she'd deserved better. In the end, he'd let her go and part of him had been relieved.

He'd put Sherdana's needs before hers. He'd done the same with Olivia. Only this time there was no certainty that he'd made the right decision. No sense that a burden had been lifted from his shoulders. His daughters were the only bright spot in his future. His mother wanted him to consider who would become his princess, but he couldn't make that decision until he spoke with Olivia and saw for himself what was in her heart.

Olivia took on the challenge of the palace stairs at a sedate pace, but was uncomfortably short of breath by the time she reached the first landing. Several maids trotted past her, but none of the staff paid her undue attention. Still, she felt like an interloper in the place where she thought she'd spend the rest of her life.

Relaxing her grip on the gaily wrapped packages containing china dolls, Olivia forced herself to keep climbing. As beautiful as the dolls were, giving toddlers such delicate toys was probably a recipe for disaster. But Olivia wanted to share with the girls something special. The dolls were just like the one her mother had bought for her and not lived to present the gift.

In her heart Olivia knew it was selfish of her to want them to remember her. First their mother had died and now they faced the loss of someone else they relied on. It was too much change for ones so young. At least they would still have their father. Olivia was comforted by how much Gabriel loved his daughters.

In two days the twins turned two. The party Olivia had spent weeks planning had stirred the palace into new heights of frantic activity. As much as Olivia wanted to go, attending was out of the question. Even though she knew the twins would want her there, they were undoubtedly the only members of the royal family who would.

Who could blame them? Olivia knew the end of her engagement to Gabriel had driven the media into a frenzy of speculation about whom he might choose for his next bride. Social networks had blown up with news about the top two candidates. As long as Olivia remained in the picture, the news outlets would stir the pot. It was better if she disappeared from Sherdana. But she couldn't go without saying goodbye to Bethany and Karina.

Her slow rise to the second floor gave Olivia lots of time to remember how golden her future had seemed the first time she'd ascended these stairs and to brood about the handsome prince who'd never be hers.

Coming to the palace was a risk. She might run into Gabriel and lose the modicum of peace she'd made with her situation. At the same time, she was foolishly excited at the thought of running into Gabriel again. Even knowing they could never be together didn't stop her from longing to see him one last time.

It was irrational, but she'd been hurt that he'd heeded her desire for no further contact after her surgery. She'd broken things off. While part of her was relieved that he'd honored her wishes, her less rational side had resented Gabriel for taking her at her word.

But what truly upset her was, after everything that had happened, she continued to crave his company. She woke from dreams where he held her close and whispered she was his life, his dearest love, and discovered she was alone. And all along, her heart hung heavy in her chest. Emptiness lingered below the stinging incision in her abdomen. Depression coiled about her thoughts, threatening to smother her. A dozen get-well bouquets brightened her hotel suite but couldn't pierce the fog surrounding her emotions.

Olivia paused at the top step and leaned on the banister to catch her breath before proceeding down the hall to the nursery. She knew the twins would be finishing up lunch and had chosen this time to visit because it limited how long she would stay.

When she got to the nursery, she stopped just inside the

doorway, but didn't see the twins. Instead, Gabriel occupied the space. Her heart gave a giddy leap. He sat on Bethany's bed, a silver frame in his hands, fingertips tenderly resting on the face of the woman in the photo. Marissa.

His expression held such sorrow, his mouth drooping in regret as she'd never seen before. Her heart wept for his obvious grief, but the tears that sprang to her eyes weren't for Gabriel; they were for herself. She'd believed him when he claimed to be over Marissa, but three years later he continued to grieve for what could never be. Was that how she looked in those unguarded moments when she thought about all she'd lost? Was this what it looked like when a heart shattered?

Suddenly this errand didn't seem like a good idea. She should have let Libby bring Bethany and Karina to the hotel instead of returning to the palace. But the media had camped out in front of the hotel in the hope that she'd comment on her broken engagement. During the short walk from lobby door to car, Olivia had worn dark glasses and a wide brimmed hat to prevent the photographers from catching a newsworthy photo of her. Olivia couldn't put the girls in the middle of the chaos.

"Olivia!"

Gabriel's head snapped up at the enthusiastic cries coming from behind her. His gaze crashed into hers. She wobbled beneath the triple impact of the twins wrapping their arms around her hips and the raw emotion in Gabriel's eyes.

The twins' demands for attention offered her no chance to react to what she'd seen, but she was glad. Remaining upright as they pressed against her became that much harder thanks to the bulky, delicate bundles she carried.

Gabriel stepped forward and took the packages from her. "Girls, be gentle with Olivia. She's been sick and is very fragile."

The glow in his eyes warmed her head to toe as he extricated her from the twins' enthusiastic embrace. She had a hard time looking away.

"Don't like sick," Bethany proclaimed, her lower lip slipping forward.

Karina gave her head a vigorous shake.

"I'm much better now, but still a little sore. Like when you skin your knee how it takes a while to stop hurting."

Karina bent down to touch Olivia's unblemished knees. "Hurt?"

Olivia laughed. "No, angel. My knees are okay. My hurt is here." She pointed to her stomach.

"Can we see?" Bethany demanded.

Olivia gestured toward the packages Gabriel had set on their beds. "Why don't you open your birthday presents instead."

"Birthday."

Olivia smiled past her sadness at having to go home to England and never see these girls again. "They are very special. I hope you like them."

While the girls tore into the wrapping, Olivia watched them, but her attention was captured by the tall man who stood so close beside her. It seemed the worst sort of torture not to lean into his strength and forget about the past week. But the twinges in her abdomen kept her grounded in reality.

"That was a lovely gift," Gabriel said as the girls fell to exclaiming over the dolls' hair and wardrobe.

"Something for them to remember me by." Emotion seized her by the throat. "I didn't realize leaving them was going to be so hard."

"You could stay longer."

Olivia flinched at how her heart leaped with hope. "I can't, and it's not fair of you to ask."

Why would he even want her to stay? He knew as well

as she did that having her around would create problems for him both in the media and in his search for a bride.

"A lot of things haven't been fair lately." He brushed her hair off one shoulder, grazing her skin in the process.

To Olivia's immense shock, desire sparked. How was it possible after all she'd been through? She looked up to see if Gabriel had noticed her reaction and to her dismay, he had.

"Olivia." His deep voice rumbled in his chest, creating a matching vibration in her. "We need to talk." He found her hand with his.

The slide of his fingers against hers made her heart race. "I think we've said everything there is to say."

"Maybe you have, but I have a few things you need to hear."

Olivia's gaze shot toward the twins. To her relief, they were oblivious to the charged undercurrents passing between her and Gabriel. The girls had been through enough and didn't deserve to witness them arguing. She turned her back to them and pitched her voice to carry no farther than the foot that separated her from Gabriel.

"Don't do this. There's nothing you have to say that I want to hear. What I need is to leave this country and forget all about you."

"Can you do that?" he murmured, his free hand cupping the side of her face, his tender touch bringing tears to her eyes. "Can you forget me? Forget how it was between us?"

Harsh emotions sandblasted her nerves raw. "Would you want me to do otherwise?"

"Yes. Stay and fight—"

"Fight?" The word gusted out of her on a bitter laugh. "I have nothing left to fight with. It's gone, Gabriel. My ability to bear children. My chance to be a mother. I'm nothing more than a shell." An empty shell without him. "I just want to go home and forget."

Forget how his smile transformed her.

Forget how it felt to fall asleep in his arms.

Forget how much she loved him.

"Can you?" He cupped the back of her neck and pulled her gently against his powerful, muscular body. "Can you forget me?"

Her pulse danced with erotic longing. She tore her gaze away from the sensual light in his eyes that drew her like a candle in the darkness. How was it possible she could want him with such intensity when the parts that made her a whole woman were gone?

He lowered his voice to a husky murmur. "Because I will never be able to forget you."

It wasn't fair of him to tell her that. To tantalize her with longing for what could never be.

Contact with him seared her from breast to thigh. Her incision burned the way it had during those first few days, reminding her that she'd have a permanent mark on her body that would never let her forget.

"Maybe not forget," she told him, keeping her voice soft to hide its unsteadiness. "But you'll move on and be happy."

Before he could respond, they were struck from two sides by the twins. Sandwiched between them, Olivia had no way to escape Gabriel. He saw her predicament and a predatory smile curved his lips before they descended to hers.

Sweet sunshine washed through her body as she surrendered to the delicious drag of his mouth against hers. This was where she belonged. To this man. And these girls. The family she craved.

Her whole world contracted to Gabriel's kiss and the twins' hugs. A great rushing sound filled her ears, drowning out her inner voice and all the reasons why this couldn't be her future. Loving Gabriel had never seemed so easy.

Outside pressure didn't exist. She was free to express herself, to tell him what was truly in her heart.

*I love you.*

But she never uttered the words because the girls clamored for their own share of Olivia's attention as the kiss fell apart. Her lips tingled in the aftermath as Gabriel held her close a moment longer before letting her step back.

"Tea party. Tea party," Bethany called.

Karina seized her and pulled.

It took her a couple seconds to realize that the girls were referring to the small table set up near the window. She shook her head. "It's your nap time."

"Girls, Olivia is right. Hattie will read to you after you lie down."

While it hurt to kneel and give hugs and kisses to each of the toddlers, Olivia braved the pain for one last goodbye. By the time they had been persuaded to let her go, Olivia's sorrow had rendered her mute.

Gabriel seemed to understand her distress because he waited until they'd descended to the grand hall before speaking. "When are you leaving?"

"My final doctor's appointment is later this week. I expect to be able to travel after that."

"You really should come to the twins' birthday party. You planned everything. It's only right that you be there."

Temptation trembled through her. It would be so easy to agree, to prolong the final parting for another day. But what good would that do? She'd have one more memory to keep her awake at night.

"I think it's better that we said our goodbyes now."

"I don't agree." He took her hand and stopped her from leaving. His gold eyes were somber as he met her gaze. "Bethany and Karina will be sad if you don't come."

His touch made her want to turn back the clock. If she'd not been so rash as to stop taking the pill against her doctor's order, she would be marrying Gabriel in a week. Then again, the burden of producing an heir to the kingdom would still be weighing heavily on her.

"And I'm not ready to say goodbye," he said, interrupting her thoughts.

She delighted at his words, until she recalled how he'd looked at that photo of Marissa. Three years ago he'd turned his back on her and chosen his country instead. Olivia had seen the way he'd been tortured by that choice every time he looked at his daughters. Was he hoping that putting his country's needs second this time would somehow redeem him for failing Marissa?

She eased her hand free. "You already have. The second the story of my fertility issues made it to prime time any chance of us getting married was gone." She touched his arm in sympathy. "People in our positions don't belong to themselves."

"That's true," he murmured, seizing her chin and forcing her to look at him. "You belong to me."

She jerked away and took a step back. "I don't." But her blood sang another tune. She was his, heart and soul. There would be no other.

"Deny it all you want, but I was the first man who made love to you. The first man you loved. That sort of bond may stretch but it will not break."

Her pulse rocked at his use of the word *love*. Did he know the depth of her feelings for him? She'd not been particularly careful to guard her emotions during those long hours in his arms. Had he figured out the truth or was he simply referring to the physical act of loving?

"Why are you saying these things? Do you think leaving is easy for me?" She spied the front door and knew her reprieve was mere steps away, but she had a few hard truths to deliver first. "I was planning on making my life here with you. It hurts more than I can say that I can't marry you. Asking me to stay is completely—"

"Selfish," he interrupted, lifting her palm to his lips. "You're right. I am selfish."

When he released her hand, Olivia clenched her fingers around the kiss. His blunt admission had dimmed her frustration. This impossible situation was of her making. If only she'd told him of her fertility issues. He never would have proposed. She never would have fallen in love with him.

"You have a right to be selfish sometimes." Her smile wobbled, and then steadied. "You are a prince, after all."

"And yet it's not gaining me any ground with you, is it?"

She shook her head. "I'll come to the twins' birthday party."

It wasn't what she'd intended to say, but her heart had a mind of its own. Knowing she would never be able to take it back, Olivia remained silent as Gabriel escorted her to the waiting car and handed her into the backseat.

As the car rolled down the driveway, Olivia knew she'd been a fool to come here today. Obviously she hadn't learned anything these past few weeks. Gabriel held a power over her that was nothing short of dangerous. Thank goodness he would never know how unhappy she was without him because she had a feeling he might do something incredibly foolish.

# Twelve

For the next two days leading up to his daughters' birthday party, Gabriel worked tirelessly to bring Christian up to speed on all the things that might come up in the next two weeks. After his last encounter with Olivia, he'd decided to take himself off the grid for a short time. Olivia's stubborn refusal to continue their relationship had forced Gabriel into a difficult position. Sherdana needed a royal heir. He needed Olivia. The opposing forces were tearing him apart.

On the morning of Bethany and Karina's birthday, Gabriel put his signature on the last report requiring his approval and went to have breakfast with his daughters. As usual they were full of energy and he smiled as he listened to their excited conversation.

It pleased him that Karina spoke more often now. Maybe she'd never be as talkative as her sibling, but as her confidence grew, she demonstrated a bright mind and a sly sense of humor. He had Olivia to thank for the transformation. She'd coaxed the younger twin out of her shell with patience and love. As attached as the trio had become, Gabriel was worried that Olivia's leaving would give rise to the girls' feelings of abandonment.

Scooping Karina onto his lap, he tickled her until she whooped with laughter. Could he make Olivia understand that there was more at stake than an heir for Sherdana?

Perhaps today's party would be the perfect opportunity to impress upon her how much she was needed and loved.

The festivities began at three. A large tent had been erected on the expansive lawn just east of the palace. A band played children's songs nearby and a dozen children jumped and twirled to the music in the open space between the stage and the linen-clad tables. Beyond that was a balloon bouncer shaped like a castle. The structure swayed as children burned off energy. On the opposite side of the lawn, their parents enjoyed more sedate entertainment in the form of an overflowing buffet of delicacies and free-flowing alcohol.

The crowd was a mix of wealthy nobility and leading businessmen. Gabriel stayed close to Bethany and Karina as they ate cake and played with the other children, keeping an eye out for Olivia as the afternoon progressed. She didn't arrive until almost five.

Looking pale and very beautiful in a light pink dress with short fluttery sleeves, she moved through the crowd, smiling politely when she encountered someone familiar, but otherwise avoiding eye contact with the guests.

Gabriel snagged a pair of wineglasses off the tray of a passing waiter. It was a chardonnay from one of Sherdana's finest wineries and he remembered how Olivia had wanted to tour the wine country. He added that to the list of things he'd promised and never delivered.

She caught sight of him when she was thirty feet away and very much looked as if she'd like to run away. Besieged by the memory of the kiss they'd shared in the nursery and the longing he'd tasted on her lips, Gabriel knew the only way to circumvent her stubbornness was to demonstrate the power of their passion for each other.

"I'm glad you came," he told her, as he drew close enough to speak. "I was beginning to worry that you wouldn't."

"I almost didn't." Her expression was rueful as she accepted the glass of wine he offered. "But I promised that I would."

"Bethany and Karina will be very glad."

Her gaze moved to where the twins were running with several children close to their age. "They look like they're having fun."

"All thanks to you. The party is fantastic."

"Libby did most of the work."

"But you are the one who came up with the concept and organized everything. You have quite a knack for party planning."

"In London I was on committees for several charities. I've done several large events, including children's parties. And speaking of children, I should probably say hello to Bethany and Karina. I won't be able to stay at the party long."

He inspected her face. Shadows beneath her eyes gave her the appearance of fragility. "Are you in pain?"

"Just tired." Her wan smile held none of her former liveliness. "My strength is not coming back as quickly as I'd like and I'm not sleeping well."

Gabriel tucked her hand into the crook of his arm and led her on a slow, meandering journey toward the twins, extending the amount of his time in her company. The tension in her slim frame troubled him and Gabriel wished he could do something to bring back the happy, vital woman she'd been two weeks earlier. He'd never felt so helpless.

Before he could bring her to where the twins were holding court, his daughters saw them coming and ran over. As they threw their tiny arms around her, Olivia's smile grew radiant. But there was sadness, as well. Sadness Gabriel knew he could banish if only she'd let him.

Hyped up on sweets and attention, the twins didn't linger long. After they'd raced back toward the other children, Olivia sidestepped away from Gabriel.

"I've taken up enough of your time," she said. "You have guests to attend to and I need to go."

He caught her wrist, preventing her from departing. "You're the only one I care about."

"Please don't," she pleaded in a hoarse whisper. "This is already so hard."

"And that's my fault." This wasn't a discussion he wanted to have in the middle of his daughters' birthday party, but he had to try one last time to reason with her. "Let me at least walk you out."

She must have seen his determination because she nodded.

Instead of leading her around the palace, he drew her through the doors leading to the green salon where they could have a little privacy.

"I'm sorry I didn't handle things better between us."

When he stopped in the middle of the room and turned her to face him she sighed. Looking resigned, she met his gaze. "You handled everything the way a future king should. I was the one who was wrong. I should have told you about my past medical issues before you had a chance to propose."

"What if I told you it wouldn't have mattered?" Gabriel lifted her hand and placed her palm over his heart.

"Then I would have to insult the crown prince of Sherdana by telling him he's a fool." She tried to pull her hand free, but he'd trapped it beneath his. Her tone grew more impatient. "You need an heir. That's something I can't give you."

"Unfortunate, yes. But that doesn't change the fact that I chose you and I'd committed to building a life with you. I'm not ready to give that up."

"That's madness," she exclaimed. "You have to. You must marry someone who can give you children."

Gabriel scowled at her response. "That's what the country needs me to do. But I'm not a country. I'm a man. A man who is tired of making everyone else's priorities his own."

"You don't have a choice," she whispered, blinking rapidly. "You are going to be king. You must do what's right. And so must I." With surprising strength, she wrenched her hand free and turned to flee.

"Olivia." He started after her, but realized nothing he could say at that moment would persuade her to change her mind.

Releasing a string of curses, Gabriel pulled out his cell phone and dialed. When the call connected, he said, "She won't budge."

"I'm sorry to hear that, Your Highness. The arrangements you asked for are complete and awaiting your arrival. Are you still planning on traveling the day after tomorrow?"

"Yes."

With the upheaval of the past several weeks, this was probably not the best time for him to leave the country, but he'd let the impossible situation with Olivia go on too long. She'd been right to say he didn't have a choice about his future. Fate had set him on a path and he needed to follow it to the end.

He found his parents together in the garden. They were strolling arm in arm, pausing here and there to greet their guests and enjoying the warm afternoon. He almost hated to spoil their peaceful moment.

"It was lovely of Olivia to come today," his mother said.

"She wanted to wish Bethany and Karina a happy birthday."

"You spent a lot of time with her." The queen's voice held a question.

Gabriel wondered how much his mother knew about his intentions. "It was her first social appearance since our engagement ended. I thought she could use the support."

"Of course. What happened with her was tragic and we cannot be seen turning our backs on her." Although the queen had spoken sympathetically about Olivia's plight, her priorities were her family and the country. "But you must not encourage her."

A bitter laugh escaped him. "She's well aware that I need a wife who can have children. If you think anything different, you don't appreciate her character."

The queen gave Gabriel a hard look. "Of course."

Gabriel shifted his gaze to his daughters. A trio of pre-teen girls were chasing the twins through the gardens. They laughed as they ran and Gabriel's heart lightened at the sound.

"I wanted to let you know," he began, returning his attention to his parents, "that in a couple days, I'm going out of town for a week or so."

"Is this the best time?" his father asked, echoing what Gabriel had been thinking minutes earlier.

"Perhaps not, but I have the future to think about and Sherdana still needs a princess."

The king frowned. "What about the state dinner for the Spanish ambassador?"

"Christian can take over while I'm gone." Gabriel forced his shoulders to relax. "I'm not the only prince in this family, you know. It's about time my brothers remembered that."

"I'm glad to hear you're ready to move forward," his mother said. "Can you give us some hint of your plans?"

"I'd rather wait until everything is finalized before I say anything."

"Very sensible," his father said and Gabriel wondered if the king would feel that way if he had any idea where his son was going and why.

Two days after the twins' birthday party, Olivia sat in an examination room, awaiting the doctor and fighting sadness. She was flying back to London in the morning. Back to her flat and her friends.

Her return would be far from triumphant. She'd been stripped of the ability to have children and because of that lost the man she loved. Thinking about the future only intensified her grief, so she'd spent the past few days finishing up the tasks she'd left undone such as the finalization of the menu for the hospital's children's wing gala taking place the following month and writing to cancel the invitations she'd accepted when she was still Gabriel's fiancée.

After ten minutes of waiting, Dr. Warner entered the room and interrupted her thoughts. Olivia was glad he accepted her assurances that she was getting along just fine in the wake of her hysterectomy and didn't voice the concern hovering in his expression. If he'd encouraged her to talk about her emotional health she might have burst into tears.

"Everything looks good," the doctor announced. "No reason you can't travel whenever you want."

"I'm leaving tomorrow," she said.

"Make sure you check in with your regular doctor within a week or two. He should be able to assist you with any side effects from your procedure and recommend a fertility specialist."

"Fertility specialist?" she echoed. "I don't understand. I can't have children."

"You can't bear children," the doctor agreed. "But your ovaries are intact. It might be possible to harvest your eggs and freeze them in case you decide to pursue motherhood in the future."

"I could be a mother?" Olivia breathed, overcome by the possibility that something she'd longed for with all her heart could still come to pass.

"You'd need to find a surrogate," the doctor said, his eyes twinkling. "And of course, you'd need a father, but it's certainly a possibility."

"I never imagined…" Her voice trailed off.

"Medical science is making miracles happen every day."

The doctor left her alone to dress and Olivia went through the motions in a daze. Her first impulse was to call Gabriel and tell him her news. Then she imagined how that call would go.

*Gabriel, I have great news, I might be able to be a mother, after all. It's chancy and it will involve another woman carrying the baby, but it would be my egg.*

Could a country as traditional as Sherdana accept a prince conceived in a test tube? And raised by a mother who hadn't actually carried him inside her for nine months?

Could Gabriel?

When Olivia returned to her suite at the hotel, she couldn't stop pacing as her mind spun through her options. Possible scenarios crowded her like desperate beggars in need of coin. Staring out the window at the river, she held her phone against her chest and searched for the courage she needed to dial Gabriel's number and tell him that she loved him and find out if he was willing to take a risk with her.

The sun had set by the time she dialed. With her heart pounding against her ribs, she counted rings, her hope fading as the number grew larger. When his deep voice poured through the receiver, telling her he was unavailable and asking her to leave a message at the tone, she held her breath for five seconds, then disconnected the call. She really didn't want to share her news with his voice mail.

Next, she tried Stewart. This time, she got through.

"I was trying to get ahold of Gabriel," she told his private secretary. "Do you know if he's in the palace?"

"No. He left two hours ago."

"Do you know where he went?" A long pause followed her question. Olivia refused to be put off by Stewart's reluctance. "It's important that I speak with him."

"I'm sorry, Lady Darcy. He has left the country."

"Did he go to Italy?"

Stewart paused before replying. "All he would tell me is that he had something he needed to do that would impact the future generations of Alessandros."

Olivia's stomach plummeted as she pictured Count Verreos and his beautiful daughter from the twins' birthday party and recalled the familiarity between her and Gabriel. Had they reached an understanding already? Was she Olivia's replacement?

"Is there any way to reach him?" she asked, desperation growing as she suspected where Gabriel and gone and why.

"I've left him several messages that he hasn't returned," Stewart answered, sounding unhappy.

"How long was he planning to be gone?"

"A week to ten days. Before departing, he left instructions that you should be given use of the royal family plane. It will be available to take you back to England tomorrow."

"That's kind of him." Although disappointed that Gabriel had at long last accepted their relationship was over, Olivia wasn't deterred. "But when you speak with him, would you tell him I intend to stay in Sherdana until we can speak face-to-face."

She hadn't believed Gabriel when he'd insisted this wasn't over between them. If only she'd known how right he was a couple days earlier.

After hanging up with Stewart, Olivia called her father and gave him the news that she was staying another week, but didn't share the real reason. To her relief, he didn't try to talk her into coming home immediately.

With nothing to do but wait, Olivia had an early dinner and took a walk in the private walled garden behind the hotel. Instead of enjoying the picturesque charm of the boxwood hedges and urns filled with cascades of bright flowers, Olivia grew more anxious with every step. What if Gabriel was proposing to Fabrizia Verreos at this very moment? A painful spasm in her chest forced Olivia to stop. Gasping for air, she sat down on a nearby stone bench and fought to normalize her breathing. She focused on the fat blossoms on the peach rosebush across the path from her. Closing her eyes would have allowed her mind to fill with images of another woman in Gabriel's arms.

A vibration against her upper thigh provided a welcome distraction. Pulling out her cell phone Olivia saw Stewart was calling. Her pulse hitched as hope bloomed.

"Prince Gabriel called me a few minutes ago," Stewart explained. "He is unable to return to Sherdana at the moment, but when I explained you intended to linger until he came home, he asked if you would fly to meet with him tomorrow."

It was what she wanted, but based on her panic attack a moment earlier, she was thinking that perhaps Gabriel intended to tell her in person that he was moving on.

"Of course." Afterward she could fly home.

"The plane will be waiting for you at ten. I'll send a car to pick you up."

"Thank you."

Olivia hung up and continued her walk, plagued by worries.

What if she didn't reach him before he proposed to Fabrizia? What if despite the passionate kiss he'd given her the day of the twins' birthday he wasn't willing to risk the unconventional method needed in order for them to conceive the next generation of Alessandros?

Pushing everything out of her mind that she couldn't control, Olivia concentrated on what she was going to say to Gabriel about the change in her circumstances. By the time Olivia returned to her room, she'd rehearsed and discarded a dozen ways to convince Gabriel they could have children. In the end, she decided the best argument was to tell him she loved him. And she was grateful she only had to wait hours instead of days before she could speak the truth of her heart.

The next morning saw her staring out the window with blurry vision as the royal family's private plane taxied down the runway. Plagued by uncertainty, she hadn't slept but an hour or so. Lulled by the drone of the engines, she shut her eyes and didn't realize she'd drifted off until the change in altitude woke her. Glancing at her watch, she saw that she'd been asleep for nearly two hours.

Stretching, she glanced out the window, expecting to see Italy's lush green landscape, but what greeted her eyes was shimmering blue water. The plane touched down smoothly and rolled toward a series of private hangers.

"Where are we?" she asked the copilot as he lowered the steps that would allow her to disembark into the foreign landscape.

"Cephalonia," the pilot answered, carrying her overnight bag down the steps to a waiting car. He handed her bag to the driver. "Greece."

"Thank you," she murmured to both men as she slid into the car's backseat. Although why she was thanking them, she had no idea. If they were kidnapping her, this was the oddest way to go about it.

"Where are we going?" she questioned the driver as he

navigated along a coastal road cut into the mountainside with a stunning view of the sea.

"Fiskardo."

Which told her absolutely nothing. The only thing she was certain of at this moment was that she was nowhere near Italy and Gabriel. What sort of trick had Stewart played on her? Was this some sort of plot to get her out of the way while Gabriel did his duty and secured himself a new fiancée?

If that was the case, Stewart better be the villain. If Gabriel had orchestrated this stunt, she was going to be even more heartbroken. Pulling out her phone, she dialed first Gabriel, then Stewart when the former still didn't answer. She had no luck getting through.

As soon as she arrived at her destination, she would figure out her next step. If this was Stewart's gambit, she would find another way to get in contact with Gabriel. Perhaps the queen would help.

With nothing to do for the moment, Olivia stared out the window as the car descended from the mountains and drove down into a seaside town. She'd never visited any of the Greek Ionian Islands before and acknowledged the scenery in this area was spectacular. At least Stewart had been kind enough to find a gorgeous place to squirrel her away. As the car navigated through town, she glimpsed the whitewashed houses with their flower-draped balconies and wondered if her final destination was one of the lovely hotels overlooking the harbor. Her spirits sank as they passed each one and came to a stop a short distance from the waterfront.

They were met by a handsome swarthy Greek in his midfifties who flashed blinding white teeth in a mischievous grin. Seeing his good humor restored her own. She followed him along the cement quay, lined with chartered sailboats, believing that there had to be a happy ending to all this adventuring.

"I am Thasos," he said as he helped her onto a luxurious thirty-four-foot cruiser.

"Where are we going, Thasos?" she questioned, accepting the glass of wine offered, glad for it and the tray of Greek food that awaited her.

"Kioni."

Another name that rang no bells. With a sigh, Olivia munched on bread, dolmas, cheese and olives while the boat sped out of the harbor. If she'd thought the water had appeared beautiful from the coast, it was nothing compared to the sparkling blue that surrounded her now. A short distance away, another island loomed, a great green hulk adorned with olive trees and cypress. Few houses dotted the mountainsides. She would have worried about being in such a remote area, but the bustle of the town they'd just left behind told her she hadn't been brought to the ends of the earth.

After polishing off a second glass of wine and taking the edge off her hunger, she stared at the coastline as it passed. Ninety minutes on the water brought them to another harbor, this one shaped like a horseshoe with three windmills on one side of its mouth.

"Kioni," Thasos explained with another wide grin.

Olivia sighed, wondering who was going to meet her here. Could she expect another taxi ride? Perhaps the plan was to keep her moving until she cried uncle. While Thasos maneuvered the boat toward the cement seawall that circled the harbor, Olivia gazed at this town. Smaller and less busy than Fiskardo, it nevertheless had the same charm. A few houses clustered close to the waterfront, but most clung to the side of the mountain that rose above this scenic harbor.

Everywhere she looked vivid purple and magenta bou

ainvillea vines brightened the whitewashed buildings or
rched over the steps that led to the homes perched on the
illside. Silence descended as Thasos killed the motor and
ne light breeze brought the clank of cowbells to her ears.
But she doubted the steep terrain was suitable for cows.
More likely the bells she heard belonged to goats.

She stepped off the boat, helped by Thasos and another
man, who claimed her bag for the next part of her journey.
Olivia followed him for about thirty steps before she spied
a tall, familiar figure coming down the street toward her.

Gabriel.

His white pants, pale blue shirt and navy blazer gave
him the look of casual elegance. Her heart jumped in her
chest as the wind tousled his hair. He slid his sunglasses up
on his head as he approached and gave her a gentle smile.

He wasn't in Italy proposing to the daughter of an Italian
count. He was here and from the expression on his face,
he was very glad to see her.

# Thirteen

The unguarded expression on Olivia's face when she spotted him made Gabriel the happiest man on earth. He was her white knight come to rescue her from the dragons. The fact that he was towing a donkey instead of a black charger hadn't made an impact on her yet.

"What are you doing here?" she demanded. "You're supposed to be in Italy."

He shook his head. "Italy? Where did you get that idea?"

"Stewart said you had gone to do something that would impact future generations of Alessandros. I assumed you meant to…propose to the daughter of Count Verreos." She touched the corner of her eye where a trace of moisture had gathered and a ragged exhale escaped her.

"No. I came straight here."

"Does Stewart know where you are?"

"No. I knew he wouldn't approve of what I intended to do."

"That's why I don't understand what are you doing here and why you dragged me all the way to Greece by plane, across an island by car and now here by boat."

"I needed some time to prepare." He grinned. "And I thought you might be less likely to argue with me if you were tired."

"Argue about what?" she demanded, her gaze drawn

toward the small donkey that stood beside him, ears flickering lazily forward and back. "And what are you doing with that?"

Gabriel patted the donkey's neck. "It's traditional for Greek brides to ride donkeys to their weddings."

"Bride? What are you talking about...?" Her voice trailed off as she noticed the donkey came equipped with a riding pad covered with flowers. "You can't be serious."

She sounded aghast, but hope glowed in her blue eyes.

"I'm utterly serious. The church and the priest are waiting for us. All you need to do is hop on." Seeing she wasn't fully on board with his plan, he caught her around the waist and pulled her body flush with his, taking care to treat her gently. "Marry me." He drew his knuckles down her cheek. "Please. I can't live without you."

Tears flooded her eyes. "You love me?"

"I love you. I adore you. You're my world." He peered down at her in surprise. "Haven't you figured that out by now?"

She took his hand and drew it away from her skin. Her grip was tight enough to make him wince.

"What of your parents' wishes? Have you considered the barrage of negative opinions you'll face when we return home?"

"None of that matters. No one matters but us. I have two brothers, both of whom are capable of getting married and having children. There's no reason why I have to be the one who fathers the next generation of Sherdana royalty. It was different when my father became king. He was the only direct male descendant. And besides, I think it's time my brothers took on a little royal responsibility."

A crowd of townspeople and tourists were gathering on the narrow street, drawn by the novelty of a decked out donkey and the argument between Gabriel and Olivia. The late-afternoon sun bathed the town in golden light, softening the scenery. The breeze off the harbor was gentle against Olivia's skin, soothing her anxiety.

"Neither one of them is going to be happy."

"I don't care. It's my turn to be a little selfish. We're getting married. Now. Today. And I'm not taking no for an answer."

That he was ready to marry her despite her inability to give him children thrilled her, and she could no longer wait to share her news.

"There's something I need to tell you."

"That you love me?"

"No."

"You don't?" he teased.

"Of course I do. But that's not what I need to tell you."

"But don't you think it's an appropriate thing to tell your groom on your wedding day?"

"Very well. I love you."

"When you say it like that, I'm not sure I believe you."

She leaned forward and slid her fingers into his hair, drawing him close for a slow, deep kiss. "I love you."

His response was almost a purr. "Much better."

"Now are you ready to hear what I have to say?"

"Yes."

Their impending nuptials had certainly brought out the mischief maker in Gabriel. Or perhaps it was getting away from the palace and all his responsibility. Olivia made a note to kidnap him at least once a year and bring him somewhere with no cell phones and no television so they could get reacquainted.

"When I spoke with the doctor yesterday—" she gathered a deep breath "—he gave me some rather startling news."

The wicked light died in Gabriel's eyes. He grew somber. He caught her fingers in a tight grip. "Is something wrong?"

"No. In fact, I think everything might be okay in time."

"How so?"

"He thinks that a fertility specialist might be able to harvest eggs from my ovaries." She watched Gabriel carefully, hoping he was open to what she had in mind. "It would require finding a woman willing to be a surrogate, but it's possible that you and I could still make babies together."

"This is the most amazing news."

Gabriel caught her around the waist and pulled her against his body. Dipping his head, he captured her lips with his for a long, slow kiss.

By the time he released her mouth they were both breathing heavily. Gabriel's eyes sparkled like the sun on the water behind them. Joy sped through her as she realized she was about to marry the man she adored.

"Come on, let's get you up on the donkey and get to the church."

"Are you sure it's tradition?" she protested, eyeing the creature doubtfully.

"Positive."

Their parade up the steep street to the church was not the formal affair it would have been in Sherdana. There was no gilded carriage pulled by six perfectly matched white horses. No thousands of people lining the streets to wave and throw rose petals at them. But there were smiles and hearty cheers as Gabriel lead the donkey through the heart of the town.

When they reached the church, Gabriel introduced his housekeeper, Elena, who took Olivia aside to help her into the modest knee-length wedding dress with cap sleeves and a large bow at the waist. A note from Noelle accompanied the dress, explaining that Libby had come to her a few days after Olivia went into the hospital because Gabriel was planning on marrying Olivia in a small island wedding and wanted a dress to suit the occasion.

So, despite his lack of contact during her hospital stay, Gabriel hadn't accepted that their engagement was at an end. He'd still wanted her as his wife, even though his family and political advisers would counsel him to move on.

Awash with joy, Olivia clutched the note to her chest and stared at her reflection. Although the design was much simpler than the lace-and-crystal-embellished gown she'd have worn to marry Gabriel in Sherdana, it was perfect. As was the man who awaited her at the front of the beautiful Greek church.

Gabriel's gaze never once wavered as she walked toward him, accompanied by the song of a single violin. There was no doubt, no restraint in his golden eyes, only possessiveness, and she reveled in his love.

He took her hand as she came to stand beside him and she tingled in delight. Elena and her husband were the only witnesses. The intimacy of the empty church allowed them the privacy to focus completely on each other and they exchanged vows in reverent tones. When they returned to Sherdana, there would be celebrations with family and friends. Until then, all they wanted was each other.

After the ceremony, they exited the church and encountered a small crowd. Apparently Gabriel and his brothers were well liked in the coastal town and when word got out that he had come to the island to get married, many had turned out to wish him and Olivia well.

They lingered for several minutes, greeting people and accepting congratulations until Gabriel insisted it was time he took his bride home. Laughing and shaking his head at good-natured invitations to stay in town and celebrate their wedding, Gabriel slipped his arm around her waist and began to edge out of the circle of people.

"My car is this way." He took her hand and began to lead her down the road.

"Oh, thank goodness, I was afraid you'd make me ride the donkey back to your house."

Gabriel laughed heartily. "It would take him too long to carry you that far and I can't wait that long to have you all to myself."

Once he got her settled in the passenger seat and slid behind the wheel, he sat sideways in his seat and regarded her intently.

After several seconds of his attentive silence, Olivia grew restless. "What are you doing?"

"Appreciating our first private moment as husband and wife. The circumstances of the last few weeks haven't given us any time together and when we leave here, there will be public appearances and meetings demanding our time. I intend to spend every possible moment until then showing my beautiful wife how much I adore her."

Being his wife was her dream come true. Olivia smiled. "If I'm beautiful, you have Noelle to thank for that." She gestured to her wedding dress. "Have you really been planning this romantic elopement since before I left the hospital?"

"It was your secretary's idea. She knows how stubborn you can be and came to me with a crazy plan that I should steal you away to someplace exotic and marry you."

"Libby?" Olivia considered her secretary's encouragement anytime Olivia had doubted her future with Gabriel.

"She helped me with the dress and arranged the church and the flowers."

"How were you planning to get me to agree to run off with you?"

"By offering you a ride home in our jet and then bringing you here. You made things a lot easier by asking to see me."

"Did Stewart have any idea what you were planning?"

Gabriel shook his head. "Stewart's loyalty is to Sherdana. Libby's loyalty is to you." He leaned forward and pressed a lingering kiss on her lips. "And so is mine."

Olivia contemplated her new husband during the short drive to his villa, a two-mile journey around the horseshoe shaped harbor. Never again would she underestimate his determination or his loyalty to her. He'd been willing to go against his family for her. She couldn't ask for a better partner or soul mate.

Because they'd been delayed in town Elena had already arrived and was in the process of arranging a romantic table for them on the terrace high above the harbor. At Olivia's prompting, Gabriel gave her a brief tour of the villa. In the spacious bedroom they would share, Gabriel drew her toward the window and they stared out at Kioni, its lights glowing bright as dusk descended. With his arms wrapped around Olivia's waist and his chin resting on her head, he sighed.

Olivia chuckled. "Was that weariness or contentment?"

"Contentment. You will be hearing many more such sighs in the coming days while we enjoy some much needed privacy."

"We will have to go back eventually."

His arms tightened around her. "I prefer not to think about that moment until it arrives."

"Won't the media come here looking for us?"

"In the past we've kept a low profile and the people who live on the island respect our privacy." His lips trailed of fire down her neck. "Now, let's go downstairs and enjoy our first dinner as man and wife."

They returned to the first floor and accepted glasses of champagne from Elena. She gestured them out onto the terrace and retreated to fetch the first course.

"This is beautiful," Olivia commented, admiring the simple but elegant scene.

With the sunset long past, the sky had deepened to indigo. A row of white candles stretched along the low terrace wall, pushing back the darkness, their flames protected by glass containers. More candles had been placed in the center of the table, their flickering glow making shadows dance over the fine white tablecloth, beautiful china and colorful flower arrangements.

Gabriel led her to the table and helped her into a linen-clad chair before taking his own seat beside her. The romantic lighting softened his strong bone structure and brought out the sensual curve of his lips as he smiled. "Here's to following our hearts."

Olivia smiled as she clinked her glass to his and marveled at her good fortune. She never would have guessed that she had to lose everything in order to gain the one thing she needed most.

Setting her glass down, Olivia reached for Gabriel's hand.

"A few weeks ago your sister told me to ask you something. I never did."

"Ask now."

"She said we'd met before six months ago. Is that true?"

"Yes."

"But I don't recall meeting you. And I assure you I would. Were we young children? Is that why I don't remember?"

"It was almost seven years ago at a masquerade party. Given the host's reputation I was a little surprised to discover the young woman I rescued was none other than Lady Olivia Darcy."

Gabriel had been her savior. The man whose kiss had set the bar for every other romantic encounter she'd had since. "You knew who I was?"

"Not until after you'd left and Christian informed me who I'd been kissing." Gabriel's fingertips grazed her cheek. "When I kissed you that night, something sparked between us. I wasn't ready to get married and you were far too young, but something told me you were the woman I was destined to marry."

"But that was one kiss seven years ago." She couldn't imagine how a single moment in time could impact him so strongly. And yet hadn't she felt the magic between them? Compared his kiss to those that came after? "And my father approached you about building a plant in Sherdana."

"That's true, but Christian put the idea in his head. My brother is very clever when it comes to business dealings and had an inkling of how much you interested me."

"But you loved Marissa. You would have married her if Sherdanian law had allowed it."

"I never wanted to marry Marissa. She was my way of rebelling against duty and responsibility. I loved being with her, but I know now that I didn't love her. Not the way I love you."

His lips found hers and delivered a kiss that managed to be both incredibly arousing and spiritually satisfying at the same time. Olivia was weak with delight when he set her free.

"I can't quite believe all that has happened today," she murmured as his fingertips worked their way along her shoulder. "When I woke up this morning I was cautiously optimistic. Now I'm happier than I ever imagined I could be."

Gabriel gifted her with a smile of resolute tenderness. "And it's my intention to do whatever it takes to ensure you stay that way."

After disappearing from the radar for a week, and then reappearing with a glowing bride in tow, Gabriel had anticipated a media frenzy, but he hadn't expected the capital's streets to be lined with people.

In the back of the limousine, Olivia waved at the enthusiastic crowd, looking every inch a princess. But by the time the vehicle pulled up in front of the palace, her nerves had begun to show.

"Are we going to be taken to the gallows and shot?" she questioned. "Is that why everyone turned out to see us?"

"A member of Sherdana's royal family hasn't been executed in almost three hundred years."

"That's not as reassuring as you want it to be."

Gabriel squeezed her hand. "Everything is going to be fine."

"Since when are you such an optimist?"

"Since marrying you."

A footman stepped forward to open the limo's door. Olivia nodded toward a glowering Christian, who was striding through the palace's ornate main doors.

"He doesn't look happy."

"I think he's realized the trap has been sprung."

"You sound as if you're enjoying this far too much."

"Do you have any idea how many dossiers I looked through over the years, weighing my future happiness against what was right for the country, while my brothers ran around the United States and Europe following their dreams?"

"A hundred?" she offered.

"Try a thousand."

"Surely there weren't that many girls who wanted to marry you," she teased.

"Oh, there were at least three times that, but only one girl I wanted to marry."

"You really have become a smooth talker. No wonder I fell in love with you."

Christian extended a hand to assist Olivia as she exited the car and kissed her on each cheek before glowering at Gabriel over a perfunctory handshake.

"How are things?" Gabriel asked, overlooking his brother's surly mood. He kept ahold of Olivia's hand as they made their way into the palace.

"Sherdana's been doing just fine," Christian muttered.

"I meant with you. Has Mother come up with a list of potential candidates for your bride yet?"

"You really are a bastard."

"Don't let our mother hear you say that." He thumped his brother on the back. "But what do you have to worry about? Nic is next in line. The burden to produce an heir falls on him first."

"Mother's not taking any chances this time. She thinks both of us should be married."

"I agree with her. Nothing like marrying the woman of your dreams to know complete and perfect happiness."

Gabriel laughed heartily at Christian's look of disgust and followed Olivia up the stairs. As they entered the suite of rooms she and Gabriel would now be sharing, she leaned close and spoke in a low voice. "Why didn't you tell Christian there's a potential we can have children?"

He shut the door to the suite, ensuring their privacy, and took her in his arms. "I think we should keep this development our little secret for the time being."

"Are you sure?" Olivia reached up and threaded her

fingers through Gabriel's dark hair. "If it works, it will let your brothers off the hook."

"There's no reason to say anything until we have something definitive to tell."

"That could take months," she exclaimed, her eyes wide with uncertainty. "They could be engaged or even married by then."

"Making you my wife has been the best thing that could have happened to me. I think my brothers deserve to experience the same."

"You're going to force them into a situation where they have to find wives so that they'll fall in love?"

"Diabolical, isn't it?"

"They'll kill you when they find out the truth."

"I don't think so." Gabriel leaned down and silenced further protests with a deep, soul-stirring kiss. "I think they'll thank me for making them the second and third happiest men on the planet."

"You being the first?" She arched her eyebrows at him.

Gabriel responded with a broad grin. "Absolutely."

\* \* \* \* \*

# MILLS & BOON®

## Two superb collections!

**40% OFF!**

Would you rather spend the night with a seductive sheikh or be whisked away to a tropical Hawaiian island? Well, now you don't have to choose! Get your hands on both collections today and get 40% off the RRP!

*Hurry, order yours today at*
**www.millsandboon.co.uk/TheOneCollection**

0215_INSHIP1

# MILLS & BOON®

## The Chatsfield Collection!

**2 BOOKS FREE!**

*Style, spectacle, scandal...!*

With the eight Chatsfield siblings happily married and settling down, it's time for a new generation of Chatsfields to shine, in this brand-new 8-book collection! The prospect of a merger with the Harrington family's boutique hotels will shape the future forever. But who will come out on top?

**Find out at
www.millsandboon.co.uk/TheChatsfield2**

FIELD_PROMO_BK

# MILLS & BOON®

## Classic romances from your favourite authors!

**3 in 1 GREAT VALUE**

**40% OFF!**

The Jarrods: Temptation

MAUREEN CHILD · TESSA RADLEY · KATHIE DENOSKY

By Request

The Australian's Desire

MARION LENNOX · LILIAN DARCY

By Request

Royal and Ruthless

ROBYN DONALD · ANNIE WEST · CHRISTINA HOLLIS

By Request

Whether you love tycoon billionaires, rugged ranchers or dashing doctors, this collection has something to suit everyone this New Year. Plus, we're giving you a huge 40% off the RRP!

Hurry, order yours today at
**www.millsandboon.co.uk/NYCollection**

0215_INSHIP2

# MILLS & BOON®

## Seven Sexy Sins!

### *The true taste of temptation!*

From greed to gluttony, lust to envy, these fabulous stories explore what seven sexy sins mean in the twenty-first century!

Whether pride goes before a fall, or wrath leads to a passion that consumes entirely, one thing is certain: the road to true love has never been more enticing.

### Collect all seven at
**www.millsandboon.co.uk/SexySins**

ST_9

# MILLS & BOON®

*Desire*™

**PASSIONATE AND DRAMATIC LOVE STORIES**

## A sneak peek at next month's titles...

### In stores from 20th March 2015:

- **For His Brother's Wife** – Kathie DeNosky
  *and* **Twins on the Way** – Janice Maynard

- **From Ex to Eternity** – Kat Cantrell
  *and* **From Fake to Forever** – Kat Cantrell

- **The Cowgirl's Little Secret** – Silver James
  *and* **The Nanny Plan** – Sarah M. Anderson

Available at WHSmith, Tesco, Asda, Eason, Amazon and Apple

*Just can't wait?*
Buy our books online a month before they hit the shops!
**visit www.millsandboon.co.uk**

**These books are also available in eBook format!**

0315/51